The
Saint
of Lost
Things

Tish Delaney

PENGUIN BOOKS

PENGUIN BOOKS

UK | USA | Canada | Ireland | Australia
India | New Zealand | South Africa

Penguin Books is part of the Penguin Random House group of companies
whose addresses can be found at global.penguinrandomhouse.com

First published by Hutchinson Heinemann in 2022
Published in Penguin Books 2023
001

Copyright © Tish Delaney, 2022

The moral right of the author has been asserted

Typeset in 11.76/17.15 pt SabonLTStd
by Integra Software Services Pvt. Ltd, Pondicherry

Printed and bound in Great Britain by Clays Ltd, Elcograf S.p.A.

The authorised representative in the EEA is Penguin Random House Ireland,
Morrison Chambers, 32 Nassau Street, Dublin D02 YH68

A CIP catalogue record for this book is available from the British Library

ISBN: 978–1–529–15868–7

www.greenpenguin.co.uk

For Liz and Tom, with all my love.

And for William McPhilemy, 1921–1995.
Never forgotten.

CARNSORE

Chapter 1

There's an auld stone under the tap outside that must have been plump and round when Auntie Bell and me were first sent to live out our days in Carnsore. It's hollowed out now. Years, the guts of thirty-three years in total, of water dripping on to it from the mains and from the rains have left it with a permanent puddle at its heart. I didn't notice it back then. I would hardly have noticed it if it was travelling at speed towards my face, but these days I find myself staring at it, this precious gem. I should rescue it, really. I should move it to a safe, dry place where it can keep what's left of itself; but safe, dry places are in short supply in the deep dark Northern Irish countryside of West Tyrone, most especially in Carnsore.

We have a nasty bungalow, Auntie Bell and me, which has been wedged in to a corner of bog as many miles away from my Granda Morris's good land as he could get us. Good land is reserved for beasts. Beasts bring in money. This is your place, he said as he shut the door on us. He likes people to know their place. This is *your* fault, Lindy, my aunt said as he drove away. A huge evergreen forest that has its roots in Donegal comes right up to our back yard, blocking out the light better than a cliff. At the front we're cut off by a deep brown burn that flows no more than forty feet away from the door. We have to overlook it, its reflected clouds and its stony bridge, to see the long road to the disappointing town of Ballyglen.

Auntie Bell planted a few rose bushes one year in a rare excursion into gardening and we get the odd pink bloom when the north-east wind forgets to howl in from the Blue Stack Mountains in June. They didn't look right sitting pretty amid the rushes and the rocks anyway. This rectangle of pebble-dash and slate and white plastic windows is what we call home, even though we know Granda Morris could turf us out any day if the notion took him. He's a man with a weather system all his own, a face like thunder and fists like lightning.

It's hard living on your nerves; tiring mostly, with a bit of fear-laced boredom thrown in. I don't *have* to stay here, of course, with or without Auntie Bell. I don't *have* to wait for the next time my grandfather's black eyes fall on me, but somehow I just do. Every day I wake up, I think to myself, this is the day, the day I take the lonely walk to Ballyglen and never come back. I do make myself chuckle. Every day comes and goes and I end up crawling back into my bed as soon as the chill of the evenings set in. I'm not a child. I'm a fully grown coward. I'm to suffer alongside Auntie Bell in her reluctant role as sole carer and to keep my mouth shut while I do it.

Auntie's job was to keep me under surveillance. I was not to break free again, once was enough. I was too much like my mother, who abandoned the mothering ship early; too much like my father, who we don't talk about. He's a traveller, not of the world just the roads of Ireland, a king of the long acre. I've never heard his name, though he has plenty of labels. He's a gypsy, a tinker, a knacker, a pikey, and plenty worse besides. I heard all of them from Granda, so I was well-prepared for what I was to hear at school. It bounced off me, the abuse of amateurs. Granda doesn't have any truck with men who don't own land, who don't work it but who want to borrow it from time to time without paying their proper dues. It's not *decent* to use land when it's not going to be handed on.

One of the things that will make his fists form fast is the reality that I am his rightful heir. Indeed, I am his only heir, but I'm so tainted that he's had to make alternative arrangements. He's against anything of mixed blood – mongrels, Catholic and Protestant unions of any kind, Romany filth coming anywhere near a girl who was reared to be good. That I'm a bastard born under his roof is more than he can stomach. That he kept me and my mother is the single thing I have never been able to understand. His threat to put me and her out to the open road where we belonged was part of our daily bread.

Thanks to Bell's tender care, I have no heirs myself. She drops it into the one conversation a week we have with others, alongside her big empty laugh that only ever lets people know she doesn't find too many things funny. *Lindy and me are child-free, aren't we, Lindy? Aren't we happy?* We are, I say as I laugh big too, to make it a good story and to not spoil the fresh cream cakes. The fresh cream cakes appear on the day we have our visitors, a Saturday, only ever a Saturday. Ah, the sweet and sour of lonely living, the sugar and spice. *Lindy and me made a special excursion to Diamond's, didn't we, Lindy?* We did, I say, with a smile that offends my face.

Diamond's is the bakery and it's the best shop for a real treat. We go on the morning bus for the workers every Friday because neither of us can drive. They don't bother to look up any more, too embarrassed. I reward anyone foolish enough to check me out with a direct stare and a freaky-deaky smile it took me hours to get right. Bell failed her test five times; I never took a single lesson. Cars are for people who have places to go. We sit in the first seat for two that we can find. Bell always has the window. I take the aisle and all the clumps from elbows and handbags that go with it. We get into Ballyglen for 8.30 a.m. That gives us four long hours to kill before the lunchtime bus shuttles us back. It's too long in a town with one instant coffee shop.

I can list the contents of every aisle in the Co-op. It's a game I play. When I see other women searching for stuff, I like to step in, uninvited, instantly recognised, unwanted. Flash bleach, is it? You need the last aisle but one at the back of the shop. There's a special offer on Brillo Pads, I roar after them, even if there's not. To my mind, unnerving people is an act of kindness. Why shouldn't they get to share the experience of feeling ill at ease in the world? I deploy the freaky-deaky extra wide as they back away with only their net shoppers for protection. Bell smiles too, though she's not part of the game. She thinks that me talking to people is a sign that I'm improving, bless. It's no wonder we've both been branded as a couple of sandwiches short of a picnic, the mad Morrises from Carn Hill.

At least we own the Hill. Well, Bell and me don't *own* it, never will. Granda owns it and a hundred other acres to boot. Farming this land is the only thing that keeps him alive. Not because he loves it but because he's too much of a hateful fucker to die and leave it to his brother Malachi. No one could guess how old they both are because they're made of iron, from the set-square jaws to the hard ridges of muscles on their still straight, strong backs, the last of the big men.

The visitors, 'the wimmin', are Mrs Martha Kennedy, Mrs Kitty Barr and Mrs Deirdre McCrossan, and I've known them since I was seven years old. I am not allowed to use their Christian names, too forward, too close to behaving like an equal when I'm not. They know it, I know it. I'm strictly second-rate. My voice rattles the whole lot of them; it's my mother they can hear when they thought they were shot of her. Mrs Kennedy is kind, Mrs Barr is a bitchy bitch and Mrs McCrossan is a muck-spreader. That was my way of telling them apart then and I've not changed it or my mind since.

The wimmin are the same age as Bell, seventy-two. Mrs Barr, the bitchy bitch, is right at the top of my list of people to hate. She's a broken record. Every single Saturday we have the parable of her getting married at eighteen and going on to have twelve children, through God's will. It's as if He was in the room, sowing the seed Himself. She's so proud that they were all *single births*. Motherhood (within Catholic marriage) is the second summit that I've stopped Bell from reaching and I mustn't be allowed to forget it. Bell's chance at a career

Search, renew or reserve
www.buckinghamshire.gov.uk/libraries

24 hour renewal line
0303 123 0035

Library enquiries
01296 382415

Buckinghamshire Libraries and Culture

#loveyourlibrary

@BucksLibraries

95100000406157

ABOUT THE AUTHOR

Tish Delaney was born and brought up in Northern Ireland at the height of the Troubles. Like a lot of people of her generation, she left the sectarian violence behind by moving to England. After graduating from Manchester University, she moved to London and worked on various magazines and broadsheets as a reporter, reviewer and sub-editor. She left the *Financial Times* in 2014 to live in the Channel Islands to pursue her career as a writer.

Also by Tish Delaney

Before My Actual Heart Breaks

was the first summit. Another gift from Lindy Morris. She was made to give up the nursing job she was forced into at Gransha, the big psychiatric hospital in Derry, to look after me. I've been there quite a few times. Can't say she missed much. We call it the Clinic to make it more palatable as a destination.

Oh Bell, they say, you're a pure saint on the sod! Aren't you lucky, Lindy, to *still* have Bell, they tell me when they've rolled a mouthful of sponge and jam into a ball small enough to speak through without risk of spitting or choking. I am, I say, I am *steeped* in luck. More tea, anyone? There's more in the pot? I can make it fresh if anyone's particular? More cake? More of anything? If you're hungry in this house it's your own fault! Or thirsty! More big empty laughter. We should be millionaires; we've found a way to stretch time. A morning feels like a month.

We cram around the small coffee table in the front room. Out of sight, knees are touching, which stresses everyone out. My legs are too long. I take up too much room. It's a plague being tall. I didn't have any choice in it but still I can be made to feel greedy, greedy for what? Long bones? Everyone but Martha tuts as their indecent length demands to be accommodated even though I keep them off to the side, glued together. Bell tuts loudest. She thoroughly enjoys being a ladylike five foot, five inches to my six foot of hateful flesh.

9

Being too big is the one trait I copped from Granda Morris so it cannot be denied that I am kin, filthy mongrel or not. On the tabletop, there's not enough room for cups and saucers *and* side plates, so the lumps of cake must be held tightly while they're not being chewed because once a piece of cake fell from my fingers, frosted cream side down on the rug, and the resulting stampede for dish rags while Bell screamed and pointed and jigged about just made it not worth the calories.

We could sit around the dining table in comfort but Bell considers this *common*. Dining tables should only be used for hot food and/or special occasions such as Christmas or Easter. I'm not sure how she came to that conclusion. So we have evolved to pick up our slab of flour and eggs from the central serving plate and to return it there when we need a mouthful of tea. It's not overly hygienic and everyone sighs with boredom if a half-eaten slice tumbles over into someone else's half-eaten slice.

If it's *my* half-eaten slice, Mrs Barr downs tools and declares she's full to bursting, couldn't eat another *bite*. It only takes a timely kick of the table to make it happen. Big feet have some benefits. She might as well run through the house ringing a bell and shouting *leper, leper* at the height of her lungs. But she can't catch what I've got. Not a single one of them has had the guts to look or comment on my shameful neck. They could hardly miss the now-healed pink perfection of it when they have to look up to see my face. I've taken to flinging my head back for no reason other than to rattle them. It's not going to fall off, hardly hurts any more, but the shudders of them tell me they think it'll roll under the china cabinet at the first opportunity. Bad Lindy for trying to set her head free.

When 'the party' is over and we all feel a bit sick, it's my job to *clear away. No, no, you all sit where you are! Lindy will clear away, won't you, Lindy?* It's not a question. I'm the juvenile in the room, although I'm only younger by twenty odd years. How do they manage when I'm in the Clinic? By rights, I should come back to a mountain of crockery. The wimmin pull all their much daintier limbs to safety while I collect the cups. I have a tray that could let me clear away in one hit but I do it one or two cups at a time just for the craic. That's the problem with not paying for your skivvy. You can't complain. It amuses me no end that they won't speak until the table is empty. It's more proof, as if any were needed, that I'm prone to making a meal of things.

Mrs Kennedy is the only one who ever follows me into the kitchen. Her kindness has followed me all my life, the guardian angel of my dreams. She takes my side even when it's not sanctioned. She's saved me a thousand times – from myself and from others – and she's still convinced that I could leave, that I could venture out just for two weeks even. It's a little holiday that I need. *Lindy, any more thoughts on the little holiday?* she asks low. *You should give it some thought, you'd not* know yourself *if you could just make it to the Donegal coast and breathe in the sea air.* I don't know myself here, I think as I nod to show her I'm still thinking about it. A little holiday? The Donegal coast is forty miles away. I could crawl there if I dreamed it would make the slightest difference to me *not knowing myself*; instead, I make it sound like flying to the moon on a Frisbee to keep it firmly in the future.

Mrs Kennedy offers her usual whispers of 'fond memories' of my mother when I'm banging the cups and saucers down on the draining board. She can't bear to let her go, which pleases me as much as it pisses me off. It's her way of letting me know that she's forgiven me for my latest episode, though she keeps her eyes firmly off my neck. Disappointingly, the cups and saucers don't break today. I won't be able to enjoy Bell sitting down with her tube of superglue and her tongue hanging out in concentration to restore the tea set to its full complement. They went to school together. Primary school *and* secondary school, says Martha every time, in case I can't grasp the long history of the fondness.

- I don't know about going so very far ...
- It's not far, not really. All you'd have to do is get a bus?

- All I really need is a few hours on my own ... just to see how it feels.
- I understand, I do, but maybe it's a bit soon to risk it?
- Please help me, Martha. Please? Just get Bell off me for an hour. Please come tomorrow. I don't know if I can stand much longer than that.

Martha Kennedy looks at the kitchen door while her hand flies to her chest to steady her heart. We mustn't get caught plotting. We have cream carpet in the front hall – an unnecessary extravagance in a house floating in muck – and a policy of stockinged feet indoors as a result, so Mrs Barr, Mrs McCrossan or Auntie Bell could be at your shoulder before you knew it. They would not approve of any plans for a break, no matter how short. Martha loses her nerve and goes back to the wimmin. None of *them* have fond memories of my mother; none of *them* think all I need is a little holiday. They know that I'm well off. They were all at school with her too, primary school *and* secondary school.

She was alright at primary school, just one of the gang, impossible to tell apart from Bell. But the rot started not long after they'd failed the 11+ and they all ended up in St Theresa's Comprehensive. She was known for her pranks, but she went too far one day during Domestic Science, in a bid to save sweet Martha from the horror of a Biology lesson which came immediately

13

after on the timetable. Martha had always dreaded it when the scalpels came out and some bit of long-dead flesh was fished out of a jar of formaldehyde and staked out on the cutting boards to be dissected. Thinking she would kill two birds with one stone, Mammy robbed that day's defrosting bull's eyes from the science lab and popped them into Kitty Barr's shepherd's pie for the pure devilment of it.

The cookery teacher, Mrs Prendergast, did not care that Mammy had only been trying to help out her friend when she found the gelatinous blob on her fork. She was halfway through her weekly mantra – a girl who cooks well is more use than a girl who looks well – when she gagged. Mammy was sent to the Principal for the strap and – Kitty Barr always screams this line – she didn't even have the *good grace* to cry. Her distress slips down my throat like a spoonful of warmed honey. Mammy's victories are my victories, and I love it when it's Mrs Barr's cheek we have our boot on.

The Incident of the Eye in the Pie comes up at least once a month. Its retelling is designed to make *me* feel guilty but I don't. I know the bit they always leave out. It was Martha, of course, who tell-taled. *She was thoughtful, Lindy*, she says, *not wicked, not really*. On the bus on the way home, Kitty Barr was still mortally wounded. She cried and whined and carried on until she had the attention of the whole bus. She was the injured party; my mother was the one swinging the axe and not even feeling terrible when it was the least she could do. Mammy bided her time, waited for the noise to die down so that Kitty Barr wouldn't miss a syllable.

– I don't know why you're making such a fuss, Kitty-cat? Weren't you grand after eating those frogs' legs?

Once, just once, I sniggered when the story resurfaced within a fortnight. God, I wish I hadn't. Deirdre McCrossan reared up at me like a rabid dog, baring her teeth and frothing at the mouth, her tea raining down on that Saturday's treats from Diamond's, unnoticed.

– You've not much call to be laughing, Lindy Morris! Not all of Babs's little jokes were so funny! She was bad to the bone, if you ask me! If only you knew what she *did* …

– *That's enough*, said Kitty Barr, her face on fire.

– It's not enough! She needs to understand that her mother had no idea how to behave! NO IDEA!

– I'll not warn you again, Deirdre McCrossan! Leave the past where it is!

It had taken ten minutes for them all to recover. Much smoothing down of skirts and clearing of throats accompanied the news that Deirdre McCrossan didn't know what she was talking about. There was *nothing* to talk about and it was lousy form to suggest there was. My aunt was mute. It wasn't her style not to join in the fun of ripping Mammy apart every chance she saw. Babs wasn't here to defend herself, let that be an end to the matter, said Martha, patting my hand, like I was freshly bereaved. What stunt had my mother pulled that hadn't ever been dragged out for analysis on a Saturday morning? I was shaken up, it wasn't like them to change the script, but it was Bell who went deathly white. She stayed like that long after the ruined party was over.

It's time for the wimmin to leave. They all have grandchildren to look about now that they're retired and have nothing better to do. People seem to really love children these days, so I'm glad for that. I was a seen-and-not-heard child, who was warned to stay out of sight. They all gather in the front hall to put themselves back together again. Coats first, then scarves, unruly grey hairs are tucked out of harm's way or secured under a hat or headscarf. It's autumn but there's always the possibility of an icy breeze.

With all hands shook and backs patted – we don't kiss in County Tyrone no matter how deep the regard – bunions are forced back into their shoes in the porch. When no one is looking, Martha catches my hungry eye and gives the briefest of nods. Oh my heart! I knew she'd cave in under the weight of her own compassion. Bell will be removed and I will be free to rummage through every inch of Carnsore. My aunt has buried something that I need.

Everyone straightens as a unit and the moment is gone. The nod is stored inside my guts, where I keep all my best secrets. We wave through the fastening of seat-belts and the endless revving and reversing of Mrs McCrossan to get off the street as if we might never see each other again. The waving stops the instant they cross the stony bridge. They'll be back at the same time, on the same day, next week, Saturday, 10 a.m. until midday sharp. They have not overstaying your welcome down to a fine art.

We stay on the step, arms crossed tight enough to smother breasts, until they're just a dot and we're near dead with the late-September cold. Most of the country-side they drive through is Morris land. It stretches from the towering trees behind Carnsore all the way to the crossroads where big Protestant farmers the Johnsons' lush pasture starts and across to Granda Morris's house. The road dips away from Auntie Bell and me, past fields of rushes, bracken, nettles, granite boulders and low tumble-down stone walls. My grandfather owns a lot of acres but only half of them can be grazed. That half sits all around his square farmhouse, all the better for him to watch over it and cod himself he's the Big Man.

That half is where he keeps his cows. The rest is where he keeps a few tenacious sheep. He's been in trouble with the Department of Agriculture for neglecting both sets of beasts, because people around here are only too glad to dob him in. He blames any lack in himself and his abilities to feed and water his dumb animals on the lack of sons produced by his wife. Her reputation as a sub-standard incubator is known to the whole townland when he's had a Guinness too many and blathers to anyone who doesn't turn their back on him quick enough in The Forge Inn.

Any man who thought to mention that Gabriel Morris was a useless fucker went home with a busted lip. For a useless fucker he's still very fast on his feet. They shouldn't risk getting him all riled up just for the craic. He's as mean as a snake but he's ninety years old, the last of the sturdy breed, the last of the barrel-chested men. Surely he's going to break a bone and be off his legs at some stage soon, God willing?

Although we're both glad to see the tail lights disappear into the valley, the bungalow shrinks another inch when we close the door. It's as well they left when they did. A fierce freezing blast full of fast-flying pine needles threatens to chip more pebble-dash clean off the walls before I can get the front door closed. Bell and me always turn to look at each other, unsure for a minute what to say or what to do next when we've only got each other again for six straight days. Did I mention she's my mother's twin? They were identical but I still spotted it straight away when she was made to replace her sister, Babs. Seven-year-olds are not stupid or blind.

I have the same thought every time I stare back at her. She looks like my mammy but she isn't. I'm so jealous that they had each other from the very beginning. I'd kill to not be an only child, never mind the joy of having a hand to hold in the womb. Only children are lonely children, a cross I have to bear. It's the trees that snap us both out of it, they creak and moan and remind us the bungalow is on shaky ground, and we turn to one of the endless jobs that make us feel life has a purpose. There's never a shortage of dust to dust.

It's flimsy, this would-be home, but it's what was built for us when my mother's disappearance came home to roost and so we stay on. Four mean bedrooms that just fit a double sit off a corridor that's so mean it only allows one person to travel at a time. It ends with the bathroom door and every time I open it, I feel like I'm going to step into another house instead of the shower because Granda hung a panelled outside door that he found cheap somewhere and second-hand.

Bell and me both sleep at the back and share the wall between us. I can hear her breathing when the wind drops enough. I can hear her startle awake when a fox breaks out its high-pitched yowl. If the foxes come too close she throws her hairbrush at the window in a bid to scare them off. It doesn't work. I can hear her great, gassy sighs when she can't sleep at all. I make no sound. The two rooms at the front are all made-up and kept neat in case anyone happens to snoop through the curtains. No one has ever had cause or desire to stay here.

There's two cream cakes left over. Bell and me do that on purpose, buy and put out more cakes than they'll eat. It makes us look generous and it makes them watch their manners. Not one of them would reach for a second helping, no matter how much it was urged on them. Mrs Kennedy is the weakest link. She's heavy around the middle and wobbly under the chin so she has to suffer the plate being passed in front of her nose several times. It's Bell who baits the snare. *Are you sure, Martha? Are you absolutely sure you don't have room for another one? What about a half a piece?* My part in the hunt is to stand up and offer to get a knife to cut it in two and force her hand, though I hate doing it. She has to state for the record, categorically, that she couldn't eat another morsel if they paid her a million pounds.

Bell usually throws her hands in the air at that point and announces that she has no idea what's wrong with them all. The cakes are bought for this day *with a glad heart* and she'd only be delighted if they'd all eat up. She's a brilliant liar. I sit back down as soon as I can because I feel sorry for Martha Kennedy and her red face. They're hoping to shame her thin. It won't work, she's built round a sweet tooth.

Bell pushes her cream cake into her mouth as she salvages the paper doily for next week. I do the same. I never save food. Someone could beat me to it. I learned that in the Clinic on the only real little holidays I've ever had. There's not much to look forward to now as Granda only gives us a lift to Sunday Mass once a month and tomorrow is not the day. I have the gossamer hope that Martha won't let me down tomorrow evening but I try not to dwell on it in case it vanishes.

It's another full three weeks before Bell and me are back on the rota for doing the flowers for the altar. It'll only be for one glorious Sunday so October will feel long. Doing the flowers is great, blending the yellows and creams with the greens is peaceful. The parish priest, Father Boluwaji, likes the way I let the ivy tumble out of the vases and trail to the marble floor. He likes a lot of things about me, much to the disgust of the wimmin. He's the one who allowed me on to the rota, putting all their noses out of joint. He's been able to spare me from three trips away in total and I might let him spare me again. We meet up now and again for what he calls a chinwag. I love him for that description alone.

It's two months after that until we're on the door at the Parochial Hall when the Omagh Players come back. This year they're putting on *Dancing at Lughnasa* for a night before Christmas, which should be a gas. We're 'volunteering', in that Mrs Barr has told us we're working the cloakroom if we don't blot our copybooks before then.

I might try to read again tonight if I can convince Bell to watch the Saturday-night dross on her own. She won't take it well. I'll hear every step she makes on the corridor, every sigh until the sighs turn into tears and then into a tantrum. *Do you want to break my heart? Do you? Is that what you want, Lindy? To break my heart again?* It's hard to take that level of emotional blackmail because one more minute watching the rubbish on television is one more minute than you can stand.

Bell loves a talent show or a reality show, which kills me. All those flashing neons and noise for what? To throw light on other people's humiliation? I don't know why they put themselves through it. Standing there, willingly taking criticism while everyone applauds? It gives me the shakes while it makes me glad that I have no talents to showcase. I can't sing, I can't play anything, I can't even Irish dance. All of those things were denied me because my mother was a bit of a show-off. She'd stand up and give anybody a tune if asked and she never could stop herself from jigging about. She took after some aunt of Granny Tess's who ran off to Dublin to try her luck in the Gaiety Theatre. There was no need to encourage such shamelessness in me.

Apart from anything else, I already stuck out in a crowd, a head and shoulders above everybody else; there was no need to draw extra fire. That was The Word according to Bell and for the longest time she made it sound like she was protecting me. And now she's glued to this exercise in shamelessness as if her life depends on it. I can't abide the fact that she seems to genuinely care what happens to strangers.

But I will try to get a half-hour with my book and tea before the waterworks start. It's not much to ask when you've somehow made it to fifty and the only thing on your mind is being sixty then seventy, then eighty and then dead. I'd kill myself now but I don't want to prove them all right.

Chapter 2

The curtains in my room are flowery, they sport a kind of large red peony, repeated in great bunches. The light from the moon makes them look like dried blood. Around 3 a.m. some nights, I decide it is Bell's fault that I am still here. I can't dare blame myself for being weak. I already hate myself enough for two lifetimes. I need someone to help me carry the burden and there's only Bell. How does she keep me here? There's no locks on the doors, no bars on the windows, but when I wake up in the middle of the night she might as well be draped over me wearing chainmail and lead boots. It's a paralysis I've felt often, but it never scares me any less, though I know it's only in my head. I'm pinned to the bed, can't even move my arms, only my eyes work, roving from side to side in my head like a demented doll. When I can't lift the eiderdown, panic sets in. The sheet and blankets weigh a ton. I'm buried in cotton and wool. In the dark they are heavier than six foot of clay.

Tonight is one of those nights. It followed this evening when Bell couldn't stick to our usual performance of pretending we're happy enough. She started to snivel as soon as I put my mug on a tray before she could switch on the garbage she loves and trap me in the front room to watch it. A tray means that things will be moved to the bedroom. I need the tray because it stops Bell from tugging at my arms. It's my shield. When I picked up the book I wanted to read too she breathed in so sharp that anybody listening would have suspected a slender knife had been pushed through her from back to front. I carried on, she in tears, me in inches.

I edged out of the kitchen. If I got my foot on the sliver of corridor, I might get the length of my door before she broke. I've lost a thousand mugs of tea this way, standing with my tray against my chest as a milky skin slings itself from lip to lip. Tea delayed like that leaves a darker mark on the china, takes extra elbow grease to restore.

- Why? That's all I need to know. *Why* would you sit down there by yourself?
- I just fancy an hour with my book, Auntie Bell. Honestly, that's all.
- You'll ruin your eyes, then where will you be?

I'll be in the dark, I suppose, but instead I pull the corners of my mouth upwards and try to leave again. The sight of my back makes her renew her efforts and I don't even touch the doorknob before she rushes at me, the tea spills and a corner of the paperback soaks up the damage before I can save it. I need a bigger shield. I need Martha. Please God, let her come. Let it be tomorrow.

– But what about *me*? I don't want to sit alone as if I have no one or nothing of my own!

Ah, there it is. Bell's no one or nothing monster has been pulled out from under the bed. Don't think that Bell's monster is the 'he' of normal fairy tales, 'he' is a 'she'. 'She' is the mother who opted out of rearing me herself thereby ruining Auntie Bell's chances at some other imagined perfect world. My mother is the reason that Auntie Bell has no one and nothing of her own. All she has is me, ungrateful me, who can't hand her my life in return for her old life. I can't give her back the first ten years that would have made all the difference. By the time I was seventeen, she was thirty-seven and practically nailed on the shelf. I doubt she was ever dusted before she was left on there for good. Now she has me to blame for thwarting her. I have nowhere else to go. She has nowhere else to go. Somehow this is my fault instead of Granda Morris's, who cleared the path to our current situation.

Even the huge evergreens that mark the boundary of what we were given and what we were not given to call our own for however long it takes us to die lean in to hear what I will say, how I will justify my existence. I can feel them bend over the little house, covered in needles that they can rain down in a heartbeat, carpeting the whole back yard with scented irritation. We all wait – me, her and the dark forest – for the next stand.

– I'll only be *half* an hour then, how's that? By the time you get a cup of tea and settle yourself on the sofa, the time will have gone by.

– Alright, alright.

I'm on the other side of the door before she can rake up any more history. A slug of the tea tells me it's lukewarm but bearable. I won't get any reading done. There's no time, it's ticking itself away, I can hear it day in, day out. Every room in this house has at least one clock in it. They all tick. There are three in the front room alone, the one that cuckoos hangs over the mantelpiece, the one that chimes hangs on the back wall and then there's a gold one with rotating balls inside a glass dome on the sideboard that tings. They all call out the number at the top of the hour and make sure you don't forget the half-hour. Every second is waiting to be wasted in Carnsore.

This bungalow has taken the name of the whole townland because there isn't another house for ten miles. It's built on a slip of a plot that could never be properly drained of the bog water that keeps the brown burn swollen. Black mould creeps above the skirting boards to remind us every day. Providing the house was a trial. Granda Morris never misses a chance to mention how much hard fill it took to get the foundations to stay put. He and his brother Malachi – who had the great good sense to only produce sons – had carried the breeze blocks and mixed the cement and put the roof on before the walls were plastered. Unlike Granda, I can tolerate Malachi well enough, though how they worked together without killing each other for as long as it took to raise a house is another cosy family mystery.

They used the same blueprint as Malachi's and when I think about the fact that there is an identical house sitting somewhere with the same pebble-dash, the same huge three windows to the front and the smaller four windows to the back, it makes me sad down to my bones. They're both narrow enough to be annoyingly narrow. I've only been to Malachi's once but walking down the same thin corridor to use the same claustrophobic bathroom and to look into the same bedrooms had one big difference: there's no dust swirling in the air. In Carnsore it can feel like I'm inside one of those snow dome ornaments that's been picked up and shaken so hard that the flakes never settle. The motes get into our eyes and clog our noses. This is our place. The place we stockpile our dead skin.

The cuckoo starts to sound, the chimes join to bury the ting, which means it's eight o'clock, time for a talent show, whether I like it or not. I should have used my thirty minutes better. I should have looked in the mirror and tried to see whose eyes were looking back at me today. Brave eyes, blank eyes, twitchy eyes? They're always pale blue, they're always my father's eyes. They're hard eyes to meet without flinching. I can tolerate them on the days I have my freaky-deaky smile practice but otherwise they're best avoided.

– Lindy? Lindy? Are you there?

– I'm here, Bell, just coming.

I look back at the bed with its beige bedspread, at the bare cream walls and blood-flowery curtains. A Sacred Heart glows in the dull red light from an electric bulb fashioned into a flame. One day Himself will see the back of me, so help me God. For tonight He'll bear witness to me throwing in the towel again and ending up back on the couch. I reach for the wasted mug of tea. It's queer how some half-hours fly by while others drag themselves along your nerves and last a week.

– Lindy? Do you want more tea before the craic starts?

– We'll need something to sustain us, Bell.

29

She means make the tea. I click the kettle on and the little bulb on the kitchen's Sacred Heart dims just a touch to remind me that we are at the end of the line. The telegraph poles have stalked their way to the edge of the forest but no further, further is another country – the Republic of Ireland just a mile away. The white lines in the middle of the roads disappear and a line of grass replaces them, that and potholes the size of frying pans. Donegal, our nearest neighbour, is where Bundoran is, on the west coast, and Martha thinks it's the greatest place on earth. With its slot machines and merry-go-rounds, it sends her all aflutter. When she tells me for the hundredth time about the amusement arcades before remembering it's all about the sea air and me finally, *finally*, clearing my head, I always smile. She doesn't know that I've been there already. I've seen the Atlantic, smelled its brine. It is one of my many secrets.

Mammy took me there when I was five; I remember being on the beach and being allowed an ice cream. I remember the sand was wet when I thought it would be dry. It's like an image glimpsed while flicking through a magazine: it's a perfect day, we're both smiling and he's there. The giver of the pale blue eyes. I was small but I knew he shouldn't be there, he was not allowed, like picking your nose or slurping tea or letting one shoe rest on top of the other. Scuffed leather was a slapping offence. *Don't tell anyone, Lindy! It's a secret.* Mammy's secrets were always rebranded by Granny Tess as bad habits that had to be stamped out. The stamping could be brutal. I knew to keep my mouth shut.

She had taken me out for a walk, down the grassy lane from Granda Morris's. She'd been letting on that we were only going as far as the big oak tree in the ditch; maybe we'd pick a few flowers and stick them in a jam jar full of water when we got back. She often put them under Granda Morris's nose but he never said they were lovely or welcome, he only ever said that flowers belong in a field, she should know that at least, even though she was daft enough for two women.

We hardly ever went for a walk and she certainly never had a day off. She had *jobs*, endless jobs – in the fields, in the scullery, in the garden. She had been made to stay at home and look after her mother while Bell was forced to go to Derry to earn a living and send the bulk of her wages home to pay Granda Morris back the cost of rearing them both. Granny Tess, or him, had picked the wrong daughter for the wrong job for the wrong reasons. They knew they couldn't trust Mammy to behave when she was clear of their watchful eyes and she'd always been hopeless with money. She would have been brilliant at being out in the world and meeting people and Bell would have been much happier lurking about the hearth, more obedient bitch that she was.

Mammy hated being kept back, Bell hated being sent away, and they ended up hating each other as much as they hated their parents for the mess. She had to fight for every minute of freedom she wanted and the day we escaped to Bundoran was one of her finest few hours. Is it strange that I can remember that more clearly than meeting my father? We'd kept going at the big oak, we'd climbed the ditch and run the length of the field, and she'd shouted that soon we'd be in Donegal on foot. She hadn't told me that he'd be waiting. I'd been frightened when he stepped out from behind a tree, throwing a cigarette butt into the hedge before he waved silently at us, but Mammy had just screamed as she ran to him, dragging me by the hand.

I was good at crossing my heart and hoping to die and swearing on the Bible that I wouldn't repeat anything she ever told me. But she was right not to trust such a small child. If she had even hinted that I would get to see the *ocean* I wouldn't have been able to contain myself.

Mammy leapt into his arms but he didn't stagger. He was big, straight and tall as a tree, with colourful string bangles on both wrists. I'd never seen colourful string bangles on a man before. His hair was black and long, it grew down past his shoulders, and I'd never seen that on a man before, either. (The Morris men even kept their huge thick necks free of fluff.) But apart from that, he looked like an ordinary man, not the devil he had been painted by Granny Tess. I'd heard so many words thrown at him, gypsy and tinker were the nicest but Mammy wouldn't ever let me repeat them.

– Come here, Lindy, this man is your daddy!
– Hello, girl, he said. You have the look of my people, right enough!

She laughed again, as if me having the look of his people was something funny. He turned to his truck, clattering the tools and bits of wire on to the floor to make space for me. Mammy said it was grand although it was dirty. *Don't waste any time cleaning it, let's go. For God's sake, get in, Lindy.* I didn't move. We should be getting back before we got caught. He picked me up as if I was nothing and plonked me down on the back seat where my feet dangled above the mess. His eyes were pale, pale blue just like mine.

The smell of an evergreen Magic Tree has stayed with me. It flailed about under the rear-view mirror as we dipped in and out and tried to swerve the potholes. I remember him making sure that my day out was a hit. *Sit up, girl! You don't want to miss Barnesmore Gap.* Bits of Mammy's black hair streamed out of the window along with the smoke from both their cigarettes and their laughter when I kept pointing out sheep. There were *so* many of them, like white dots on the steep green hills.

– She'll be counted out before we get there at this rate, he said. Has she never seen sheep before?

– Well, she doesn't exactly get out much. Da's not keen on her being spotted. Bad-tempered auld bastard. At least she gets to school and back now and that's her lot.

– Jesus! Has he not eased up at all?

– No, he hasn't eased up at all.

He'd shook his head then and she'd stared even harder out of the window. I watched them ignore each other for the rest of the ride. They didn't come up with any plan to get me out more. We were in jail together. She would pay for her breakout. I might too. And the thought of Granda Morris's black eyes landing on me made me weak. I wanted to go home but Mammy wouldn't hear of it. I tapped at her shoulder and whispered we should go back. She shook me off and I started to cry. She'd never shook me away before. I was going to the seaside, whether I liked it or not. The man that was my daddy said nothing.

She's never far away from me, even now. I can feel her hair trailing through my fingertips, the skin of her palm dry and cool in mine, her soft lips on my forehead. Her smell was tobacco and talc and the Johnson's Baby Lotion from a bottle that she used to take off her make-up. She never saw anyone but she was always ready to be viewed. She had a cough from the Woodbines that

34

she robbed from Granda's packet when I shakily promised her he wasn't looking. It made her scrabble for the edge of the bed in the middle of the night and sit up until the worst of it passed.

I watched her collarbones heaving and tried to forget what Bell said about the pure badness of fags every time she lit the end of a new one with an old one. *People with lung cancer are blue-black by the time they die, blue-black!* I hated the thought of Mammy's lovely face going blue-black and I told her so. I don't want *you* to have a blue-black face in the coffin, I'd say, turning towards her in the double bed. We were always close. She'd laugh and give me an auld tickle and tell me to never worry about it, she'd be the best-looking corpse in town.

We were caught out when we came back from Bundoran. Mammy had cried when the man that was my daddy had taken her arms from around his neck and pushed her back towards Carnsore. We stumbled through the dark night, through the forest with branches scraping us and roots tripping us. The nettles that grew in great swathes around Southfork got us more than once. She had wiped the sand off my shoes and hid the sweets we'd bought in the shed but it was no good. Granda was waiting. I was thrown into the front room with Granny Tess while Mammy paid for her pleasures. You're not an only child, Granny Tess had hissed at me that day and plenty of other days before she died, far from it, there's plenty more little blue-eyed bastards where you came from! I loved the thought that I had kin. I longed for a brother who would grow up and hit Granda back. As of that day, I had a daddy she didn't know about. I would find the rest of them when I grew up.

– Lindy, the judges are on the stage!

The kettle clicks off in the same instant; Bell and her chosen instrument of torture welcoming me back from my first little holiday. My life has boiled down to being Bell's retainer and making fucking tea while underhand clocks and shit TV kill the hours when I'm not at my shit job or in the Clinic. I need to look into my father's eyes again. I want to touch someone who doesn't have Morris blood. I've been lonely all my life for a loving pair of arms wrapped around me. I need to ask him why he abandoned us both. All I have to do is track him down. All I need is his name. I might as well wish for pine trees without needles. Somewhere around my heart, a sickening flutter tells me to call Father Boluwaji for a chinwag, and soon. He's sworn to me he doesn't mind. We all need to fashion a shelter before it rains, Lady Lindy, he says.

– I'm coming, Bell, don't want to miss the judges!

She's all set up on the far seat of the couch by the time I kick the door open to let myself in with the millionth tray of tea. Between us – because my seat is the seat nearest the door in case she needs anything fetching – is a plate piled high with Viscount mint-fondant biscuits. This is her contribution to the night's entertainment. My heart cheers up a beat when I remember that she might be winkled out of Carnsore tomorrow. That and the meltdown she'll have if Martha can keep her nerve. Please God, let Martha keep her nerve.

Bell likes to peel each Viscount carefully so as not to rip the green foil. Next she picks off the chocolate so she can have that before she licks away at the sugary mint layer as if it was a lollipop. It's a messy business. When she has the biscuit consumed, she smooths out the little metallic square over the fabric of her skirt with the front of her fingernail. She doesn't have to look down as she folds it into a perfect little boat that's never going to be put to sea. She lines them up along the edge of the china cabinet, her armada.

It's one of her habits to do three or four things at once. Right now she's pretending to be thrilled by a fat boy who can really sing but who won't make it because he's fat; voice or no voice, faces and bodies are everything. I learned that early. Long legs don't always carry you to where you want to be. She's also eating more biscuits, making boats and making sure that I stay put. She believes that some terrible sin is committed simply by sitting in a bedroom before it's time to go to sleep. I've no clue what she thinks I get up to when I'm not allowed to keep my door closed.

I do know she scopes the whole place out when I'm at the Credit Union. I leave traps for her to step into when she trespasses. A book on the bedside table which I've placed exactly 4cm from the edge, a pair of knickers tucked under a jumper. She can't tolerate that or me leaving anything inside out. She puts it all right and we never let on it's happened. It's as much fun as we've had since we came to Carnsore.

I witness the poor saps on the programme fall one by one and another hour goes by according to the cuckoo and the chime and the ting. I find the commercial breaks very long because Bell has two questions she uses to make what we say to each other pass as a conversation.

– Any more thoughts about going back to work?
– Any news from Miriam?

I never have any thought about going back to work other than I don't ever want to go back. I'm an admin girl at the Ballyglen Credit Union when I'm well enough to go in. They were forced to employ me to keep me out of the Clinic and it shows. There are five other people who are also going slowly out of their minds but they've the sense to keep it quiet. They count as normal as a result. None of us speak to each other until the Christmas party forces us all into a room with plastic tumblers full of warm fizzy wine. We play Secret Santa and every single year I get six bath cubes which are on sale for £2 in Kelly's Pharmacy the whole year round. I either smell or I work with cheapskates and I'm still not sure which.

I do tell Bell every time about the six bath cubes before I stack them in the bathroom cabinet to gather dust. She's always totally surprised that I've made 'such good friends' at last. She must forget for eleven and a half months that I barely said more than hello and goodbye to them. She must forget that she was the first person to drill into me that I shouldn't make friends. Friends can get to know you and you don't want that. You want to keep your head down and hope you're not noticed. That's not easy when you're tipping six foot tall and a traveller's bastard into the bargain. The good Christians of Ballyglen are choosy on which neighbours they love as well as themselves.

Miriam says the Credit Union's where they send dull people to die, but she doesn't mean me, *not me*. I'm not dull, just deep. It's a different sort of affliction, more acceptable. I love that she tries to put a positive spin on it, even though we both know it will never work. There is nothing positive about sitting behind a desk bored out of your mind and feeling tense in the same instance. At any moment someone could ask a question, work-related or otherwise, and then we freeze, hares in the crosshairs. We resort to chocolate bars when it gets terrible – when you have a mouth full of Toffee Crisp everyone leaves you alone.

Miriam is Miriam O'Dwyer, now Mrs Miriam McPhale. She's the one true friend I do have but she's knee-deep in her grandchildren now the same way she was knee-deep in her own children thirty years ago. We went to primary school and secondary school together. I was foolish enough to think that when we got away together from bollicky Ballyglen we'd stay away together. She's the only one who understands why I like to tear a little hole now and again. I know it's only to let the poison out, she says, and point-blank refuses to entertain any of the chat about me being disturbed. She clings to the word 'deep' and keeps paddling.

Where do the years go? she asks me, often with a laugh, and I laugh too and shake my head over the mystery of it. I had hoped she would be around a bit more, but she's been down south in Galway to look after a set of twins that her daughter Sally produced using IVF. The world has become strange. Miriam spent her entire life trying not to get pregnant and her child has paid thousands of pounds and as many hours bawling about the fact that she can't even have *one* all by herself.

I miss Miriam. I don't like her not being around the corner. Of course, she's always convinced that I'm on the mend and tells me constantly how she never worries about me. Never. In her mind, I'm a survivor. She prays for me, she says, every night without fail, unless one of the gorgeous babies takes her attention. I don't hate her for it; she's always had a soft heart and she'll save a corner of it for me. It's her face and that of Father Boluwaji's which often stopped me from doing anything really silly.

Now it's a small suitcase that is keeping me going. I'm going to find it tomorrow if Martha can stand by me one more precious time. Granda Morris pitched up with it two months ago. He never came to Carnsore. He let himself in, it was his house even though it was our place, and from the front room where I'd run to hide, I saw him shove an old brown suitcase into Bell's reluctant hands. They'd whispered in the hall. I heard him say that *he* didn't know what to do with it but he was *sick and tired* of moving it from one corner of the loft to the other. The very sight of it was making him itchy. Bell would need to go through it, he was washing his hands. She'd made a dirty track along the yellow paint on the wall when she'd dragged it quickly out of sight. Granda snarled when he realised I was at his elbow.

– That's nothing for you to worry about, girl, d'y'understand?

I said nothing but inside my head the words that I wanted to hawk at him, gathered bile. I'm no *girl*. I've made it into my fifth decade, no thanks to you, you vile fucker. Silence enrages him. I smiled as his face purpled.

– I'm just having a clear-out. Southfork is full of auld rubbish!

Southfork was my mammy's joke, I wanted to roar at him. Do you remember *her*? Do you remember your *daughter*, my mother? Barbara was her name, and she called your stupid house Southfork when you built some stupid pillars at the end of the stupid dirt track to the stupid front door where you'd nailed your stupid brass lion-faced door knocker. Do you remember when we all used to sit watching *Dallas* and laughing about JR's shenanigans and yer wan Sue-Ellen walking about drunk as a skunk in a bikini and high heels and perfect hair and how looking at it seemed to bring us together for an hour a week? One sweet hour.

Sometimes the laughter would stay with us for the rest of the evening and we'd have hot chocolate and no shouting matches before bedtime. I wanted to roar but the women in the Morris family don't roar. He doesn't like being reminded of me, I'm the reason he has no one to carry his name. I stole the lives of both his daughters. I dare to move an inch closer to him and I stand and gawp because he hates it so he finds a way of putting me at a distance.

– Have you forgotten your manners, girl? I could use a mouthful of tea!

– Yes, Granda.

I backed away into the kitchen even though I knew he'd soon *suddenly* remember he had no time to stop. The names he called my mother when his blood was up after a few whiskeys still land on me every day like punches. When he was done calling her names he'd start on my father. Then it was my turn. He could fit so much hatred into the word bastard, it was a wonder it didn't burst his mouth before he could spit it out.

Bell had come back out of her bedroom. They had whispered some more, he most likely making sure she knew that they had been caught trying to cover something else up. I heard her telling him to stop fretting, that Lindy wasn't half as clever as she thought she was, and I suppose he nodded although they both knew I was twice as clever as either of them. I heard him sigh. It wasn't like him to be agreeable. *I just can't bear to open it. You know? Given what it is?* Whatever it was, I could feel Mammy, agitating to break out of it like she'd fought to get out of every corner. I had to free her. Bell whispered some more about him not worrying, she would take care of it. I heard the Holy Water fount swinging on its nail when he blessed himself for the road home. I took the kettle off the range when the front door slammed.

I licked every biscuit on the plate before I put them back in the packet; only Bell and Granda Morris eat

Hobnobs so I like to give them a little something back at every opportunity. Bell reappeared after about ten minutes, pinched in the face and blotchy around the neck, and doing her level best to forget that she'd just been handed a bomb, a ticking time bomb that she knew I would spend every spare minute I had to find.

It joined its song to the cuckoo, chime and ting. It was the tinkle of my mother's laughter and I kept my ear out for it. Bell didn't leave my side. She even stood at the top of the corridor when I went for a wee. She was grey from tiredness because I stayed in the bathroom for ages practising my freaky-deaky. It's the perfect opportunity. The laments of her as she lay in the room with her bomb amused me no end for a while. She feared that I'd sneak past her in the night. After a week of watching, I heard her dragging what sounded like her chest of drawers around when she went to bed. She was strong as an ox for an old woman, like all the Morris breed; it felt like she would live for ever. I was gratified when she pulled a muscle in her stupid septuagenarian neck and at least then the furniture noises stopped.

When nearly a month had gone by and I'd still not laid my hand on it, I tipped over. It was the longing, I suppose – the longing for some connection to Mammy, however shaky. I put on my very own special talent show for Bell. I hit my mark just inside the kitchen door and didn't reply to several calls from her. She came looking, all flustered after doing a quick check of her bedroom to make sure it was empty.

When I had her complete attention, I drew the meat knife from one ear to another, not deep, not deep at all, just deep enough to scare Auntie Dearest towards a fit of screaming and praying to God to be delivered of me before she got a hold of herself and called an ambulance to hurry me back to the Clinic. I hate wasting their time but some of my episodes need stitches and some don't, and Bell can't be expected to know the difference even after all these years. It healed nicely, a fine pink line just under my jaw. Doctors are so good at the stitching these days. They tell you over and over again that they're the best, that there won't even be a scar. One more scar won't make a blind bit of difference to me.

Martha came! The month I spent in the Clinic melted away as the headlights of her car swept around the living room. I hadn't needed to beg her to come and take Bell away. She knew that the days and weeks after I'd been away were a trial all their own. Bell would be in such a terrible state after surviving on her own in Carnsore for a month, the loneliness eating at her, tearing chunks. As soon as I got back, she had to let me know the extent of her suffering. She didn't want to be delighted because I was such a nightmare but I was better than nothing. As soon as the ambulance drove off the street, it was time for The Wrong Child speech.

There had never been such a wrong child. I was the worst, the worst of the worst. It was a wonder I had been spared. There were other children who had been denied life yet here I was, sucking up God's good air. There were children who mightn't have grown up to be ungrateful. There were children who wouldn't have been hell-bent on breaking her heart. I remained silent. No point in stoking this particular fire. I never laughed. I never cried. I just took it and waited for the finale.

– What are you? Lindy? What are you?

– I'm the wrong child.

As soon as those words left my lips, Bell would relax as if she'd been darted by a tranquilliser. She had to hear it or we couldn't carry on. I was the wrong child, but I was home to keep her company.

Martha had hit on asking her to the bingo. She'd made sure there was no room in the car for me and Bell would have looked ungrateful to the point of rudeness if she had refused. Mr Kennedy was behind the wheel, his knuckles white even though he was stationary. She'd also roped in a couple of chubby ladies I'd never met, all three of them tried not to startle when I bent down and waved in at them with one of my better freaky-deakies. When someone, anyone, drives out all the way to Carnsore you can't say you're not in the mood for an outing.

While Bell combed her hair and picked out a cardigan with pockets big enough to hold four bags of sweets and a selection of pens, Mrs Kennedy winked at me and said she hoped I'd be alright on my own. I could have hugged her. I mouthed the words 'thank you, Martha' and she winked again. No one had done anything so thoughtful for me in a long while. It was amazing that she'd buckled so soon after one of my episodes. But that's the beauty of Martha, she was willing to free my hands even after the terrible thing I'd done.

Bell was so put out, it was comical. She finally emerged with two bright red spots of annoyance on her cheeks and tears already tripping over them. In this bungalow, only one of us was allowed to be top dog at a time and it was never my turn to wee on the tree.

- Come on, Bell! It's only the bingo in the parish hall not Timbuctoo!
- I know *that*, Martha! I just wasn't expecting to be out *this* evening!
- Surely that makes it all the more craic?
- Aye, aye, sure! Lindy, I won't be long, okay?
- You go and enjoy yourself, Auntie Bell. I'll be grand here.

She didn't trust me, not a single inch, but she had hardly strapped herself in before the car took off at

47

some speed so she'd no other chance to warn me to be good, to not over-exert myself, to maybe have a little nap. A niece that's napping can do no harm. The St Bede's Parish Hall Bingo on a Sunday evening waits for no woman. I watched the tail lights disappear over the stony bridge before I ran to Bell's room.

Aside from passing the hoover over it twice a month when it was my turn, Auntie's place of rest was off-limits. My mother sang out to me. She was close. I stood in the doorway and wondered just how close. The bed was tight-made, very neat corners – a nurse's set of corners. The sheet turned back in a perfect rectangle was pink against the once-white of the bedspread. The pretend-wood wardrobe was closed, its oval mirror covered in a fine veil of dust. The curtains billowed towards me when the wind raced through the evergreens and another thousand pine needles landed in the back yard. The smell of Bell came lightly, a mix between Lifebuoy soap and warm nylon.

A chest of drawers holds a black-and-white wedding picture of Granny Tess and Granda Morris. They had married when they were just seventeen. Why were they in such a rush to be miserable? Granny Tess was standing slightly behind the chair where he sat holding a blackthorn stick, all the better to beat her with if she ran off. She didn't look inclined to do anything so self-preserving. She had a point on the cuff of her long-sleeved dress that covered the whole back of her hand. A ribbon with the Sacred Heart was pinned on her left breast. God is the only jewellery a decent girl needs.

The Big Man's jaw was square and hard like it is now, and him hardly more than a boy. The eyes were cold and dark under the heavy brow on what was supposed to be the happiest day of his life. He had a tweedy suit on and high laced boots that looked as though they would have Blakeys nailed to the toe and heel so he could be heard coming a mile off while saving his shoe leather. They shone, polished no doubt for many minutes the night before, just like he always did on a Saturday night in Southfork ready for Mass in the morning. He would only polish his own shoes, the rest were left to Mammy. The cuckoo let me know I had no time to waste dandering about in memory lane. Bingo only takes an hour.

Bell's bed was the only possibility. It was a divan and I pulled out the two drawers at the front. One had nothing but high, neat piles of cold linen sheets for the use of laying out the dead. The other had equal amounts of white net curtains with various patterns, polka dots and butterflies, vines and roses. What was she collecting such flashy curtains for when no one so much as drove past never mind walked? I pushed both sets of useless material back into place.

Slumped against the bobbles on the eiderdown, I tried not to drag my thumbnail up the inside of my wrist to make just a little tear, when it comes to me. There are two drawers on the *other side* of the bed! The mat must be carefully rolled up to preserve the dust and when I drag the bed out on its castors, there's a funny smell that I can't put a name to. The closest I can get is toilet water, the kind that Granny Tess used to douse herself in, lavender with something even more sterile flowering underneath.

The drawer on the right is a mess of clothes and papers, which surprises me. Bell is not given to untidiness. There's a winter coat mothballed in plastic, a few jumpers, one of them is a bright pink, which Bell could never wear. Too close to the colour of her face. I can't leave a big brown envelope unopened. It is full of photos jumbled together. Tess again, still young, still stern. Bell, young, Bell in her school uniform, Bell in her nurse's uniform, Bell having a smoke. Bell having a smoke, the *hypocrite*. I lean in to make sure that it is Bell and not Babs, but even through the grain of 1970s Polaroids I can tell it isn't the right woman.

Right at the bottom is a pair of monogrammed gold cufflinks with the letter 'V' on them and a matching tiepin in a black box. Who is this mysterious 'V'? We don't know anyone called 'V', do we? It was a present of its time, stamping ownership on people. You're my

'V' and don't you forget it. I snap the velvet coffin shut and put it back. Who is V, who is V, who is V? I chant as I pull out the left-hand drawer.

It has the suitcase, which is nothing for me to worry about, part of an old man's clear-out, something that Bell will know how to dispose of. I pull it out and settle it on my lap. It's an old brown leather thing with a hard handle and two latches to either side that slide back under my thumbs. The fools! They didn't have the sense or wherewithal to lock it. It too is full of clothes. I see the lace stitched along the hem of an old gypsy dress covered in white and red flowers. It was *hers*. I remember it, I remember her joking about it. *Would I pass as a gypsy girl, Lindy, now that it's all the rage?*

There's a jumper I know, Granny Tess knitted it when there was talk of Mammy being allowed back to Mass. I don't think she ever wore it. There are blouses and … I don't often scream out loud. But some screams hit you like an ice bath. Underneath are clothes I had at seven. A few tattered little blouses and a pair of shorts. I pull them out and hold their tiny shapes up to the light. I had been small once. *I just can't bear to open it. You know? Given what it is?* Of course, it was summertime when she packed it.

My heart starts to hammer. If I'm not careful the screams will start and not stop. I need to get the suitcase off my body where it's starting to feel like I'm nursing a millstone. I pat the layers back into shape, understanding that I'm too worked up to memorise how to put it all back again in order. Bell mustn't know I've been elbow-deep in things that are none of my business. That's when the muffled sound of a biscuit tin rings out.

Several layers down is a square box that has two white dogs with their tongues lolling out, one has its paw on a blue ball and the words 'Half-time' written above its ears. The cuckoo, chime and ting force my hands to slip it out. It has to be hers. I lift the lid to find it full of paper. I can't put the box back, nothing will make me put it back, *nothing*. It will be hard evidence that I'm a thief, a sneak, a spy; it will be further proof of my bad blood, me the wrong child. I tidy the clothes. I plant a kiss from my lips to my fingertips on the lace of her dress, close the lock and slide the suitcase back into the drawer.

The bed is back against the wall and I'm eyeballing it to see if there is any change in its appearance. I unroll the rug with its dust intact and escape with my prize. My room is out as a hiding place, both spare rooms are out, too spartan. Every inch is already accounted for in the kitchen, the front room is the same. Bell has all day every day to search for it and she'll be on a mission to outfox me.

I hit on it! The turf stack. Bell won't go near it where it's piled high against the big shed wall, too many spiders and earwigs. She's terrified of anything with more than four legs. Carrying coal and turf are my jobs, so I will have good reason to go and fill buckets and baskets. In November, the cold weather will start in earnest. Before that I'll be sweeping pine needles off the path then I'll be pouring boiling water on the step to clear the ice and by December the snow will come for a week or two. I weigh the biscuit tin and its promises in my hands. It could be weeks before I can find enough peace to get to the bottom of it. I must ferry it to safe ground.

The shed will soon be absorbed by the evergreens but the heavy wooden door swings out after a couple of good tugs. I pick a spot to the bottom right of the stack. A white box is easily spotted. An old navy apron that I use to keep the worst of the grass stains off me is still on the hook. I double wrap it before putting the box on the concrete floor and covering it with turf. A large horse-shoe-shaped turf that I can almost swear I recognise from the first footing marks its place. A boomerang made of peat. I lean against the block wall at the end to settle my painful heartbeat. I'm not used to so much excitement.

There is a flicker of hope burning in my chest that would account for the heat spreading through me. I breathe in through the nose, out through the mouth, in through the nose, out through the mouth, just how they trained us to breathe in the Clinic. In and out, in and out, thinking nice calm thoughts, thoughts calm enough to block out the unique itch of tightly wound crêpe bandages. It doesn't take long because my mother's hand is back in mine.

I'm boiling the kettle and spooning loose tea into the pot – already heated – when Bell bursts through the front door and treads muck across the good cream carpet she's in such a rush to get at me. She's all bingoed out and in a bad mood. She brings with her the smell of cigarette smoke, a thing she has always claimed she hated. Her eyes flit from me to her bedroom door and she runs to check if she's been invaded. There is no immediate evidence, but fault must be found somewhere. She comes close to put her hand on the teapot to check it's been warmed and I'm glad to be a step in front of her. She can not tick me off.

– Good time?
– It was alright, same faces, same games ...
– Did you win? Did Martha win?
– She's Mrs Kennedy to *you*! And no, she got nothing either. Waste of money, that's all it is. I'd have been better off at home.
– Well, you're back now.

We watch the BBC news because there isn't much on before we switch over to RTE to watch the Irish news, old habits die hard. Both of us are tucked up in bed by eleven but one of us is happier than she's been in a while. I have a new secret or two tucked away. Bell is two-faced, I have proof. There must be something in that box which unnerved Granda Morris enough to move it and to move it dangerously close to me. He and Bell know how devious I am. I got the deviousness and the wild hair from Mammy. What had I got from the man who was my daddy apart from the blue eyes? Neither of them know I'd seen him once; I am so good at keeping stuff to myself. Even when Granda started on me that day after Bundoran, I didn't break. I'd heard Mammy swear it over and over again. *He wasn't there. He wasn't there. He wasn't there.*

I smile in the dark before I let myself feel the burning enjoyment of my other big secret, the old one, the stone that's always in my shoe. Auntie Bell has been swearing pure lies about me over the cream cakes for years and years. I wasn't child-free at all.

Chapter 3

It took two days for Bell to admit she'd been robbed. I was so glad when she finally said something because I was beginning to believe I'd had another one of my dreams, the ones that seem so real that I can touch them. Did I dream that I had found a set of bits of paper that I would fashion into bunting given half a chance? I had scratched a horseshoe shape just to the right of the light switch in my bedroom so that I would not forget my turf sign, but it swam in my eyes when I stared at it too hard and I had a job not to resort to the razor blade taped to the bottom of my metal bin to help me concentrate. The biscuit tin cried out to me but I couldn't get to it for a good long while yet. I was the Queen of Patience.

I am in the kitchen washing lettuce for the salad tea, enjoying the sound of the eggs boiling in the saucepan, when she comes to stand beside me. She is a tuning fork that has been bashed on a table's edge, her agitation reverberating around the eight foot-square walls. I am all serenity. I smile and go back to my work, blotting each leaf between two clean tea towels: wet lettuce really spoils a cold plate.

– Lindy, I've lost something ...

– Oh aye? What?

– Oh ... it's hard to describe. Shall we just call it a Box of Tricks?

– Well now, Bell, if I see a Box of Tricks I'll let you know!

Never show concern or curiosity when you're involved in a crime, that's my motto. Bell bristles some more but she can't give too much away or the lid on all sorts of boxes will fly open and all the skeletons will dance across the lino before we can herd them back in. I might join them just to see Bell's face as I dip and whirl?

– I'll find it, Lindy Morris!

– I'm sure you will when you remember where you lost it. One egg or two?

– One's plenty for any *decent* person.

My hands don't shake as I lay out my lettuce, slice the tomatoes, make little rolls of the Limerick ham with its shocking orange crumb crust and open the eggs to enjoy the brilliant yellow yolks, one for her, two for me. I am not decent. We'll have it with Salad Cream, hot potatoes and silence before the six o'clock news. When we cast down our eyes for a second, by way of Grace, I send up a prayer for Martha Kennedy, even though I know there's no one listening.

Bell on the back foot is a treat. Halfway through the meal she finds cause to complain about the way I have rolled the ham. I should know by now she doesn't *like* the orange breadcrumbs on crumbed Limerick ham from the supermarket. Sometimes she thinks I operate out of *pure badness*. I down my knife and fork while she trims and refolds the dead pig meat to her own taste, then we both plough on to the end.

I pop half an egg with a big extra squeeze of Salad Cream straight into my mouth to drive home my badness. This makes Bell cry and run for the safety of the sofa. Only the news will settle her; the sight of Donald Trump doesn't have that effect on many people but she always had peculiar tastes. She's done her best, you see, her absolute best, always to keep me on the straight and narrow, but I'm still twisted. Only a satsuma-skinned lunatic in a scary wig can console her now. God bless America.

I have a new game. I read my book in the living room while Bell watches the television. This strategy has been in place for a fortnight already. She can't complain I'm not keeping her company, she can't complain that she

58

has no one or nothing to call her own as I'm right beside her with my feet up. She doesn't like it one little bit and has taken sighing to Olympic-gold levels. Father Boluwaji would be so proud of me. I've built myself an invisible lair and Bell is at a loss how to break into it. She sniffs around and around, trying to find the door. It's *wrong* to sit in a room with a television streaming shit and be able to block it out. And doing *two things* at the same time? Must be the Devil himself working through me, she says as she straightens her skirt and dusts crumbs off her chair and readjusts her breasts where a bit of one of them must have sprung free. The left one seems more prone to a touch of the Houdini's. She's always pinging her bra with the thumb of her left hand.

I knew she'd not take to this new stage in our long, complicated relationship so I've a little play rehearsed, for her ears only.

- I find the words on a page comforting ...
- I *understand* that. I can *read*. But this is *The Chase*? This is *Bradley Walsh*? How can you block *him* out?
- Don't you find that the voices get inside your head?
- WHAT? What voices?
- The voices on the TV? They all join up inside my head and create this awful racket. I find myself thinking about strange stuff when they all speak together? Is it not the same for you?

59

I wish her mouth wouldn't fall open so far. It makes me want to cross the room and see how many biscuits I can fit inside it before she gets a hold of herself. She shakes like a sheepdog that suddenly remembers he's taken his eye off the sheep. She needs to get me safely back to my pen before I run over a cliff. All the phrases come pouring out, familiar as a Hail Mary, and twice as pointless.

– Well now, Lindy (cough). You'll need to *calm* yourself (cough). There's nothing to be gained by *that* kind of talk (cough). You don't want to be getting the doctors involved again, do you (cough)? Your Granda Morris will have a hissy fit if he has to take *any more questions* when he's in town (big cough). You know he can't take the shame. Especially from Protestants!

– I suppose you're right, Bell.

– I am right, I am right. Of course I'm right.

I'm not surprised she's struggling. If I break out again, it'll be proof that she's not up to the job of keeping Lindy Morris out of sight and out of mind. She only has this one job so she mustn't fail. It comes with a free house, free locks on the doors to which she alone has the keys and a free hand to report whatever she wants about me to my darling grandfather. I go back to my book, placid as a lamb, and it's not long before I hear the wrappers coming off a pair of Caramel

Wafers. She passes me one without a peep and I take it in gracious silence. I love Caramel Wafers, so sweet and satisfying.

We're both watching the nights draw in and I've been making noises about tidying the back shed. The turf stack is falling down, I say often. I'm going to have to do something about that, sooner rather than later. Bell nods, the information is seeping in and I will wait for a dry day. Spiders run for cover on dry days and she will be hunkered down behind closed doors and windows in case they cross the twenty yards and reach the house.

There have been no more of my episodes. I've made sure of that. She relaxes when a few weeks have passed and we get on with ignoring the fact that I took a knife to my own throat. If I catch her snooping on me, I cock an ear as if there's someone chatting to me from the ceiling but I don't answer back. Sometimes I feign surprise. *Oh, Bell, it's you*, I say, *I thought I heard something.* I keep it to that and a good blast of the freaky-deaky; this game has to be played with a subtle hand. She can take me in with one glance. The faintest trace of blood on a hankie or a piece of clothing would have her nerves out on stalks, but I have become a model niece. I can wait another lifetime to have a nice long stretch with the Box of Tricks. I want to be able to sink my teeth into it and never let go. Its song stays strong, cuckoo, chime, ting, tinkle.

I wake up, I make the tea, I make my lunch as I have decided all on my ownsome to go back to the Credit Union, only three days a week for now but days of my choosing. Good Lindy. I have a sandwich, always cheese. I take the bus that turns at the edge of the Carn Forest and enjoy the luxury of a window seat all the way into Ballyglen. I like the expanse of green running to the hills and the huge white clouds racing above it. I sit for six hours wishing it were only two hours that didn't feel like twenty. I try to keep the chocolate bars to one a day and rotate them, though every day could be a Lion Bar day if I wasn't disciplined. Monday KitKat. Tuesday Turkish Delight. Wednesday Lion Bar, oh happy day and midweek to boot. Thursday Toffee Crisp. Friday Double Decker. I come back on the same bus and I make the tea like I was never out of the house.

The town of Ballyglen is small, too small even for the Credit Union. People around here don't like borrowing money in case word gets out that they're in bother. We all sit at our desks shuffling papers and shuffling figures and shuffling back and forth to the filing cabinets as if it mattered. They all steer clear of me, especially when I'm just back from the Clinic. They smile, tight little smiles that don't show any teeth, in case I startle and run from the building. I've never done anything showy but if I even sneeze violently they all look up from their desks in alarm. They think, like most civilians, that pain makes a sound, but it doesn't.

The best day I can have at work is the first day back after a flip-out. Fear has a smell; it's Imperial Mints and sweat on the women and greasy hair and sweat on men. I'm asked a hundred times how I'm doing and I tell them I'm doing fine. They don't care and neither do I as long as we all keep it polite.

The Credit Union is a two-storey house painted white which sits at the fork at the top of the town. The road to the left leads out to Carnsore, the road on the right leads out to Carnsore the really long way round. For some reason the front garden was left when it was converted into an office building of sorts and on both sides of the path a particularly nasty colour of pink hydrangeas bob their heavy round good-for-nothing heads. I really hate hydrangeas, especially pink ones. The Main Street has a news-agents where the nominal boss Siobhain gets her Imperial Mints and her family-size bar of Cadbury's Fruit & Nut every day and her *Grazia* magazine once a week. She believes she has class.

It has a huge Co-op store, a hardware store founded in 1865 and last painted in 1864, Leehy's drapery, Kelly's Pharmacy, Diamond's the bakery and coffee shop and Scraps Fish Bar, which sells the deep-fat-fried mince-beef pies and chips that my colleague Declan McIvor has managed to spill down his shirt front without noticing every single Friday. I count them, one splat, two splats, three splats. I've never had to go above ten, not even the day his tomato ketchup sachet exploded and his solution was to wear his jumper for the rest of the afternoon in a hot July. It's a good job nothing much puts me off a Double Decker.

I have my cheese sandwich at my desk when they've all fled to sample the delights of the strip or to run home for a bite to eat in one of the two housing estates that were built at the other end of the town. I don't like the housing estates – all those windows looking on to flat tarmac drives and paved front gardens with maybe one sad pot of geraniums or maybe nothing growing at all. Purgatory picked out in pebble-dash and grey coins of discarded chewing gum. I make a mug of tea and roll my chair back and prop my feet up on the wastepaper basket. It's a glamorous career.

There must be a rota somewhere drawn up by Boss Siobhain that dictates whose turn it is to stay with me. It's someone different every day who says too loudly why they have to work through as they roll their eyes and laugh a bit too much. I feel so sorry for Declan McIvor when his turn falls on a Friday. He spends the whole time blocking the window with his enormous arse while he looks in the direction of Scraps Fish Bar and I can't even apologise for keeping him from his one true love, chips. Where do men get trousers that size? The next time I go into Leehy's, I might just ask.

They're very good to have me at all as I'm on doctor's orders to 'have a purpose' and to 'not get too isolated', not a fantastic CV. Auntie Bell says the money's very handy to bolster her pension when she sees it landing in our joint account. If I need anything, I only have to ask her and we'll go together to buy a jumper or a pair of shoes.

I'm not sore on clothes. I have three pairs of trousers and about four tops that I wear to work, a pair of jeans and a few jumpers for home and set of overalls when I need to work outside. I've been repairing the overalls in front of Bell when I've had enough of my book or enough of her sighing fit to lift the roof. I've sewn the pockets back in place and tightened the buttonholes. The right knee needed a patch and I did the left one to match. Don't want to be lacking style as I'm mucking out the chicken coop.

Back in front of the dreaded television in the evening, Bell wonders why I can't keep myself still. My hands always have to be 'at' something. I have turned a page in my book. Amazing criticism, this from a woman who you might find named under the word *fidget* in the dictionary. The left boob has worked itself loose again and is rammed back into the brassiere. Poor auld boob, it must be black and blue. She still hasn't found the Box of Tricks and her temper shows it. She's never done picking at me like a cross hen. But the Box of Tricks has had the opposite effect on me. I am as unruffled as a lake on a breathless day. I sit and wait for the right moment and, praise be, it comes as so many things do, in the form of a death. Always a good sign, I think.

Mrs McCrossan's mother decided to die at a rather inconvenient time. Mrs Barr is away for all three days of the wake – a last-minute bargain coach trip to Medjugorje to stand in awe at the foot of the Virgin Mary statues – and Mrs Kennedy can only do the first day and night as her and Mr Kennedy are long booked into a nice boarding house in Downings. It's their anniversary, she keeps saying, and she won't be budged on her romantic break because the deposit is non-refundable.

There is only one option, Bell must step in to help with tear-drying and tea-making and she may have to stay the whole night if Deirdre McCrossan can't pull herself together. Her mother was in her nineties so it was hardly a shock that she had a stroke and never woke up again but apparently her grieving daughter is carrying on as if she had fallen off an international stage when she was ballet dancing. The wimmin are unimpressed by her heartbroken show. There's been a lot of sniffing, even in the telephone conversations.

I will not be going. I am not good at wakes. One glimpse of the waxen faces and gnarled hands bound by rosary beads for all eternity and I could be back in the Clinic. I'm always convinced they're going to wake up. I imagine them sitting bolt upright and demanding to know why everyone's gorging on tea and biscuits right in their bedroom. A little shiver runs down my spine when I remember how Jack Gallagher, the undertaker, puts too much make-up on them, the women and the men. The lipstick is peach for both genders; he must have bought a job lot of it somewhere. I get my mind off the cold, hard lips double-quick time in case they open and tell me what's on the other side.

So Bell must attend. She's in a tailspin the like of which she might never recover from. It's the suddenness of things that upends her. Without time, she can't organise a minder for me. I will be off the leash for hours.

I help her gather the essentials – water from St Patrick's Well blessed by Father Boluwaji on the last feast day, hankies, mints, back-up Lourdes Water, black cardigan, apron, rubber gloves (for the washing-up, not for anything to do with the remains) and finally she's ready. Granda Morris is beeping the horn on the street to let her know she's keeping him back. He has better places to be than stuck out here with one of the two idiotic fucking bitches left in his life. Every honk adds to Bell's distress.

– You'll be alright, won't you, Lindy?

– I'll be top, Bell.

– There's plenty of ham in the fridge and a couple of tomatoes that could do with being eaten because they're on the turn ...

– Ham and rotten tomatoes for tea, got it.

– Oh Lindy, now I didn't mean that!

– Bell – you have to GO! Granda Morris won't wait.

She climbs in to the tractor and I hear her getting an earful about how it's not his fucking job to taxi her about, even though there's a fucking dead woman involved. Women are two a penny and still not worth the money. She nods and nods her agreement as she's joggled off the street. He won't come back to check up on me, it would be too bare with just the pair of us eyeball to eyeball. She wouldn't tell him about the missing Box of Tricks in a month of Sundays. He'd blow a gasket if she failed him again. I see them cross the stony bridge. I wait for the next cuckoo before I take off.

The turf stack is how I left it with the horseshoe turf. I lift it up like a chalice and set it to one side. The biscuit tin is there with its little white dogs and their blue ball. Should I bring it in to the house and devour the contents or keep it out here? If Bell managed to get a lift home, if her services weren't required, she could be back in half an hour. I hope that Deirdre McCrossan is howling loud enough to be heard on the moon. I hope she needs twenty-four-hour care for a week, although, of course, she'll be dropped like a hot potato as soon as the funeral is over. No one can help you grieve, it's a traditionally lonesome activity.

I settle down against the brick wall with it on my knees. Every sound carries for a mile out here, I'll hear her and have time to run back to the kitchen. The lid makes a satisfying little metallic pop. The top layers of the box are photographs of my mother. There's a shot of her in her school uniform. Her wild curly hair has been parted and brushed down into an uneasy-looking frizz with two hair clips on either side. Her face says a thousand words and not one of them happy. She *loved* having her hair wild and free, and it suited her that way. It's never particularly suited me; it's too much when it's perched on a six-footer.

There's another picture of her and Bell together and the same torture has been applied to her mop of curls. Who would have done that? Granny Tess or themselves? As always I am struck by their similarity – only Bell's eyes are more placid, she looks like a schoolgirl whereas my mother looks like she could rise up out of the chair and fly at any moment. The wimmin have often sniffed at her flightiness but I like the thought of her as a bird.

69

There are two more pictures of them side by side, in identical Holy Communion dresses and in identical Confirmation dresses. I can pick my mother out without thinking about it. That would be the problem with twins, especially twins making their way through the Sacraments – you can't throw one away or you'd lose the other. The Communion dresses look home-made. They're plain, no frills, white knee socks and white shoes with white buckles. Both of them were slight, knobbly knees and slim wrists, a clip with three daisies holding on their lace skull caps, long ringlets springing free.

The Confirmation dresses must have come from a shop. They're pale blue with a velvet band around the chest and a droopy fabric rose. Leehy's would have been stacked high with ankle-length nylon in the run-up to Ballyglen's Confirmation season, 1956. Now the girls are starting to divide. Bell is taller – starting out on her journey of being the slightly larger version of the two. Granda would decide that only one of them deserved feeding. He liked to watch one of them choke on their cheap mince and spuds while the other one watched and wished it was her. It was usually Mammy who watched Bell. *I could get through it without crying so it was easier on us both*, she told me. Maybe she was brave but maybe she was foolhardy to skip so many meals; maybe she knew being smaller meant being harder to spot.

There's a photo of Mammy with Martha Kennedy. She was pretty but already running to a bit of chubbiness in the face. They're slung around each other, widest of wide smiles, terrible cream Aran jumpers alive with cables and knots. They have their backs to a hedge that could be any of a hundred hedges around here. *I have such fond memories of her. She was thoughtful, not wicked, not really.*

There are postcards, too, from Martha Kennedy from her beloved Bundoran on the Donegal coast – she had a summer job and wrote to Mammy every week. *Dear Babs, Hope everything is well with you?* The news was always the same, she was busy waitressing, the tips were pretty good, the Yanks didn't seem to know they didn't need to tip, the seaside was the best place in the world, even though it never stopped raining. She's going to send a letter soon. *All the best for now, Martha.*

After four or five postcards, I find the promised letter. It's another round of breezy news, dated August 1964, so Mammy would have been eighteen, two years before I was born. Right at the bottom just before the 'best regards' the word America screams off the pale blue lined page. *Soon, we'll be away to America. It's hard to imagine the times we'll have.*

The pounding blood in my ears is coming from my heart and I remember again to breathe in and out, in and out, nice calm thoughts. Of course she would have wanted to fly across the wide and beautiful Atlantic. I had wanted the exact same thing when I ran away myself at the same age. I couldn't *wait* to get away. Granda Morris did *not* approve and swore I would get no help from him, no money, no lifts, no hope of any rescue if I got into bother. Granny Tess didn't give a rat's ass if I went and never returned and Bell cried herself into a fever. Her skin was still on fire the day I had to touch my face to hers by way of goodbye.

I would have hitchhiked all the way to Larne dragging my holdall behind me if I'd had to but in the end Miriam's brother drove us all the long way up the Belfast road to the port to get the boat to Stranraer and the never-ending, stinking coach all the way to London Victoria railway station. I felt so young and yet beyond ready to step into a city I had only ever seen on the television. For a minute we're all on the same page. My young mammy and a young Martha and me all about to hit the ground running and live happily ever after.

I hear the low moan of the evergreen trees as they move this way and that as the evening draws close. They must often want to pull their roots from the bog and be away some place else too, some place where they don't have to stand in water while it rains down in sheets.

Mammy would say, *Let me show you a funny thing, Lindy! Look, it's raining sheets!* And sure enough, even though I was small I could see the rectangles of rain racing each other across the dark hills. *Stop filling her head with your nonsense,* Granny Tess would answer from the corner where she sat darning. I looked over at her, her thick legs in thick brown tights disappearing behind the big bag of wool in every colour of the rainbow. She was fixing stitches on to her circular needle, red wool filling a hole in one of Granda's grey welly socks. I wanted to shout at her to *just go away* but Mammy must've felt me stiffen. She pulled me against her in a forbidden hug. *There's hardly anything wrong with showing her the sky.* Granny Tess said nothing, suddenly too busy mending and making do.

She's close to me today, lovely Mammy. I can feel her leaning in to kiss my neck. I can see her dreams rear up out of the box and parade themselves across the dreary turf shed covering it with colours. The blue of her favourite scarf, her worn-out green tweed coat with the horn buttons on the pockets, the blue glint on her long black hair. I hate that she's not here; I miss her so much some days that she's an ache that takes up the whole of my chest.

There are a few other papers in the box: report cards that show she was a good enough student. Some ticket stubs from the Astoria Ballroom in Bundoran for various dances, Big Tom and the Mainliners, says one, Brush Shiels, Horslips. Some old pink cardboard raffle tickets, a miraculous medal with 'Cloth which has touched the tongue of St Anthony of Padua' printed on the paper it's pinned to. Where in God's name did she find *that*? The patron saint of lost things and licker of cloth?

Right at the bottom of the box, under a handful of small pearl buttons, is the document Granda Morris had to produce when I went to the grammar school. (No one said well done when I got the 11+ because now I would cost them even more money to rear.) It was so forbidden that he drove me there himself and handed it over to the Mother Superior.

The trip was so *long* and so *silent*. He didn't even bother with one of his eight-track cassette tapes of terrible country and western music. Johnny McEvoy was the pits, but I'd have killed to hear him that day. A thousand green fields rolled by outlined with stone ditches, ditches with trees in, ditches with the giant metal feet of electricity pylons standing either side of them as they stretched over the hills and far away.

I'd never been in his company for more than five minutes alone in my whole life. And suddenly there I was sitting on the back seat of the car while he drove the twelve miles to Strabane and up the Curley Hill to Mount Carmel Convent Grammar School, waiting outside the office for twenty minutes – both of us uncomfortable on too-small plastic chairs, breathing in the smell of wee and sandwiches in the first-year cloakroom.

We had our allotted twenty minutes with Sister Joquina, who checked me for horns and nothing else, and then we had to endure the twelve miles home again. I was thirsty, I was hungry, I was car sick, but I never said a word. I didn't have anything to vomit. He'd gone to a lot of bother to stop me seeing my birth certificate. And now it lay in my hands.

Paper is so delicate, so light even when it has a cast-iron secret. Mother's maiden name: Barbara Anne Morris; Profession: Housewife; Father's name: Linus Quinn; Profession: blank; Gender of child: (F); Name: Belinda Jane. Date of birth: 20 May 1966. Time: 2.09 a.m. Linus Quinn is written in what must be my mother's hand, he is an addition.

I was official, documented. Mammy didn't even give me my own name. She called me Belinda so I had to share with her twin. I'd never had the sense to ask her why she did that, give me Bell's name. Bell got the good syllable and I got the tail end, I was Lindy from the start. And he was Linus Quinn, of no profession. Maybe she wanted to give me a hint of his Christian name when she knew I'd never carry his surname? Hello again, Daddy! I'm Lindy to your Linus. It's been a long time. Why did you never come back just once to check up on me? Oftentimes, I could have used another day out at the seaside. Was it Granny Tess, Granda Morris or Bell who kept me from him and him from me? I stroke the paper where her name is, where my name is, where his name is, the family that should have been.

Bell cried like a spoilt child the day she put it into the envelope to send away for my passport. She didn't like it that soon I wouldn't be her toy any more. She cut her lip when she licked the glue to make it stick. I handed her a stamp and she licked that too. I didn't trust her to post it for a second. I demanded she hand it over and when she didn't, I mithered her until she pulled on her coat and walked the mucky lane to the main road. I was a dog at her heel. I've no idea where I got the cheek to be so bold. Without a passport I could never get away. The pair of us sat stony-faced as the bus lolloped along, smacking against the low branches of sycamores and the scratchy fingers of hawthorn hedges.

We were stopped at an Army checkpoint and the British soldiers came along the aisle eyeballing all the men where they sat rolling their cigarettes so they could keep their eyes down. We were all put out a mile before the town. We had to walk through a long line of other soldiers twirling this way and that to make sure there were no snipers, no bombers, no youngsters with a variety of missiles ready to take out one of their number.

Bell, who couldn't stand the soldiers with their guns on the best of days, reminded me what a traitor I was on this truly terrible day. I was surrendering to being British like a filthy, unprincipled coward. I said nothing when I prised her fingers off the envelope and dropped it into the unknown insides of the red post box. For weeks afterwards she watched the road like a hawk. I wasn't home when the postman came with the packet holding my dark blue British passport.

Bell left the passport on the kitchen table and took the birth certificate. She'd always opened my letters, although they were only from Miriam. When she heard me coming in to claim my first ever ID, she ran down the stairs and threw the door open, face puffy, every cell dripping with hatred. *Don't bother putting me down as next of kin*, she said with venom. *You're nothing to do with me! Don't bother putting me down either*, said Granny Tess from her chair next door, *accursed turncoat*! Granda Morris had slapped me good and hard when he was told I'd applied for a British passport instead of an Irish one. It wasn't political. Belfast was quicker than Dublin and I needed to get on the boat sooner rather than later.

I'd rarely missed my mother more than I missed her on that day. Staring like a gom at the passport that was supposed to set me on the path to a different life. I had no one to claim me. In the end, I wrote B. Morris,

Southfork, Cavan Road, Ballyglen, Co. Tyrone and hoped that the RUC or the British Army or whoever did that sort of thing would make one or other of my reluctant relatives collect my body in the event of an accident or an emergency.

I wake up on the floor of the turf shed when it is dark as pitch. I hate it when that happens. One minute I'm soaring, the next I've crashed. The cold has seeped into my bones. I scramble around the walls to throw the switch for the light. All my treasures are laid out in a semicircle where I've been sitting. The birth certificate is at the top, to the left of it the photos, to the right the postcards and other bits. I don't recall setting them out like that, like a game of Solitude. Sometimes my hands work without my mind.

I check the time on my watch, 8.30. Bell will hardly be home tonight. The wake will be in full swing. It's a bonus no one lives near us, she won't be able to get a lift as it's a big ask for someone to come all the way to the border with Donegal and it's such a long, straight, lonely road. I have enough time to read everything again, to soak it up like a cake in syrup. I have a father. I try out the sweetness of it in my mouth. I've read my father's name. My father is called Linus Quinn. He's tall and straight and strong as an oak tree. He might remember me, he might not. I can remind him. I have the look of his people, right enough.

I look down at my semicircle and feel what I'm sure is a wash of happiness, though it's been a while. I slide back down the rough wall and hover my hands over the papers, as if I could divine more delicious detail that way. Look at me, getting all gypsy-headed! It is only then that I see the paper tucked tight into the lid. How had I missed it? Hungry eyes usually see so far. I get a fingernail under it and fish it free. Although it's shaking, I can read it. Mother's maiden name: Barbara Anne Morris; Profession: Housewife; Father's name: Linus Quinn; Profession: blank; Gender of child: (M); Name: Patrick Joseph. Date of birth: 20 May 1966. Time: 1.48 a.m.

I feel myself lift off from the cold floor. I am unmoored. Floating high above a house where Time has stopped, even though some man-made machines still cuckoo, chime and ting. I see the evergreens being shaken by the wind and hear them creak as they let loose another hail of pine needles. I see them land and already start being rolled into piles on either side of the concrete of the back yard as the October wind follows them down. It doesn't seem possible that something as real as concrete could even exist. Then time flies backwards, back to where the strange story of Lindy Morris started in earnest.

I was never designed to be all alone. I was one of a pair. I had a brother. What had happened to him? Had a son been good enough for Linus Quinn but not a daughter? Was he just as rotten as Granda Morris on that score? What else had Mammy never told me? The enormity of the secret gnaws at me for a minute until I remember I have the same one. It's not impossible to bury a whole baby, it's not even that difficult. I'd managed it. I'd had good reason.

But why had Mammy taken that road to hell? Where was he, my brand-new big brother? Then I know, I can just feel it like a key turning in a lock. The little rectangle to the side of the Morris grave that I'd pointed to so many times.

— Who's in there, Mammy?

— Just an angel who fell to earth.

— Why is there no headstone?

— Angels don't need headstones because you can never forget them, no matter how hard you try. You just keep him in your prayers so he can go back to Heaven one day, alright?

— Alright.

I'd prayed for our dead every Sunday for the eighteen years before I escaped Ballyglen for London and I'd never known my brother was on the list. I bloody my knuckles on the rough concrete floor as a voice from the past reassures me that you can't miss what you've never had. What a lie. You can miss what you've never had every cuckoo, chime and ting of the day.

Bell would have known about Patrick Joseph. Granny Tess would have known about Patrick Joseph. Granda Morris would have known about Patrick Joseph. Malachi and his mob would know. Kind Martha, Kitty Barr the bitch, the muck-spreader Deirdre McCrossan, even Miriam's mammy would have known. He was buried on consecrated ground so he had been baptised. The priest would have known, the priest's housekeeper, the undertakers, the grave diggers, the whole townland of Carnsore probably knows. Maybe even the dull fuckers at the Credit Union know? I have been segregated.

Mammy might have told me the truth when I was older. She might have told me if she'd got older. I wish for the millionth time that she had lived. Auntie Bell wishes she had too. She still hates wakes because she's practically seen herself laid out and prayed over. She explained it to me in one word, as 'peculiar'. *It's very peculiar, Lindy, to see your mirror image in a coffin like that! Oh, and the way she died! Too terrible!* She must have thought about the worms eating her sister's face, must have wondered if the flesh was blackening and falling from her bones, if her teeth were bared. I know I did, I still do. On the worst of days, her jaw falls open with a click. She doesn't speak, not a word, not even goodbye.

Grief is a room. Someone helpful told me that at the Clinic. We think we can escape it. We've locked it and walked away a hundred times, a thousand times, but the slightest nudge will have the door springing open and try as we might we still have to walk through it. The dark inside it beckons. Its ceilings are high and the walls are miles apart and the feel of it never changes. Its detail never fades, the edges only ever get sharper, the air thicker and harder to breathe. My room has Mammy in it. Mammy in a wooden box resting on wooden trestles. I am seven, she is twenty-seven, exactly twenty-seven. She died on her birthday, her and Bell's birthday. Had there ever been a cake? Or a celebration of any kind to mark their birthday?

In my room, Bell is crying in the corner, she can't stop. Mammy's friend Martha Kennedy, too. She has been trying to hug me all night but I will not be touched, not by her or anyone else. Kitty Barr is carrying trays of tea around and Deirdre McCrossan is following behind with plates of biscuits and buttered scones. They all look sad as they look from me to each other and back to the box but I don't care.

Mammy lied to me. She had said we would never be parted, not for any reason. But she was already on her way to Heaven without me. She had said she wouldn't be blue-black in the coffin. She said she would be the best-looking corpse in town. She's not. I can hear

82

everyone whispering about how terrible she looks, how terrible that she hadn't been more careful. But then, she'd always had that wild streak. Poor Tess has been sedated, that little thing there is her daughter, aye, *that daughter.* Oh shame, shame, shame, they say, rattling their rosary beads. I wish Mammy would wake up and tell them all to go away, but it's been three days already and Mammy hasn't woken up, not even once. Bell says she's not going to ever wake up again and Martha Kennedy cries some more every time she says it.

Granny Tess had screamed the house down when the RUC came. Granda Morris was away at the cattle mart so she had to deal with them herself. She had sworn an oath never to speak to one of them, them or the UDA, but here they were now, muddying her good clean street with their rotten boots. I was outside playing because I wasn't allowed inside until Mammy came home again. I had my coat on. Mammy had buttoned it up for me and said, *Be good, Lindy. I'll be back as quick as a wink!*

It was early, so early that the light was still milky and I could see her breath coming out as white clouds when she turned to wave at me, bye, bye, bye. I had a bit of bread and jam in greaseproof paper in my pocket to eat in an emergency. Granny Tess would likely not call me for dinner but I wasn't to worry. Mammy would be back before then and she'd see to it that I got my fair share of brown fish and spuds. The days were long in August, I had to remember that, I should play about and think what colour I wanted my bedroom in the new house painted. I already knew – yellow was my favourite, yellow like the sunshine in my picture books.

She was off to look for a house. There was one in Donegal she had her eye on. We needed a house and soon. There had been a few almighty rows over the past weeks and we were both in danger of being put outside for ever. Granda had promised that we were for the road. We were nothing but bloody gypsies so the road was all we deserved. Mammy was going to fix it, though; she was going to fix us up a place to live happily ever after.

I played about outside for hours. Granny Tess had at least allowed me my porridge before lifting the latch on the back door and pointing to the back yard. It didn't come with a lovely coating of brown sugar like Mammy's did, but I said nothing. I swallowed my last spoonful of salty milk and went where she pointed.

– Where's that mother of yours today?
– I don't know, Granny Tess!
– Hmmmmm, well, she needn't make a habit of leaving you here. I have enough to do without dealing with her mistakes. Out!

The armoured car stopped at the front door when everyone knew that the kitchen door was the way in for friends. The RUC men had a job getting Granny Tess to answer it; they knocked and knocked and knocked. But it was the sight of the priest that made her open the door. She let him cross the threshold, though the RUC man had to stay on the doorstep. The screaming started a few minutes after that. I'd never heard such a sound and could hardly believe that it was Granny Tess that was making it – she was never done telling me to be quiet.

The RUC man asked me my name. Lindy Morris, I says. And what's your mammy's name, Lindy? She's called Babs, that's short for Barbara Anne, I says. Right, right, he says, and puts on his cap with a sigh and a rub of my curls and leaves me all alone on the street. The doctor comes next, Dr Moore. Hello, Dr Moore, I says. Hello, Lindy, he says, shaking my hand, I'm sorry for your troubles. He takes one of his lollies out of his pocket and gives it to me. I don't have any troubles but I love lollies. I've only just peeled it and started to suck when Granda Morris comes back.

- Get that out of your mouth! This is not a day for sweets!
- Dr Moore gave it to me …
- I don't care. Get rid of it and get out of my sight! Run!

I ran all the way to the big barn at the back of the farm. I wanted my mammy. She hardly ever left me for this long during the day. She often slipped out at night when I was safe and sound and feeling sleepy in the big bed with her. It was one of our secrets. She liked walking in the moonlight and I couldn't go with her because I was only small. When I was a big girl we'd go together and we'd lie down beside a ditch and watch the stars spinning around. But Granny Tess and Granda Morris could never find out because otherwise they'd want to come too and ruin all our fun. I crossed my heart and hoped to die that I wouldn't ever tell them; they were the *last two people on earth* I'd want to come along.

My stomach growled and I got colder and colder, but still Mammy didn't come. I watched the yellow squares of light coming from the kitchen windows but no shadows moved across them. She can't have found the house in Donegal where we were going to live or maybe she had to clean it up first before she came back to get me? Maybe she had to buy some stuff for the dinner and was even now walking back across the border to scoop me up and take me there for chips and sausages and a runny egg?

Would I be able to have Miriam in my new house? She wasn't allowed in Southfork because we had enough mouths to feed. And I wasn't allowed to go to her house because even though her people *said* it was okay for a gypsy to come in to their house that's not what they really *thought*. I lay down at the bottom of the stack of hay bales and pulled another one in front of me to make a room of my own. All I had to do was wait.

It was the next morning when Bell finally came to find me. When she shook me awake, I was cold and hungry and started asking her where my mammy was, but she wouldn't say. All she said was that Mammy wasn't coming back but I had to get up now and come inside. She held my hand too tight in hers and took me back across the yard. Uncle Malachi was there, standing outside smoking a cigarette with Granda Morris. They both eyeballed me and I was worried that I would get a slap or two for sleeping outside. I hadn't meant to be bad, to break the rules, and I hadn't even been smart enough to see the stars spinning round, but they let me pass.

– That's going to be a bigger problem now, says Uncle Malachi.

– Aye, says Granda Morris. It is.

Bell made me toast and piled it high with butter and sugar because Granny Tess was nowhere to be seen. The whole house was quiet without her and my mammy. I was to have a bath as soon as I was finished eating, God knows what might be crawling on me after a night in the barn, the whole place was alive with bugs and ticks, never mind the filthy rats.

The big old tub was filling up with water and she poured a capful of bubble bath into it. Bell stripped me down to my vest and knickers, stopping a minute to turn my palms up and to kiss me quickly in each. Something was very wrong to be getting kisses instead of smacks. I wished I knew why she was crying so that I could make it better. *Don't cry, Auntie Bell*, I says. *Mammy'll be back soon.* She took off my miraculous medals and closed the nappy pin carefully before she turned to me again. Her eyes were red as beetroot.

- You need to be looking nice and neat today, Lindy, d'you understand? I'll do your hair in plaits and you're not to fiddle about with them and set that hair of yours off into a mad frizz ball, okay?
- Okay. Where's Mammy?
- She's on her way.

My room started a matter of hours after that. Auntie Bell wasn't as gentle with the hairbrush as Mammy but she was better at plaits so I tried not to squeak every time she ripped out a knot. I was dressed in my Sunday best though it was only Saturday, and made to sit and wait on the stairs. You'll know when to come down, says Bell.

I couldn't see what the men were carrying in at first. They had a terrible job turning it so that it would go into the living room, head-first. It was a box with goldy handles and a carving of the Last Supper on the lid. Granda Morris let out a roar at one of them to be careful when it bashed into the door frame and I knew there was something terrible going on when he let Bell reach for his hand.

Every time my mammy tried to hold his hands he pulled them away from her and held them above his head, out of reach, and she'd have to stay on her knees in front of him crying because she was so angry. *He never listens to me, Lindy! He just won't listen.* He pretended she wasn't there, every time she moved her head to block the TV he'd move his to see past her. He looked like a cowboy surrendering to a sheriff but she didn't ever have a gun.

Martha Kennedy, Deirdre McCrossan and Kitty Barr all filed in, followed by loads of neighbours, so I climbed down the stairs and some of the people made way for me. There was a man on either side of the box, each of them undoing two screws at a time and I was level with it when the lid came off and there Mammy's face was. It looked all melted. And why didn't she move or smile at me when I'd been waiting for her for two whole days? I put my hand on her forehead to see if she was sick but she wasn't hot, she was cold. Granda Morris roared for Bell.

– Get *her* out of here!

– Well, she has to see at some stage!

– Not now, not bloody now when everyone's watching!

Bell pushed her way through the shocked faces to reach for me but she didn't realise how tight I was holding the side of the box. When she yanked me the whole thing wobbled and everyone let out a kind of *Oh*. The men shot to their feet to steady Mammy before she spilled on to the carpet. Some were for letting me stay; I was only small and I must be confused. Others were for taking me home with them until it was over, but I was already home.

I saw Granda Morris's tall, wide shape turn away from me. He was like a granite block standing stone. I'd often heard him described as a rangy man and I thought that meant a man who was content to sit in front of the range until Mammy put me right. He's six foot, five inches, and every one of them rotten, she said. I was shoved in to the kitchen and Martha Kennedy started trying to hug me. From the hall, I heard a couple of the big men chatting in low voices but not low enough.

– That Gabriel Morris is nothing short of a fucking bully!
– He always was and always will be, forever more, Amen! Still, you've got to feel sorry for the auld fucker on a day like this.
– Not too sorry, he treated both those girls like dirt. I don't fancy that wayne's chance of ever seeing another drop of loving kindness.

The people stayed for three days. There was a lot of praying and a gallon of tea handed around. I listened to what they thought. It was so sad, she was so young. It was so sad about me. Sure I was only a little thing. Who'd look out for me now? They'd heard that my grandfather would never be able to swallow the disgrace that his daughter – God rest her soul, we know we shouldn't speak ill of the dead – had tangled with the travelling community. They'd hardly try to claim me back at this stage? You never knew with travellers, some of them were the salt of the earth, some were not. Mind, some of the people sitting round this room were dirty rotten bastards, rosary beads or no rosary beads blessed by God. Granda Morris's head snapped round like someone was calling his name.

It was extra sad for Bell, what a *day* to lose your twin sister. Oh, and what a *way* to lose your twin sister. She wasn't lost, she was right there in the box in front of their hungry eyes, I wanted to say, but somehow I knew they didn't want to hear from me.

Auntie Bell was terribly upset. I'd seen her beating her hands against a complete stranger. Maybe she was mad because the stranger hadn't queued up to get in to the house, he hadn't dipped his fingers in the Holy Water fount, he hadn't pumped Granda Morris's hand and said sorry for your troubles. He'd been hanging about smoking cigarettes near the big barn, he walked up and down, up and down in a pale green suit. He was no farmer. He had on shiny black shoes that he'd managed to keep the muck off.

I slipped out and looked at him up close. I'm Lindy, I said. Are you scared to come in? He stared at me like I was a ghost but finally he said that he wanted to talk to Bell, could I be a good girl and go and get her? Her and only her, because it was a secret the thing they needed to chat about. When I whispered to Bell that there was a man outside, she shot out of the back door like a greyhound. She crossed the yard and he threw his cigarette down and ground it out with his shiny shoe.

She walked right up and started pounding on his good shirt and tie. He didn't even try to stop her and she tired herself out pretty quick. She sort of slid down but when he picked her up by the elbows she was all done being helped up. She pulled her arms away and came back into the kitchen. His mouth said *Bell, Bell, Bell* but she didn't stop. He just watched her go. I'd never known that there were men who wouldn't slap you as quick as look at you. She caught me nosy-parkering at the window and yanked me back towards the hell of the wake.

– What did you just see?
– Nothing, Auntie Bell! I saw nothing, nothing!
– Keep it that way, Lindy! If I ever hear you so much as mention this I'll tan your hide, dead mammy or no dead mammy!

I never saw the stranger again. When I looked back, he was gone, disappeared without paying his respects.

That night, I was lying alone in me and Mammy's bed. It was cold. I was so lonesome. I wanted to be downstairs with her but Granda Morris was keeping watch by her remains. Uncle Malachi was down there too. They kept a chair between them and passed a bottle of whiskey to and fro as the need arose. I could hear the clink of the glasses being filled. The rest of the house was silent; it felt damp even for August. I watched a moth warming itself on the light bulb, landing and flying, landing and flying until it got burned. The only sound was the sobs coming from Bell's room. I slid to the floor and padded down to her. She probably only needed a hug and I could use one myself.

She had her back turned to the room, face jammed against the wall. As soon as I spoke she uncoiled herself and crossed the bare floorboards to shake me none too gently by the arms. There'd hardly be hugs after that.

– Auntie Bell?

– Get out!

– Don't cry. There's no point in crying. It doesn't make anything better. Mammy said—

– Don't ever quote what *Mammy* said to me, d'y'hear me? And why are you crying now? Hmmmm? If it's pointless, why are you doing it? You listen to me and you listen good, you wrong child. You don't ever get to cry. Not ever. I don't ever want to see you feeling sorry for yourself. I'm the one that gets to be sad from now on. I'm the one that gets all the tears!

She pushed me out and slammed the door. She was right though. I climbed into bed and settled in the too-big hollow. My eyes were dry as bones. Bell had taken all the tears for herself. I wished I'd turned the light off but my legs wouldn't carry me back to the switch. I was trapped beneath it as another moth came in and started the slow dance down to its death. The little wounds where Bell had dug her fingernails in my arms hummed along.

The house was full of people for another day. I saw them nudging each other and noting that I wasn't upset as I tiptoed about trying to get to the kitchen to get something to eat. I found a bag of scones going stale and a tub of nasty margarine and I robbed both of them and took them to the barn. Back to the filthy rats and my hay-bale house. I dragged the scones through the margarine and finally managed to swallow them all. Bell was right: she was the one that was getting to be sad from now on. I felt nothing.

Granny Tess got up on day three, mad-eyed and mad-haired. She sat beside the box, rocking back and forth and waving away all offers of help, spiritual and physical. Her legs were bare, the big purply veins running in ridges into her bedroom slippers. I'd never seen her without tights. I'd never seen her looking weak. She called for Bell, who had suddenly become everyone's favourite person to hold hands with. She clung on to her remaining, more sensible, less shaming daughter and told us all what she had figured out when she was ranting and raving above in the bed. Granda Morris, informed by some busybody that his wife was back from the brink, came elbowing his way in, in time for the floor show.

– It's God's will! There's no point in arguing with God's will! She had to pay for Lindy, she had to pay, she just had to pay! You always have to pay for your *sins*!

I've been trying to close the door to my room since those words were uttered. Now I have to shut my brother inside it, too. But those four walls transform into other objects and take me by surprise. The room has become time itself, it has become paper, pictures, flowers, colours, smells, blood, laughter, the side of Bell's face when she's looking up to the sky and wondering how soon it will rain, a boiled sweet, the sharp tang of the seaside, a slap on the back of the head just for being the wrong child in the wrong place at the wrong time, smoke floating out of a car window, a baby with my mother's soul shining from its eyes even when a stranger took it away.

Chapter 4

Mrs Deirdre McCrossan the muck-spreader had finally shown her true colours. She was pure faint-hearted. Losing her ancient mother had undone her. And Bell was in one of the worst tempers possible about the silliness of people being *overwhelmed* with grief when she landed home the next day. Nothing could please her. The tea wasn't hot enough. When it was hot enough it wasn't sweet enough. She didn't know why she was even drinking tea as it was likely there was tea flowing in her veins after the night she just put in. It was *despicable*, may God forgive her for complaining when He'd spared her to live another day in health.

It took a full hour of gold-standard whining about the types of carry-on she had just witnessed before she calmed down. Auld Winnie Mallon had shown up in a rainbow-knitted hat she'd bought from the Foyle Hospice Shop and hadn't had the decency to take it off when she went up to kiss the corpse. One of the mad beaded ties had got snared in the rosary beads wrapped around the cold fingers and Bell had to unravel the mess. *No one* tried to help her. Winnie Mallon had taken a fit of laughing at her and tried to waltz her across the room when she'd been freed. Imagine someone being mad enough to *dance* at a wake even if they had Alzheimer's? I nodded that I had at least that much imagination just to move her on.

Deirdre McCrossan had fainted twice. No sooner had someone revived her with a nip of whiskey but she was back on her feet and ready, willing and able to shame herself afresh. Bell would *never* get over it, never, ever, ever. She'd been through worse – *a lot worse* – and never made such a mess of herself.

With that she eyeballs me up and down and demands a detailed itinerary of events since we parted. I wheel out the detested books, a nice bath in some of that smelly stuff the Credit Union Secret Santa so sweetly gave me, an early dreamless night. But Bell is no pushover, she's already noted the black bags under my eyes, the fact that I've pulled deep ragnails on my thumbs and fingers, that I told her I called in sick to work because I didn't want to miss her coming home. She knows when I'm lying, I know when she's lying. Neither of us says anything because that's the game and without the game we have nothing.

She knows I've been at the Box of Tricks. I can see the panic in her eyes. Does she know about Patrick Joseph's birth certificate? I hate her for not telling me. I've always had the bones of Mammy's life, but now it was fleshed out and flesh can hurt. The children at school had been armed with the knowledge she'd drowned and they let me have it with glee the first time they had a chance.

They were known as the Lace Lakes, a pretty name for an ugly place. She had followed one of the rough roads through the bog and tripped and fell into one of these massive craters made when the British Army blew up all the roads to shut down the border. The craters had all filled with brown water and when I imagine that water filling her beautiful mouth and nose I am almost standing there myself, watching, unable to help, unable to reach out and take her hand. I choke with her every day on that water.

A farmer had seen her green coat floating out behind her and run for help. She'd been fished out by the fire brigade while the RUC watched. She'd only kissed me goodbye and pulled my little coat tight around me a couple of hours earlier. *Be good, Lindy. I'll be back as quick as a wink!*

Why had she left me so early that morning? She had wanted to cross over the border to get to Donegal not for a house but for *him*, Linus Quinn. He must have been back on the scene. He would be the only way for her to get a different roof over her head and mine. Him being close by would account for the screaming matches and the sight of Babs on her knees in front of Granda Morris. He would not tolerate having the name of Morris disgraced again.

Accidents happen. That's what people say when they hear my name even now. Oh, you're Lindy Morris? Losing someone like that must be terrible, they say, so sudden and so unfortunate, but *accidents do happen*. That's what their mouths say but their eyes give away the fact that they've heard Mammy was trouble who begat more trouble by having me.

Bell never speaks about her twin's death. After it happened, she was summoned back from Derry and her job – and presumably made to abandon the mysterious 'V' – and tasked with breeding all the worst traits of Babs out of me. She was never mentioned unless it was to hurt me.

I was not encouraged to speak, sing, dance, recite, read, study, to look up from the ground more than once a day – anything that would keep me in the muck where I belonged was good. Every tiny mistake – a spilled drink, a torn dress, a skinned knee – would see me sitting eye to eye with the Sacred Heart in the front room. Granny Tess would vacate after she'd put out the fire so

Jesus and me could be alone for hours at a time. He'd look at me and I'd look at Him. I wondered was He that bothered by a robbed sweet when His heart was already wrapped in barbed wire and set on fire?

She still won't talk about it all these years later. We won't ever really talk. How will she cope when I ask her if that rectangle of holy ground really is my brother? How will she let me know what took him? I'm not strong enough yet. I've already decided to ask Martha about Linus Quinn; she won't lie to me, and it's as much as I can handle. Bell and me move on to much more important stuff. Do we need any groceries? We're both sure we have enough stew in the freezer for another two meals at least. She has a notion she might take up Aran knitting again when the winter comes, it's such a dreary season and it would remind her of *dear* Granny Tess. Those red geraniums in the front window need dead-heading too. While we're thinking of all things house-proud, we might as well wash those windows. Bell's just going to have another scout round for her Box of Tricks, it can't have gone far, she says as if to herself but so that I can't not hear her. If you could describe it to me I could you help you, I tell her. Two sets of eyes are better than one. Only then do we both have the grace to smile – not with teeth, our lips are sealed. We're well matched in a host of ways.

*

We both attend the funeral for Deirdre McCrossan's mother. Either I've done a good job of looking contained or Bell's not going to let me out of her sight for even an hour. I like going up to the old granite block that is St Bede's Catholic Chapel and the parish priest, Father Boluwaji, is such a good shepherd. Lady Lindy, my Lady Lindy, here she comes, he says with his sing-song voice. There's always time to start over, Lindy, always time, he says when I leave him and our chinwags. I let the soft hope of it being true rest on my shoulders.

Today he has on his white vestments and a violet sash while he waits for the remains of Mrs McCrossan's mother. Bell doesn't like him crossing from the chapel door to where I'm standing to say hello. She redoubles her grip on my arm in case I get away. Bell doesn't like anyone killing me with kindness. He must be really *something* to reconvert me to priests; I thought that I had had my fill of them in London. I get time to smile at him before everyone has to turn and stare at the spectacle of Mrs McCrossan howling like a banshee and that's *before* they slide The Matriarch out of the back of the hearse.

Father Boluwaji leaves us to try to contain the emotion flowing freely under a sky that threatens nothing but rain, the sort of rain that can soak you to the skin even though you haven't felt it land. Bell tuts and tuts, and her tuts are picked up and echoed by several of the other good Christians who are here to pay their respects.

Martha Kennedy, fresh back from her romantic weekend, is tut-free and may even be feeling a bit sorry for Mrs McCrossan, who has lost her marbles entirely. Everyone around here knows that death will always call, we learned that in The Troubles when a person stepping out for a pint of milk or a dance or a quiet prayer in the chapel might never step in again. It was always the low, lonely moan of the siren down at the fire station that let us know that a bomb had been planted or a bullet had found its target.

I feel sorry for Mrs McCrossan in a small way, something about the way she is draped between two men like a ragdoll reminds me of my worst of times in the Clinic. Is she being held up or held down? She mightn't know herself as her good black shoes are trailed up to the front of the altar where she's dumped in a sodden little ball of pain, hiccupping and choking and making a decent stab at pulling herself together. The entire congregation pretends they can't hear her wailing. Bell, still welded to my side, nudges me to drive home her disgust.

Everybody has to die; we're informed of that fact from a young age. We're supposed to suck it up as the dearly departed fly off to Heaven to be seated on the right side of the Father. It's what Catholics are born for, to die and then live happily ever after in Heaven. Catholic Heaven, to be precise; we wouldn't encourage any other religious types in there. Grief is supposed to be a muted business, therefore, and Mrs McCrossan the muck-spreader has really let the side down.

The prayers are familiar as salt on my tongue. The incense is swung across the coffin so that it can seep through the air. You're next, it promises, you and you and you, rolling towards us and our mortal lungs on little grey puffs of smoke. I take it in. Father Boluwaji looks solemn as he sprays us like so many weeds growing in the pews, and we bow our heads. I must ask him if we can have another chinwag soon. Finally, the auld doll is blessed enough to be buried and we all fall in line behind her as she's borne aloft to the hole waiting outside.

All of a sudden, I catch sight of Miriam on the opposite aisle of the chapel. I hadn't known she was coming home, never mind coming to the funeral, and my heart swells as a big daft smile spreads across her face. I want to push everybody out of my way to get to her but that would be unseemly. I shuffle inch by inch until we reach each other at the back door. She gives me enough strength to shrug Bell off and we grasp each other's hands – together again at last.

– Are you going to the tea in the Parochial Hall after? she asks in a whisper.

– I am now, I whisper back.

We snigger and stay arm in arm right out to the graveyard. *Don't worry about me, Lindy Morris,* Bell hisses in my ear as she passes by, hooked now on poor Mrs Kennedy as they battle their way to the front. I've let her down. I use the precious time without her to catch up with Miriam, darling Miriam. Galway's grand but it's not *home*. She's the same as always, just *delirious* to be back in Ballyglen, though she already misses the little twins; they're gorgeous, she says, and the love she has for them shines out of her eyes like a diamond. How I adore this friend of mine. How lucky I am to have her. How I wish she didn't get homesick every time she leaves this dull-as-fuck town. How I wish she'd stop using the word 'twins' as if it was just something that happened.

We make a plan for her to come to me. I explain that my high-flying job at the Credit Union is now complete with flexible hours and she roars. She knows that'll be easier because Bell will feel included even though she won't be. Over the years, Miriam and me have mastered a whole new level of chitchat – we can use a thousand words and say nothing and there won't even be a short gap in the conversation. We wear Bell down with our unrelenting chirpiness and she gives up and goes to bed. It's no use to her if all the stories she hears are going to be *happy*. Only bad news cheers her up.

The date is set for Tuesday for us to run over all the old ground, the old times, the craic we had in school dodging the wrath of the nuns, the craic we now imagine we had in London before Miriam just couldn't force herself to stay another day. Her heart was in Ballyglen and she had to go back to it. If she hadn't loved her family, if she hadn't left me there, I might have kept my baby.

LONDON – 1984

Chapter 1

I had never seen Miriam cry until the day she showed me her boat ticket. It was one-way back to Larne. We'd barely been in London three months. She was pining for her parents, the sweet and kind O'Dwyers, who in turn were pining for their sweet and kind daughter. I'd not had a word from Southfork and that suited me fine. Her letters came in every week and Miriam would read them, sat on my bed in the nurses' home. She didn't say much, she didn't need to when I could hear her tears hitting the paper. I prayed that she would rally. After all, it had been *her* idea to leave Ballyglen. It had been *her* idea to carry me along. I wouldn't have had the chops to even think it by myself.

We were eighteen *at last*. We thought that Duran Duran were the greatest thing on ten legs and that we might bump into them on the pavement. We were such eejits but Miriam was on a mission: meet Simon le Bon before he married somebody else, somebody who couldn't even dream about loving him as much as she did. She'd *no* clue how much I loved him. She saw the advert for nursing auxiliary workers in the *Ulster Herald*, she cut it out and showed it to me and I nodded, wide-eyed at her cheek. They would take girls our age with no experience and they'd train us up to be angels of mercy. A job, any kind of job, was brilliant, but a job with accommodation was too much to refuse. We wouldn't need to stay for ever once we found our feet. All I had to do was get myself a passport. So I proved myself evil beyond a shadow of a doubt when I got a British one, a traitor to my Nationalist grandparents, who couldn't grasp that all I was, was in a rush.

They were still smarting that Sinn Fein's Gerry Adams had been shot and wounded in Belfast by the Ulster Defence Army in March. And here I was, rotten me, practically *condoning* British Rule in Northern Ireland. Granda had come home two or three times in the weeks that followed the shooting, spitting the word he reserved for all things Loyalist, *cunts*. He didn't need to explain himself – not to three bloody fucking women – but for once he couldn't stop himself speaking to us. There was no one else.

He'd had to stomach gangs of young Protestant lads taunting him and other Catholic men with shouts of *UDA all the way, UDA all the way* as they went about their business in Ballyglen. There wasn't a damned thing he or any of them could do about it. It had to be swallowed when the young lads were flanked by the dark green uniforms of the RUC. He didn't like being taunted; he'd had enough of that from his own people when my mother had disgraced herself. The only thing he hated more than Protestants were travellers. At least Protestants worked for a living.

All I remember is the pure excitement of having the application form for The Royal Hospital and Home for Incurables on West Hill in Putney, London, England, and the application form for a British passport sitting side by side. Now life begins. Escape beckons. The police in England didn't carry guns. There would be no Saracens, no roadblocks, no bomb scares, no stop and search. My tiny mind couldn't stretch far enough to imagine walking down a street and not knowing every single person on it. I would soon be living a spy-free existence. I could do as I pleased, wear what I wanted. I might meet someone who wanted to kiss me? I might even take a drink and go to a disco or a dance and nobody would tell Bell, Granny Tess or Granda Morris. The only word was *joy*, pure, pure joy. I could see why people jumped for it.

Bell took to her bed but I didn't buckle. She took to refusing food, sitting through a score of dinners sobbing until Granda Morris told her to shut her silly mouth or he'd shut it for her. She took to hovering in my bedroom door, and asking me if I wanted to *destroy* her. She, who had given up *her* life for *me* when I needed her! Who was going to look after *her* now? Now that I was just going to *disappear* like my mother before me and leave her entirely exposed to Tess and Gabriel Morris?

I said as little as possible and soon enough we were heading for the boat. I hadn't much to carry as I'd used up every penny I ever saved to get the ticket – £26 – to get all the way to London. In my holdall were a couple of tops, a few pairs of navy knickers and socks from my school uniform and a spare pair of corduroy trousers. Anyway, Miriam and me were beside ourselves at the idea of shopping someplace other than dull-as-dishwater Leehy's when we got our first wage packet. We were going to get *style* – if *Smash Hits* was anything to go by, London was full of it.

Granda Morris left early on the day of my departure. Granny Tess refused to look up from her knitting. I looked from her to Bell, who was standing in the hall like a statue – a statue with the hiccups – and I crossed to where she stood and just touched my forehead to hers. She hiccupped another sob before she ran for the kitchen. The door slammed with a ferocious bang when Miriam's brother drew up outside and honked the horn.

I could still hear her crying. I knew, without seeing, that she had her bum against the wood and that she was bent double, elbows on her knees and her fists in her eyes. She always cried that way, like she was being battered into the ground with a frying pan. Nothing would make me check that I was right, that she was broken. I was out of the front door like the teenager I was. Though my heart was burning at the back of my throat, I threw on a smile and jumped in.

I'd said my goodbyes to Mammy. She was buried near the back of the graveyard at St Bede's. I walked there in the heat of a July day, the tarmac was bubbling and the smell of it mixed with the sweet smell of grass cut for hay and the pink spirals of honeysuckle in the hedgerows. The day I visited her, my feet were aching in a pair of fawn desert boots and so was my heart. I didn't want to be even further away from her but I wanted to get out, to meet people and to find Simon le Bon for Miriam. I kneeled on the little border of marble that had been put around her grave and read the headstone, the smallest one in every direction. *Barbara Anne Morris. August 24*[th] *1946 – August 24*[th] *1973. Rest in Peace.* I picked out one of the sharp white stones that lay on top of the plastic keeping the weeds down and slipped it in my pocket. I'd carry it to England; I'd carry it with me always so she could experience life with me. The sun blazed down on the crown of my hair. The wild black mane of it was hers, the white face, too, but not my blue eyes. I wanted to give her something; I *needed* to give her something in case she thought I'd ever forget her. I was leaving her to the tender care of Bell and Tess and that other lousy bastard, her father. He never so much as dipped his knee at her grave. At least she had her unnamed angel to keep her company. He'd been lying to the right of the Morris family plot for as long as I could remember.

I cast around and found an old jam jar that had been left on a neighbouring grave and filled it with water from the tap at the side of the chapel. As I came back I picked every dandelion I could find growing in bright yellow clumps along the sides of the paths and stuffed them into my jam jar until it couldn't hold any more. It wasn't much but it was all I had, my wreath of sunshine weeds. *I'll be back sometime, Mammy, I promise*, I lied.

I don't know why Miriam and me ate Yorkie bars at every service station on the M6. Maybe it was because the white-bread sandwiches were already curly on the shelves of the motorway shops? Whatever, I puked mine up before Birmingham and she couldn't even join me because she was so sick. The whole coach groaned but

I wasn't the first and I wouldn't be the last. We'd loaded up on cans of Coke and crisps, unsupervised for the first time in a lifetime. Waynes running mad on an outing! The whole chat was about maybe seeing Buckingham Palace one day and shouting at the Queen how much we hated her. Although now that I was a British citizen I wasn't sure I was allowed to shout at the Queen.

After ten hours we couldn't feel our bums any more, never mind speak. I thought we'd never see a house again but I woke up just as the coach juddered and died out at a traffic light. The driver turned the engine a few times and it shook itself back to life and we carried on. By that stage all the young wans were sitting up and looking out the windows. Big patches of clear glass were rubbed clear of the condensation, although the stink of fag smoke and old tea didn't budge. The older wans, mostly men who had clattered bags of tools into the racks above the seats, kept their eyes down. They'd seen it all before. They were back to break their backs on building sites and roadworks, so any novelty had worn off. When we finally pulled in to Victoria coach station everybody was keen to get out. We all stood on crampy legs, holdalls against our chests, and jostled to get out for our first taste of London air.

The tube station was a walk away and we did it accompanied by the sound of pneumatic drills and lots of Irish accents shouting at each other from diggers and trucks and yellow tents. The whole place was under construction. We stood in front of huge panels flipping the names of towns that we'd never heard of – Brighton, Haywards Heath, Dorking, Portsmouth Harbour, Gatwick Airport – until we realised that there was *another* station called Victoria. You're in Victoria railway station, says the woman we stopped and asked, you need Victoria tube station. She couldn't have been snottier if we'd paid her for snot, and Miriam hung on to my arm in case we were broken apart by the crowd. So many people! Where were they all going? Why were they in such a rush? It felt as if every soul in Ballyglen had stepped out of their houses at once. Their faces swam past us like angry salmon.

– We've made a mistake!

– We haven't, Miriam, we'll get the hang of it!

– What if we never get to the hospital?

– We'll get to the hospital!

I didn't believe for a second that we'd get to the hospital but I was used to Miriam looking after me. Now I found myself in the unfortunate position of having to look after her, I had to say something. I thought of Bell. What would Bell do? She'd go in somewhere for a cup of tea, so I guided the jumpy Miriam across the big smooth floor and into a café. Jeepers! The price of the tea! But it was worth it, we calmed down and the lovely

Indian man behind the counter showed us a tube map, showed us how to figure it out, where to get a ticket and wished us luck. He was delighted that we'd come so far to be nurses – London always needed nurses. I'd never seen a man in a turban before, let alone *spoken* to one. Granda Morris's head would explode.

We found the tube, the right line *first time*, got ourselves to Putney and asked the way to West Hill. Behind high black railings, an old mansion house painted pale green and white declared that it was the RHHI. I'd never seen a more beautiful building and I was going to be working inside it. We looked up and read the arch of cold metal that stretched high above the side entrance gate – The Royal Hospital and Home for Incurables. Jesus. *The sight of that must cheer them up from the ambulance*, I said, and Miriam managed a smile. Nurses' home to the right, the paper sign said. Today's intake gather at 1 p.m. in the Hall 'to commence a week's orientation period'. We'd made it.

I was going to be under a new roof that night, one of my own making, and I might just have felt free for the first time. We ran arm in arm through the double doors and queued up with all the other girls, except that they weren't all girls. Some looked to be women as old as forty and they were every colour under the sun. Miriam and me tried not to stare but we had rarely seen another living, breathing soul that wasn't white.

We had only ever been concerned with the thin line between the equally pasty races of Catholics or Protestants and now we were in the middle of Jamaicans, Filipinos, Chinese, Koreans and Ghanaians. I could learn to be different by making friends with these people. They might tell me about the world and what it was like to be a part of it.

The nurses' home was long and low, two-storeyed and made of red brick. The hallway was wide and beyond it we could see a double staircase. A sea of blue tiles, pale cream walls and strange smells washed towards us. A fat man was handing out keys faster than a priest with sweets. I got the room just beside the front door, which would be locked every night at midnight by the porter. He was called Colin and I didn't like the look of him one bit – he walked up and down as much as his big belly would allow him, every inch the fox in a chicken coop.

– Hello, there. Where are you girls from?

– Ireland! says Miriam.

– *Northern* Ireland! says me, in case I have to show the shaming passport.

– Irish girls, is it? Lovely! I'm always glad to see a few white faces coming in!

Miriam and me looked at each other. We were white for sure, maybe too white, but what did this dickhead expect? We never get more than four days of consecutive sunshine in Tyrone so we'd hardly show up with a tan?

He pulled keys off a metal ring and handed them to us, all the while making us feel sick.

- You're a big strong girl, aren't you? I bet you could break a man's lap given half the chance?
- *What?*

Miriam snatched her room key and we backed away from the green scum on his dentures and that smell wafting off his cardigan, something like ear wax but worse. She was on the second floor so we went to my place first and slammed the door on Colin's beady eyes. A single bed – I could tell straight away that my feet would stick out the bottom – with white linen and a hospital blanket marked Property of RHHI on it, two towels with the same stamp and a gloriously empty wardrobe with ten wire hangers hanging in it.

Tomorrow we'd start five days in a classroom and then we'd be let loose on the wards. Before that, though, we'd get our uniforms – nursing auxiliaries got three sets of pale blue checked dresses and two pairs of white rubber shoes. We were going to be tending the sick. It was so romantic. My heart swelled with pride. I saw myself wiping fevered brows and holding hands and looking sympathetic. I was going to have a job and a room with a lock and key. Miriam and me were standing on the lip of an excitement volcano and we could hardly wait for it to erupt.

Chapter 2

The classroom was great fun. We learned how to lift people, how to make beds and to not interfere with patients fiddling with each other in the corridors unless one or other of them looked distressed. Apparently this place was an actual *home* and everyone was entitled to a sex life. Miriam and me blushed down to our roots and watched the ceiling with interest. Rule number one was to treat everyone as we would wish to be treated ourselves – let respect and dignity reign, said the little sandy-haired male nurse Kenny who was training us and making us love him for his Scottish accent.

The ordered days suited me. Best of all, they ended. I'd always had so many jobs to do at Southfork, ones that Bell suddenly remembered as soon as I sat down. Now, Miriam and me wandered down to Wandsworth

Common and to Putney Heath most afternoons. One night we walked all the way through Putney and looked at the River Thames. We didn't cross the bridge but the lights on the other side looked pretty. Everyone had somewhere to go and each of them produced an umbrella every time a few drops of rain fell. It was gas, they wouldn't last ten minutes in stormy Tyrone. The pubs were full; we walked past the Railway Tavern on the corner every night and listened to the voices rising above the cigarette smoke. We longed to go in and see what kind of craic it was, but we had no money to spare, not a bean until that first paycheque.

We'd each bought a big loaf of white bread and a half-pound of butter, and I had got a pot of strawberry jam while Miriam got a packet of cheese slices. We could swap out what topping we had for our breakfast, lunch and dinner toast when we were sick and tired of eating the same thing day in and day out. Every time we ventured into the kitchen the Filipino girls would be in there cooking up an exotic storm, they looked at us with pity and laughed with good nature when we waved our flaccid bread slices around. The black girls lived on balls of savoury semolina and fish, plates of it piled high. They ignored us every time we said hello. How would we learn to be cool?

Miriam guarded a load of change that she used to call home with every night from the phone booth. She was in there as long as she could be until someone banged on the door and told her to get out. I asked her to get her mammy to call Bell and tell her I was fine. I missed her in a way, but I didn't want her voice in my ear – she might cry or, worse, she might not. I was happy now and I didn't want her to ruin it either way.

Every night when I lay down, the sounds of strangers talking in their own language and flip-flops on the corridor filled my head. Doors banged and keys jangled; now and again someone would bark with laughter and someone else would tell them to shush their noise. The big double doors beside my room banged shut and rattled open, bottles clinked and people sighed, glad to be finishing their shifts. I had Miriam above me, hopefully dry-eyed though she was looking a bit sadder with every day that passed. It was more soothing than the deepest, darkest countryside. Home, such as it ever was, seemed far enough away for me to relax.

It only took us two weeks to understand that we were nothing more than donkeys. Donkeys in pale blue and white squared uniforms. My uniform was way too short so I made it worse by wearing thick white tights so I could lean over beds without passing out from embarrassment. I had left a world of work and orders behind me when I escaped Granda Morris and Granny, but the misery of it had followed me. I had to do everything I was told without complaint. Miriam was allocated to Women's Ward Main on the third floor – *That's mostly geriatric,* said Nurse Kenny from behind his clipboard – and I was sent to the Rehabilitation Unit in the Alexandra Wing. *Lots of heavy lifting, Lindy. You'll be perfect for it.* I was a big strong donkey. It was a bit more modern, built at the back of the hospital and down a long, long corridor. I got over my romantic notions of being an administering angel pretty sharpish.

Within minutes, I was tying bits of sticky plaster around men's willies before I put on the condoms that led to the wee bags, and I'd never even seen a man's willy before. Within hours, naked body parts lost the power to shock. Within days, heating up six saline enemas in the sink was all in a morning's work. At the end of a fortnight, clearing away the fallout from six saline enemas was second nature.

I just got on with it. Miriam seemed unable to separate out the different parts of herself like I could. Every day after a long shift and a much-needed long shower, we'd meet in my room, where Miriam took the end of the bed and I took the headboard so we could eat our white-bread toast and exchange notes. She felt like she was working among the dead, they were all long-term institutionalised and she couldn't cope with the sad, sad histories. *There are people in here who have epilepsy. Just epilepsy, and they've not been outside the grounds for years.* I soothed her as best as I could, she'd always had a soft heart. The phone calls home were getting longer.

The more I tried to fend off her misgivings, the more frustrated she got with me because I simply wouldn't call home. If only I'd call home, I'd remember how good home was, Miriam said with a totally straight face. I burst out laughing, thinking she'd join in, but she didn't. Bell was telling everyone in Ballyglen what a wastrel I was. I had run off and never looked back. I didn't care about her. She had squandered her life for me, and now look, she was all alone. I could imagine her holding up people just trying to get a few groceries, standing with a cabbage in one hand and a few rashers in the other and a howling Bell blocking their exit. I found myself agreeing that calling home sounded like a good idea so that I wouldn't lose the only friend I ever had. I'll do it, I said, knowing that wild horses wouldn't drag me to the phone booth.

I felt sick when the ward sister, Sister Smith, summoned me to her office. I hoped I'd done nothing wrong, but all she wanted to know was whether or not I was Catholic. She knew that *people in Northern Ireland* had some issues about religion, but when I declared which side I was on, it was the right side to be assigned to Father

Vincent Donnan. He was an English priest who had been bashed on the head by a lorry when he was out on his bike. Bell had always warned me to stay away from priests, but I couldn't tell my boss that. Men of the cloth shouldn't have temptation put in their way, she said. I'd no clue what she was on about. What could men who had taken a vow of celibacy, poverty and obedience want from anyone?

But every man of the cloth I had ever met had scared me, from the one or two who came to primary school to scare us before the First Confession to the ones who dropped in to the convent to scare us before we left. They were worried that we would most likely continue the rot of abandoning Ireland for foreign climes and opportunities. They were even more concerned that we carried on our *Faith* when we got there. We were to make it our *duty* to find out where the nearest Catholic Church was and to attend it *religiously*.

Miriam and me had done that, too, as part of our no-money and need-to-fill-time activities: it was Our Lady of Pity and St Simon Stock on the Hazlewell Road. I'd no intention of going – my second act of rebellion in a lifetime – but Miriam went and reported that it was nothing like St Bede's in Ballyglen, not as fancy. There were hardly any flowers on the altar and only one nice statue of the Virgin when the whole chapel was *named* after her. She'd lit a candle to keep me in God's good books. She did not approve of me abandoning my religion so easily after all we had been through in the Six Counties. It took me a minute to swallow the laugh that was bubbling inside me at her pious face and shined shoes and preachy voice. It took me another minute to realise she was serious. The girl who had found joy in everything was fading.

Father Donnan's lights were on but there was no one in the sacristy. When I gave him his lunch he stood up and blessed the bread. When I popped tiny bits of it into his mouth he said Amen. When I wiped his face he leaned into my hand like a love-starved dog. I had to bathe him, shave him, dress him from the undercrackers and vest up, and every time I kneeled down to tie his shoelaces he put his hand on my head, his lips moving over the familiar prayers. Sister Smith was glad she finally had someone on the ward who could understand his mumbo-jumbo and I nodded like a good donkey. I could not get over the fact that he was *just a man*.

I worked mostly with Yasmina. Yasmina was from Jamaica and was not weighed down with fears of doing, saying or being the wrong thing. She wore a hot-red petticoat underneath her cold-blue uniform and just rolled her eyes every time Sister Smith told her off about her huge, dangerous earrings being 'a little garish for work purposes'. We had been paired for several bouts of saline enemas and all they entailed, and she was moved to say that I was a good worker, which made me nearly cry with gratitude. I wanted to be good. She was tiny and round and I leaned down when she needed to order me around so she wouldn't get a crick in her neck.

I was also desperate for someone who wasn't Miriam to *like* me. I needed a back-up plan in case Miriam and me fell out. I didn't want to swap being all alone in Ireland to being all alone in England. Yasmina had finally started talking to me when she realised I wasn't standoffish, that I was just shy to the point of being mute. *Open your mouth, chil'! What's the worse can happen?* she would say when I whispered to her about how I was worried about seeing Father Donnan all naked and wispy as a baby chick when I propped him on the commode. It didn't seem right to see a man of the cloth with some of his cloth around his ankles. Maybe it was even a *sin*? She just roared with laughter, her big belly rocking and her mouthful of chocolate biscuit and malt in danger of flying across the common room. *Ain't nobody in this world shit pink,* she said. *No body, cha!* Just sitting beside her bolstered my heart.

Chapter 3

I rang Bell after six weeks and wished I hadn't. Miriam wore me down. *Everyone needs to speak to their family, Lindy, even you.* I only did it to please her because she was not settling in like I had, and it was starting to show. Yasmina had pushed me to the other girls on the ward and now I had a gang of people to talk to, to laugh with, even though I was still timid. A gang of people who knew nothing about my history. Miriam had had no such luck up on Women's Ward Main and still sat sullen and shy when all of us from Rehabilitation met in the kitchen. She picked at her cuticles while I showed off my new and overwhelming desire to open my mouth, chil'. What's the worse can happen?

I'd hardly finished my hello when Bell started screaming. If Miriam hadn't been manning the door to the phone booth I'd have slammed down the receiver and run, but escape was barred. I had to listen to what my aunt thought of me by this stage. The word ungrateful cropped up several times; spiteful, rotten, selfish a few times. She had *always* taken my part against Granda Morris and Granny Tess when they told her I wasn't worth the shoes I stood up in. Had she?

I couldn't remember much defence of my character, but now wasn't the time to argue the toss. She went on and on, quoting her saintly parents as if I'd never encountered them in the flesh. They had washed their hands, after everything they had done for me, given me a home when *plenty* of other grandparents would have put me out on the street. I'd never been what they wanted. I was part of a bad deal. The wrong child. They wouldn't be even slightly surprised if I never bothered to come back again. Probably I wouldn't even bother coming home for Christmas! They were beginning to think I had forgotten what a debt to them I had. Did I know what it cost them to rear me in *every way*?

I said as little as possible, her words slicing through the thin skin I'd grown like paper cuts. I'm sorry Bell, I'm sorry Bell, I'm sorry Bell. She was taking the brunt of it now, now that I had left her there all alone, all the hatred they had for my mother rained down on her head. I could have been a nurse in Derry or Omagh or anywhere close to home where I'd have been of some use to my *own* people, but it wasn't good enough for *Lindy Morris*. I thought *I* was something special. But I wasn't. I was nothing more than Babs's little bastard. She wished she hadn't risked the *one chance* she'd had at a life for me when I obviously wasn't worth it. The gloves were off.

The pips went at last and Bell was cut off mid-whine. I sat a while in the phone booth, my ears ringing. The walls were painted a pale green and it smelled like dust and old perfume and sweet wrappers. This was where everyone else rang home because they were loved and missed. This happy little cell witnessed people promising to speak to each other soon, sending their best wishes to other family members. Maybe they even gave and got love.

It was breathtaking how miserable she could make me feel from such a distance. I had crossed the Irish Sea but she could still reach inside and twist my guts.

– Alright?
– Sure. You were right, Miriam. They were waiting to hear from me.
– See, I told you! I told you you'd feel better as soon as you got back in touch.
– You're a genius, Miriam O'Dwyer.

The first paypacket finally arrived. The excitement of having some money and getting it out of a hole in the wall nearly cheered Miriam up. We celebrated by going

130

to the Railway Tavern. We sipped half-pints of lager that made us both want to puke. The barman suggested that lime cordial might help and that was even worse. I proposed we try something else, a gin and tonic maybe? A vodka and coke? Miriam scowled her no. Lager was cheap and that way we could save even harder to go *home* and we didn't want to risk getting drunk on spirits, God knows what might happen. We might have a bit of fun, I thought to myself, fun that I felt I'd earned, but I said nothing. And what was this about going home? We'd only just left home and as far as I understood it, we were supposed to stay away. For ever.

It was Sister Smith who told me about the IRA bomb in Brighton. The only TV was in the common room, and we didn't like to go to the common room. Every time we even poked our noses around the corner it looked too crowded. The IRA had planted a bomb in the Conservative Party Conference to try to kill Margaret Thatcher, and Sister Smith wanted to know what *side* I was on? The IRA were Catholics, weren't they, like Father Donnan and me? What did *I* have to say about the fact that *they* had just killed five innocent people and wounded plenty more?

I hadn't a clue what to say. Granny Tess and Granda Morris and even Bell were raging Nationalists. There was no discussion of the rights and wrongs of *the situation* in the Six Counties. They just knew it was wrong that our country of Ireland was being ruled with England's help and that warranted no other reference to history or facts or reality. Any talk of *talks* on the radio was quickly followed by the news that *talks had broken down*. I'd felt at home in London, I was a stranger among strangers here. People largely left me alone and being left alone was fast becoming my favourite thing. Walk down the street, no one says hello. Poke about a shop, no one says hello. Don't buy anything, no one sniffs or grumbles or badmouths you to the next customer. Pat a plane tree, no one tuts and reminds you're one of the mad Morris breed. But now what? Would people start shouting things after me in the street, things like *murderer*?

Sister Smith was waiting and I had no defence. Yasmina rode to my rescue. *Leave the chil' alone! She got nothing to do with this thing!* She pushed me past Sister Smith's office with her big bosoms and set me to sorting out the breakfast trays. The smell of kipper swam up my nose but I swallowed hard and got on with my day. Yasmina winked at me and I winked back, relieved someone had my back.

I had Richie to deal with after that. He was thirteen and had been fished out of a swimming pool long after it was safe to fish him out. Just looking at him burned my heart. The word 'drowned' could still hit my throat like a fist. Someone had managed to revive him but he was so brain damaged that he was curling up into a ball no matter what the physiotherapists did. Every morning he was stretched and pulled into a kind of ordinary shape but every night he started turning back in on himself. His mother had stopped coming. She used to come in and shout at them to all stop hauling at him, to just leave him to die, Yasmina told me, matter of fact. But we couldn't do that, we had to keep hurting him for his own good, even though he was never going to get better.

I sat through the midday briefing with Sister Smith, my face on fire. None of the other girls mentioned the bomb, thank God. On the agenda was notice for all of us that Richie's time in the rehab pool was going to be doubled, and I shivered inside at the thought of his wild-eyed face as he was strapped into the hoist and lowered into the water. Father Donnan was going to be allowed back to the Parochial House for respite visits when a nun could be freed up to care for him full time.

That afternoon, with a cheese sandwich lying in my stomach like a breeze block, I tidied up Father Donnan, knotting his shoelaces and trying not to notice the dry skin falling from his shins like snow. I did up his black cardigan buttons, knowing he'd undo them in five minutes. His soft hands and thin fingers never rested; the kind of hands that had never done a real day's work, Granda Morris would say as he rubbed his own calluses with Snowfire. I got a hat, scarf and coat out ready – he was going out for an hour, and though it was nowhere near as cold as County Tyrone, there was a chill to the air.

It was Sister Smith who spun me round and nearly into the outstretched hand of Christopher Campbell. He stood among the specially adapted furniture and wheelchairs that make up a room in a home like this, dripping with rude health. He had startlingly white teeth and startlingly dark hair, a couple of things that always appealed to me. And we were eye to eye. Bliss. It's so hard finding a boyfriend when you're six foot.

Although not a word came out of my mouth, my mind sang a little song from the playground, one of Miriam and my favourites as we jumped rope. *Lindy and Christopher sitting in a tree. K.I.S.S.I.N.G. First comes love, then comes marriage. Then comes Lindy with a baby carriage.* Sister Smith gave him my name.

– Hello, Lindy. I believe you've been doing a sterling job with our friend here?

– Aye. I mean, yes!

– Is he all ready for the off, then?

– Yes, he's ready.

I rammed the hat on to poor Father Donnan's head as Christopher Campbell fixed his feet on the footplate of the wheelchair. They were only going to do a turn of the grounds and would be back in time for tea at four o'clock. I watched the tall shoulders walk down the corridor, the dark head dipping down now and again to check that the cargo was secure, and then he disappeared. Sister Smith had to tap me on the shoulder to stop me gawking after him. There was such a tremendous shine on his hair.

- Miriam, what do you think of my hair tied back like this? Does it make me look a bit young?
- Lindy! Have you been *listening* to a word I've said?

She was in a total panic about the IRA thing. Five people had been killed, loads more injured and Margaret Thatcher wasn't even dead, now she'd hate Northern Ireland with a passion. I saw the tears rolling down Miriam's cheeks and I knew we were doomed. She would never stay here now; this was the excuse she'd been waiting for to get back to bastardy bollockin' Ballyglen.

- Miriam – nobody's really said anything, have they?
- No, but that's not the point. They'll look at us differently. It'll be like being at home again and being caught on the wrong side of the divide. If we're going to be that scared, I'd rather be actually *home*.
- I'm not going home.

Miriam's whole face shouted 'what' but the word itself did not make an appearance. I'd taken myself by surprise so she must've been nearly ready to pass out.

135

I'd always relied on her to stand out front, to make me acceptable even to myself, but nothing, not even her, would make me get back on that coach to Stranraer.

It wasn't the journey, which was still fresh in both our minds, it was the truth that she would go back to her lovely family, who would be skipping and jumping and baking cakes in-between hanging out the bunting, and I would be lucky to get a grunted hello. She'd run up the path and the whole O'Dwyer clan would pour out and try to hug her all at once. She'd be enveloped in love and relief that she'd come back home and could now live out her days with all of her own wans.

I, on the other hand, would fall immediately into the whipped-dog category. It would be said that I'd tried to make something of myself and failed, and now here I was trailing home with my tail between my legs. Here I was expecting to be taken back in, maybe even cared for? Here I was mistakenly thinking that Bell and Granny Tess and Granda Morris would even open the door when I'd made it all the way down the rotten nettle-flanked lane to Southfork.

– But Lindy, you have to come home? Bell'll kill me if I land back without you.

– I'm not going, Mim. Certainly not for Bell and not even for you!

She nodded, understanding that somehow in under three months I'd found enough strength to stand on my own. I'd nearly stopped stooping. There were girls at the RHHI who had crossed the globe for these jobs and we'd only crossed the Irish Sea. There were people here who couldn't speak English, people who had every intention of making their lives here, and I didn't see why I couldn't be one of them. It was then she produced her ticket. London Victoria to Belfast, one way. She'd had it for a month and hadn't known how to tell me. She was miserable.

Miriam couldn't cope with any of the stuff we saw here. She didn't like dribble, phlegm, bunions, varicose veins, dentures, gnarly toenails or twisted joints. Couldn't stand to hear them crying, sighing, farting, vomiting, coughing or struggling to breathe. Last week, three of the poor old dears had passed away in the same night and when Miriam came on shift, she'd been made to help wheel them down to the mortuary.

When she got down there she was left alone to wash them. The other two nurses didn't tell her what was expected of her, they were too delighted to be playing a trick on the lone Paddy. Two of the dead had families, one didn't have anyone left, hadn't had a visitor or letter for years. She could do the minimum for her because no one would ever see her again. Rose Gould, Celia Jacobson and Anka Beliek – she was the one who had no one left.

It was going okay, peeling off the thin nightdresses from the thinner bodies, throwing out the soiled nappies and the net knickers and trying to comb what was left of their hair. Then one of them moved! Actually moved a few inches and let out a sound, a kind of awful, low moan. Miriam was never going to be able to unhear it. She'd run like the Devil was behind her, down the long corridor and all the way out of the hospital, up to her room where she'd scrubbed her hands until they were raw.

Poor Miriam. She was crying most of all because she couldn't remember which one had moaned. She was panicking in case it had been Anka Beliek trying to make herself heard, and she'd been abandoned by the last person to ever hold her hand, Miriam O'Dwyer, good Catholic and genuine angel. I tried to tell her that anyone would have run screaming out of a mortuary if an officially dead person grumbled, but she didn't want to hear that.

She wanted to hear that she could escape. This place would haunt her until the minute she could put her arms around her own dear mammy. Only then would she be able to sleep. Only then would she feel safe. And the very next day, when she'd eaten her body weight in home-made bread and jam and drunk a bucket of good strong tea, she would go to confession at St Bede's with Father McGarrigle himself to tell him everything. When he wiped her soul clean, she was going to settle down in Ballyglen and never leave again.

– Oh God, Lindy! I just want to go *home*! I want to go back to *my own people*!

I wished her all the luck in the world. What else would I do when I valued the burning desire to be somewhere else? I understood that I'd say goodbye to Miriam when we'd both hiked back to London Victoria station. It would be late at night because she'd pick up the overnight coach and suffer the bum-numbing ride back to Scotland then the boat across the sea to Ireland. I'd wave until the tail lights disappeared from sight. Then I'd be on my own for real. Then I could do whatever I wanted and no one, not even my best friend, would know what I had to say for myself when I started to speak.

Chapter 4

I knew that I would miss Miriam more than I could dream I would. With the clock ticking down, we'd 'done' the sights. Buckingham Palace was disappointing. Surely the Queen could afford something a bit fancier? We scared the pigeons into the air in Trafalgar Square and tried to sit on the lions' heads. I'd thrown a 10p into the water to make a wish and watched a tramp fish it out almost as soon as it landed. I wished that we'd see Simon le Bon before it was too late. We'd had silly pictures taken in photo booths. Mine was all pouty because I'd been pulling Adam Ant faces and hers was covered in smiles because I'd made her laugh. I tucked mine into the little mirror above my sink. And now she was gone.

Oh, how she'd cried! She nearly undid me, so much so I had to dig my fingernails into my palms. We'd been so brave right up until she had to join the queue. I checked she had her passport, her ticket, her holdall bulging with presents for the family, her *Smash Hits* magazine with Paul Young on the cover. We loved him almost as much as Duran Duran. We'd hung on to each other as she wept, as if we might never meet again. The coach left only the stink of diesel and an empty feeling in the pit of my stomach. There wasn't so much as a single hair of her head visible, although she'd promised she'd wave until her arm ached.

She'd have to do that hideous journey without me by her side. I told myself she'd be sad until Birmingham, she'd perk up by Liverpool and as soon as she smelled the saltwater in Scotland she'd be practically home and that would only ever make her happy. The trip would be even worse done in the cold of early November. I wondered just how many years it would be before we met again. Would we be *old*, maybe even in our thirties? Would I invite her to my wedding? Would she invite me to hers, even though she must know I'd never go back to Ballyglen again, not even for her special day?

I walked back alone, Victoria was a bit dodgy at that time of night, but I was worldly now. I sidestepped the drunks and strode to the tube station. I ignored the hundreds of people all around me. I'm alone now, I thought, quite alone, and I'm fine. I could even feel a little swirl of excitement way down low in my guts. It was romantic – Belinda Jane Morris doing just fine on her own two large feet, thank you very much.

The walk up West Hill was lonely, but not impossible. The RHHI was dark against the sky, and I stopped in the east gateway to look over at the pillars by the grand central door. I'd never even bothered to walk under the covered gangway as the ward where I was – the hoity-toity Alexandra Wing for Research and Rehabilitation – was round to the right. When I looked back, Christopher Campbell was standing in front me; he'd just left Father Donnan and now he'd found me. That's what he said, I'd been found.

– Look who I've found!
– Hello!
– What are you doing out looking at the stars all alone, Nurse Lindy?
– I'm not a nurse, not yet anyway ...
– A woman with ambition! I like that!

He suggested a drink and I nodded and fell into step with him right back the way I'd just come. I wished I'd had the sense to put on lipstick or a spray of perfume like Mammy. I wasn't ready to be viewed and I'd not much to say for myself, but Christopher Campbell didn't need much by way of conversation, he chatted almost to himself about the hospital, Father Donnan – such a sweet and gentle soul, a real man of God – how Irish nurses were the best nurses in the world and suddenly I was sitting with a gin and tonic in front of me in the Railway Tavern, which I must have asked for unless he was a mind reader. It was bitter but it was cold and I liked that I had ice cubes to look at so that I didn't have to meet his eye.

Christopher, for I was indeed to call him Christopher, worked as a bookkeeper at St Simon Stock's among many other jobs, so that's how he'd come to be friends with Father Donnan. The staff had been devastated by the accident; they all hoped and prayed that he'd make a full recovery. I thought of Father Donnan giving out the words to the Eucharist while he had his bare bum on the commode. Did they know he had forgotten how to use a knife and fork? Did they know he got so agitated at night-time that he swore like a docker, much to Sister Smith's amusement?

Had no one ever told them he liked running his hands over our boobs or even between our legs if we forgot to pin his arms before we leaned in to wipe his mouth? I had a flash of 'the staff' on their knees saying the rosary and asking God to reverse his irreversible brain damage. They were begging up the wrong tree.

– Miracles do happen!

– They do, Lindy, they really do!

Christopher bought us another round and I listened to him talk. His father was dead, an early heart attack. His mother had struggled to raise him and his two sisters but she'd done a good job, or so he hoped anyway! I waited for him to declare his Irish credentials – it was what everyone did as soon as they heard my accent. It seemed that everyone's mother or father was Irish, every single one. Or their granny or grandfather. They all longed to go there one day, it sounded like a fantastic place, but they'd have to go to the South, of course, they'd heard the North was still a bit rough. Far from the IRA bomb in Brighton making us outsiders, we found ourselves living among kin.

Everyone hated Margaret Thatcher, that probably helped, but I couldn't be sure trying to murder her was acceptable? Thou shalt not kill, says the fifth Commandment drilled into us for the Catechism. I always remember that because it was the one after Honour thy father and thy mother. I'd always thought that both of those commandments should be a bit higher up the list of dos and don'ts. God always had to be catered for first.

My fingers froze to the second glass of gin and tonic as he explained that one sister was a teacher, the other one was a nanny, so they had both, in their own small ways, carried on his darling mum's caring genes. Christopher Campbell was not Irish, his people were from Scotland originally, Glasgow to be precise, and he had visited the city quite a lot when he was younger. He loved Celts. Boy, could he find stuff to say. He was off and running down the lists of things he loved about Celts. In Ballyglen people would be backing away and warning everybody else to run for the hills, there was a slabber on the loose.

He paused, at last. It was my turn to speak. I had no *Mummy* to pull out of the bag so I latched on to the last thing he'd said. He was Scottish, even though he had the poshest English voice I'd ever heard.

– Are there any *English* people in England?

– Oh Lindy, I knew you'd have the gift of the gab!

He was going to walk me home, back up West Hill. To make sure I was *safe*. If he could guess how many times I had dreamed that someone would want to keep me *safe*, he might have been more careful with his words. But Christopher was not short of words, he had enough chat for three men, none of them interesting. Good job he had those teeth and that shiny hair.

He didn't stop at the east gate but took me right up to the double doors. He even came through them and stood a minute in the hall of the nurses' home until stinky Colin started to rattle his keys. I told Christopher he'd better go as my room was just beside him. He was delighted. That's handy, he said, you'll be first out if there's a fire. He didn't want me to burn to death. How lovely, was all I could think, as he asked to see me in another few days. I could listen to him chat some more bollocks in the Railway Tavern.

Hours later, I burned with embarrassment not because I'd wanted him to kiss me, but because I'd forgotten Miriam, my one true friend. She had been wiped completely from my thoughts in the last couple of hours. What kind of self-centred mare was I? Had Bell and Granny Tess and Granda Morris been right all along? I tried to imagine poor wee Miriam in the greyish yellow light of an all-night coach, bunched up and inviting cramps with her knees pulled up to her chest, but I couldn't. Every time I pictured the light, Christopher Campbell stepped into it and soaked it all up.

I couldn't wait to see him again. I'd never had a chance at a boyfriend before. There was something fluttering about in my chest, not my heart but definitely something with wings. Even Miriam noticed the change in me when I spoke to her. I called after two days to make sure she was okay. Mrs O'Dwyer picked up the phone and shouted for her to come quick, it would be costing me a *fortune*. You will take care of yourself, won't you, Lindy love? she begged before Miriam took the phone.

She was fine, so happy. Her parents had invited half of Ballyglen over to welcome her home. Bell had refused to come, the two senior Morrises, Tess and Gabriel, must have been busy too. But what about you? says Miriam.

– I'm fine!

– What's up? You sound funny.

– Nothing's up, nothing at all. What would be up?

– I don't know. I suppose I thought you'd think better of staying there all on your own and maybe follow me back. But you're not going to, are you?

– No, I'm not going to.

We parted on promises of weekly phone calls and maybe even a letter or two. She advised keeping in better touch with Bell, who had been badmouthing me to every single person who had time to listen, even the priest. Her own dear mammy had had to practically hide under the table at one of the Parish Church tombolas to avoid being interrogated.

There had been another sectarian incident in the square at Ballyglen. One of the boys we'd been to school with, Padraig Gallagher, had caught alight when he'd dropped his petrol bomb on his legs. It had been destined to break and burn brightly against the side of a passing Saracen. He would be scarred for life – she'd heard talk of the loss of an eye, an ear, some fingers. It was a double tragedy when he'd been so handsome. And it had confirmed to her entirely how much she hated nursing, she couldn't stomach the *damage*.

She'd always fancied Padraig Gallagher, but like me, she was a good girl, a girl who wasn't allowed out much given the fact that Ballyglen was a bit rough. In my case, Granda Morris wasn't so worried about me being caught by the casual sectarian violence. My mother had been impossible to keep in and look how *she* had ended. I knew I wasn't locked away for my own safety but for his peace of mind. Bad dogs need to be tethered.

I could have told her about Christopher Campbell, but for now I just wanted him all to myself. I imagined him boring the arse off Bell, Tess and Granda with his minty breath and mountain of dry facts and posh English accent, and the three of them being too shocked to run away. They did not like forward people. I swallowed the smile so fast I got the hiccups.

Chapter 5

Without Miriam to keep me company, I spent hours in front of the mirror. I peered at my face, trying to see what he saw, but all I could see was 'not good enough'. The hair was too unruly, the eyes too blue and too wide, the mouth too full; I was a frog, a pasty frog with no nice clothes. I pulled myself apart and hit my head against the glass when I finally understood I could never put myself back together again. So I was more nervous than ever when Thursday rolled around and I had to present myself in the Railway Tavern at seven o'clock.

By seven thirty I was still sitting alone in the corner. I felt sick down to my stomach. I should have known he wouldn't come, should have known he was only messing with me. Bell was right: people could *feel* that there was something wrong with me, I was not what any decent man would consider wife material. A hefty man called Barney from Dublin was leaning in and making jokes about me being stood up when he got patted on the shoulder and asked to step aside. It was Christopher!

He couldn't apologise enough for being late, only he had got caught in a meeting at St Simon Stock's and he could hardly just run out, though he had dearly wanted to. I refused every sorry and lied about how I had been grand to sit in a bar by myself and then I took to laughing at myself too much, the biggest, saddest clown in the whole room. He got me another gin and tonic and walked from the bar already drinking from his pint of Guinness. He wiped the froth from his lips as he sat down and smiled and I thought my heart would burst, I was so glad.

We chatted mostly about his day, and when my day finally came up I waved it away so he could keep talking. I still didn't like to repeat many of the things that went into making my day. Father Donnan featured a lot because I had made sure to give him plenty of extra attention. I confessed that Sister Smith didn't seem too keen on me. I told him all about Miriam deciding to leave, our sad parting at London Victoria coach station, how it was strange to phone Ireland and to find out that Ballyglen was ticking along just as it had always done when it already felt like a different life for me. Christopher nodded and nodded, he understood everything.

– So, you're all alone in London Town, Lindy?

– I'm all alone in London Town!

– Well, we might have to do something about that.

I stopped breathing to hear what his plans were to save me from being all alone but Hefty Barney was back. Him and some of the other lads wanted a few rounds of Twenty-Five Card Stud and they could use another couple of hands. There was money involved but it was just for fun not for fleecing. When Christopher answered him, every silly notion that I'd ever had of being fancied, of being wanted, of just being *liked* came true.

– Tell me, if you were sitting with this beautiful
   girl, would you waste your time playing cards for
   pennies?

We fell into step with each other easily. Over the next few weeks we met every Tuesday and Thursday outside of the hospital. We'd been to China Town and eaten sweet-and-sour pork, the maddest thing I'd ever tasted. Deep-fat fried and practically glowing orange. We'd had a night in the Tin Pan Alley Club on Denmark Street. We'd watched *Once Upon a Time in America* with Robert De Niro because I loved the Bananarama song about him waiting and talking Italian.

I didn't like the film so much and Christopher was not too impressed with the violence. It hadn't been entirely my idea to see it but I still felt terrible, like I'd made a mistake. He was definitely a bit sensitive about all sorts of things. I'd been back to Trafalgar Square late at night with him and he'd been upset by all the poor homeless people who had to queue up for food and a bed for the night at the hostel at St Martin-in-the-Fields church.

There was no doubt he was a bit of a Holy Joe, but I was glad he was kind and a good Catholic boy – it would make it a lot easier for us to get married. At least, Bell wouldn't be able to scream at me about bringing home a Protestant, even though she would find fault in his lack of Irishness. And Granda Morris would never accept him and his accent, *never*. It would be the equivalent of asking him to have a beer with a British soldier. I just hoped Christopher knew what he was letting himself in for when he took me on. He was letting himself in for the wrath of the whole Nationalist Morris Family. Of course, if they hated him, that would suit me down to the ground too. I could stay away from them and Ballyglen for *years* at a time.

I did wonder when he would kiss me. He always saw me home, straight to the door, and waited outside until I opened the curtains and waved him away. I didn't want to be brazen, but I hoped he knew that I would *love* to be kissed by him and only him. I hung back and thought of extra things to keep him on the threshold, but he wouldn't bite. Lying in bed I'd replay the evenings to see where I was going wrong. Was I dull? Was

I stupid? Was I too quiet, too noisy? Did I have on too much cheap perfume? Had I talked about *Smash Hits* too long? Would he rather have someone dainty, who didn't hobble along beside him in shoes deliberately bought a size too small?

I got to thinking it was because I always changed the subject when the subject was my family. He wanted to know about them. I didn't want him to know about them. This was a new country, a new life, all I needed was a new family.

– So what does your mother do?

– She's dead.

– Oh Lindy, I'm so sorry! What happened?

– Cancer.

– And your father?

– God, did you see the double-page spread on Paul Young in this month's *Smash Hits*? It's a brilliant read!

He wouldn't want to see me again if he knew I was illegitimate, so I went for stupid and he frowned at me often but we carried on somehow, two people tolerating each other as best they could.

I wasn't used to men who didn't shout, to men who asked me what I wanted to drink or eat. I wasn't used to men who were chatty, who were gentle and patient. He called for me once and I wasn't ready and instead of roaring at me that he had better things to do than waste his life standing about waiting for a *bloody fucking woman*, he just smiled and sat down in the hall. There's no need to rush, he said, the man who made time made plenty of it. This man opened doors and let me pass through them first, he held coats so that I could find my sleeves without fumbling, he made sure all of me was inside the tube doors before they slammed shut. This same man won't ever kiss me. *I'll die an old maid if I can't figure out how to make the first move.*

Wednesday was so long. The morning refused to end. I'd brave the savoury mince and mashed potatoes in the canteen and Yasmina'd sit with me eating her cooked fish and semolina, working the bones around her mouth until they popped out between her lips when she'd line them up along the edge of her Tupperware like a comb. She didn't like brown English food, it had *no bite, cha*!

In the afternoon, I still had Father Donnan as my special project. Reading to him really calmed him down, so I brought in my back catalogue of *Smash Hits*. He leaned back in his chair with his hands joined in prayer and closed his eyes as I told him about Madonna – he'd always say a little prayer when he heard her name – about Frankie Goes to Hollywood, Annie Lennox and Hazel O'Connor. As he dozed, I imagined standing between the concrete pillars that marked the start of the long lane down to Southfork. The strip of grass that grew down the middle, straight as a ploughed furrow no matter what the season, moved past me as I ventured closer. The nettle lawns to either side. The second-storey windows always picked up the light and reflected the clouds racing by. The roof was dark slate, bobbled with moss and spotted with lichen. The walls once painted white now stained with muck and manure.

The far chimney had grey smoke rising from the range in the kitchen, which was always lit. The door was left open in the summer and closed with a rolled-up meal bag applied against the draughts in the winter. I might even have felt a bit homesick until I looked inside. There's Granny Tess chewing a wasp! Auntie Bell sighing and floating about the place looking for something to find fault with! And just when you thought it couldn't get any colder, enter Gabriel Morris, the head of the family, ready to ill-treat the pair of them just for being alive.

– Miss Morris!
– Yes, Sister!
– They're short up on Women's Ward Main so I've allocated you to them. Off you go! You're up there for what's left of the day.
– Yes, Sister!

She hated us daydreaming, but I bet she wouldn't have sent Yasmina for the same crime. I saw the look of disgust on her face before she twisted poor Billy Idol into a figure of eight and popped him into General Waste. It was a good job I'd already ripped out the poster of him and his lovely white hair and stuck it on my wall or I'd have *died*.

Women's Ward Main on the third floor was where Miriam had discovered her horror of all things geriatric. I walked as slowly up the stone stairs as I could, stopping on the landing to look out at the houses all in darkness on the other side of West Hill. It was only four o'clock, the November nights were closing in. The plane trees were nearly bare and their big startled shapes were lit up in the headlights of buses and cars. I still got there eventually.

The ward sister was friendly, Sister Julie Walsh, and I was to call her Julie. She was afraid I'd have to be a bit of a self-starter because there was such a shortage of hands and there were twelve ladies in need of their tea and then in need of the potty and then they'd have to have an early night because there was even fewer auxiliaries around for the late shift. She pointed me at the three-tiered dinner trolley and left me to match the meals to the mouths. Before she disappeared she called over her shoulder.

– When you've fed all the ladies in here, we have to see to Mercy. If you get to her before me come and get me and I'll give you a hand.

– Yes, Sister, I mean Julie!

Miriam had told me about Mercy. I'd hardly been able to believe her, though she couldn't tell a lie. Just as

156

I shivered at the thought, a long low howl travelled up the corridor and pushed the goosebumps out of my skin like needles. A few of the old girls got agitated and a few more started shouting for someone to make the noise stop. Julie's voice rang out. *Mercy! For heaven's sake, pipe down!*

Miriam had been shaken to the core by her first sighting and couldn't wait to tell me about it so I could be terrified too. We'd set ourselves up with chocolate bars and mugs of tea to better analyse her living banshee. We'd shivered and made a sign of the cross, even though we were hundreds of miles from Ireland and the heart of civilised London was beating just across the river.

We'd been reared on stories of black dogs at wakes, devil dogs who were waiting to claim the souls of bad people, the bogeyman who sat on every bridge all the better to drag you under, and the banshee was the biggest threat of all. She came with death on her breath. Always a white-faced and silver-haired woman, the sound of her keening was a sure sign that a soul would be taken to Hell. Miriam was as freaked out as I'd ever seen her the day she first had to nurse Mercy.

The spoon I was moving towards the gummy mouth of one Mrs Alice Kent shook so much when the wailing got louder that I dropped a big splat of bread soaked in Horlicks on her bed jacket. I mopped it up as I told her again and again how sorry I was, but nothing registered on her face so I laid her back gently against the pillow and went when Julie called out for me – she had got to Mercy first.

She was at the far end of the corridor in a small room that would have been the nurses' room on any other floor. Julie stood aside to introduce her and I wished that she hadn't. Mercy could never be unseen. She had tried to kill herself, Miriam had told me with wonder in her voice, and it had left its mark. She'd thrown herself in front of a train, taking off from a metal bridge that spanned the tracks. She'd stumbled and fallen sideways. The train had hit her hard on the head, damaging the eye socket and smashing the cheekbone. It had taken her whole left arm, her whole left leg and her right leg below the knee. She couldn't speak any more and watched the world with such sad wet eyes that they couldn't be met. I could taste how hobbled she felt.

Julie explained the unique problems of handling her. She had to be secured to the chair or the bed because otherwise she could slip off, and although she wasn't all still with us, she was heavy. We hefted her up and even though I was as white as a sheet, Julie left me to feed her. I tried to spoon some rice pudding into her mouth but her tongue worked and worked to push it back out. I'd only taken my eye off her for a second when she hit me. It didn't hurt nearly as much as one of Granda's but it shocked me. I wasn't braced. The rice pudding was scattered and so were my nerves. I was rubbing at my cheek when Julie came back.

- Sorry, Lindy! I should have warned you that she gets a bit angsty around new people.
- It's okay, it's okay.
- Aren't you naughty, Mercy, hurting poor Lindy like that! You know what has to happen next?

Julie rolled her eyes at me and smiled as if she were standing over a badly behaved child. We got a sheet and swaddled Mercy like a baby before we strapped her against the chair. Sitting there among her many pillows, she looked sadder than anything I'd ever seen before. We had removed the one limb she had left and she stared at us like a kicked dog. The scars on her skull shone through her grey hair on the left side, and her eyes had murder pouring from them in salty tears.

It was no wonder Miriam had run back to Ballyglen. She had been among the dead and I among the living this whole time. I teetered again, it was not too late to bolt; if I got back to Bell before Christmas she might be glad to see me? Well, not *glad* but maybe not sad? We'd managed to have something resembling fun over the years; we'd always made the Christmas pudding together, then the Christmas cake, which we'd feed with brandy for a fortnight before we rolled out the lovely slabs of marzipan and fitted them all around it like a sweet blanket. Bell mixed the icing and I spread it on, making sure to pull up plenty of snowy peaks to hold the silver balls we used to decorate it.

One year, Granda Morris had a slice forced on him by Granny Tess and he said it wasn't bad. Bell and me had been so delighted you'd have thought he'd just handed us the moon and the stars when all he'd done was not roar at us for a change. But with the word 'Christmas' in my memory came the face of Christopher. He was a man who smiled and chatted and wanted to make sure nothing bad happened. He was so different, he could make me different, he could save me from a life like Bell's – a life of duty and dust. He was *steady* – Ballyglen speak for dull but worthy enough with it – a plough horse not a race horse, but a horse none the less. Beggars can't be choosers.

Mercy eyeballed me. I had to get some fluids down her because she had ripped out the last three feeding tubes and the scabs on the end of her nose told me it was none too gently. She wanted to die with every fibre of her being; it was the only thing she would gladly swallow. I closed in with a sippy cup of water.

Tomorrow I would see Christopher and all of this would be worth it, this new life I'd made in this new place, these new dreams. Tomorrow everything would be bearable again. I could steal a look or two at his lips as he yammered on and wonder what it would feel like when they finally rested on mine.

Chapter 6

The River Thames was so lovely at night. It lapped against the sides of the walkways and it was hard to tell that it's grey. The reflected lights rippled and danced. Christopher and me were walking along the Embankment after meeting for a drink in the Polar Bear off Leicester Square. It was not a happy walk, even though coloured light bulbs were strung through the trees for the Christmas that was coming. We'd had to finish our drinks and leave when I started to behave badly. He had noticed the bruise on my cheek straight away and his face was all concern. I told him how it had happened, about Mercy, about how we were keeping her alive against her will.

He listened and nodded and I hoped he would kiss me or at least hold me close. I wanted to be steadied after another whole day being allocated to Women's Ward Main. Mercy had been doped overnight and couldn't wake up enough to have a mouthful of food forced on her. Julie was as breezy as ever.

– We won't have any bother with our Mercy today, Lindy, she's had her pills.
– She's actually asleep?
– No, not asleep, just ... not so alert.

That she had been drugged seemed worse than letting her have her rage. She was a prisoner, trapped inside her broken body with its broken mind in that horrible arid room. And there was I with my syringes of pulped apples that she didn't want ready to squirt into her mouth. If I was her, I'd lash out. If I was her, I'd find some way of getting myself to the window so I could have another go at flying through the air.

Christopher did not agree. As far as he could see, the hospital was doing the right thing, life was precious, given by God, and only God could take it away. Maybe, he said, Mercy is being given time to atone for what she's done?

– What did she do?
– Oh Lindy! She tried to take her own life. That's a sin.
– What's happening to her now is a sin too. If you could see it with your own eyes, you'd understand. It's cruel.

– I do understand. It's not her time yet. Don't work yourself up, Lindy. This is your job. You chose to help these people?

– I'd never even been inside a hospital until I came here. I'd no clue what kind of things would be asked of me. You only see the nice side of it – you don't know what goes on behind those feckin' curtains!

He breathed deep at that. He didn't like girls who swore. And I could tell by the way he gripped his pint that I was to finish my drink too, now. And then I was walked across the flashy madness of Leicester Square, through the crowds of people clapping along to a busker, past the closed doors of the National Portrait Gallery, past the hungry souls queuing for food and shelter at St Martin's and across the road to Charing Cross station before we dropped into Villiers Street. All around us people were shouting, laughing, kissing, running to and from the trains, *living*. And I'd never felt more alone.

A gap had opened up between him and me the width of a person and that person was Mercy. We carried her through the open end of Embankment tube station and out the other side. I counted five benches in the shape of sphinxes with angel's wings before he spoke, a record silence for him. I'd no intention of opening my mouth in case I destroyed my last chance with him. I had to understand what I was saying was *wrong*; in fact, what

I was *thinking* was wrong. He'd assumed that I was a good Catholic girl. Jesus!

I'd come to the boil so often – over losing Mammy, over inheriting Bell, over Granda Morris and Granny Tess – and I had always judged it best to walk away and scream silently in a corner, but not this time. I'd often been told not to speak. I'd certainly been told not to dream. But now I wasn't allowed to *think*? With one good hard yank on my leash he'd lead me back to suffer the hearth in Southfork.

– You're a dull man, you know that?

– Lindy ...

– You make me *sick* with your preaching. You're so perfect. I don't know why you even want a girlfriend?

– A girlfriend? What are you talking about?

I left him and the river then. I ran all the way back to the tube and got myself through the barriers and on to the first moving train I could find. I wished Miriam was still there so I could tell her what a fool I'd made of myself. I'd fallen out with the first boyfriend I'd ever had over less than half a woman.

Now I was travelling in the wrong direction across a city I hardly knew. What had made me think that I could ever make my life here? I turned around eventually, wading against the waves of people who knew the routes like the back of their hand. As I was rocked through the tunnels to Putney I wondered where I had kept that anger for so long. My mother had been fiery, so my temper was never tolerated for a second in me. *You don't want to turn out like your mammy, do you, Lindy?*

I started up West Hill, as miserable as I'd ever been. Some of the Filipino girls were having a party in the kitchen. Delicious smells and giggles poured out from where they all sat on the tables, flip-flops dangling. They were doing each other's hair and plucking each other's eyebrows and talking fast and loud. I watched them awhile with a heavy heart until I made for the cold sheets in my room, property of RHHI.

I scrubbed off the silly make-up I'd put on with such hope earlier. I was copying Sheena Easton and I'd gone mad overboard with lipstick and eyeshadow, half of which I'd rubbed down my face. There was only one thing left to do and that was hope for sleep. I lay down with a cold flannel across my eyes to bring the puffiness down and listened to the sounds of this place I called home.

What had seemed as calming as an ocean wave three months ago now grated like a nail dragged across a blackboard. How could someone make so much noise *walking*? How could they keep laughing after what we had to endure on a daily basis here?

When the sound of the tap-tap-tapping came at the window, I didn't hesitate for a second. Throwing the flannel to one side I pulled the curtains, pulled up the sash and stuck my head out. And there he was – Christopher.

– Can you come out?

– No, it's freezing. Come *in*, for God's sake!

He climbed in one long leg at a time and we found ourselves face to face in a very small space. I only had on a T-shirt so I quickly wrapped a towel around my waist to hide the terrible milk-white legs. There was nowhere to sit except the bed and Christopher said he wanted to talk. He was all whipped up and had a lot he needed to tell me. Big gaps opened up between his words like he was making them fresh. I wanted to wait, I did, but when it was obvious he'd come to make up with me, I thought, why put him through it? I can forgive him right away. I had my lips on his before he could stop me.

After only a few minutes I could hardly remember when I hadn't been kissed. We were naturals, he leaned in to me and I leaned in to him like we'd both fall flat on our faces if we didn't. It was lovely, everything I'd dreamed of, a real connection. When he got too hot he stood to get his coat off but when he looked back at me on the bed he just stripped all of his clothes off and got in beside me.

The feel of him all soft and warm alongside me was too much and I gave myself away in a heartbeat. It hurt, of course, I knew it would, but it wasn't too bad. I'd put up with worse. I held him as he slept, his head heavy on my collarbone. I kept my hand in his shiny hair and pulled the blanket up around his shoulders. I had done the right thing at the right time and we'd wasted no precious minutes worrying about it too much. I'd always wanted to feel peaceful, to feel loved and now I did. When Christopher stirred, I held him closer still and said the words I'd been saving up for a lifetime. I'd not said them since Mammy disappeared quick as a wink to find us a house to live in happily ever after.

– I think I love you.

– I suppose you do, Lindy.

Christopher knew so many things. He must have known that I would be out of my mind with worry to not hear from him. I was left on Women's Ward Main for a fortnight. Dealing with Mercy didn't get any easier and every time I looked into her hollow eyes I remembered she was the reason we'd quarrelled. I swaddled her before every feed and hated myself every time I forced another spoonful of mush on her. I breathed in the air that Mercy breathed out. I was glad she couldn't spit far as I wiped the fruits of my labour off her chin.

I missed Father Donnan's release. When I came back Sister Smith told me right away and she looked a bit sorry for me. I even got a shoulder squeeze. I know you'd grown fond of the old boy, she said. Don't worry, that nice young man says they have a lovely place all set up and ready for him and he'll have a whole nun to himself. I took the kindness as best I could but I'd lost my chance of seeing Christopher so I could ask him what I'd done to keep him away.

After that night, when I thought I'd made him mine, I woke up and he'd gone. I had let him slip out of my arms. I didn't worry. He would be back in touch before next Tuesday and we'd carry on being boyfriend and girlfriend. He'd been as eager as me to go to bed. Bell had warned me so often about being forward and I'd upped and slept with a boy without so much as a backward glance. I felt quite modern, another step away from the old me. The me who was always waiting for a clump on the head, the me who never had an interesting word to say for herself. I sent up a prayer of thanks for London's anonymity. I could do whatever I wanted and not a word would get back near Southfork.

When Tuesday rolled around and I'd not heard from him, I waited for Thursday, which also came and went and saw me lying alone in my room, staring at the ceiling. I ran through what we'd done in this very bed to see if I'd done something wrong. I'd stayed still, I'd made no fuss when he hurt me, I'd told him to go ahead, it was okay to tear me, it was only me. When he was finished I didn't ask him if that was it, it had been quicker than I'd expected. I'd told him I loved him because that's what you're supposed to say after you've done the wicked deed. It rolled around and around my head, the reality that Christopher didn't *know* me and yet he still didn't want me when I'd been as obedient as I could.

He didn't know I had traveller blood. He didn't know the rotten bastard that was Granda Morris, whose shitty reputation could carry him across five townlands. As always when the loneliness hits, it's Mammy that comes back to keep me company. I hear the tinkle of her laugh as she tells another tale about Granny Tess. Granda had always hated the fact his wife was *short*, not something she could have kept hidden from him at any stage. She'd told Mammy once in a fit of bad temper, *I wasn't standing on a bloody chair the first time he asked me to waltz.* Mammy and me had roared at the thought of tiny Tess balancing on her bird legs in all her finery at the back of a dancehall.

Over the years, there had been countless remarks made on her failure to produce any more children, as if the twin girls had been enough to clean her out, useless bantam that she was. He hated me for the opposite reason. I was too tall for a girl, he couldn't see past me. *You're blocking the light from the window. Sit down, for fuck's sake, bloody girl. You're making the place look untidy. You've cost me more in shoe leather than you're worth*. I was terrified he'd been right all along, that I had flaws that even strangers could see.

I went back to the mirror and tried to figure out what Christopher saw. A tall girl, slightly too wide in the shoulders, pale blue eyes, long black hair mostly tamed now by the discovery of conditioner, a full mouth that managed to look forlorn. I was plain at best. I smiled as wide as I could but it didn't change anything. I just looked a bit mad. *Tell me, if you were sitting with this beautiful girl, would you waste your time playing cards for pennies?* Men are liars, screams Bell from the past.

I forced myself in to work every day. I was always worried until I knew that I was safe on Rehabilitation. Mercy and Women's Ward Main were more than I could face. It was Yasmina who noticed the moping.

– What's up, chil'?
– Remember that man who was friends with Father Donnan? He took me out a few times …
– He keep you home a few times, too?
– Once, only once.
– Once is all it take. Be careful there. You don't want to get mixed up with those Church men.
– He's only a bookkeeper.
– Bookkeeper? That's all Church men interested in, money, cha!

I wanted to ask her if I was owed some sort of explanation. Why had he left me all alone in London when

170

he'd said he'd do something about that? I could tell by Yasmina's face she was all done doling out advice.

I'd still not told Miriam; she didn't need to know a single thing about Christopher Campbell. Good job I hadn't humiliated myself by cracking on that I thought someone fancied me. This left all of her focus on getting me to ring Bell. My aunt had started to call the O'Dwyer house every few days. She cried down the phone when she wasn't screaming down the phone, and it was getting on Miriam's mammy's nerves.

– Please, Lindy – just call her. Just *once*!

– I will, of course, one of these days.

– No, Lindy – it *has to be* today. We can't handle the stress and strain any more. She thinks I left you bleeding in a gutter somewhere.

She went on and on in the same vein. It helped to block out the sadness that Christopher had lost interest in me. Bell having her little breakdown was nothing to do with love for me; it had to do with her fury that I had been able to carry on without her by my side.

That's when it hit me. I'd not been able to imagine a world without Bell for eleven years. She had taken over my life so completely that I didn't really live it myself, I had been led by the nose. But now look! I was doing okay in a separate country. If I could survive Bell Morris and her beloved parents, I could survive Christopher Campbell. If he was only going to be more proof that I wasn't good enough, I could live without another serving of that bile.

I said goodbye to Miriam with a much lighter heart and before I could change my mind, I called the number in Southfork. I could take Bell on. *Don't let Granda Morris pick up, don't let Granda Morris pick up, please God, just this once have him guarding the phone against his bloody fucking women.*

   – Hello?

   – Hello, Bell.

   – Lindy! How could you do this to me? Don't you know I've been out of my mind with worry? I've been climbing the walls. Your granda has been spitting nettles about it and Tess has made my life a misery. They blame me for how you've turned out. Me? It's hardly my fault!

   – I'm doing fine, Bell. Thanks for asking. Before you go off on one, could I beg you to stop calling the O'Dwyers? I'll call you once a month from now on, but you have to stop torturing them, do you understand?

   – It's so typical of you to take this out on me. What was I supposed to do? Just pretend it was alright for you to disappear clean off the face of the earth?

It took quite a few of my good, hard-earned 10ps to pick her off the ceiling but we parted on semi-decent terms. *Promise me you're going to Mass, Lindy! Don't give up your faith!* I stayed a minute afterwards in the booth to settle my heart. There were scores of numbers written all around the wall where the phone was nailed. To call Australia add ++00, said one, why would you want to, said another with an arrow and a question mark.

The corridor was quiet, no one was waiting. The hall was lit with its dim green light, the kitchen was empty. The soft sound of the traffic ploughing up West Hill could just be heard. The river wasn't far, the widest, deepest, greyest river I had ever crossed. It was proof that I lived in London and I was going to live better. I was going to live as me. If that meant being all alone here for another few months so be it. I went to bed and slept like a well-fed, well-loved baby.

Chapter 7

Lindy, Beverley but call me Bev, Donna and Susanne. The four of us were out on the town and deciding between Tequila Sunrises and Orgasms. We'd been thick as thieves since we'd all been trapped on Women's Ward Main for a whole week together. I'd met them the day after I decided to be happy. Bev and Donna were Aussies. Me and Susanne were Paddies, although she was from the Republic, Galway to be exact. I had had the job of introducing them all to Mercy and I'd been so calm that they thought I was super cool.

I watched their faces register all the many horrors of Mercy's life. You'll get used to it, I said, as she got her hand free and swung at them. I swaddled her up as gently as I could and showed them how to get the mush into her cheek so that some of it could slip down before she managed to push it out. It was agreed by all three of them after one shift that I was 'fucking amazing, mate'.

I took their 'fucking amazing, mate' and their dread of Mercy and turned it into a night out, which turned into a few nights out every week and now we were out drinking under the Christmas lights that burned rainbows in every bar in town. We'd crossed the river to find a bar that did cocktails, dolled up to the nines. I'd bought myself a pencil skirt and a dangerous pair of high heels and discovered that standing out in the crowd was a good thing. Bev, Donna and Susanne were all insanely jealous of the long legs I'd been hiding for a decade. All the rest of the talk was of just *how much more fun* we were going to have.

Susanne was put out because she was going back to Galway, which wouldn't be even half as much craic as being here, but she had no choice. She had been summoned and the hideous coach ride from Victoria to Holyhead to Dun Laoghaire was uppermost in her mind, that and missing out on all the shenanigans of me, Bev and Donna. We told her to dry her eyes and then we clinked our Tequila Sunrises and sip by sip she stopped sulking.

I had been signed up to work Christmas Day and all the other crap shifts, and Sister Smith was glad about that. Bell was *not* pleased and I had to remind her that she had often worked unsociable hours; she could hardly forget Granny Tess not speaking to her for a month the first time she missed Our Lord's Birthday? Certainly it was the worst Christmas I ever had. The first one without Mammy was when Bell was working out her notice in Gransha and my grandparents just glared at me as if I was Judas Iscariot made flesh. Granny Tess had allowed me to draw close so she could tell me a secret. *Do you know why Santy Claus is giving Southfork a wide berth this year? It's not because you're the worst child, it's because he doesn't exist.* She could have waited until I was eight.

I'd agreed to working New Year's Day, too. Bev, Donna and me were going to see in 1985 in style. We'd heard the thing to do was hit Trafalgar Square and splash about in the fountains with a crowd of other lunatics, even though it was freezing. Bev and Donna cracked up in hysterics when I said I wasn't worried about catching my death, I'd be far more likely to die from alcohol poisoning. I was a riot. Susanne went back to sulking and had to be coaxed out again with another round of Tequila Sunrises.

Being in a gang was the best thing ever. I stopped short of getting a perm when all three of them did. We all liked a lacy blouse with as big a bow as it could support. They thought I was class because I stuck to my passion for dungarees in the brightest yellows and pinks I could find when they erred towards red. We all agreed that it was a tragedy I couldn't borrow any of their shoes, but big feet were the price I had to pay for being so damned leggy. I pretended to be unbothered by life at the RHHI, by life in general and by life as a single girl. I'd told them about Christopher Campbell and we'd all decided that he wasn't worth bothering about. He didn't know what he was missing was their verdict and I had to agree.

Life was good enough. The work was routine, some days were better than others, but I had a certain confidence now in my abilities which saw me dropping my shoulders and raising my chin. I could talk to relatives when they broke down, I could organise the newer girls and show them the ropes. On the rehab ward it wasn't so bad, there was hope for some of the patients even though it was slim, but long stints on any of the other wards meant more and more alcohol at the weekends and sometimes even during the week.

Me and the gang joked about it when we bought litres of cheap vodka from the shops and doused it with orange juice. We had bed picnics. Not a single vegetable passed our lips, there was no room, we were so full of crisps, peanuts and biscuits. It would soon be payday, I'd go straight to the supermarket and buy a whole bag of lettuce. That would do the trick and it would be cheaper than buying new jeans.

*

Relatives started to show up as 25 December came round. They were armed with presents of soaps and flannels, pyjamas and dressing gowns, as advised by the hospital – stuff that was useful. We had a big tree all lit up and covered in tinsel in the corner of the day room and Sister Smith let us have the radio on for the Christmas favourites. Band Aid was played every hour. Do they know it's Christmas time at all? asked my faves Simon le Bon and George Michael. I was so proud that Bob Geldof was Irish like me and he need never know I had a British passport. We were looking forward to having our roast turkey and ham in the canteen, which was criss-crossed with paper chains made in some of the wards where the long-term patients had been put to use cutting and sticking and linking yards and yards of them. It *is* the season to be jolly.

Increasingly I was pleased that I had made this move. I had friends now, girls who took me as they found me. There was no dark backdrop to my life, no aunt nailed to a cross, no grandparents dripping with hatred, no absent father, no shame because that father hadn't stuck around to tell me his name, never mind give me his name, no mother found floating in a lake. These girls had no memories of me and I loved it. Here, I was a clean slate.

Working in the RHHI for months as a nursing auxiliary made me realise I didn't want to be trapped in a hospital for ever, so I had my eye on night school. I could see myself in a nice clean office, dressed in little skirt suits of the kind I saw being walked around town. I'd trade in my latex gloves for perfect red fingernails.

The thought of Christopher Campbell intruded now and again, but as Susanne often said, it would have been a pure freak to meet the right man the first time around the block. With my looks and my figure, I'd not be short of admirers. She'd had a couple of boyfriends herself, saw nothing wrong with bonking them and then moving on. Gotta try before you buy, says Bev, and Donna nods over the rim of the vodka bottle. We were all so worldly and wise for eighteen.

As pure rotten luck would have it, I was sent to Women's Ward Main almost as soon as I got to work on Christmas Day. Julie was off so the next ward sister over, Sister Chen, told me and three other stand-ins to 'do our best'. All three of them dodged into the side wards and I knew that I would have to cope alone with Mercy. I could hear her from where I stood, drowning out the jingle bells.

Mercy wasn't alone. A woman of about thirty sat beside her, a box covered in reindeer paper on her lap. She had the same long face, same wide eyes, same hank of straight hair, though hers was still blonde. They both looked up when I came in.

– How long has she been trussed up like this?

- What?
- Her arm! She only has one arm and she's not even allowed the use of that?
- I'm sorry! She pinches, you see, and pulls hair and …

I didn't have to cast around for any more feeble excuses because the woman burst into tears. She fell back into the chair and sobbed, great back-rounding sobs, and Mercy moaned along in time. I wished Julie was there, maybe she could have explained it better. It must be terrible to see someone you love hampered like that, but we had to stop her scratching the nurses. I'd never liked doing it. The worst feeling in the world is being made to feel even weaker than you already know you are.

- I really am so sorry. Please don't cry.
- I'm okay, I'm okay. I just can't stand it. You can understand that, can't you? That I can't stand it?
- Yes, I can understand that.
- You got a mum?
- No, she's dead. She died in an accident when I was seven.
- God, you're so lucky. Trust me, there are plenty of things worse than death. Like this, for example. Stomaching this, year in, year out.

With that she tucked the parcel of reindeers down the side of her mother's chair and looked at her for another minute. I waited for Mercy to get a hug, maybe even a kiss, a loving touch of some kind, but the woman just sighed and walked away. Mercy kept her eyes on me, unaware she had been abandoned once more.

I took out the present and tried to get her to look at the wrapping before I opened it. Hand cream and a new T-shirt, pink, size small and it would still drown her. The word drown blew up inside my head like a bomb. The picture of Mammy lying peaceful and pale in her coffin rose to the surface. I tried to never let that happen. It hurt to see that stillness in someone who had paced rooms, swung me around to the records she liked on the radio, who had climbed out of windows and down drainpipes, who ran for the forest any chance she had. She had to get her dose of moonlight. Would she have folded in on herself if she'd failed to die outright? Mercy let out a terrific howl, which brought me crashing back into the equally unpleasant here and now. I dropped everything and took off.

I shot past the other girls who had gathered in the corridor, past Sister Chen, down the stone stairs and out into the fresh air. The whiff of Brussels sprouts pouring out of some vent close by reminded me that Christmas should only come once a year. Later, I'd sit in a canteen with people from every corner of the globe and we'd all be super friendly for today. This year I would get to spend it without Bell, Granny Tess and

Granda Morris grinching and that had to be a plus. I'd never got used to spending it without Mammy.

I'd got myself to a place where children wanted their parents dead and parents wanted their children dead, another madhouse when I'd just escaped one. I was tired to the bone of the work here, it was wearing me down. What I did was as insignificant as a tick on a boar's back. The reality of this place had got into my guts, making them churn and heave, the movement was dislodging long-buried damage. And it was *still* better than being within striking distance of Ballyglen.

I pulled myself together. My New Year's resolution was *happiness*. I'd book those classes in night school. I'd make myself into someone different. I'd forget Christopher; the girls were right, he wasn't worth bothering about. I might even have disliked him for being such a soft lad if I hadn't been so desperate. I'd bury the past in even deeper graves and look to my future. One day, I'd outrun every last skeleton and live happily ever after.

CARNSORE

Chapter 1

Bell is blowing out her nostrils like a bull who's just spotted me skipping across his field. I have set up the tea things in the kitchen, deliberately breaking Bell's rules of only eating hot food off the table. Miriam will be here in half an hour and Bell can hardly contain her bad temper at having me choose this day of all days to play up.

- You know we *always* take tea in the front room?
- That's what *you* and your friends do, Bell. Miriam will be fine in here with me and you're welcome to join us.
- Well, you're a piece of work, Lindy Morris! Inviting people into my house and dictating to me where they'll sit!

– Surely it's my house too, Bell? After all, I'm the reason it was built?

It's getting easier and easier to shut Bell up. The Box of Tricks and the news that Patrick Joseph existed have made me bold. I was not alone from the off. I smile sweetly as she tries to pick her jaw off the floor. His life has added to the story of Mammy, he has fleshed her out. She, too, went through the agony of losing a son. I also have a father and I'm going to bore Bell out of the room and ask Miriam if she can help me find him. She won't be able to cope with sitting in the kitchen for long when we have 'company', so I'll be able to pass over my tightly folded piece of paper with his name written on it. Ballyglen is so small and yet so full of gossips that someone will know someone who knows *something*.

I've been to Diamond's to get half a dozen fresh cream cakes and I can't wait to see Bell's face when I put them out. Right now they're hidden in their white cardboard box and sealed with an inch of Sellotape. I've made a few sandwiches too – cheese, of course – and Bell has somehow managed to survive her earlier horror that they have no lettuce or tomato in them. If anyone had heard her analysis of my character for shunning salad, they would have thought I'd just nailed a kitten to the wall.

Miriam's always on time so she comes in to the tune of cuckoos, chimes and tings at midday. Her face lets me know she can feel the temperature in the house and it's nothing to do with the fact that a chilly breeze is blowing down the valley from Carnsore. She hangs her coat and shucks off her shoes and pats her hair back into place and breezes on through to the kitchen to greet Bell with a huge smile and news about the weather. It's threatening to rain, apparently.

While I heat the teapot and warm the mugs (another sin: no cups and saucers), Bell complains that the upcoming play *Dancing at Lughnasa* is not to her liking. She'd rather something a bit more weighty, something like *Many Young Men of Twenty*, which was just the ticket in her day. Miriam should be on the stage herself, she does such a good job of not letting Bell know that she'd give a cloud of hungry midges a run for its money in terms of being annoying.

I slice the Sellotape on the cakes and flip the lid up to reveal our cream horns. Bell cannot abide them – they flake apart in pure badness just as you're trying to enjoy them. The shrieks of her! I'd not have gotten better value by turning out a bucketful of spiders. She has to go and lie down to see if she can figure out why I have turned out to be the Devil incarnate with my cream horns. Miriam and me keep the giggling to a minimum. No point in getting too cocky. Tea poured and two cream horns each shoved down the gullet in record time and we can catch up. Miriam's news is taken up with the details of her twin granddaughters, their tiny dresses, the amount of stuff that has been bought for them, enough to rear six children. My heart swells every time she says 'twins', but I am not going to tell her. Bell is going to be the first person who speaks with me about Patrick Joseph, whether she likes it or not. I have trouble keeping up with which one of Miriam's six children produced which perfect offspring. I find that nodding covers all such lapses.

I love watching Miriam when she talks. Her face lights up as it describes hugs, kisses, tiny toes, wind, smiles that could be wind, real smiles, shitty nappies, boke, screaming colicky fits, which all give her joy in equal measure. I tell her about finding Bell's Box of Tricks. We giggle about Granda Morris having to force himself across the threshold of his house of middling women to get shot of it. The giggles die down when she asks me about the Clinic. Of course, she would have heard. Some secrets get kept in Ballyglen, some do not. She tells me again that I'm deep while I tip my head so she can inspect the scar running from one ear to the next. You'd hardly see it if you didn't know it was there, she says, and I agree. It's a bagatelle.

When I finally tell Miriam that I found my father's name in the Box of Tricks, she gasps. Without a minute's hesitation she throws herself headlong into a plan to help me find Linus Quinn. She knows someone who knows someone who knows a family of Quinns on the other side of the border; she'll start there.

- This is big, Lindy! Huge. Give me wan of those sandwiches to settle my stomach.
- There's no guarantee he'll be pleased to see me.
- Of course he'll be pleased to see you! Why wouldn't he be pleased to see you? Aren't you gorgeous and smart and all the other things a daddy would want?
- Maybe?
- Trust me, Lindy. I know you couldn't possibly understand it because you've no children, but every parent would welcome a second chance. It's one of those mad things, you just *can't help* loving your own waynes.

I'll never learn to stop giving happiness an inch. The little swell of my heart is replaced by a stab. I wish I could tell her that I did have a wayne of my own, that I had loved him and I'd give my arm for a second chance. But I never could, never. Even Miriam wouldn't be able to grasp how I had given him up. The yarn I'd spun myself when all I'd done was save my own skin. The little razor blade sang out to me from the bottom of the bin in my room at the end of the corridor. I like to picture it there, it and its promise of relief. But I held on to the chair in the kitchen until my fingers nearly snapped.

Miriam ate another cheese sandwich and talked with her mouth full of how she was going to go straight round to her friend as soon as she left here. *We'll dig him out, Lindy, don't you worry*. She needed another couple of mugs of tea to fortify herself then she was up and bouncing out of the back door with hopes and promises flying around her head like butterflies. She'd be back soon then we'd be cooking on gas.

The cheery beep of the car horn fails to raise Bell so I take my chance to step lightly past her door and into my own room. I pick up the bin but instead of tipping it up and freeing the sharp metal edge of my saviour, I hold it against me as if it was a baby. I rock it gently and try not to crush it, to memorise its every detail before someone comes to take it away. I try not to cry when it doesn't become real, doesn't cling with its little hands, doesn't make its little sucking noises. Nothing or no one can make me give it up this day.

I will not let it out of my arms. If anyone tries, I can use it to cut myself; I'll divert them with screams and blood and make a run for it. I'll get myself on the other road, the road I should have chosen that would let me be with it always. I climb into bed with it and pull the beige eiderdown up over us both to keep us warm. As I drift, content for a rare moment, I hope Bell will sneak a peek through the door later. If she finds me in bed with a bin, it'll really put the willies up her.

The dream that comes is an old friend. It lets itself in and sits down in its usual chair. It is my son, fully grown

now. He is thirty-three this year. He has kissed a beautiful girl goodbye, a peck on the cheek. She is always a
version of Bev or Donna with their tanned limbs and
wide smiles, a girl who makes him glad to be alive.
They part company because he is on his way to see *me*.
He is fine-boned and light-footed. He makes his way
along the streets I knew in London. We meet on a corner under a giant plane tree. I walk beside him as he
talks about his day. He has a nice clean job in a nice
clean office because he was sensible and listened to his
mother. I am always Mummy *not* Mammy. He says it
just how Christopher Campbell said it. *Mummy*. We
link arms because the traffic is heavy and we need to
keep each other safe from harm. He talks to me in his
lovely posh English accent, he wants to eat Chinese
food and sit with me awhile in a nice pub drinking beers
and gin and tonics. He wanders off to look at a shop
window. But then a red double-decker bus drives
between us, and when it passes, he's gone.

That's when I always wake up, heart breaking and
nerves shot to pieces. It's as well the dream doesn't give
me time to look for him because I know he isn't there,
there is no shop window, there is no street, there is no
way back even in dreams. The metal mesh of the bin
has pressed itself into my face, it hurts just enough. I
put it back in its place beside the bed and pat it. It was
a good baby while it lasted. Did the people who took

him on give him a new name? I never get to shout his name in my dream but it's always on my lips. I had taken only one look at his mop of thick black hair before I called him Kieran. That's all I got to give him in the eight weeks we had together.

Chapter 2

Saturdays roll around too quick. Bell and me are standing with the door open to welcome the wimmin even though the late-November winds are burning our cheeks with the cold. Today Mrs McCrossan has rejoined the fold, dressed top to toe in black, with a black armband that she took off her coat and pulled on to her jumper in case we forgot she was in serious mourning for the morning. But Mrs McCrossan *has* pulled herself together, a fact Mrs Barr is delighted by. She's made it her mission to explain to Father Boluwaji that he can expect higher standards from other grieving parishioners just in case he thinks of bolting back to Nigeria and leaving us all without a shepherd.

Bell's pupils dilate and fix on Mrs Barr. It's unbelievable that she has managed to breach the security system at the Parochial House *singlehanded*. Father Boluwaji does not encourage gossip or favouritism, but if he's going to be influenced, then Bell wants a slice of the action. She's off and running on her desire to 'do more for the chapel'. The rota for doing the flowers for the altar is far too busy, she whines, we could do with doing away with *half* the women on there. She wants an additional four Sundays a year. She decides she's hampered in her lofty ambitions by having no car when I remind her that she has no licence so no car is not the problem. That gets me a trio of such violent intakes of breath the living room nearly empties of air. It's cheekier by the day, I'm getting.

Mrs Kennedy nods and nods but dives in with a timely reminder that soon it will be all hands to the pump for *Dancing at Lughnasa*. It should draw quite a crowd so we'll be busy on the doors and helping with the costumes. But even dear, kind Martha can't divert Bell from her misery today. She hates the play, she says; why anyone would be interested in the shenanigans of a bunch of Irish women who sit around bemoaning their lot, she has no idea. The wimmin look out of the window in silence.

The problem is she *did* see me sleeping with the bin. It had the desired effect of shredding what's left of her peace of mind. She's still not found the Box of Tricks and I'm getting more difficult to control with every hour that passes. I almost felt sorry for her when she tried to talk about it, *almost*.

– Lindy (cough), do I need to worry about you?

– Me, Bell? Why would you worry about me?

– You were sleeping with a (cough) bin in your bed.

– A bin?

– Yes, yes, yes, a bin! God's sake, don't pull every word out of me like a rotten tooth! You were sleeping with a bin! Why would you do that? Why?

– How did you see me sleeping with a bin? Are you spying on me again? You know you've really been twitchy since you lost your Box of Tricks? What was in there anyway? What was Granda Morris trying to hide this time? It must be something huge? Something that's meant to stay buried?

Many a cuckoo, chime and ting passed before she recovered. She wasn't used to having the tables turned on her and she didn't like being questioned. Could she know that I'd found Patrick Joseph as well as Linus Quinn in that suitcase?

I feel rather than hear the wimmin tearing the arms and legs out of Father Boluwaji as they pull him this way and that over the cream cakes like spoiled brats with a ragdoll. He's airborne for the bulk of the two hours, a prize that must be won. Every single one of these women probably knows about my brother, I think to myself, as their outrage over dead flowers grows. It's soon time for me to clear away but not soon enough. *Lindy will clear away, won't you, Lindy?* They pass their cups and saucers and I take them one by one into the kitchen. Martha follows me in when she sees I'm on my last run.

We roll eyes at each other and smile. A high-pitched discussion on the pros and cons of moving the choir from the balcony to the altar rails reaches us from the living room. It will buy us some time for a chat. She mentions her cure-all trip for me to Donegal like she always does and I say I'm thinking about it like I always do. Then it occurs to me she's been there a lot, she probably knows a lot of people, she's probably always known a lot more than she's told me.

– Martha, did you know Linus Quinn?

– Oh! Lindy! Where did you get that name?

– I found some papers. Do you know him? Do you know where I can find him?

– I'm not sure that's such a good idea! It was all so long ago, he could be dead, he could have moved on. You were never even meant to *hear* that name … Oh!

– I'll find him, Martha. I will.

I pass her a plate from the soapy basin and she dries it up. One day soon I'll ask her what my mother had *actually* done. I know she'll know that too but I can't risk upsetting her any further today. I hear Martha tut softly to herself over the ruckus from next door. What's so wrong with hearing a name? I've heard his and Patrick Joseph's and I've not had to be sent off to the Clinic for a little holiday.

Mrs Barr is adamant the choir should be in the balcony, that way the beautiful sound of the hymns could waft down into the congregation just as they have done for generations of Catholics. Bell is in the opposite camp. She thinks that the good God-fearing people should be able to see choirmaster Liam Foley on his guitar and the singers opening their hearts and souls up to Heaven.

Mrs McCrossan says she doesn't really care where they sit but they should be more thoughtful. It was the *singing* that totally undid her during her mother's service. If it hadn't been for the opening bars of "Nearer, my God, to Thee", she might have made it through without disgracing herself.

That's enough for Mrs Barr. She's never been a fan of people wriggling out of bad form. I hear her push her chair back hard with her formidable calf muscles. She declares that it's time they all left to get on with their day and perhaps it's way past time for a break in this particular routine! Bell and me will have one less thing to fill the week but we will all meet the first Saturday *after* the play to discuss whether or not it has been a raging success. It's only three weeks away.

*

When the phone goes on Sunday afternoon, Bell answers and blushes to her scalp. It's for me, not her. I assume it is Miriam but she doesn't say a word when she hands over the receiver. Father Boluwaji's lovely voice curls itself into my ear. He's remembered that we are due one of our chinwags, it has been far too long since we've sat down and set the world to rights. We agree that tomorrow is as good a day as any. He'll have the kettle on, he says, and my heart lifts.

I'll walk the six miles to St Bede's, even though it'll be bitterly cold every step of the way on what was always the bog road. It is long, straight and narrow like the road that runs to Carnsore before it too crosses the border into the Republic. The big evergreens will lean out to watch me leave, the lip of a leafy wave which never spills over. We're all living on the edge of a new country. One that agreed to peace on Good Friday 1998, thirteen years after I came back from London. One that has run out of Catholic priests born and bred on either Irish or British soil. One that watches Stormont in Belfast and Westminster in London with equal suspicion.

Bell hovers, waiting to hear what I'm up to now. I tell her I have a cake to bake. She won't get to taste it, though, because it's for Father Boluwaji, and the frustration that she's not the centre of anyone's attention makes her twist her fingers while she comes up with a hundred reasons the cake will fail. It won't rise. The eggs aren't what they should be. She's not sure if there's enough gas left in the canister to sustain this ridiculously extravagant gesture.

How would I know what Father Boluwaji likes and what he doesn't like in the cake department? It's not as if we're *friends*, he's *only* being kind because it's his job. I'll go to all this trouble and expense only to find he'd much rather have something decent from Diamond's. Something he could actually eat.

I have years of experience of blocking her out. If I had listened to her I wouldn't have got out of bed after the age of eight. She hemmed me in with shame. It must have been such a bonus when I made it to twelve and shot up two feet overnight. After that, I was trapped inside a body I could hate, one that she helped me hate, one that would only ever get me the wrong kind of attention. Children are all tall now, even the girls. I see them strolling around on their long legs, tossing their perfect straight hair, and I hope they don't take that confidence for granted. I'd had about twenty-four hours all told in London when I wasn't peering down at the world and waiting for it to rear up and smack me in the face.

I weigh out my flour, my sugar, my dried fruit. I beat my eggs and drop in mixed spice. I put my Stork margarine in the saucepan and scoop out one tablespoon of treacle and another of golden syrup to all melt together. Bell's between my shoulder blades like a knife and, God, dear, dear, dear God, I'm so tired of her. Today's recipe has three different spices I could add but I'll only pick one. Linus and Patrick Joseph can wait together. I get a handful of flour and throw a thick layer of it on to the worktop as if I'm going to roll out my mixture.

– What are you doing that for, Lindy? You know you
    don't need to do that for a cake, that's for a scone.
    For heaven's sake … stop messin' there!
– It's not for the cake, it's for you, Auntie Bell. A gift.
– A gift? Have you lost your marbles again?

She comes to inspect her gift. I've dragged my finger through the flour and managed to come up with a very neat 'V'. It takes her a minute but she meets my eye. For victory, I says. Her face floods with blotches and the cuckoo calls out the hour. I know I'm being unkind, when I see how I can shake her to the core. I don't enjoy the fact that I've done it; she's old and vulnerable, though she doesn't show much sign of either complaint. She wants our ghosts to stay dead. I want them alive and with or without her help I will have them back.

She won't answer, she can't answer. For once she doesn't make a single sound before she turns her back on me and walks unsteadily to her bedroom. She'll know that cats don't get put back into bags without someone being torn to shreds. I picture her, shoes kicked off and then tidied into a neat pair, lying on top of the covers wondering how I have turned out to be such a bad girl when she gave up her *entire* life to make me good. I only realise that the freaky-deaky is on my face when it starts to ache.

I should break the habit of the last three decades and confess my sins to Father Boluwaji next week. He's keen for me to turn my face back to God. To be able to bask in that glorious light, I'd have to wheel out a lot of lying, cruelty, deception, deviousness, theft, cowardice, and many more beasties for my absolution. A home-made fruitcake won't make a dent. I'm not sure I'm ready for it and I know Father Boluwaji isn't either. He believes I can be *saved*, although he never specifies from what. I assume it's the old trusty eternal damnation? But to dodge that I'd definitely have to tell him about how I killed Granny Tess.

Chapter 3

I like the Parochial House. It's tatty and homely and not stuffed with spooky statues like it was in Father McGarrigle's day. He was a great fan of having people take to the stage to recite or dance or sing. He had cleared out the storeroom in the hall to house all the costumes and props and lumps of scenery he used over and over again. All the spare Virgin Marys, St Francis of Assisis and St Brigids had been moved to line the hall before they were placed around one of the sitting rooms. The result was a hundred mournful plaster eyes locked on yours and nowhere to run to in case you knocked one over and they all tumbled like holy dominoes.

Father Boluwaji is delighted with his cake and runs off to hack two big slices off it and make a pot of tea.

He doesn't have a housekeeper so we're blissfully alone, no danger of a busybody with her ear to a glass on the wall. He says we'll need the tea to be strong because he has something specific to discuss, *a family matter*. I suppose Granda Morris has been to complain for the sake of complaining about Uncle Malachi, about Bell, about me. I'm delighted that he's buttered the fruit cake; I like a person who doesn't give a fig about health. We clink our mugs and cheers each other.

My many little holidays at the Clinic have taught me a few things. Never try to tell your whole story at once, it's better to keep it as a series of still images rather than letting it run on full tilt like a film. One frame at a time is plenty and allows you to pull back when you feel as if a hot poker is sizzling on your skin. But if someone says 'don't be alarmed' then it's time to brace yourself for a body blow.

- Now I don't want you to be alarmed, Lindy, but I've been contacted by someone who wants to get in touch …

- My father! My friend Miriam's been asking around! She must have flushed him out! Oh! So he wants to see me? Really?

- No, Lindy, not your father, although I know there has been some pain there too. No, this is from … your son.

- My son?

– Yes, the boy you had in London. He's had your name for two years and now he feels ready to meet you in the flesh ... Lindy? Lindy? There's no need to panic, really, you will find no judgement from me and you will find no judgement from him. He has forgiven you ...

– Forgiven me?

Father Boluwaji nods and nods, his face is animated with a mixture of kindnesses. He even manages a smile. I am forgiven. I am not judged. But I am exposed. I will be punched to the ground by Gabriel Morris. I am shaking like a leaf. Bell will sink me with tears. I am spilling tea on the already stained rug at my feet. I will destroy Miriam's faith in me. I am not ready to discuss my shameful secret with my priest. I am not ready to meet this perfectly imagined son of mine. I never dreamed that he would want me back in his life in such a concrete way. I'd always been happy with keeping him hazy.

Imagine the mess if he showed up in Ballyglen? He'd be in the shops with his English accent asking everyone if they knew where the Morrises live. He'd smile his perfect smile and explain that he was given away by his unmarried teenage mother in England and now he had come home to roost. He had my name; he'd say it out loud, not knowing it was a touchpaper. He wouldn't be able to understand just how *small* small towns were, how could he after London?

The words would hardly be out of his mouth before someone would ring Southfork – not to destroy me but to destroy Gabriel Morris. A golden chance to rub his rotten bullying face in the muck would never be missed. Granda Morris would load his shotgun and drive as fast as he could down the long, straight bog road to Carnsore. He'd come into the kitchen and Bell would drag me out by the hair of my head. *Slut. Whore. Bitch.* The words he used for my mother recycled now for me. Like her, I'd have to pay for my sin.

I feel the sick hit the back of my throat and I run to let fly a hail of sultanas and currants. In the sudden silence that follows, I understand that Father Boluwaji is beating on the loo door. He's lying to me when I thought he never would. *It's going to be okay, Lady Lindy. It's going to be okay. It's going to be okay.* I gave up my whole life so that my Kieran wouldn't have to suffer being another Morris bastard. I couldn't look after him then and I won't be able to look after him now. Granda Morris will hurt him, his tender skin will be lit up with slaps, his sweet face will bloom with bruises. It can never be okay. Kieran cannot be allowed to come here, it's not safe.

There's nothing left to puke up, I'm empty. I remember how tired the patients were in the RHHI after they'd been sick. I remember the jumpy weeks when I realised why I often felt so sick myself. I'd written it off as a series of hangovers fixed with too many crisp sandwiches.

- Lindy? My Lady Lindy, you must come out some-time? Apart from anything else, that's the only lavatory in the house!
- I'm sorry, Father.
- I'll put the kettle on for more tea. You join me when you're ready.

What a lovely man. Too lovely for Ballyglen. When I've cleaned all around the bathroom, using wads of toilet paper, I finally have to look myself in the eye. The mirror is set high, high enough for a man to shave in, so I can't dodge it. I look like a woman on her way to the hangman's noose, so I gather the imaginary rope in my fist and yank it a few times letting my tongue loll out, but making fun of myself has never been enough of a release. A small pair of nail scissors offer themselves to me from Father Boluwaji's shaving mug. They're sharp and perfect as I sit on the toilet lid and draw the blade along both inner thighs. There's no blood, just a pair of pleasing red welts which should hurt long enough to get me back to the table.

- Are you alright, my Lady Lindy?
- Yes, Father.

Father Boluwaji settles himself to tell his story, the tips of his fingers tapping until he can find a way to start without making me run over the hills and far away. He'd been contacted only the day before he called Carnsore because 'the matter' had become urgent. This boy of mine has always known he'd been adopted in London. He had lost both his parents in a short space of time, now he was curious about his real parents.

When I breathe in hard, Father Boluwaji looks up at me and my white knuckles where I'm clinging on to his chair. He begs me to relax so I stop chewing the inside of my cheek and offer him a watery smile. When he's as sure as he'll ever be that the danger of having a woman faint on him is over, he continues.

I let his voice flow towards me while I imagine my son walking by the River Thames with his head down, his heart heavy. He has on a smart, dark overcoat which just makes his hair look even darker. The leaves from the plane trees flutter down and hundreds of people rush past him, unaware that he's been short changed. He looks lonely, I recognise the look. I used to see it on Mammy's face when she gazed out at the acres and acres of green fields all around us. *It's just fodder, Lindy*, she'd say, *just fodder.*

The thing is, my boy is delighted that I'm Irish. Father Boluwaji's voice hangs on the 'de' in delighted making it a song – deeeelighted. It has cheered Kieran up beyond measure to know that we'll have so much common ground to stand on. Cheeeered. My friend has stopped to try another smile. Everyone in this triumvirate is happy but me. I'm trying to understand what he's saying and it sounds like he's saying that my son has been brought up in Ireland.

- I don't understand? He's a London boy, isn't he?
- He has been less than 40 miles from you since he was an infant. His first adoptive mother died when he was only eighteen months old in London, a terrible heartbreak, but his father soon married a girl from Derry who convinced him to come back with her and the baby to Derry. They were farmers too, Catholic farmers, so he also shares your faith. He's a credit to them, he sounds a very sensible young man on the phone. Very ... what's the word now they use around Ballyglen? Steady! That's it! He sounds steady.

Bell is waiting for me when I get home, nose against the glass of the front-room window. It's been tipping down with rain but I hardly felt it batter me all the way home. I'm later than expected, as after my bit of news, I went to sit with Mammy and Patrick Joseph for a while. The day she was buried I had to be dragged away. I was sure that my father would come for me now that she was gone away to God but though I scanned every face, I saw no long black hair, no startling blue eyes or arms with string bangles reaching out to scoop me up. I'd howled the place down until Granda Morris came over and gave me a good hard slap across the jaw to stop my nonsense. Nobody tackled him, though a few of the bigger men refused to stay and shake his hand by the graveside.

I should look after her plot better. It's overrun with dandelion stubs and sow thistle, even though it's been a bitter winter so far. My brother's little rectangle has nearly been swallowed by tall marsh grass. I tried to rip it out, but the depth of the roots fought me. He was holding on to his roof so I left him in peace. The neighbouring graves are already sporting Christmas wreaths, real holly set in oasis rings and topped with plastic flowers. It's a good choice: the wind would rip the heads off anything more delicate.

I'm sure Babs is fine with her once-white stones and crop of weeds; she never did care much for frippery. I touch the stone I've carried with me for thirty-four years to the pile where I think her feet might be to recharge it, to give me strength. *Help me, Mammy! What am I going to do about this boy? How am I going to keep him hidden? How am I going to make sure he doesn't break cover because he'll be shot down and I'm not equipped to patch him up again? What happened to your boy? Why did you never tell me when you had the chance?* She was never big on guidance and my knees aching against the marble remind me I might as well go home.

Bell is gagging to know what went on. She even stoops to getting me a towel from the airing cupboard to dry my hair to soften me up. The warmth of it and the heat of the range thaw me enough to feel and I bite a chunk out of my cheek to keep my feet on the ground. Do I want tea? Scones? They're fresh out of the oven. That's how she got in *her* day when *she* was all alone with nothing or no one of her own, ha ha ha. She baked. Imagine it, Lindy, being reduced to baking because you're desperate to fill the time. *We're like clones, you and me, with our silly baking!* I pity her somewhere deep down in my soul because she doesn't know that life could get even worse. She could soon be a great-aunt to another Morris bastard, which would bring her nothing but more pain.

Father Boluwaji had wanted to drive me home. His gaze stayed on my back all the way to the graveyard but thankfully he didn't follow me. He had held my hand in both of his for a moment too long and I'd only just got away without breaking. After he'd told me the whole story of my son, and told me again that I had done nothing wrong in his eyes, though he couldn't speak on behalf of the Church, he had me hang my head and take a blessing. It was one I knew and I mouthed the words. *God, grant me the serenity to accept the things I cannot change, courage to change the things I can and wisdom to know the difference.* I did well not to puke again.

Bell is jigging about from one foot to the other. After I'd drawn my 'V' in the flour she had maintained radio silence for the entire evening. There had instead been a tsunami of wounded wafting about. She made her own dinner, she made her own tea, she stepped around me if I put myself in her path. I'd read in my bedroom for hours without interruption. But now she has a speech ready. Now, when I'm at my wits' end, classic Bell. It is for my ears only, not Miriam O'Dwyer's or any of my *pals* down at the Credit Union. She likes to keep her private life private, if that isn't too much to ask?

Once upon a time, in a life far, far away, she, Belinda Margaret Morris, had had a *beau*. God alive! Only Bell could make the word *beau* even more annoying than it already was. He was called Vincent Murray and she was fairly sure he would have popped the question until he came across the existence of my mother and me. Vincent was a strict churchgoer and didn't want to be marrying into the likes of us. The story ends with a sniff that states once again for the record it was my mother and me who had ruined her entire life. Not just once or twice but every day in every way since.

– What do you mean 'us'?

– You know what I mean, Lindy! Don't act the cod!

– You mean you were dumped because my father was a traveller?

– He was worse than that. He had his way with your mother when he knew he couldn't marry her! What else would a good holy man like Vincent Murray do?

– He could have done a hundred things. He could have realised that you and Babs weren't the same person. He could have understood that I didn't get to pick my father. He might even have come round to the fact that a person is surely allowed one mistake in this life even in this shitty family?

– Oh! You look just like that mother of yours when your blood's up! Vicious!

And that is the end of that particular discussion. As soon as I speak up, I become Mammy. Mammy the bad girl. There is never a way out of this particular hole. Instead, we both adopt the strategy that has worked in the Family Morris for as long as I can remember – pretend there was no row. Say whatever nasty thing you want then put the kettle on. No need to apologise. My mother was vicious. I was too. Bell was a saint, a wronged saint. Is now the right time to ask her about my brother? Should sainted aunts not cough up the truth once every fifty years or so?

I look at her face, my mother's face, and want to rise and strike her hard enough to rattle her dentures. It's a good job I can tell when she's lying. There's a bit more to the story of Vincent Murray, but God only knows if or when she'll spit it out. Her face goes all wistful as she rewrites the truth in her mind. She's quite the actress. So am I. So was Mammy. So is Granda Morris, he's been pretending he's not a rotten brute for years. So was Granny Tess before I finished her, she kept up her tough-old-bird act until she realised that I wasn't going to change my mind. So is my son. The genes, good or bad, will out.

My boy, Father Boluwaji told me, is an actor. He's in the Omagh Players, who are coming to Ballyglen in a week's time. He's leaving the Players immediately after this performance, it's time he left behind any notions he ever had of acting being anything more than a hobby. For that reason alone, he hopes I'll see him, the last time he'll stand on a stage for the rest of his life. He has three sons of his own. He married an Omagh girl and he's been racking his brain as to the best time to drop by and see his biological mammy. Imagine his delight when he realised he would be right beside me in Ballyglen? Sometimes the stars align, Lady Lindy, said my sweet friend.

Bell wants to know if I visited Babs's grave, and if I did, how did it look? *Like a grave* seemed the obvious answer, but instead I say it was fine. It's still right beside the little fallen angel we're not ever going to talk about, I should have said, but she's extended the olive branch so it would be churlish to rip it out of her hands and clout her with it. We must get a Christmas wreath the next time we're in town, I say, and she nods, though she thinks flowers for Mammy is a waste of precious money.

She wants to know if I met anyone, if there was anyone in the chapel, did I go in to light a candle? What Bell really wants to know is what I might have spilled to Father Boluwaji in the way of family secrets. I wish I could tell her that this time Father Boluwaji was the one doing the spilling. But we have come to a deal. He would explain to my son that our reunion will have to be so low key that not even he, our go-between, would notice if he was standing right beside us.

Kieran had been allowed to keep his name. I was *cheeered*, it had suited him from the start. He was Kieran McCreedy and he would make himself known to me on the night of the play before he went on stage or maybe after. He was certain that Ballyglen would be his last tread of the boards. He was playing the part of Gerry Evans, the rogue who has left one of the five sisters pregnant and unmarried. We would shake hands but not for long. There would be no hugs or kisses, there would be no hint that our paths had ever crossed or that they ever would again. He knew that I was troubled, that I had been troubled since I came back from London without him, but that I had managed to keep the source of those troubles to myself. How could he know that 'troubled' didn't exactly cover everything that had happened in my life?

He agreed to the wisdom of keeping the lid on the pot. His parents had made no secret of the fact that being uncovered would be a problem for me. He had been coached in *my faith* by good steady people. My notes had said that I was a modest girl from a good Catholic family.

He sounded like a good boy, a kind boy, a boy with tiny boys of his own, a boy who got to grow up in an Irish city rather than an English one, so at least he was without the burden of land, land and more land. If I had done only one thing right, it was to set my son free from the Morris clan and their obsession with Morris land. Land that was hard to work, hard to turn into a profit of any kind, but land that could never be given up. Land that would soon have to be handed over to his brother Malachi who had not been cursed by a clutch of bloody fucking women. Granda Morris's life was blighted with us and he wouldn't spread the rot by leaving us a single acre.

I had managed to eke out thirty-three years of being treated like filth so Kieran could live free. In just over a week I would touch his skin with mine once more and it would all be worthwhile. Would he still feel like a beautiful gift that slipped through my fingers?

LONDON – 1985

Chapter 1

It's July and London is so beautiful as I walk along the river. The plane trees are in full leaf above the mottled green trunks and I breathe them in, I breathe them in with the smell of the Thames and the joy that I'll be having my baby next month. All the prayers and sermons I've endured over the years about the Virgin Mary being with child make me smile now because that's how I feel. I feel *I am with my child*. I knew I was pregnant around Eastertime when I couldn't face looking at a Cadbury's Creme Egg. When the dot of unnaturally yellow slipped and slid about in the white fondant I had to run to the bathroom.

Instead of panicking outright, which is what I always thought I'd do before I left Ballyglen, something settled on me, something peaceful and warm, when it became a reality. I was glad that soon I'd have someone to call my own, soon the word 'Mammy' would be back in my life. I was free from Carnsore apart from the now-monthly call to Auntie Bell, who must be sleeping beside the phone in the hall she gets to it so quick. The only bad side effect as far as I could tell was that I finally discovered what it was to feel *homesick*. A phone call to Miriam should knock the worst of it on the head. I liked picturing her smiling when she heard my voice.

Though I knew I would never go back now, what I wanted more than anything was to *be home*, to be back in Southfork, which was a strange sensation. Not to hear the abuse that played in my head 24/7. Not to live there again, but I just wanted to stand in the kitchen for ten minutes and remember being there with Mammy. Like the days when we made butterfly cakes, my job was to put the pretty paper liners in the baking tray. The sugary smell of them cooking in the range joined up with the smell of the buttercream that was beaten and ready for when they came out added up to a kind of peace that lasted until Granda came home.

Then the little cakes stopped looking pretty with their hundreds and thousands and started looking like an afternoon wasted, an afternoon when we both should have found something more useful to do. She'd stick her tongue out behind his back and poke her fingers through her hair to make horns when he glowered at the cakes and then glowered at us. I couldn't even laugh I was so scared of giving her away. I'll never be done missing her.

She would have helped me with the baby. She wouldn't care that I had let myself down. She'd be full of plans for escape, full of stories about how we were going to be alright one day, the day we left Southfork behind and headed off to be with my father. She never said he loved us but she said that she loved him and she'd come to understand that was enough. The baby kicks out and stops my silly dreams. She's not coming back but I'm not totally alone any longer. I'd never leave this child, never. I wrap my arms around it and pray that it will be happy and healthy. I pray that it will never be discovered. I hug it to me and it twists and turns with delight. I can't wait to see the little back that I can feel moving under my skin.

The months rolled by so fast. I had had to put the thought of going to night school out of my head. Although the RHHI wasn't for ever, I had a roof and I had my friends, I had a job, I had a room that was no longer a cold white cell. It was papered all around with posters from *Smash Hits*, hundreds of lovely smiles and kind eyes beamed down on me every time I rested my head. I went to sleep with the smell of fresh Blu-Tack and old beer in my nostrils from the plastic cups the gang threw into the bin as they bid me and the bump goodnight. There was no doubt I was content. I had fallen in love with London, even though it had not given up Simon le Bon.

I was high as a kite on its many joys and freedoms. I'd hardly thought about Christopher Campbell. He had been wiped out by the city's familiarity, its smells of petrol wafting through parks, its trees growing straight out of the paving stones, the hundreds of different little towns that were squashed into it all, trying to stay different. When I looked at the Thames I didn't think of him any more, I thought this is my river, this is my home, and I never want to leave. I didn't care if I ever saw another green field full of bloody cows again as long as I lived. My child would be English and I'd send him out to school in good clothes so no one would ever laugh at him for wearing hand-me-downs.

Susanne, Bev and Donna were open-mouthed when I told them at the end of March, but Bev and Donna recovered in record time. In their worlds parents forgave, parents wanted to help, parents would understand that a girl might make a mistake, parents would grumble and moan and give out, but when the baby landed they'd all be gaga for it. They were teary that I wouldn't be just down the stairs any more. I wouldn't be able to let them in when stinky Colin locked the door in pure badness, I wouldn't be coming out for drinks in the pub, maybe for months. Even then I'd only appear when I could get a babysitter. Susanne didn't gush. She knew that Ireland, Catholic Ireland, was a world away from Australia. She reckoned my family would come round, eventually. I smiled and nodded, we both knew she was wrong.

Susanne, Bev and Donna listed the many reasons why it was a tragedy to lose me but high up on the list was looking after Mercy. I'd grown quite fond of her and I'd pop in and sit for ten minutes even if I wasn't working Women's Ward Main. Her daughter never came back after Christmas. The gang promised to visit me in the Loreto Convent Mother and Baby Home for Unmarried Mothers on Well Street because I couldn't stay on in the nurses' home when I left work. That such a place existed at all cheered me up no end. And I wasn't surprised that it had such an unashamed name in England; I was ready for any institution after the Royal Hospital and Home for Incurables.

Sister Smith sorted it all out for me when I told her I was 'in the family way'. She had lost many of her best trained donkeys to illegitimate pregnancies over the years. It was a pain but *life* was always preferable to *death*. She liked to stream us according to our religion; after all, we'd been paying for the Loreto with the pennies collected on the Catholic Church's begging plate since we were children. I nodded, feeling sure she was right but not really understanding what she was so het up about. Plenty of girls before me had managed and I would be no different. There would be people, well, mostly nuns, in the Loreto to offer me any advice and help I needed. They were old hands at this palaver. Sister Smith would be glad to have me back if I could manage on the wages to get a flat and a child-minder and still afford the bus fares as the nurses' home would also be off-limits post-baby. I'd turned out to be a very good worker.

I wasn't planning on being back but I didn't tell her that. Now that Granda Morris wouldn't be around to call me a beggar, I planned on collecting Child Benefit and Family Allowance from the British government he hated. I already loved this tiny baby. How would I be able to ever leave it out of my arms? We would not be parted until it was time for it to go to school – that's how it had been for Mammy and me and it would be the same for my child and me. We'd be inseparable.

Chapter 2

There are twenty-three plane trees between the Royal Hospital and Home for the Incurables and the door at St Simon Stock's. I lost count of the number of traffic lights and zebra crossings by the time I crossed over at one of the big avenues, though I'd promised myself to focus on every detail except my fear until I was face to face with Christopher Campbell again. He'd know as soon as he saw me why I needed to see him. Even with my best, baggiest Bananarama dungarees on, it was fairly obvious.

It was Susanne, Bev and Donna who talked me in to going to St Simon Stock's. Money's going to be tight and he'll want to help you out, Bev said, and the other two nodded. I didn't want his money, but I did want him to know this baby. Susanne went as far as to say that he might do the decent thing and marry me, but the other two didn't nod. We all knew Christopher Campbell wasn't going to make a decent woman of me even if I wanted that.

They all agreed that he deserves to know, that he might like being involved. I thought of my own father, who I met once on my jolly day out in Bundoran. He'd seemed so ordinary, nice even, when I had built him up to the size and strength of an ogre with Granda Morris and Granny Tess's help. I'd missed him before that day and missed him twice as much after that day. Surely it was worth the face-burning embarrassment of letting Christopher know I was as green as the grass for getting caught if he'd at least *talk* to this child a few times a month?

I'd made it into the chapel. The June weather in the city was almost unbearable, so much warmer than County Tyrone, and I needed the familiar chill of the nave. Miriam was right, it was a very plain space compared to St Bede's, no over-the-top stained glass or heavily framed Stations of the Cross, but it smelled the same, of wax and incense. The House of God can lull, though; it's something to do with the light and the hush. I thought of Miriam lighting a candle for me to keep me in His good books. I daydreamed for an hour, waiting to find someone I could ask where the Parochial House was. I had a whole speech worked out for the daddy. All

I had to do was get across the fact that he mustn't blame himself, we had both been at fault, the main thing was that he would visit the baby now and again so that it wouldn't feel so alone. The leathery sound of someone stacking hymn books made me look round. Christopher frowned in recognition as he made his way towards me. I'd speak but I've been gagged by the dog collar, silenced by it as I've been silenced by several of them before. As far as I knew they were still reserved solely for priests not bookkeepers.

There are still twenty-three plane trees between St Simon Stock's and the Royal Hospital and Home for Incurables. I picked them up like crumbs to find my way back, blinded by insults and my rank stupidity. Christopher always did have a lot of fine words at his disposal. When he'd yanked me out of the pew and down the aisle to put me outside his chapel, he'd let me have all of them at speed. The traffic had rolled past us up and down the Hazlewell Road just a foot away and not one driver or passenger would be able to guess just how fast I had crashed to earth.

Daft *bitch*, silly *whore*, thinking that I'd be able to make any calls on him or his time. No one would believe me, not me the six-foot clown who didn't even *try* to keep her legs together. He'd make sure that anyone who found out about me and this baby would know it was nothing to do with him. What had I expected him to do? Say no when it was offered to him on a plate? He was only human. Bell had warned me to stay away from priests and I hadn't even been smart enough to spot one when it was practically tattooed on his forehead. Every cell in my body bloated with the hatred I felt for myself and my inexperience. Christopher was just hitting his stride. Girls like me were always the same, they filled up with self-pity when self-loathing was a more suitable choice. His face was all twisted with disgust and I hadn't even opened my mouth. I was every repulsive inch the idiot he described.

Where was the boy who held out coats and opened doors? The man I had imagined sitting in the kitchen at Southfork confounding my aunt, my grandfather and grandmother with his lovely posh voice and clean, soft hands? The man who I hoped would show them that *someone* wanted *me*, someone who could understand that I wasn't vermin? The memory of Granda Morris in a rage, beating at the deep banks of nettles growing along the path with a walking stick, came to me. With every slice of it through the air, I had felt my skin light up, even though I was behind the glass of the kitchen window.

Christopher told me there would be no money, not for anything, although he could see I was way past the stage for an abortion. There would be no demands made on him for any reason. He already had his vocation, his life was God's.

Did I dream for a second that I, Lindy Morris from the bogs of Ireland, could compete with God Himself? There was only one answer to that so I finally found my voice. No, I said, of course not. That pleased him. I had seen sense. Indeed, he had helped me see sense, he had the wisdom to do that and he calmed down and let go of my elbow. He had always known that, at the back of it, I was a good enough type of girl, a bit too trusting maybe, but I'd soon learn.

– You'll need to make a confession, Lindy, before the ... before, yes?

– A confession?

– Yes. Go to your own priest and offer up your sins. Absolution is the key.

He wished me the best of luck with it as he kept his eyes firmly on the orange and red bricks of his church. The thing was, you see, that with Father Donnan off waiting for his healing miracle, he might get this parish now to call his own. He would be in charge, the captain of his own ship. The people around here really loved him, respected him, he had proven himself more than capable of taking on the large, wealthy flock. *That's all Church men interested in, money, cha!* I walked away from him and his firm Christian values and willed myself to not trip over my big clown feet.

I could hardly shout that all I wanted was for him to see the baby. To visit, to talk, to tell it a story now and again. I knew what a gap was left when a father was absent. How much a child longs for the two people who are supposed to love it more than anyone but who just weren't keen enough on the job to stick around. I thought of what a huge risk Mammy had taken to show me once to the man who was my daddy. A single day at the seaside was not enough. I could hardly shout that Christopher could do with half an hour in the confessional himself. But mostly I didn't shout because you can't shout at Catholic priests, they're a cut above, untouchable even after they've deigned to be touched.

CARNSORE

Chapter 1

Bell did something today that put the heart right across me. She walked in with one of Granny Tess's old coats on. For a second, I thought the auld bitch had finally come back to haunt me. She'd often remarked that I would be the death of her, little did she dream that she'd be right. Now I must tell Bell *immediately* what I think of the bouclé wool coat with fraying hems that is – like everything owned by Granny Tess – too short for her and too tight. But she's managed to button it and it's helped with her terrible posture as it's pulled her straight.

– That's a rare treat for the eyes, Bell.

– Do you think so? Really? I do like it but, now DO
  NOT LAUGH, Lindy Morris, I still think Granny
  Tess will rise up and shout at me for me for touch-
  ing her good stuff!

– I suspect she'd have been back by now, Bell, if she was going to bother coming back at all.

It was Granny Tess who discovered that I'd been pregnant. We had been home alone because she'd been feeling under the weather from the minute I appeared back on the doorstep. I had given her a headache, one that no amount of Mrs Cullen's Powders tipped delicately under her fissured tongue could shift. She left the blame squarely at my door and made sure everyone heard her do it. I was the hex.

I'd come back to Carnsore in time for Christmas without my boy. He grew all in the last month. Me and the other girls in the Loreto Home for Unmarried Mothers were waddling about but, mirror, mirror on the wall, I was the biggest of them all. My whole body still ached, not just my heart. The birth had been hell, Kieran was bigger than anyone had thought possible. It had been hours, which turned into nearly two days, and I'd not stopped screaming the whole time. In the end, there was a change of staff and one of the young, tired doctors came in and cut me. I can still feel that scalpel, the blessed relief it brought along with the sweet, searing pain. The first time is the best time in a myriad of ways. I was resurrected.

Kieran was born not too long after that, but I still had some screaming to do. He was taken away to be weighed and tagged. I fell back under the less than tender care of the young, tired doctor to be stitched up. A midwife had warned me that the doctor had made a terrible mess of me and the stitches were all wrong. She whispered that 'things' could be fixed after the next baby and I'd nodded like I had a clue what she was on about. She gave me a glass of orange juice, the most delicious thing I had ever tasted until they brought Kieran back to me wrapped in a blue blanket. When I touched my lips to his head he instantly became as essential as air. I knew him. He was as familiar to me as my shadow. He was my soul. How did I let him slip away?

With Bell away to the bingo for the night, I had to stay out of Tess's sight, which also meant staying away from the fire, so I ran a bath to keep warm. I eased into it, glad of the veil of bubbles and the smell of roses. I closed my eyes and soaked until the heat went out of the water, but when I sat up the stretch marks puckered and bunched beneath my breasts. They were a dark map of everything I had done wrong.

I leapt out as quick as I could to escape the memory, making a puddle on the old, cold lino. I shouldn't have run to my room. I was still heavy with baby weight and the sound of me pounding across the landing roused the poorly Granny Tess from her darning chair. She started by shouting from the bottom of the stairs for me to stop galloping about like the bloody horse I was. Her head was fair bursting with the throb that was in it.

Her and Bell had barely spoken to me in the week since I darkened the door at Southfork. There had been plenty of tense meals in that cold farmhouse but the sound of four people chewing and trying to swallow was much worse. I'd got an *oh, you're back then* when I stepped into the kitchen, dripping wet and frozen. The workers' bus had left when I was still in two minds whether to get on it and travel the ten miles to the end of the lane at Southfork. When I couldn't get any colder standing in the doorway of Leehy's dreadful drapery watching the Saracens, the tractors, the cars, trucks and bikes all carrying someone with somewhere warm to go, I set off on foot, dragging my holdall, empty now of my bright London clothes.

They both played it cool but I knew they were terrified about what Granda Morris would say when he heard he had a traveller back under his roof. Nothing welcoming or kind was the answer. Before I had time to cover myself, she was at the door and as was her custom, she didn't stop to knock. If she wasn't as light as a sparrow she wouldn't be able to flit about so fast. The sight of me and my dark map made her reel back and she knocked against the picture of the Sacred Heart that hung in the corridor. Jesus was still rocking above his electric candlelight when she ran for the stairs.

I pulled some pyjamas on over my wet skin. I waited to hear her reach for the phone, but she didn't. There was no sound at all so she must have collapsed into her armchair to digest what would happen next. Would she march me to the priest or to her husband? She'd have to do something as the Morris matriarch; her deep faith would demand it. I could not be left unpunished. Was it worse to abandon an illegitimate child than to take it home as proof that you were lacking in moral fibre? Whatever, I'd need to try to head her off before Bell got home. Bell would not come out of this well either, my failings were her failings. We were both due a whipping.

The stairs, which hadn't creaked once for her on the way up, screamed with every tread of mine on the way down. The front-room door was closed. The hall was lit with just the red glow under the ground floor's Sacred Heart. We'd had fried eggs and spuds with raw onions, silence and butter for the dinner and the greasy smell of them still hung in the air, though I'd washed the plates and the pans up as soon as we were finished. I only had an hour to make a case for myself if I ever wanted to have another meal in this house. I knocked the door.

– Granny? Granny? Can I come in? I can explain …?
Well, I can't really explain … Granny? Please can I come in?

I'd have to risk entering without permission. She was on the floor; her head had come to rest on the mat in front of the fire with just an inch to spare. She'd missed the hard edge of the hearth, which would have meant a quicker, surer death. Her face told me she'd had a stroke. One eye blazed with fear but the other one had already started to dull. Her speech was gone, which was fine because I'd heard enough from her over the years. She waved her right hand from where she lay as if to hurry me away. The other arm hung limply behind her. I had a sudden memory of Mercy and of how much I had wanted her to have her wish of death.

I watched Granny Tess's face twist when she realised that I wasn't going to run for help. I cleared some newspapers and other rubbish off the sofa and lay along the length of it, relishing the feel of the bobbles on the material. I'd wait with her, though, it was the least I could do and it wouldn't take long. I'd stayed with many an old woman passing her last night on this earth in the past year, one more wouldn't hurt. My parting gift could be kindness, more in an hour than she'd shown me in a lifetime.

The clock ticked and the room grew colder as the last turf she'd thrown burned low. Her feet in her old brown felt slippers were close to the bag of rainbow-coloured wool in the darning basket. There was so much of it, skeins and skeins that would now be wasted as Bell and me don't darn. She wouldn't teach us, wouldn't let us into the magic kingdom of repairing socks, it was hers alone. Her throat rattled but soon enough, she was silent. When I touched my fingers to her wrist she was warm but on her way to the Heaven she'd hoped was kitted out for her all her days.

I stood and watched the end of the long lane for headlights. Bell had got a lift with Martha Kennedy, who had stepped in with her kind heart to make sure she got out of Southfork at least once a week after I had disappeared to England. Granda Morris was at a whist drive somewhere in Donegal, he didn't trouble us with what time he'd be in. I listened out for the wail of the banshee, for the sound of a black dog slavering and digging at the door, for a series of knocks, but nothing stirred to come and fetch Tess's soul.

By the by, a beam of yellow light showed between the gaps in the thorn hedge before it swept left between the big concrete pillars and started its journey to the street. I turned back for one more look at my grandmother, her eyes were closed and I didn't fix her skirt where it had rucked up at the back exposing her spindly legs. Poor little bantam. Instead, I stepped back into the hall, closing the door softly behind me and walked as sedate as I could to my bed.

The sheets were cold; it hadn't been the right kind of night to remember to fill a hot-water bottle. Martha tooted the horn when she left. I imagined my aunt smiling and waving her off, safe home, God bless. By the time Bell had banged the kettle down on the range and gone in to check if her mother wanted a cup of tea I was braced for the scream when it raced along the corridor.

Chapter 2

I started cutting the stretch marks after Granny Tess's funeral as I'd never be stupid enough to let anyone see me or them again. They've faded to white now, though some are still edged with silver. I might have to revisit them after I've touched Kieran again. The closer he gets, the heavier my heart lies, the easier my stomach buckles. It's such an effort to hide it from Bell, who's a bit snotty with me because I'm *not excited enough* about the Players coming to town. She has no idea what's wrong with me. I've always loved seeing the stage in the drab Parochial Hall come alive, to make itself into another world for a couple of hours. Normally, I'd be cheery at the thought of such an extravagant diversion, but life has nothing to do with normal at the moment.

I even had to take the unprecedented decision to abandon my fabulous career at the Credit Union for a solid couple of weeks. I got bored of ringing in every day. Sitting in that dull space is more than I can face. Although sitting in this dull space means more time with Bell. This particular little holiday has enraged my dear aunt. She doesn't want me to develop freeloading habits. My mammy had a tendency to please herself which I should look out for. Siobhain was sympathy itself when I called to say that I wouldn't be around, but she was so keen to get to the part that I shouldn't rush back that she nearly fell over. Her and Kevin and the rest of the jolly team wished me all the best and a speedy recovery. I hadn't even said I wasn't well. They all hoped I'd be tiptop for the Christmas party, it would be the usual cracker.

So, I'm home all day with hours to kill. Cuckoo, chime, ting. Thinking about the past brings it right to the door, it comes traipsing in and sits beside you, staring and staring and waiting for answers. I know I've had thirty-three years between Kieran and now but it has shortened itself into a few standout days. Granny Tess's demise, Bell and me being shifted from Southfork to Carnsore and the several little holidays I had to take in the Clinic bloom like flowers at the end of a long tunnel that's filled with long-boiled tea and talking about nothing. It's as well the Tyrone rain forms itself into so many shapes and consistencies, if Bell and me didn't have the weather to analyse we might have come to blows years ago.

Granny Tess is buried in a new plot on the other side of St Bede's, as far away from her daughter as she could get. She had bought the plot herself, although we had no idea where she got the money. Granda never gave her a penny more for the housekeeping than he absolutely had to, but she had scrimped it together somehow. How high the chair had flown over her head the day that old Father McGarrigle delivered the good news! She had her six foot of ground to call her own, even though she'd only get four foot, four inches of use out of it. He was hardly off the street when Granda finally boiled over. He'd sat like a bear through the tea and scones before he gave Tess the warning shot. She ducked the chair but a framed picture of her sister sitting outside St Bernadette's shrine in Lourdes with a hundred other pilgrims caught her on the lip and the blood from it ruined the holy scene lying in pieces at her feet.

He'd had the gall to sit beside her coffin and take all the condolences he didn't need. Repeating back what was said: she was a good woman, she was a good worker, she was a good wife. Every time he was reminded she was a good mother, a good grandmother, good enough to take on Babs's *little girl* and rear her up with the family, he eyeballed me. He couldn't know that I'd let her slip away, but those black eyes weren't fooled by the doctor's talk of natural causes, not when I was in his house with my dodgy gypsy ways.

Maybe I had to be removed because he was a tiny bit afraid of me? Most widowed men would pray that a daughter and a granddaughter would stay close by but not Gabriel Morris. He roped Uncle Malachi in before the first wreaths on his late wife's grave had withered. The foundations were dug for Carnsore and no amount of Bell's tears would sway him. We were going; he had done his time with bloody fucking women. We should be grateful he was decent enough to provide us with a roof of any quality over our heads.

It was impossible to imagine living anywhere else in the countryside around Ballyglen. Southfork was big and damp and uncomfortable but it was familiar. Every room had its own personality. The living room hid its lack of warmth with an open fire that sparked and hissed. The bathroom was bare, an ancient scratched bath and a square of badly fitted lino, a wooden rail where we hung a clean hand towel every week. I assume the others used it, I never did.

The bedrooms were all the same, a double brass bed dulled from years of neglect, a crucifix nailed at the head, the Sacred Heart on the back wall, a chair in one corner, a small table with a lamp in the other. The curtains were a different set of flowers all spun on a brown backdrop. Blue roses in Granny Tess's room, green barley shoots in Granda's room, yellow dahlias in Bell's and daisies in Mammy's and mine. They were all that was left behind with the beds when we'd packed up our belongings – we were to get new curtains for the new house, it was only right and fitting we'd have fresh flowers.

We'd rarely seen him so happy. He breathed life into a word I first heard in London, 'chipper', before I knew it wasn't just the place where chips were sent down ready-fried from God. Always an early riser so that he could see to the beasts, he was gone before sun-up. Uncle Malachi's van trundled past the end of the lane about an hour later. Between them they had strung up the plumb lines, and the breeze-block walls were climbing higher every day. Granda had helped him build his mediocre bungalow now he had to help Granda build our mediocre bungalow. They both had had good practice on sheds, a house for us would be a doddle and would hardly need to be any grander.

Bell had dinner ready for both of them by twelve thirty. They discussed the bricklaying progress to pass the time and in this way we found out when the lintels went in, that there was to be no garage, we would never have a car, that Granda Morris had found seven second-hand doors that would do well enough. He didn't need anything flashy, something practical and cheap was just the ticket. Bell just ladled out more spuds and stew and tried not to let either of them see her crying. She couldn't believe she was going to be driven out of her own home.

I saw bits of furniture accumulate in the turf shed. An old table and four chairs, two armchairs that had seen better days, but I didn't tell her because we still weren't on the best of terms. She'd hardly had time to get over the horror of me walking in like a drowned rat when her mother had died. She was torn between needing me to comfort her and hating me, when Granda had had the wisdom to point out that I alone was the stress and strain that had brought on his wife's death. Neither of them cared to remember that she had been knocking back high blood pressure tablets since Mammy died and plenty more tablets of every colour beside that. There were sleeping pills, pain pills, stomach pills, laxative pills – the woman was a walking pharmacy. She had stepped out of herself to cope with the grief and she never did come back as strong. Neither of us dared voice that she lived on her nerves, braced for the next row, the next rant, the next blow.

Bell informed me – after several weeks of prayer – that she had decided it couldn't be my fault that Tess had shuffled off, but it was *entirely* my fault that she, St Belinda Margaret Morris, was being ousted from the family home. She, who had given up her life to stand in as my mother, she, who had sacrificed her nursing career and *a lot else besides*, was now going to be put out to pasture at the very end of the Green Road. No one would drive all that way to see *her*. No one would care that this was none of *her* doing. No one would be able to understand that all she had ever done for every single person in Southfork was her very best and now look at *her*. Abandoned at the edge of the border with a niece who had failed in England instead of blossoming, instead of making something of herself – how was she supposed to cope with such a heavy, dull liability all by herself? I had no answers.

A cardboard box of second-hand china appeared in the turf shed, an ancient gas cooker with years of grease and stains, a coal scuttle, a wardrobe with an oval mirror, a wardrobe with a darker section of wood that should still have had a mirror, another armchair in a different shade of pink. It was all horrible and dated and whiffed a bit, but I looked forward to the day that I was even further away from Ballyglen, even further away from Southfork and even further away from Granda. I didn't really want to be incarcerated with Bell, but we don't get to choose our cellmates. It was only the guts of six months before we had to pack up whatever we wanted to carry into this new world. We had one crack at it only, Granda Morris wasn't going to waste his time trailing our rubbish up the Green Road in dribs and drabs.

Uncle Malachi handed over his trailer and Granda Morris hitched it to the back of the tractor. It was already half filled with a pair of old brass beds with spring bases and stained mattresses although they were covered with a tarpaulin, more for shame's shake than concern for keeping them dry. The bedding was rolled in bin liners, a saucepan, a frying pan and a kettle had been freed up from the spares kept by Granny Tess and they dinnled all the way up to the lonely foot of Carnsore.

Bell and me rattled along with them, the wind whipped hair into our eyes where we sat opposite each other on the wheel hubs, miserable bookends. I held a pot of soup steady between my feet, the last supper we'd cooked at Southfork. She kept her eyes pinned to the walls, then the roof then the chimneys of her childhood home until it was lost in the trees and the hedges that petered out the further we rattled on. The greenery gave way to granite walls and granite boulders and rushes, and soon we caught sight of Granda's little project. It looked small and mean, a grey rectangle stranded in a muddy puddle. To its back, a wall of evergreens stole the sky over Donegal. Just to the south of it a wide, deep burn reflected back the grey clouds in its brown bog water. The piles of earth that had been displaced sat in mounds all around it, already sprouting dandelions and thistles, nettles and rough grass. The trailer made it over the stony bridge with a crunch of the chassis and we were home.

We'd never set foot in the house until we carried our boxes and suitcase up a gangplank that had been wedged with a lump of granite to get us over the puddle that still gathers by the front door because the site hadn't been drained properly. Uncle Malachi and Granda hadn't found the time to build the front door-steps or the back doorsteps and only three of the rooms had plaster. The kitchen was a pipe sticking out of the wall with a tap on it. There was no heating and no carpet but it was watertight. It would do for us, said Granda. Malachi and him would get round to the 'finishing touches' if and when it didn't interfere with farm work.

I'll never forget Bell and me trying to put the beds back together, she crying, me shaking because my body still felt so weak, the tenderness that it had lived through showed no sign of receding. When we finally managed to make the frames stand up, we went down the corridor to heat the soup and warm our guts. Neither of us had thought to bring a box of matches. We'd never been in a house without matches before. It was the final straw for Bell, who screamed out as she kicked the saucepan across the concrete floor and had to limp after it when she'd given her toe such a bang. Little orange flecks of carrots and pearls of pearl barley landed here and there and my stomach growled. It would be better to have cold soup instead of no soup at all, but I said nothing.

– I hate this place and everything in it! Do you hear me, Lindy Morris? *You* have brought me to this. I belong in Southfork!

We stood eyeball to eyeball for five minutes but we both knew there wasn't much we could say or do because there had never been much we could say or do to stop Gabriel Morris in his tracks. It was his way or the highway. I didn't even bother to nod. We parted company to put sheets and blankets on our separate beds. I assume she lay awake most of the night looking out of the dusty curtainless windows and listening to the then-strange sound of the evergreens creaking and moaning in the wind.

We were both standing in what would be the kitchen, aching, upset, red-eyed and hungry, when Granda dropped off a small box of groceries and the poor auld hens the next day. The sight of them scratching and clucking around in the dirt and the nettles of the building site seemed to cheer him up. He had cleared out all the bloody fucking females from his life in record time.

Chapter 3

Time always races in when you don't want it to. Though I tried my best to slow it down, it tore past me, like a small boy chasing a ball, unstoppable. *Dancing at Lughnasa* had come to Ballyglen. It was a big favourite and the Omagh Players were the best for miles – it was going to be packed. Father Boluwaji had rung Carnsore to offer Bell and me a lift to the play. She was made up at the thought of stepping out of the priest's car in full view of *everyone*. It would be her red carpet moment if Mrs Barr, Mrs McCrossan and Martha were anywhere they might witness this modern-day miracle. He was, of course, only worried about getting *me* there. I was the baggage that needed to be delivered safely to the door of the Parochial Hall. Kieran had been phoning him on a daily basis to check that I would be alright on the night.

My son's nerves grate along my own in the same way his cries could make me crawl into a corner and cover my ears when we were both young and raw. I'm far from convinced that it's going to be tolerable, but my lovely nodding, smiling friend has redoubled his efforts to reassure me that it will be wonderful to meet my steady adult son once more. Woooonderfuuul. Would he cut the nods and smiles in half if he realised that I had slept with one of his own? Of course, I'm far from special these days in terms of the scandals being uncovered in the dear old Catholic Church, it's riddled with rot. Here a sadistic nun or ten, there a brace of priest's children being paid for with money begged from the pulpit, everywhere a paedophile.

I've hardly closed my eyes these past days trying to imagine what my own little sin will look like. I don't remember much fine detail about Christopher Campbell; he was tall, dark and could talk and talk and talk. I can only remember the words he used on the steps of St Simon's Stock because they cut so deep. For years, Kieran has been a version of him with bits of eyes and noses and smiles and dimples that I've borrowed from actors on the telly that I've liked. I've built him out of other people's skin and hair and teeth and bone because he was so unformed when I left him, just a soft bundle of smells and squeaks. I've had to allow myself to see him get into a car in Omagh, watch him drive down the

Drumquin Road, make sure he stops at all the dangerous crossroads and slows down for the bends. I feel I
know the roads well, though I've mostly experienced
them in the back of an ambulance. But for all my conjuring he still has no face. It slips and slides so fast that
I can't grasp it.

Father Boluwaji is outside. Bell runs for her best hat
and Granny Tess's coat. I tuck a straight pin behind my
lapel for emergencies and we're both soon being driven
over the stony bridge and down the long road to
Ballyglen. I let Bell sit in the front so she can be spotted
more easily by her public, and she's like a kid at
Christmas – well, Christmas in somebody else's house.
The greenery picks up, the potholes get fewer and far
between and it's not long enough until we're parking
just outside the main door. The local builder, Larry
Patricks, is swearing at one of his apprentices as they
try to wrestle the big banner saying *Dancing at
Lughnasa* on to the hooks under the fascia boards. His
'fucks' and 'bastards' ring out across the packed car-
park and the sneaky last-minute smokers all gather
together to enjoy the free show.

The hall has a stone porch with a window to either
side and a glass panel in the door glows weakly yellow.
I'm glad I've not eaten because I feel sick, but my head
is light and I sway a little as the reality of what is about
to happen quickens somewhere deep down in my guts.

My son is on the other side of that wall. I will soon get to *see* him. I will soon get to *touch* him. He will soon get to see and touch me. We are going to hold our hands out to each other and pretend we're nice, polite strangers. Father Boluwaji guides me forward with a warm paw on the small of my back and I have no option but to take the next step.

Bell has toddled ahead, desperate to give out the *news* of how she got to town. I stroke the little pin before I brave the ticket booth.

The sound of Larry Patricks toppling off his ladder makes the ten smokers, me and the priest all gasp at once. We run past the Parochial Hall and out through the side gate but he's already standing and waving a fist at one of the younger lads when we get there. We hear 'fuckin' eejit', 'fuckin' gom' and 'I'll give you fuckin' *slipped*' in rapid succession in among the sniggers. I'm glad to have the distraction of it, be it ever so short. The feel of the rare laugh in my throat makes me think, just for a split second, that tonight *is* going to be okay. Kieran will play his part beautifully and with Father Boluwaji's help my son and me can meet again on less dangerous ground at some stage in the future. I'll get away with my indiscretion.

The hall is buzzing, and judging by the look on Mrs Barr's face, Bell and me should have got here earlier. Her eyes are blazing, her jaw clenching so hard the

dentures will be dust before the interval. I've no energy
to waste on her and her bloody-mindedness tonight.
I've only opened my mouth to force out an apology and
get her off my back when Bell bursts back through the
door and into the porch. She's white as a sheet and
before she can try to explain, I hear Mrs Barr barking,
half anger, half glee.

— So, you've seen him too?
— My God! Oh my God, oh my God!
— There isn't a single soul in there who hasn't com-
    mented, not *one*!
— Who is he?
— You'd better ask the one person who might know!

They both turn to me. Bell is crying silently. Mrs Barr
is glowing with rage. The sound from inside the hall
grows, a wasps' nest of stings waiting to happen. I try
to get out of the porch door but Father Boluwaji is
blocking it with his bulk and his smile. The smile slips
when the other door opens and my son fills it. A few
faces have the bad manners to rubberneck around the
door when the noise dies down. We all freeze – my aunt,
my old enemy, my beautiful priest and my Kieran.

He couldn't be anyone else's but mine. Everything
about him screams my sin. He is a big rangy man, six
foot five and wide built, with thick black hair and eyes
black as coals. He smiles, unsure of himself, and I can
tell even then that this doesn't happen often. He is made

of granite. He owns the space he takes up with ease. I've seen that face before; it's a replica of the wedding photo on Auntie Bell's chest of drawers. He doesn't have to speak, I know his voice will be deep enough to bury me. Of all the faces I have ever plastered on him, I've never dreamed for a second that he would be the double of Granda Morris, his twin, the spit out of his rotten mouth.

Chapter 4

The smell of the tea brings me round. Father Boluwaji had whipped us out of the Parochial Hall and into the Parochial House. Bell has upgraded her shy sobs for a set of howls that will have every dog in the parish joining in if we can't settle her. We're all missing *Dancing at Lughnasa* – all of us except Kieran – for a sad little play all our own. Father Boluwaji acted fast but not fast enough. Mrs Barr was able to tell Bell that the good folk of Ballyglen had clocked him straight away. He even walked like Gabriel Morris, he spoke like Gabriel Morris, he couldn't be anybody's blood but Gabriel Morris's. Martha had managed to get Mrs McCrossan to stay behind, a small mercy. She couldn't stop Mrs Barr, and I listen to all three of their raised voices. They have been quarantined in the front room full of holy books and crucifixes. I am confined to the kitchen until they all calm down. Father Boluwaji is refereeing as best he can.

I never even got to touch Kieran. Seeing him was too much. The sweet, handsome English boy of my growing-up dreams had been washed away in the blink of an eye and replaced with the bogeyman of my childhood. He hadn't stepped forward to shake my hand as it was obvious something had gone badly awry. He knew he was the eye of the storm so he bowed out, literally, reversing back through the Parish Hall door and closing it gently in front of him. He was indeed as steady as promised, he had not waded in or thrown his weight around. He had acted, which meant he read and understood life; he was likely to be gentle. Please God, I prayed to the God who had forsaken me, let him at least be gentle and good, this lost boy of mine.

Someone has slapped Bell. I hear the familiar sound of a hard palm against a soft cheek and the sudden silence it is designed to bring. I can't have her hurt like that, not any more and not on my account. I put the tea down and make it to the front room on jelly legs in time to see Mrs Barr rub her fingers to take the throb out of them. Bell has cupped her hand over the welt that's forming like I'd seen her do a thousand times, quietly, as if she deserved it.

– Why did you do that, you vile bitch?

- Don't dare speak to me! You've proven that you're a bigger tramp than your mother ever was! At least she kept her wee bastard!
- She did and look what joy it brought her! You treated her like filth every day after, right up until she died and then you practically danced on her grave!
- Good riddance to bad rubbish!

Father Boluwaji does his best to keep us apart but I lunge and manage to rip a gratifying handful of hair out of her, enough hair to make her roar like a bull and run behind poor Martha for safety. Martha's face tells the whole story; she is sad down to her bones that I have let this happen to me, that I have let this happen to Bell. She is cradling a glassy-eyed Bell against her chest and shielding Mrs Barr from the murder in my eyes. And, may God bless her for ever, she still finds the will to offer me a smile.

- Is he really yours, Lindy?
- Yes, he's mine, Martha.

I dearly want to be alone with poor Bell, to try to explain to her how it had been, what had happened, but even I can see she is in a worse state than me. And I have hardly dared tell the story to myself. I might have to practise it, see if I can force the words out of my mouth. It is trapped inside me, a tumour taking up the space where a clump of happiness might have grown.

'Bell,' I say, but the word has hardly left my mouth before she starts to shake and cry again, all the shock suddenly gone. Father Boluwaji rides to the rescue.

He suggests that I stay in the Parochial House while Martha and Bitchy Barr take Bell to one of their homes, where she would be safe when the news gets back to Gabriel Morris. They've had a conflab about it in the hall. The inference is that not even Granda Morris would storm the priest's house, so I will make it through the night. He turns me away from the three women who have all been wounded in their own way and leads me towards the bottom of the stairs. I don't say goodbye.

- I'll make sure Bell's alright, Lindy, says Martha to my back.
- You don't have to promise that dirty hoor a single thing, says Mrs Barr.

Chapter 5

I haven't spent a night out of Carnsore for any other reason than the Clinic in over thirty years. It's strange to be in someone else's home. There's a funny smell in the room I was put in. Dust mingled with something … holy. An oil of some ilk, something herbal that has soaked into the bare floorboards. It rose up with every footfall as I paced up and down in the darkness wondering how, *how*, had I managed to reproduce Gabriel Morris? The man who treated me like a pariah my whole life, a man whose death is one of my constant desires. He has been regenerated. The dreams of Kieran making his way in London, stepping happily off the pavements and mingling with the crowds on the King's Road or wandering up and down Petticoat Lane were wiped out in a heartbeat. I'd been living on lies all these years.

Father Boluwaji had come home late and I was frightened by the sound of another man's voice until I realised it was only Larry Patricks, still walking, talking and swearing. He'd been roped in to witness that the priest had spent the night in the chair in the kitchen. They talked into the early hours, Larry Patricks airing his tall tales, Father Boluwaji joining in with a few short asides. 'That was some fuckin' vigil, Father,' Larry Patricks said as he slammed out this morning, the dangerous hours of darkness and the potential for mischief now past.

I have to face the music. I have to climb down the stairs and walk into the kitchen. Father Boluwaji only has forty-five minutes before he has to set out to unlock the sacristy – can't leave the altar boys shivering on the granite step. I've had hours to plan what I'll say to Granda Morris when he comes beating at the Parochial House door. I didn't come up with anything. What punishment would he deem worthy for the mongrel bitch and her mongrel pup? When I realised that the worst he could do was return me to Carnsore to live out the rest of my life, I sat down and knocked my head against the single iron bedstead until it throbbed. Then I realised he might do the opposite. Bell and me could be turned out at last, the mean bungalow locked up with all our dust inside it.

The sound of a whistling kettle makes its way to my door and my stomach growls. I was going to have sweets in the interval of last night's play, followed by a hearty bowl of stew when I got home. I'd have met my son, it would have been as fine as I was promised, it would be over and I'd be able to eat. Not for the first time did I marvel at the way the human body can let you down. Just when you think it's coming near time to end it, the thought of a mouthful of hot tea and a heel of scone will make you wait for one more day – just one, you tell yourself, as you put the razor blade back in its secret place.

He's at the cooker, lapping fat over the yolk of an egg he has in the pan, the old brown teapot is under a knitted cosy and slices of loaf bread are curling on a plate. He's rumpled in his sock soles but he hums along to a tune from the radio that's perched by his head on a shelf. Why had he lied to me? Why did he tell me it would be alright? How had I been stupid enough to trust anyone again? What had he said to my boy who got to see me looking like a terrified rabbit last night? Your mother's mad and the whole family is tinged with it?

– Hello, Father.

– Lindy! My Lady Lindy, you've lived to fight another day?

– Seems so. What happened? What did Kieran do?

– Come sit and let us talk.

Kieran had stolen the show. He's a fine actor, when the whispering died down and everyone had stopped nudging each other when Gabriel Morris's big thick gravelly voice popped out of him with a Derry accent, he had carried on as if nothing at all was wrong. He had such confidence; many a lesser man would have buckled under the strain and called a halt to proceedings, but not my boy, he stood his ground and made himself heard.

I absorb these details as I watch a fried egg being delivered, glistening strangely on a bare plate. Father Boluwaji realises his mistake and lifts it again with a fish slice to pop a slice of unbuttered bread underneath it. He's pouring the tea, which will presumably help me to swallow it when he tells me that Kieran spoke to him after the curtain fell and is more determined than ever to meet me. My son says it must be soon, I am not at all what he expected.

What did he expect? Some sort of monster? How does a woman who can give up a baby look? Just like a woman but with a chunk missing, a wound that no one can see, a wound that never heals but rots and leaves its poison in every corner you turn your face to.

I am being told that there will, of course, be other difficulties. There have already been several comments and questions. Father Boluwaji has done his best to wave them off as if they were nothing, but we should be in no doubt that Gabriel Morris will find out by the by. I nod, trying to imagine how Granda could hate me more, understanding that it is a gift of his – his ability to hate me is as bottomless and dense as a bog.

A week after Mammy died and Bell had returned to Derry and Gransha in tears, knowing that she had to hand in her notice, I was outside Southfork. I had been put there by Granny Tess and told not to come in until I was called. The last thing she needed in her grieving state was the sight of me – it was enough to tip her over the edge, knowing that she couldn't put me out of her sight *forever more, Amen*. One of the hens had laid and its cuk, cuk, cuk stopped me from wondering how long it would take me to walk the long lane to the road and the even longer road to the town when I'd never done either by myself. Collecting the eggs was one of Mammy's jobs, she had to check them every day and wash them in the rough sink in the back kitchen before putting them in the big green bowl in the larder.

I could do her jobs, that would make Granny Tess and Granda keep me. I could be useful. I gathered the eggs, five of them pooled in the hem of my skirt as I walked as carefully as I could to the sink. I mustn't crack a single one or it would prove that I wasn't up to the job. Granda was standing by the corner of the barn. He covered the ground between us so fast I didn't have time to shake. He knocked my hands away and all the eggs smashed on the muck. And then he beat me. My ears burned as he knocked me one way then the other.

Filthy, thieving, tinker bastard! I was not to let him catch me stealing eggs again. If he ever saw me in the yard, he'd take me into the log store and show me how sharp the axes were. A tinker without fingers would find it a lot harder to lift his property.

I'd shouted so long for him to stop that Granny Tess appeared. As they both stood looking at me where I knelt, I threatened through the pain to run away. I'd run away and I'd never come back. Never! She rolled her eyes but reassured me that no time would be wasted looking for me. He also had better things to do with his days than check the ditches for vermin. They both turned away at exactly the same moment, perfectly in tune on my worth.

Father Boluwaji is still talking, the gentle purr of it guides me back to the room, to my already cold tea and his plan to act as a buffer between me and my grandfather. He believes he knows what he's dealing with because he also believes it's a simple question of negotiation. Gabriel Morris does not negotiate.

I hope Granda doesn't find Bell before he finds me. I don't want her hurt on my account. It's been years since he's had a chance to raise a hand to either of us, but if she's not ready with reasons, with excuses, with sound explanations, he might boil over and scald her where she stands.

The telephone rings in the hall. Father Boluwaji rises to answer it, silent without his shoes. I use his absence to bin the egg and the tea and to clear away both sets of plates. *Lindy will clear away, won't you, Lindy!* His mumbles and yes, yes, yeses carry on for a minute or two before the receiver clicks and he turns back to me. The news is not good.

– He knows, doesn't he?

– Yes, my Lady Lindy, he knows.

Chapter 6

We have to go and get Bell from Martha's house. I'd do anything to let this cup pass over her but, as always, we are going to be treated as a unit. Granda Morris has *requested* we both show up at Southfork to hear what he has to say on the subject of having and giving away illegitimate babies and dreaming that it was a secret that would lie buried for ever. When Father Boluwaji yanks on the handbrake, the net curtains are torn apart and Bell's haunted eyes appear on the other side of the glass. She's a picture of misery. She knows why we're here and she knows she'll have to come quietly. The door inches open and Martha is hiding behind it. Every other pair of curtains in the row opposite is pulled and several shameless faces are gawking, ready for the show.

It only takes a few words from Father Boluwaji on what the morning's proceedings will be to make Bell whimper and I see her jigging from one foot to the other, but in the end she forces herself into Granny Tess's bouclé coat and it pulls her straight again. To me, she has nothing to say. She won't even meet my eye. But I must talk to her! I must try to tell her how sorry I am. When I ask her how she is, she snorts and barges past me. How would she be anything less than wretched?

- I never want to hear another word out of your
    mouth! You're a liar! You're a dirty cheat just like
    that mother of yours!
- Bell! That's not fair! Don't bring Mammy into it!
- She's always bloody in it! She's at the heart of every-
    thing ruined!

Martha, darling Martha, gives me a squeeze and begs me not to listen. Bell will come round, she tells me. She's overwrought; it's been a terrible, long night and my aunt has had screaming nightmares in the rare minutes she was able to sleep. She falls back on the news that 'worse things happen at sea'. For a minute I'm standing on Bundoran beach, watching the steely waters of the Atlantic rolling over the sand. Mammy is on one side of me and the man who is my daddy is on the other and I've never been happier or sadder. The day's brightness just outruns the shadow of Granda Morris.

Has it only been a few days since I picked up Linus Quinn and Patrick Joseph and Kieran McCreedy? I can hardly remember all the years I've been without them. I've jumped off a lonely cliff and landed in an ocean of men. Father. Brother. Son. Grandsons. I hope they're not more than I can carry.

Martha is still waving as Bell and me are driven away. My friend's eyes have dark hollows underneath them and red rims all around. She looks terrible but she's still not a patch on the state of Auntie Bell. She is a woman who has been filleted. The little car climbs its way out of Ballyglen in deafening silence. Now and again a tricolour painted on the road or a Union Jack flying from a telegraph pole marks the bit of the road where a Nationalist lives or a Unionist lives but all else is waterlogged fields and stone walls. I haven't set foot on Southfork for ten years at least. The hedges fly past; now and again a huge bald sycamore blocks the light and makes the air even cooler. We turn right at the crossroads and from a mile away I see Uncle Malachi's truck.

He's coming fast. He drives just like Granda Morris, like no one else should be on the tarmac. He's heading straight for us. Father Boluwaji reacts before I can scream, he swerves into the grass verge to avoid being mown down. When Malachi is past us he holds his hand on the horn until he turns at the crossroads for home. We're all shaken, even Bell, who has roused herself to see what's happened. If that's the brother's reaction, this homecoming is going to be even more unpleasant than I first thought.

– Why did he do that?
– I don't know, Bell!
– He could have killed us all!
– He could but he didn't so we'll have to carry on and face the music!

That makes Father Boluwaji smile but it makes Bell burst into fresh tears and the guilt of having pounded her hits me again. That sound she made, the pain she suffered when I confirmed that Kieran was mine, will never wipe itself from my memory. I'll make it up to her but for now I have bigger fish to fry. What I can say for myself in Southfork will dictate whether or not we have a home to go to when I'm done. By nightfall we could be out in the open, it's the best way to teach a gypsy a lesson – make him or her move on.

I remember the sight of Mammy on her knees, pleading and pleading with him for something, and him ignoring her. What had she *wanted* so badly that she had risked being so close to him? It was only a few days until she set out to find us a house and never came home again. After a bit of wheel-spinning and revving we're back on the road and it isn't looking any brighter.

The pillars come into sight like two granite standing stones marking a far from sacred place and my heart quickens at the sound of the indicator as we leave the empty tarmac to pass through them. The nettles that cover the ground between the pillars and the house look lusher than ever. A tall, dark green stinging acre. Granda Morris is already on the street waiting for us. His big shovel hands hanging straight down, no sign of the shotgun that has put paid to several hundred rabbits and plenty of neighbours' pets. Father Boluwaji switches off the engine and lets the car roll straight towards him. He gets out to help Bell off the back seat and I have to manage alone.

My mother's father is stock-still, his face a mask, but I have to close the distance between us even if it means another punch. I flinch when the first move he makes is to take off his cap. He holds it there, between his fingers, a thing that is never removed from his huge head until the second he steps past the Holy Water fount in the chapel. I wait for the first insult to fly but he stands aside and indicates with a hand that I should go into Southfork. Whatever punishment is going to be doled out, it isn't for the birds.

Even after all these years, it is still home, the home where Mammy danced into the moonlight. The only home Bell wants. The smell of tea and bought bread mixes with the smell of dust, perhaps even some of Granny Tess's dust. I walk on to the front room and when I turn to face him I'm standing on the very spot she breathed her last. It was a good enough place for her to die. For the millionth time I wish I was smaller, I wish I was lighter, I wish I wasn't the blue-eyed bastard who has poisoned them all. Bell and Father Boluwaji follow him in.

– I don't know what to say for myself, Granda. I made a mistake—

– You did! You should never have given him up, girl! Never! He's a Morris, he needs to be made back into a Morris and you need to see to it that he is!

– What? I don't understand? I don't—

– It's very simple. You and Bell are going to be fine; you'll even be welcome to come home if he comes too. I've already told Malachi that his name is off the land. We need this boy to come home now, d'you understand, girl? This is my land and it must go to my line.

I am transformed into the saviour of Southfork so fast that my lungs can't keep up. We all look at the Big Man and wait for him to sneer, but he stays sincere. I see my hand float out to take the first drop of loving kindness he has ever given freely. He has poured out four small measures of whiskey and he reaches one to me, one to his priest and one to his daughter. He raises his own glass and bids us say cheers. *Times have changed*, he says, grave as a bishop delivering an apology. A good deal had been struck and, as always, it is on his terms. He was in the market for a male heir. Kieran's three sons are a bonus. He doesn't bother mentioning the bloody fucking wife. She will form part of the job lot.

    – Did he just say we could come *home*? says Bell with far too many teeth.

    – I'm not sure that's what he meant, Auntie Bell …

    – Don't put words in my mouth, girl! I said you were welcome but only when I get the boy. The boy's the key.

All I have to do is deliver my son, this time into the jaws of a man I hate more with every heartbeat. I worry for Bell; she had no use in his plan. She shifts her weight from foot to foot, too excited to stand still, too stupid to know to not get excited. All she has heard is that she is welcome. She has wanted to come home, back to this draughty farmhouse, from the minute she was made to leave it. She has forgotten how malicious he was. This is Granda Morris, for God's sake! He can't be trusted as far as we could throw him, which would never be far enough.

    – I hear the boy even has the right faith, Father?

    – Yes, yes, he was brought up in a Catholic home—

- That's good, that's good! There's some things that can't be bred out of people and being reared a Protestant is one of them, for sure!

I risk a look at Father Boluwaji, whose bottom lip is hanging. He necks his whiskey and swallows hard and Bell and me have little option but to do the same. The burn is welcome and we cough up our disbelief.

Chapter 7

Carnsore has changed in a cuckoo, chime and ting. It has become cheery. I don't like it. Not one bit. I am upside down and back to front, but Bell is awash with joy. And she is in no mood for further conversation, it seems. She ran into the bungalow when Father Boluwaji dropped us off after we left the twilight zone of Southfork and started to pack. I waved him and his concerns away, promising that I'd call if I needed him. I had to go after her, had to pull her hands out of the drawers and explain that Kieran might not be keen to give up his own place, give up the name he was given, and to just pop down here to fulfil an old man's wishes.

– He has a wife, y'know, Bell? A wife who might not want to uproot her children and move to a farm-house in the middle of nowhere?

- She'd *love* Southfork! It's the nicest house for *miles*!
- It's not! *It's not a nice house!* Apart from the fact that it has barely been cleaned for a decade, it comes with a live-in lunatic!
- Don't talk about your grandfather like that! He's not that bad! He has his own way of doing things, that's all!
- His own way of doing things? That's how you write off a lifetime of abuse? For God's sake, Bell, get sense!
- I'm not talking to you until you remember your place, Lindy Morris! You're hardly in a position to lecture me on anything?

She squared up to me, daring me to be the bold brat that she'd given up her life to put down. I was sick of her. And now I had Kieran to consider too. All he was to her was evidence that I was no better than Mammy. While I watched, she pulled out her divan bed and got Mammy's suitcase out of the drawer. She would not open it. It was not *hers*. It was my mammy's. So convinced was I that my son would not buckle so easily that I took the suitcase off Bell's bed and marched it out to the turf shed and the spiders just to slow her down. It was still heavy with whatever Mammy dreamed she'd need for a future without Granda Morris and Granny Tess, packed on the day she died. I badly needed the December air to chill me, so I breathed it in and out, in and out, nice and slow, casting around for calm thoughts that darted away laughing.

Bell wasn't in the mood to be bossed around, however. She was ready and waiting for me in the kitchen, feet planted wide on the battleground of the lino. Her arms were crossed. She was in need of telling me what she thought of me and my son. I was always impressed by how quickly my aunt bounced back. She was a tough old girl. Shame she didn't know I was about to knock her down.

– Well? You've gotten brazen instead of ashamed since the discovery of this boy of yours?

– Which one? Patrick Joseph or Kieran?

– So, you're a thief and a hoor?

– I am! Isn't it wonderful to be so talented? What happened to my brother, Auntie Bell, and none of your lies?

– He was a cot death. Made it to two months. He was a sweet thing, Babs called him Pajo. We were all sad when he was taken. We were, really and truly!

– Is he the only reason Mammy and me were kept?

– The only reason.

A cold, sickening feeling spread through my guts. A boy for a house. A house for a boy. The boy's the key. *We need this boy to come home now, d'you understand, girl? This is my land and it must go to my line.*

We? My arse, it was never 'we'. Bell and me would be received as long as the boy was laid at his feet, a welcome mat. Kieran wasn't the first bastard boy being bargained for. Patrick Joseph had been the first, the right child.

The sadness of it hit us both at the same time and we struggled to pull out the chairs and to sit down. A lifetime of not being good enough can wear you down. I asked her to tell me more. There was nothing more to tell, she said. It wasn't uncommon in their day. No fuss was made. I knew this was the truth, I'd even heard Miriam's mammy say such things. He died, it was the will of God that he was taken and I wasn't, the entire Morris family had offered it up. We'd both had the same care. Mammy had proved them all wrong when she turned out to be a very capable mother. Even Granda had been surprised. He'd been a bit easier on them all for as long as Pajo had been around. That *was* him, the little rectangle just to the right of the family grave. We'd both been baptised in the hospital because we'd been severely underweight. Granda wouldn't stretch to a headstone. There was no point in drawing attention to another disappointment courtesy of the bloody fucking women in his life, he said.

– And what about Linus Quinn?
– Linus Quinn had been moved along by then. He never even knew there were two of you.

Bell was deflated, all her rage replaced with regrets. She could have done more to help her at the time, she says, but none of us know what sorrows lie in the future. I couldn't disagree. I was exhausted. Too much had happened too quickly. The quiet of the bungalow allowed the sad wintry sighs of the pine trees to seep in at the windows. We joined them, doing our best to exhale. I put my hand over her leathery hand and we seemed to be friends for a while, at peace, a unit bound by griefs old and new. But Bell's never been a fan of counting only the bright hours.

– You can't miss what you never had, she says. It's not possible.
– It is *possible*!
– It is *not* possible!
– It is! And stop trying to dodge the fact that you lied to me! You should have told me I had a brother once – that's big news!
– You should have told me you had a son. That's quite big news, too. News that's going to get us back through the door of Southfork!

I've never wanted to be like Granda Morris in any way, shape or form, but sometimes furniture needs to fly through the air and shatter against kitchen walls. I thought there would be a satisfying crash with splinters flying and lumps of plaster chipped off. Judging by Bell's face, she thought it would break too. But no, even a kitchen chair had let us down in our moment of need.

I had to chase after it and batter it until it broke. When the sweat was lashing off me and I'd managed to reduce it to admittedly chunky kindling, I felt more composed than I had for years. It was such a pleasant change to let the rage pour out instead of letting it turn in. Bell said not a single word. I left the wreckage and reached for a tea towel to get on with drying the pots that were on the draining board. Bell and me hadn't had time to finish the washing-up before we'd stepped out for the joy of *Dancing at Lughnasa*.

Sunday is always a long day. Bell and me try to make it special with a roast dinner but we've found we've no appetite for one today. We'd both taken a nap after we'd gathered up the bits of chair and put them outside the back door. She was good to help me. I swept up the debris and carried on to do the whole kitchen floor. She held the dustpan out for me. I walked to the bin and she skipped ahead to lift the lid. There was nothing much to occupy either of us after that, except tackling any one of a hundred conversations we needed to have, so bed it was.

I was glad to lie down, alone. I pulled my knees up so my feet wouldn't dangle over the end and looked out at the clouds racing by. It was a filthy day, though the rain falling hard on the inadequate roof of Carnsore was comforting. About forty miles away, my son and his family would be having a Sunday of their own. I tried to imagine what it would be like for him. For his wife. What would he say to this woman he had chosen from the herd to share his life about the woman who had handed him over for someone else to rear?

He was the key for Bell in the same way that Patrick Joseph had been the key for Mammy. How quickly Bell had allowed my late brother into the room! As if he was nothing worth talking about. He was the only reason I had a roof to keep off the worst of the weather but he was also the reason I became the wrong child. You win some, you lose some. I had a mother, she died. I have an aunt who lost her life because of me. I had a brother, he died before he had an inkling of life. Linus Quinn didn't even know he'd been born. Our father has never bothered to find out if I was still alive or dead. I have a son, he lived in Ireland for the whole time I imagined him in London. I have a grandfather who needs to die. I'd need to live to a hundred and two to add it all up to a happy sum.

The tiredness finally overcame me. I slept until it was dark and the cuckoo, chime, ting makes it only four o'clock. Bell slept too; we both stumbled into the corridor at the same time, bleary-eyed and slightly embarrassed by our rare foray into telling the truth. She turned for the kitchen so I followed her in single file. We don't like the night creeping up on us, it's unnerving to see the windows turned into mirrors by the deep dark outside, so we move around the bungalow and pull every curtain closed. The whole place is quieter somehow, even the pines have given up on their groaning. We're at a loss what to say next, Bell and me, delving about as we are among the living and the dead. So we do the sensible thing and switch on the telly.

Sunday-evening viewing is nearly as mind-numbing as Saturday-evening viewing but it doesn't numb our minds enough. Mine is travelling the road to Omagh and back, travelling the road to St Bede's and Father Boluwaji and back, and when I'm not keeping an eye out, I start travelling the road to the Clinic. Bell has only one journey to undertake. She's travelling the road to Southfork and never coming back. A row was guaranteed, now that we've finally got the hang of them.

– Why wouldn't he want to live in Ballyglen?

– By *he*, I assume you mean my son Kieran?

– Aye … why wouldn't he want that?

– It's not Ballyglen, it's Southfork. If he gets bogged down at the end of that rotten lane how will he get out again?

– He'll not want to get out again. Why would he?

– Because he has *a life*! He's married and has children and a house and all the other shite that goes with it presumably, and he has no reason to give it up and trek down here to be Granda's puppet?

She sulks and protests and harrumphs and agrees to go to bed ridiculously early after an enforced meal of fried eggs on toast, although she's nearly too excited to swallow them. I have to get her away from me. Of all the things she's said today it is the fact that she could have done more for Mammy that has stuck into me. And now, she is ploughing the same auld furrow as forever before as if we haven't just unearthed two brand-new children between us. I need to put her out of harm's way. Now that I know razing useless objects was such a buzz, I know even better that I'll develop a taste for it. I am itching to reach for the heavy skillet and make it light on her head.

She can't hear what I am telling her, we might not be going anywhere but she doesn't hear me because she can't bear to. Her time trapped alone with me out on the edge of Donegal is coming to a right, true end. She doesn't sleep, I hear her moving around through the thin wall between us as I lay awake too, wondering what madness the next day will bring. The dried-blood flowers of the curtains fade in the darkness and are lit up again as the sun rises, milky and unbothered by the shenanigans of two sad, melancholy old women.

*

This Monday morning, Bell is reborn, bouncing around like a teenager. She's fully back to pretending that we're happy enough and that there are no dark clouds on the horizon. She's sorting drawers that have been left shut for decades, rummaging through boxes that were mouldering in the attic. Worse, she's putting stuff in *piles*: keep, donate, destroy. I have to step around them as they grow from the carpet. She holds up a variety of things – a lettuce drier, a giant bag of giant hair rollers, knitting patterns for awful cardigans – and asks me what we ever kept any of it for when there were probably people out in Africa in desperate need. (She's never recovered from all the years she spent donating money to the missions in Kenya, Kenya having become for her the whole of the continent, brimming to bursting with poverty and pagans and the poor nuns she funded run ragged trying to save their mortal souls.) I shrug my shoulders and smile. I suspect that the poor people in Africa wouldn't thank her for any of this crap.

She will not listen to another word about the fact that I have a child. I HAVE A CHILD, a child I kept from her. I try to mention him, my Kieran, but she looks past me as if she's lost something and must get on with looking for it without delay. He has only one purpose and until I guarantee it, she won't play ball. She walks away and finds another load of rubbish to sift through. She laughs when I ask her if she doesn't want to know why

I did it, why I gave him away. It's no business of mine, she says. Granda Morris has let me slip the noose, so that's good enough for her. She has adjusted to our new circumstances with alarming ease. All she wants to focus on is that she's going home, back to Southfork after a mere thirty-three-year break.

I couldn't feel any more muddled. I found out that my brother passed away and that I had been right that he was beside Mammy. He just wasn't meant for this world, that's what's said when babies are taken naturally. King of the long acre, Linus Quinn, had been allowed in too without so much as a hiccup. Bell didn't die as she spoke his name. We are in danger of behaving like normal people. I got to walk out of Southfork without a blow of any kind, not physical, not verbal, just emotional, which doesn't count as a battle scar in Carnsore. I got offered the opportunity to be the Morris family salvation. I had drunk one small whiskey with my grandfather so I had no option but to take it. I still have to find the strength to meet my son. How will he take being asked to leave his entire life behind just because he wanted to meet his mother?

I'm distracted by a loud rap on the front door that has me and Bell clutching at our throats and checking that we have a breadknife handy in case it's robbers. No one has knocked on that front door in three decades: Granda walks in, we wait for the wimmin in sunshine and in snow to save them the formality and Miriam comes in through the kitchen. I open it with Bell standing between my shoulder blades for protection. It's a huge bunch of flowers being held out to me by a cheery-looking driver. They must be from Kieran! My son has sent me a gift. Alien tears gather in the corners of my eyes at the thought he is so thoughtful. We thank the poor man so much he backs away and roars off up the street at high speed. He'll have another tale to add to the Mad Morrises of Carn Hill.

There are so many. The colours are so lovely. The scent so sweet. I've never had a bunch of flowers before and they mean more to me than gold bars. Bell fusses while I get the scissors and cut the ribbon and we remember we don't have a vase so we have to set about chopping them down a bit and fixing them in to a series of jam jars and milk bottles. I like that I can put them in every room in Carnsore. Even ugly houses can have a little joy. The card is small, so small I nearly miss it. *All the best from your friends in the Credit Union*, it says. I've seen the shine go off a lot of things but nothing quicker than this bouquet.

Bell at least has the good grace not to crow. She even goes as far as giving me a distracting job. She has arranged a collection of torches along the chest of drawers in her bedroom and I'm invited in to give my opinion.

The curtains are drawn as she tests one, then another, to see how far its beam would reach in the blackness of Africa. She doesn't want to be sending duff stuff to people who already have more than their fair share of bother what with the droughts and those terrible, heart-breaking images of them with no food that did the rounds at Christmastime. Jesus! I close the door on her and her Christian charity.

I have to phone Kieran. I need to be steady so I select the paring knife I use for apples. As I am about to etch a jagged line from knee to thigh, one leg only as there's no need to be greedy, I hesitate. I stick it into the heart of the kitchen table instead, over and over again, until a decent tarnish appears. I'm refreshed enough for the phone. I dial the number that Father Boluwaji gave me. Kieran barks 'hello' down the line. It is like hearing Granda Morris, but I shake off the fear that he could be anything like him in other ways.

I mumble an apology over what happened in the Parochial Hall and he tells me not to worry. Then I am stuck. What do you say to a child you gave away? What do you say to a child you have to get to come 'home'? The same child I saved from that exact fate? The silence grows and we listen to each other breathing. In the end he speaks first. He still wants us to meet. He thinks coming back to Ballyglen isn't the best option. Could I come as far as Omagh and meet him on neutral territory, so to speak? I nod into the phone but manage an 'Aye, surely' when he prompts me.

His voice is deep, a no-nonsense voice, the voice of an actor. We set a day, the very next day, no point in waiting. There is a coffee shop in Dunnes. Tomorrow is Tuesday, it will be quiet. I'll walk through the knicker department, past homeware, and he'll be there. He promises he'll be on time, he'll be waiting, he knows the times of the Ulsterbuses getting into the station. He seems to know a lot of things.

He signs off with the words I always say to Miriam – keep in touch. Why hasn't she been in touch? It's been a whole day and a slice of a morning. News should have reached her by now. Will she despise me for keeping this secret? Babies are always good news, she would have said if I'd been brave enough to call her. Why didn't you tell me? she'll say. I would have found a way to help you, she'll say, and maybe she'd be right. My mind wanders back to the final days of Kieran ... the days when I didn't always keep him safe in my arms. I don't think of those days often, they're too uncomfortable.

The phone is still in my hand when I hear a commotion from the kitchen. My aunt has been pretending she couldn't hear who I was talking to. Another barrage of stuff hitting the lino makes me open the door to check she hasn't broken her blasted neck. She's wobbling on a stool to root out any clutter from the top cupboards that would slow down her return to Southfork. How many seventy-somethings would risk their hips for this nonsense?

– Bell! What are you *doing*?
– I've no idea what we've been saving all this Tupperware for, Lindy? Do you think the Africans would have a use for it?

Chapter 8

I've been to Omagh. Martha's taken me and Bell to Dunnes a few times and Miriam has dragged me along when she's shopping for school uniforms and baby-grows and cute little patent shoes for Holy Communions and Confirmations. I've not been on my own before in a bus and I enjoy the countryside clicking by like slides in a projector. It's a fine, dry day and I've done my best to look normal. The make-up I have on might be a mistake judging by the looks on the faces of my darling colleagues at the Credit Union. I had dropped in to say thank you for the flowers. None of them spoke so I filled in the time by adding that I had to go to Omagh and I know they all thought 'hospital' without me saying another word. They've obviously heard that I have added 'unmarried mother' to my CV.

- You're very good to come in, Lindy, given the, erm, circumstances, says Siobhain with her arms crossed.
- Plenty of people have done the same thing, Lindy, they've just not been caught out, says Declan McIvor through a biscuit.

That earned him a slap on the sleeve from Siobhain and he drops half his biscuit and watches, forlorn, as it lands by my feet. He should know the rules by now, do not refer directly to any elephant in any room. If an elephant is mentioned I might lock myself in the toilets. It sets me up for the day ahead, how nervous they were, how utterly desperate they were to ask for even one glorious detail that they could pass on at the Co-op. I bet I get something more exotic than a set of bath cubes this Secret Santa season now that they know that I'm not the oldest virgin in town.

The bus weaves its way through Drumquin and passes the cinema on the outskirts of town before it docks at the bus station. I push one heavy leg in front of the other to make them get me to Dunnes, to keep me going forward when all I want to do is run. Run away! Run back to 1984 when I thought I was Sheena Easton, mooning about waiting for her man who was working 9–5. Why am I not filled with happiness? Why does this son of mine not bring all the love and joy that I thought he would after all those years of imagining? My heart is still a stone in my chest.

I know as I get past a wall of yellow pansies dying in their plastic pots and walk through the automatic doors of Dunnes that the refined, handsome boy of my dreams is not waiting. He's not dressed smartly and strolling down the pavements in Soho. He's going to look at me with his grandfather's eyes. But he's reliable; as I poke my head into the café, he stands up at the back, all six foot five of him, and lifts his hand to salute me. The big square jaw drops an inch into what might be a smile.

– Lindy!

– Kieran!

– That's what you called me, apparently!

He means well, wants to crack a joke to put me at ease, but I light up, my face on fire, and he has to rush to buy a pot of tea and a terrible, blue-looking cup of coffee and a couple of scones over at the self-service bar while I sit down and try to settle myself. I had been wondering if we'd shake hands or hug or maybe even kiss, but we haven't managed any contact and now the moment is gone. I keep my eyes on the tray as he puts all the pieces, one by one, on to the table. He pulls the heads off three white sugars and pours them into the coffee, just like Granda Morris has his. I sip at mine and I hope he won't be angry if I can't swallow a single mouthful of a scone pockmarked with huge raisins.

– So, here we are.

– Yes, here we are.

- Thanks for coming to me – I didn't want to be seen back in Ballyglen until we'd had a chance to talk. The reception I got was the last thing I expected.
- Well, it's a small town with a long memory. You'd have been spotted just for walking down the street never mind being lit up with spotlights in the Parochial Hall!
- Well, anyway, I'm sorry. I never intended to cause you any bother.

I manage a smile that I really mean. I've never heard those words on Granda Morris's lips, not for my whole life, so it's good to hear them now from the next best thing. Kieran starts to ramble on then, and I sit back and listen. It seems that this boy of mine could talk and talk and talk, and he rattles off the story of Kieran McCreedy, the same script he gave Father Boluwaji. I link my fingers together in my lap as if I'm saying a prayer for the gift of serenity.

The woman who adopted him died when he was eighteen months old. I make a sympathetic tut but he waves it away, he couldn't really remember her, he says. Cancer, he says, nothing could be done to save her. His father married a girl from Derry not long afterwards and she convinced him to give up the building trade and try his hand at farming. Her parents were struggling as all their sons had given up on troubled Northern Ireland and its only reliable crop of bullets and bombs and left for England and America. They weren't coming back so that left her, Meg, next in line to take on the land.

They'd not had an easy time of it, what with his father having an English accent, but they'd seemed happy and all he'd known was the two of them working harder and harder every season. There were four more children. He doesn't bother to give their names and the dip in his voice makes me think he didn't get along with them, whoever and whatever they were. His father was a gentleman, he says, a man who always *talked* about fair play. I don't miss the emphasis. The replacement mother number two is also given nothing to distinguish her.

Life had really started for him when he'd had kids of his own. It was the damnedest thing. I wouldn't believe him but he had *twin boys* and another boy all under the age of three. I nod and smile and nod and smile and brace myself for when it will be my turn to confess. He has pictures in his wallet. They're all dark-haired and dark-eyed, real little Morrises. He has a keyring with the twins on either side of a Perspex fob which he lets swing from one little face to another. They were not identical like Mammy and Bell. They were like Pajo and me, fraternal.

He lays them all before me on the table like a card game, the twins – Laurie and Donal – at birth, them again at six months, twelve months, eighteen months, though they're bigger now. The baby, Brian, named after rugby legend Brian O'Driscoll himself, at about two months, which stabs my heart for a painful minute. He's so like Kieran at that age and the confession draws closer. Kieran points out the age of Brian in the photo without a flicker of recognition, noting how small he was, how vulnerable they all were at that age, how much they needed their mother.

– Do you have any photos of her?

– Who?

– Their mother?

– Good Lord, no! Why would I?

– I don't know – because I thought that was something that men did, carry pictures of their wife in their wallets? Is that not a thing that married people do?

– Not for me, no. What would be the need?

– Oh, right.

He's no romantic fool, this son of mine. We both take a breather by staring at the large people pushing trolleys piled high with white bread and bottles of fizzy pop down the walkway at the back. *This* is where Declan McIvor gets his big trousers from, here is where 40-inch waists made of all the polyester of your dreams could be had for £30 a pair. I swallow a mouthful of tea, it's truly cold now but it's better than nothing. I want to ask her name when I realise he hasn't given it. This girl, this wife, who has produced three sons for him but who hardly features in his talk of 'family' and his need and love for it. I recall Granda Morris's unending problem with bloody fucking women and Christopher Campbell's spit hitting my face as his hatred of me dripped on to the stone steps of St Simon Stock's. How long will I be able to keep *that* little secret?

Kieran is tapping his index fingers together, such a light tap but still it gets inside my head like a drum. He's wondering how he's going to fill the gap between me knowing stuff about him and me not telling him stuff about me. There are so many things I need to keep from him. The fact that his father was a Catholic priest. The fact that my father was a gypsy. The fact that my mother drowned when she was trying to find a way out of Ballyglen. The fact that the wimmin thought she was wicked, not thoughtful. The fact that my grandfather is nothing but an auld fucker. The fact that I am the reason my Auntie Bell has no one or nothing to call her own. My existence even made Vincent Murray the fiancé abandon her.

Kieran will find all of this out if he comes back to Ballyglen. I should make him run for the hills of Derry and never look back. I don't want him to be fooled by anything that the auld fucker has to offer but I don't want to let on that I'm not nice, that I'm not reasonable, not sensible, not someone who could be rational. I need to hide from him the most important fact of all, his mother is a nutjob, that even while one hand wobbles out to straighten a scone on the plate below his eyes, the other hand is wrapped around the sharp piece of white quartz that I took from Mammy's grave all those years ago. So long ago it was before Kieran existed. It's small but effective. I never leave home without it.

I hear him take up a big breath of air to mark the end of a safe silence. There is one more fact that he will want to know before any of the others will interest him. I brace myself for it, the question that I thought I'd never have to face, especially across a plastic table in a supermarket café where the lunch crowd have started to materialise even though it's only eleven o'clock in the morning. The smell of cooked lamb drifts our way and I can imagine it, grey and greasy and glistening in large steel trays. When I look at him, I can see there's no escape.

As I will my stomach to not let me down, I move the pictures of the little boys around the table, pairing the twins, matching all three of them as tiny babies. Every black eye is on me. Kieran leans forward. Softly enough, he asks the question that any boy in his position would, and with nothing else to hurt, I push the fine edge of the quartz under the nail of my index finger to let the blood come.

– So, Lindy, why did you give me up?

LONDON – 1985

Chapter 1

It was so lonely in the Loreto Convent Mother and Baby Home for Unmarried Mothers. It was just a holding pen. The other girls didn't talk much, either to me or to each other. We weren't here to make friends. Sister Helen, the Irish nun who came in every morning to get us up at 8 a.m. for breakfast, kept us away from each other – she didn't want any of the 'naughty girls' putting bad ideas into the heads of the 'civil girls'. After a month, I still had no idea which camp she'd put me in. It was all hurry, hurry, hurry. Get up, get your breakfast, say your prayers, get on with your jobs. The only words she had ever spoken to me were strange. Although I'd never asked, she decided to tell me she was from Mayo, you know, *proper Ireland*, and I nodded my

Northern Irish head with what I hoped was the right amount of shame.

Taking my *Smash Hits* posters down from the walls in my bedroom at the RHHI and picking all my Blu-Tack off had been the first time I realised that this was a big move. I had worked as long as I could. Sister Smith kept me on rehab and saw to it I had light duties. There had been a card with 'Sorry You're Leaving', a cake and a few bottles of Pink Lady at the end of my last shift. I'd enjoyed it well enough, but Yasmina wasn't there, she was on holiday and her laughter was a huge loss. You take care now, that stomach look like a son to me, cha, she said, instead of goodbye for ever.

I'd taken a bit of cake up the stairs for Mercy before I left for good. It was a hell of a day to discover that she would smile if you put a ball of buttercream icing into her mouth. Kissing her goodbye was a mistake. She got her arm around me and pressed her face into my baby bump. She was crying again by the time I walked away.

But staring at the blank walls and trying to shove all my clothes into the holdall made me go really funny. I'd loved this room. It was mine. It had a lock on the door. Bev, Donna and Susanne had had a leaving party in it every evening for a week. Only Susanne wasn't working when I had to hand my key back to stinky Colin. She'd come with me in the cab that dropped me at the Loreto, but the first sighting of a nun had made her bolt. I had

had to sign in on my own, say no to having my baby put up for adoption, which earned me an eye roll from the sister on the front desk. So, you're big *and* stupid, she said. I was taken to a dormitory on my own. There were six beds with a slim window in the end wall. There would be no privacy and no heating, apparently. I could see my breath as I unpacked my suddenly shaming bright pink and yellow wardrobe.

I spent the bulk of the four weeks before Kieran was born scrubbing the already-clean floor in the kitchen and the long corridor that led away from it to what was called the canteen. Six tables with six chairs each held us for our three meals a day while Sister Helen paced up and down, telling us to hurry, hurry, hurry. Thirty minutes was plenty of time to eat a meal unless we *intended* to make gluttons of ourselves when we were already costing the Catholic Church a fortune.

I called Bev and Donna and Susanne but they were busy – they had extra shifts and boyfriends and parties, and they knew I'd understand. One day soon, they'd have babies too, then we could hang out again. They all appeared to get a look at him, to comment on the enormous size of him, on how black his hair was, how perfect his toes. He bawled the place down near enough and they all three bounced him on their knees and passed him on double-quick time and back to me. He was still screaming fit to burst, his little face a ball of purple rage and pain. They ran off laughing and sticking fingers in their ears, when I'd been praying they would ask me if I was alright.

I wasn't. I'd never been so tired or felt so sore, and after a fortnight of not sleeping, the dreams set in. There were the usual ones where Mammy smiles and reaches out her hand just before she slips slowly back and under the dark water. The ones where she was beating on the inside of the coffin lid and no one could hear her but me through the six foot of heavy clay. To these two sleep-killers were added the dreams where Kieran died. I'd walk up to a crib that I knew even in my dreams wasn't mine. But when I looked into it, Kieran would be there, he'd be still, black and still, a tiny fist clamped in his mouth.

I wished someone would lift Kieran off me for a second or even better a minute. But he was always hungry; I couldn't produce or deliver enough milk to satisfy him. Sister Helen told me that I must be doing something wrong as he bucked and reared five minutes after I got him to take my breast. She tutted, a woman who couldn't feed a child disrupted her hurry, hurry, hurry schedule, and she herded me off to an even colder part of the house where I could sleep alone and cope alone while the other girls held their babies with one hand and drank tea with the other. They were all content, they were all coping, they were delighted when me and my little screaming nightmare were quarantined.

If I could keep him moving, I could keep him quiet, but my legs felt like lead and he felt like a sack of grain against my chest. My arms ached, my neck. I wished I could lie down for an hour somewhere his cries couldn't reach me. The cries took all my energy to absorb and I didn't have much left to fight my desire to put my hand over his mouth. More than once I caught myself eyeing a wooden blanket box that sat at the end of the corridor, it looked cosy, solid, soundproof, big enough to give a baby room to thrash around while I took a long, hot shower.

As the days went by, I understood. He didn't want me. I wanted him, I'd wanted him from the very first minute I knew about him, but he had decided that I wasn't good enough. He wanted to be with someone else; he was his father's son, he didn't want a silly girl in his life. Sister Helen asked me why I had *decided* to have a baby out of wedlock if I knew nothing about babies. I was so tired, tired down to my bones, so that I wanted to throw Kieran across the room to free up my hands to wring her neck. I'd had help getting pregnant. Would she like to know who helped me? A man who was still standing behind an altar not far from that dingy Church-funded house. I didn't get to say anything, of course, because she was in a hurry. She could condemn us without breaking stride and the clinical smell from her clothes was all you were left to chew on.

I was still struggling with him when she came back. I saw her strangely flattened leather shoes plant themselves not far from mine. When I looked up, she had crossed her arms and was watching me as if I was a novelty of some sort. The thing was she had been thinking. Some babies need a bit *more*. Some babies are happier with a nice *family*. Some babies just know that their life will be harder without a father and brothers and sisters, with only a mother toiling to work and rear them all alone, and that's why they don't *settle*. Some babies cheer right up when they know they're with the *right kind of person*.

I nodded, she was making sense. It would be better for Kieran to have two or more people to share the constant carrying of him. Two people could look after him properly, two people could provide for him, and I only had another two weeks in Loreto Convent Mother and Baby Home for Unmarried Mothers before I would have to fend for myself and him. The thought of trying to wheel him around a supermarket to buy food, to get that food home – where exactly would I be able to afford to live? – to get it cooked all while he was howling and needing more from me than I had to give made me start to shake. Sister Helen lifted him out of my arms and swayed from side to side as she rested him against her shoulder. As always, as soon as he was away from me, he stopped crying. The relief of the silence let me hate myself for even thinking of letting anyone else bring him up. He was mine, mine alone. The minute I snatched him back he let out a roar that ripped through my head, it was so loud I could see it as a hundred stars of blood all bursting at the same time.

Sister Helen was like a dog with a bone after that. Every day she approached me with her 'some babies' speech, and it wasn't long until the perfect couple were introduced into the conversation. The thing was, she had found a wonderful *opportunity* for Kieran, a perfect couple who would know what to do with such a demanding little boy. A couple who would love him. The first thing she gave them was a religion, you can't really build anything without a strong foundation. They're Catholics, *thank God*. After that, the more earthly parts of them arrived. They have a *nice* house, small but *nice*, very clean. This made me look down at my stained T-shirt and jeans, so many splodges of baby spit and vomit not wiped carefully enough that it was hard to tell it's not a pattern. They have a car. He has a job as a builder, she's only working part time in a clothes shop and is willing to throw all that glamour away as soon as a baby is given to them.

It would be a way to prove to these good, hard-working Catholics that God had a plan for them all along after He took her womb at the tender age of eighteen because He'd given her cancer. Into each life a little rain must fall. I would be helping God out, not an offer an exhausted, aching, lonely girl gets every day. I missed Miriam. I wished with all my heart that I had told her my secret. She would have come to me, to us, even though it would not sit easily with her faith. She had always stood by me and my blood.

I would have to think about it, said Sister Helen, long and hard. I would have to scour my conscience so that I could make the right choice. It was very simple really, Sister Helen explained. Could I give Kieran the nice, clean, already-smote-by-God parents he deserved or would I be selfish enough to keep him for myself when a mole could see I wasn't capable? Mrs Perfect deserved another miracle, an answer to her good Catholic prayers. No matter what way I looked at it, they were miles ahead of me.

I fought on. I took to hiding on the fire escape at the back of the Loreto. Not that anyone was looking for me. I had made no friends because of Kieran. I wrapped him and me in blankets so we could stay outside without freezing. As I watched the hundreds of tiled roofs and gardens flowering in their sad little rectangles, I pretended that I wasn't holding Kieran too tight, I wasn't trying to squash his mouth into my chest, I just wanted him to be quiet, I needed him to be still.

I imagined Mrs Perfect reaching out her arms for my boy and more and more it was all I wanted in spite of myself. I wanted someone to help me. Mammy came only in my dreams and just as I was about to beg her to stay, Kieran's cries would tear through even that bubble and I'd be on my feet for the rest of the night trying to soothe him. Nothing worked but keeping him on the move; he would even breastfeed if he was in motion, and I spent hours patting him on the back and trying to keep his feet from kicking my already sore body.

He was only two months old when I cracked. I'd been trying to find a place to live, the clock in the Loreto Home for Unmarried Mothers was ticking, there were plenty of other unmarried mothers who needed a bed, room had to be found. Kieran and me had had our fair share of sanctuary. I'd just had the phone slammed down on me for the fifth time in a row; landlords didn't like having to talk over the sound of a crying baby. I knew I had to leave him behind in my room but one look at him let me know he was gearing up for a screaming match. None of the other girls would touch him, he was too much like hard work with his purple face and pumping fists. I'd only put him behind the bed to muffle the sound. There wasn't anywhere else and the floor was safe enough, safer than the bed or the cot just until I made a few phone calls. Sister Helen did not agree.

I should have gone straight back to the Loreto public phone booth but with my arms empty for what felt like the first time in a hundred years, I made myself a mug of tea and took it out on to the fire escape. It was only for five minutes, five minutes. How could I know I would sleep right there against the hard railings, the sounds of the traffic just a breath away? When I woke up, Sister Helen held the cup in front of her like a chalice and informed me that '*this* can't go on'. Mothers who hide poor innocent babies, babies made in the very image of the Christ child Himself, would not be tolerated. She'd taken the liberty of taking Kieran out of the Loreto for the night, although she wouldn't say where. He had been *placed* with people who would look after him properly. I was to use the time to consider whether or not I was fit for purpose.

I didn't cry. I didn't ask where he was. I didn't beg. I felt nothing but relief. I thought, I have a whole night off; I'm going to sleep like the dead. When Sister Helen didn't get any reaction, she tutted and turned tail. I didn't waste any time following her in and running to my room. Lying down on the full length of the bed, my bones sank back into place and I was out. What seemed like a second later, the sound of the girls tripping down the corridor towards the kitchen woke me up. The stiffness in my neck let me know I hadn't even shifted position, I hadn't missed Kieran, hadn't given him a second thought.

The pure joy of maybe being able to get to the kitchen and get myself a huge bowl of porridge and milk and brown sugar and to stuff it all into my mouth, spoon after spoon after spoon of it, without having to man-handle his hot little body hit me hard. What kind of a mother was I? I shut my eyes and imagined my usual judge and jury. Useless, good-for-nothing article, roared Granny Tess! You can never trust a mongrel, said Granda Morris. Bad blood comes from the bone. I gave up my life to look after you, Lindy, said Auntie Bell, I did my best to make something out of you and this is how you repay me? By proving you weren't worth it after all?

When I opened my eyes, only Sister Helen was stand-ing over me.

– Well?

– Well what?

– What are you going to do about the *fact* that you can't look after your own child? He had a great night last night, he was no bother at all – not that *you* seem too worried about him – so it appears the problem lies with you?

– Yes, Sister ... Where was he?

– He was with that *nice couple* I told you about. They'll be delighted to take him off your hands if only you can make the right decision and make it soon. He's not the *only baby* in town, you know?

With that she was off again. I stared at the empty door and for all my conjuring, it was still the bowl of sweet, milky porridge that cried out to me louder than Kieran ever had. My stomach growled and twisted and I swung my huge, heavy legs off the bed and set out for the kitchen. The other girls stared – why wouldn't they? I was smelly, dirty, greasy-haired and minus my son as I slurped and swallowed my way through one bowl, a second bowl, a third. I was starving. I wanted eggs, bread, anything. God, anything that could build me back up to the person I was before I got here. Miriam's best friend, the capable nurse, the fun mate, the lover of Spandau Ballet and Duran Duran, the rubbish grand-daughter and niece. It took me a while, a while too long, to realise that I didn't see myself as Kieran's mother.

Chapter 2

Like sand through my fingers, Kieran was gone in a matter of days. Sister Helen was so helpful. Mrs Perfect was lined up, some papers were signed, and the few bits of clothes that I had scraped together for him were washed and ironed and folded inside a bag. He'd been on a bottle for days and was still screaming every time the last drop was drained, but without him latching on to me with his hard little mouth and flailing at me with his hands, a gap had opened up between my heart and his. He wasn't going to be mine for ever. He was going to be Mrs Perfect's. I let him go, inch by inch. When the day came, the last day, Sister Helen dressed him. She had bright white babygrows provided by his new parents so that he'd not look out of place in their nice, clean house.

He picked that day to be silent. He watched as the nun fastened the little studs which hid his delicate shoulders and sticky-out belly button from me for the last time. He looked put out when she rolled a hat on to his head, his first hat, which hid the dark mat of his hair from me. When he was all packaged up and ready to be posted, she asked me if I wanted one more kiss. I shook my head no, no thank you, and she hoisted him on to her shoulder. You can't miss what you never had, don't forget that, said Sister Helen, as if she was telling me the time of day.

As she hurry, hurry, hurried away, I saw how much Kieran had come to resemble my mother. His face had the look of hers, his eyes were full of her questions and her sadness. *I'll be back as quick as a wink*, she'd said. When the door closed on him, the sharp pain that had been stabbing at me became blunt, numb. I'd have to find a way of replacing it. I couldn't lose another bit of her, so I let the doors that had been slamming in my head for months all shut at the same time. They brought the blackness I'd needed to carry on.

CARNSORE

Chapter 1

I am standing in the bus station in Omagh, alone. Beside me some convent grammar school girls play-act in their brown uniforms. They are pretending to be embarrassed by each other's attempts at embarrassing each other. One hikes up a hem of a skirt to get a scream, another throws a textbook to the ground and declares that she's 'over crappy French', yet another is pulling faces behind an old lady who's staring into the middle distance. I shouldn't have told Kieran what happened in the Loreto Convent Mother and Baby Home for Unmarried Mothers in London, but I have so many other lies to tell him I needed the truth to lay them on. He said he understood, but how could he? How could he begin to think anyone would give a baby up just because she was tired? The retelling of it made me feel worse than I've felt for years, but worse again is the feeling that this lost son of mine is not the boy of my dreams.

The girls are ratcheting up their noise, pulling at each other's jumpers as they run around between the tired, cold, annoyed adults who just want to get home to their dinner. I've had enough; this morning's been exhausting and difficult and I can't risk their play-screams getting inside my head. I step into their path. I salute them with my bloodied hand and an immaculate freaky-deaky without saying a single word. I've always been a bleeder and it runs to the darker shade of red. By this stage, my face will be deathly pale and bluish under the eyes. This serves to make them run away. It's so easy to put people back in their box when you don't care what they think of you. I return to my place, my back against the outside wall of the waiting room, as I try to make sense of the first two hours I've spent with Kieran McCreedy, the man who could be no one else's but mine.

I had managed to half embrace him when he leaned in to hug me 'Goodbye for now'. I'd forgotten how claustrophobic being hugged is, and with him being so tall he had sort of pinned my arms down by mistake, wrapping me totally against his chest for thirty seconds while I feebly patted at what I hoped was his back with my unbloodied hand. I forced a smile before he stepped back to inspect how pleased I was by his forgiving nature. I watched him walk away, he didn't look back. I watched the shine on his black hair until he was finally swallowed by the distance between us. It was impossible to imagine him standing in the kitchen in Carnsore but that's exactly where he will be in only two days' time. That was hardly time for me to prep Bell. Her head will explode. She needs at least two weeks to panic.

I had managed to deliver the story of how I gave him up in neutral tones, gliding over the worst of my faults. I'd not told him that at nineteen I thought I'd already plumbed the depths of loneliness but that I was wrong. I'd not told him he was a difficult baby. I'd not told him that *he* was the one who didn't want *me*. I'd not told him that his father was absent for very good reasons. And when he asked what his father had done for a living, I had told the truth. He was an actor, I said, very accomplished, so he hadn't stuck around long enough to find out that he would be a father. That seemed to please him, gave them some common ground to lie on.

I'd never set eyes on Christopher Campbell again, even when I found myself living on the streets. I could have gone to Susanne or Bev or Donna, but every time I thought of telling them I'd simply handed my child over, I couldn't take the shame. I'd left the Loreto and spent the last of my money on a revolting hostel. It cost a lot extra for bloody fucking women because I had to be kept away from the hundreds of men queuing outside for a place to rest their heads. The money didn't last me long, though; I don't know how many days or weeks I lay with my back against the wall, my only company the stains on the carpet and the sound of people fighting for space outside in the corridor.

I walked to St Martin-in-the-Fields on the day they put me out for good. Don't come back, they said. If it's charity you're after you need to find a church. It was someone there who told me that I was in pain. I nodded, I think, at the truth of it. I knew what to do with pain, I was a well-trained donkey. I went from chemist to off-licence and back again and got what I needed to make it stop. I don't tell my son any of this. I don't tell him how I begged the commuters trying to get from Charing Cross station to Leicester Square for coppers, how I was prepared to step into their path and bark at them if I had to. It didn't take long to save up for the ticket I had in mind. He doesn't need to know, he's not a London boy.

I'd not told him that ever coming back to Ballyglen was the last thing on my mind but I'd found myself being talked at by an Irish nurse when I had my stomach pumped. I've no idea how many pills I took or how many vodkas or even who found me in the street, but this Irish nurse told me that there was nowhere for me but *home*. I'd have to get back on the boat. *You'll not know yourself when you're back with yer mammy for*

a few months and all this nonsense will be forgotten.
She was from Fermanagh and she knew for a fact that
*plenty of walks in the good, clean Irish air would fix
me up in no time*! She gave me the fare and made me
swear on the Bible that I wouldn't waste her hard-
earned money on anything else but a ticket home. It
was the only option on the table so I took it. I don't even
remember her name.

He kept quiet and I rattled on to the job in hand,
Gabriel Morris's decree that the boy is the key for me
and Bell.

- My grandfather, your great-grandfather, wants to
  meet you! I know Father Boluwaji tried to explain
  the situation in Ballyglen – but Gabriel Morris is
  from another time, a time when a girl mightn't be
  forgiven for having a baby out of wedlock.
- So, he's changed tack?
- Well, he's surprised us all by ... well, he's surprised
  us all ... he's taken us by surprise and says he wants
  to meet you sooner rather than later. The sooner
  the better! He comes to Omagh for the mart ...
- I'll be down. I want to see your place and I'll go to
  his place if there's time.
- You'll *what*?
- I'll visit. Gabriel Morris is right, the sooner the better. I want to meet as many of my relatives as I can
  before it's too late. I hear he's an old man?

I wanted to warn him that Gabriel Morris, old as he was, could not be trusted. That at any moment, he might turn and start shouting insults, that if he didn't think his insults were hitting home he'd deliver them again with a wallop. I knew he wanted to trap my son behind his miles and miles of stone wall and barbed-wire fences, but Kieran already had a life, a family. He would never bend to such a ridiculous whim. I had stacked all the pictures of his little boys together then, formed them into a neat pile and made to hand them back as a way of drawing a line under the day. They lived silent and clean in his wallet while his wife-with-no-name changed their nappies and made their tea.

– They're for you, Lindy, he said, your grandsons! You can show that auntie of yours? Bell, was it? And the old man – I suspect they'll get a kick out of seeing that they have a few new relatives too!

When you pray that the Ulsterbus won't make it through the traffic, that it might veer off the road at any one of the dangerous bends on the way back to Ballyglen, that's the day it makes it to the end of the long road home double-quick time. Bell was at the window from the minute I came into view. I crossed the stony bridge at my leisure. I was taking my time, I told myself, enjoying the bog cottons and dandelions that shivered in the rivers of moss running between the granite boulders. I'd nipped in to Diamond's for a box of pastries to sweeten the next few hours. There were two Viennese whirls and two chocolate eclairs and a lifetime of mistakes to swallow. It took me a minute to register the car at the side of the house – Miriam was inside Carnsore.

Bell is not happy. By the look of the snarl on her, Miriam's been talking and Bell has had no option but to listen. Lindy's had a baby, she'll have said, you have to deal with it, she'd say, people have been making the same mistake as Lindy for thousands of years, she'd say. Thank God for Miriam, now I'll have her to look after me when I tell Bell that Kieran is coming home. I'm almost glad that the clean-up has started and that half of the rubbish that's been lurking on shelves and on top of cupboards is now bagged and ready to send to the Africans. I hurry my step and conjure a wide smile; it falls short of my best freaky-deaky but it's enough to fool them both.

– Lindy! I just found out and Bell says it's true. You have a son?

– I didn't tell her anything she didn't already know. You know me, Lindy, I'm not one to gossip about other people's misfortunes.

– It is true, Miriam, and he's coming here on Thursday for a visit. Do either of you want a cup of tea? I'm parched.

They're both open-mouthed in the hall as I breeze past them with my box of treats. The little bursts of light that dance in front of my eyes when I'm about due for one of my episodes blind me for a second before I can locate the kettle. I lift it, pour water down its spout, turn and put it on before I start to reach for mugs, all while I'm talking to my lungs: breath in, breath out, calm thoughts, repeat.

Miriam is crying, the tears are pouring out of her as she advances across the kitchen with her arms open. I'm going to be hugged for the second time in a day, and it's not even Christmas. I want to tell her that it's alright, to not waste her sympathy on me, but Bell is watching, lips pursed, hackles up. Miriam clings on for a good five minutes, swaying me this way and that. It's a tiny bit mortifying but I force myself not to pull back. She's delighted for me, *really*, even though *the circumstances* are not the best. Forgive the sinner, hate the sin, that's Miriam. It's wonderful that he's found me at last and that we can get to know one another. On and on she babbles while Bell hangs about like a bad smell. She's not enjoying having to listen to someone who loves me, someone who's trying to make it better.

Miriam knows the rules of Carnsore – I am not allowed to be shown any compassion. All the damage I've done myself over the years is just attention-seeking badness, but she's overexcited and wants to hear all about him, every detail. I don't start at the beginning because the beginning is too dangerous and it's ground that I've covered once today already. I cannot walk back through the corridors of the Loreto Convent Mother and Baby Home for Unmarried Mothers again for a very long time. Instead, I confirm that he resembles Gabriel Morris, that he's tall, standing at over six feet and five inches. He's dark like all the Morrisses and even has Gabriel Morris's black eyes.

When I've run out of physical details, they wait for me to dress him with a personality. He seems a nice man, patient, kind, understanding. I don't mention his sons or his wife-with-no-name, too much new blood. I add that he's a farmer, the acting is just for pleasure, and finally they both relax, we all know farmers are the salt of the earth. And, of course, the big rabbit I have in my hat, he's a Catholic and she claps her hands with delight. Bell softens another inch too, this dreaded boy is a much more familiar creature than she first suspected, he's a boy who knows about Mass *and* cattle.

I know that at some stage she will wonder if he's a boy who might swan into Southfork as if he owns the place, when she's on a mission to get her own feet back under the table. I know that won't happen. Through the pouring of tea and sharing of buns and even a glorious minute of laughing at Miriam when she gives herself a cream moustache, there's a mosquito in my head and it drones and drones and drones and grows so loud that I can't believe they can't hear it. There's one thing I'll never be able to tell them, one thing that I'll never be able to say to anyone. I don't seem to have an ounce of feeling for Kieran McCreedy other than unease.

Chapter 2

I've been awake for four hours and thirty-two minutes now. Bell is not pacing tonight. She's snoring. With every minute that passes she's more confident that the intrusion of Kieran McCreedy into our lives is a good thing. It is the thing that will change how and where we live for ever. She went to her room early. Miriam had asked if she could speak with me alone, and far from tutting and sulking and carrying on, Bell declared she was done in. I didn't like the way her eyes shone or the nervous tongue lapping again and again at her lower lip. Miriam and me watched her pick her way down the corridor, as if she was in a minefield and couldn't guess where the next foot should fall.

We closed the door to the living room and Miriam threw herself lengthways on the sofa, her feet on the armrest. She was all smiles, and I'm struck by how unsurprised everyone is by my big surprise. Why had I worried a hole in myself? I thought there would be hell to pay, but this friend of mine, my shitty grandfather, my holy aunt and my beautiful priest have recovered from it in record time. I wish I could join them.

It's not just Kieran who has her all aglow – Miriam has found Linus Quinn. I see again his long, dark hair, his thread bracelets, the way my mother's arm touched his as her hair blew in the breeze from the open window. *Lindy, this man is your daddy!* Miriam's as pleased as punch. One relative popping out of the woodwork begets another. I'd not dreamed she would pull him out the bag so quickly. I've been waiting for forty-seven years to know more about him than bangles, and now she can paint me a portrait. He lives in a caravan that has been parked beside a cottage for twenty years. He's over the border in Donegal not far from the town of Dunalla – the word is he's been 'seeing' a widow woman who lives in the cottage but whose deep Catholic faith won't allow her to have him live in.

– I don't suppose you're that bothered any more, Lindy, but that's where he is.

– Why wouldn't I be bothered?

– Well, you have your son back now! You'll need to be keeping all your energy for him – he has to take priority. The next few weeks will be key to get you both on the right track!

— The right track?

— Yes! You need to bond with him. You're so lucky he came back – not every woman gets that kind of chance.

— A chance for what?

— To make amends. You have a lifetime – *his whole lifetime* – of heartache to fix.

— Oh good! I'm glad it's going to be something simple.

Miriam clucks and rolls her eyes. Somewhere deep down inside, she knows that I know how to behave properly but that I just choose not to. I keep her on Linus Quinn. I need the exact address, is he always there? Does anyone know about him? Has he stopped being a king of the open road? Does a caravan parked beside a randy widow's cottage still make him a gypsy? Are there any more children – someone with my blood that I could claim as kin?

Miriam wants to talk daddies but not mine. She wants to know all about the mysterious boyfriend that I've never mentioned to her, never once in all these years! I was a dark horse! She would *never* have been able to keep such a secret from me. I'd known five minutes after she'd kissed Dermot McPhale. I remember that phone call – a nurse had come to my room in the Clinic and said I had a friend on the line, a friend that wouldn't believe that I didn't want to speak to anyone that night. The noise from the Forge Inn in Ballyglen had billowed into the room carrying the smell of beer and fags and excitement to me where I sat in the sterile light of a hospital at night. She had to say a quick 'goodbye and God Bless' when the siren went off – a siren meant a fire or a bomb and a fire or a bomb meant that everyone would be going home early, first kisses or not.

I'm trying to find a good reason why I kept Christopher Campbell and his child away from her without mentioning the dog collar. My stupidity on that score alone still mortifies me. I'm saved by the loud ring of the phone, which makes us both jump. Granda Morris always waits for 8 p.m. before he places a call; he still believes that off-peak gets cheaper the later you leave it. I have to get that, I say to Miriam, who nods.

– Well?

– Hello, Granda …

– What did he say? Did he say he was coming?

– He's coming to Carnsore on Thursday. He says he'll see you if he has time.

– I knew I couldn't trust you to do a decent job! Did you even mention the land to him? Did you tell him it was his if he comes back here as a Morris? I should never have let you get to him first. God knows what kind of shower he thinks we are now.

What time will he be in Carnsore? Speak up, girl, and none of your lies!

Every time I think I can't find another drop of hate for this lousy auld man, I find one seeping in. He's going to wrestle this boy away from me, he's going to put himself and his 100 acres centre stage – the Big Man, the big negotiator, the big fucker. Bolstered by the fact that I have Miriam by my side, still stretched out like a bad cat, I treat myself to a little white lie.

– The thing is, I told Kieran how much you hate children, how the sight of them makes you likely to
  reach for the nearest big stick, so he might not take
  kindly to you landing on the doorstep. He's promised to bring all three of my grandsons, you see? So
  maybe you should wait until you're asked?

I've hardly slammed down the receiver before Miriam O'Dwyer is on her feet and punching the air. When she grabs hold of me, I let her, and we spin and spin, whooping like lunatics until we collapse in a heap laughing fit to burst.

But that was last night. Today I will have no Miriam and no cream cakes and no option but to get up and spend another strangled day with Auntie Bell. Miriam had cried her eyes out when I handed her the pictures of my grandsons. I thought she'd never stop. They were so beautiful, so perfect, such a dream come true, and I nod-ded along to the truth of it. I'd put them inside my book when I finally crept to bed. There was no need to check again that they were Morrises. Six black eyes can't lie.

The clocks let me know that the time is now 5 a.m. The dark in deepest darkest Tyrone has a density to it; it won't lift for another hour and will only be replaced by a milky glow. My mother hated this time of year, going to sleep in the dark and waking up in the dark. *It's like being a bloody bat, Lindy!* We'd giggle under the covers. She always had a torch, a big heavy square red thing that I was allowed to put on any time I felt scared. I often only had the torch for company on the nights she wanted to go out and walk about in the moonlight. *Don't tell anyone, Lindy, don't ever tell! I'll die without my dose of moonlight!*

I would never have told; keeping secrets kept you safe. I wanted her to be free as much as I wanted her to never leave my side. When you're seven, it's a decent bargain to strike – all the waking hours when Granny Tess, Granda Morris or even Bell might decide to shout at you with Mammy there to protect me or all the black hours when they were all lying in their own cells and couldn't hurt me unless I lost my nerve and cried out.

The clocks let me know it's 5.30 a.m. Thoughts of her have been bound with thoughts of him, my Kieran, for thirty-three years. In my mind, I could set them both free. She was floating out of reach, happy at last, and he was part of a city humming with life. A city that could swallow him whole and keep his identity under wraps. A city where he could make a life for himself. A city that had seen its share of bombs from the IRA but wasn't a patch on Derry where he ended up. The paltry gifts I thought I'd given him were snatched away.

Sister Helen had told me about the cancer eating Mrs Perfect's womb. God's will caught up with her in the end and exposed my boy and his lonely English daddy to Meg from a farm in Derry. Meg who had four more children and who might not have taken to a troublesome eighteen-month-old? My father was a gentleman, he'd said. A man who always *talked* about fair play. But maybe Kieran didn't see much of that fair play when he'd found himself battling with four siblings who had their parents' blood running through their veins? Blood is everything.

The 6 a.m. cuckoo, chime and ting are playing along to the soundtrack of a tractor. Granda Morris is on the street. The usual heart stitch makes me sit bolt upright. I have to pay for last night's insolence. Bell has heard him too. She hits the lino hard, too hard for a woman of her age, and gets her feet into her slippers to run and unlock the front door. We don't want him to be pounding on his own property even though no one will hear. I get dressed in the dark, taking my time. I pull on my work jeans, my work socks and my old heavy wool jumper complete with holes before I walk the corridor to the kitchen.

He's there with his arse to the range dancing a little from one wellied foot to the other and Bell is filling the kettle and asking him if he wants anything to eat. He never eats in this house, even when he can supervise us. But today is not a normal day; he agrees to a slice of wholemeal scone spread with butter and rhubarb jam. He must have decided on the way here that he'd risk being poisoned for a gawk at Kieran McCreedy.

– Are you going to stand in the doorway all day?

– No, Granda ...

– Sit down! I'm not going to bloody bite you!

Bell and me exchange looks. Neither of us are sure that he won't bite but we pull the remaining three dining chairs out, and all three of us sit down to break bread. He eats with his mouth open, every mouthful is deposited in the left-hand cheek where he works at it with his remaining back teeth while he wheezes through both mouth and nose to speak. It's an unpleasant sound but I enjoy it. A man who talks with his mouth full is a man who can choke.

– The farm needs a clean. I know the boy will come to me after he's been here.

– He said he'd go to you if he had time.

– He'll find the time. He's not going to just leave – he's a Morris. He knows as well as you do that it's a good deal!

- I, I didn't ... there wasn't much time to discuss the land ...
- No time? You had all day, you useless ...! What the hell *were* you talking about if not the land? Eh, what?
- We talked about the fact that I couldn't keep him because I had no family.

Bell can't get her fist to her mouth in time to stop the cry. A red flush is creeping up Gabriel Morris's neck and he shakes with the effort to keep his big fists pinned to his sides. He's not used to me being so reckless and none of us are used to me being in a position of power. I have the key to the success of Southfork in my hand and anyone foolish enough to rap me on the knuckles could see it flying away, out of reach over a thorny hedge. And to think, I was only kept because I had a brother. He was the only reason. I slowly cut my scone in two and spread an inch of yellow butter on it before I load it with a huge dollop of jam, enough jam to let them see again that I'm not decent.

- Rhubarb was Mammy's favourite? Do you remember?
- I remember she had a taste for anything that was bad for her!
- Yes! Yes, she did! I'm looking forward to telling my grandsons all about her! How funny she was, how she was kindness itself!

– You're skatin' on very thin ice, girl!

– Aye, but at least I'm skatin'!

Bell is crying now, the tears are dripping down her face but she makes no noise. Granda is furious, the red blotches have given way to white-hot rage. We watch each other in the many minutes of the heaviest silence I've ever sat through. I push my scone past my freaky-deaky. Granda breaks first. He likes the last word but the first word also falls naturally to him as the man of the house. He keeps them slow and steady, because he knows he's talking to idiots and he must make himself understood. Southfork had been a bit neglected since we 'moved'.

– As I said, I *know* the boy will come to me. You and her need to get the auld place into some sort of order. It's looking a bit the worse for wear.

– You need a woman's touch?

– I need a woman who knows how to dust and sweep and mop and to keep her cunt's mouth shut while she's doing it!

– We'd better get our coats on, Bell.

Bell is wearing her Marigolds. She is clinging on to the right-hand side of the linkbox and I'm clinging on to the left as we are joggled all down the bog road and back to Southfork. We are not speaking. I'd like to hit her. Hard. She ran from the kitchen and threw on her

336

work clothes and ran back to the kitchen to fill our washing-up basin with bleach, Windolene, Brasso, Mr Sheen, good cloths, rough cloths, a hunk of steel wool. Then she slipped on her Marigolds like she was a lady about to head out for a country walk. Granda Morris grunted, well pleased with his handiwork. Then the pair of them stared at me and I had little option but to rise from my chair and follow them to the tractor.

The familiar fields roll by, still washed with silver dew. It's cold and the few bits of bags and cardboard that do us as seats are damp enough to make us feel even colder. There are six fields in all to count off between the turn at the crossroads and the turning for the farmhouse. When he slows the tractor to turn left between his stupid pillars with no gate, a flock of crows rise up into the air, cawing their discontent before they settle again on the bare branches of a huge sycamore. Bell is hanging off the linkbox like a spaniel to catch her first sight of home.

Granda's assessment that the place looks a bit the worse for wear is off the mark. It looks terrible, the white paint is hardly visible behind moss, the windows are grey, and even from the street I can see a thousand spider webs trailing across them inside and out. He wants this fixed in a day? Bell bolts into the kitchen, yellow hands itching to tackle any job big or small. She would be on her hands and knees for days if it got her one step closer to being back in her old room.

She doesn't stop to think that there are only four bedrooms in total so the decreed homecoming will never mean we are going back to the bricks and mortar, oh no, there are only enough bricks and mortar to absorb a couple and three perfect little sons. Bell and me will only ever go home in the sense that we will be welcome to visit, and only then if Kieran agrees to pander to Gabriel Morris. Although I hate her today, my heart breaks. After all that we have been through, she still trusts her father. She will add it to her list of regrets, soon.

Everything is covered with mould and melancholy. Piles of *Tyrone Constitution*s and copies of the *Irish News* beige with dust and age sit here and there on the table, the chairs, the floor. Only the spot where the Big Man settles his arse every night is clear. The old couch, which has been bearing the brunt of him, sags and bags opposite the television. Pipe smoke sticks to every stitch of fabric and the only clean smell is from a bucket of apples in the pantry. The chill of the place makes me shiver. No fire is ever lit until the sun sets. Kieran will be appalled by the place if he ever agrees to come here, and I'm delighted. I don't ever want to see the two of them standing side by side. Anyway, Kieran is visiting *me* to see where *I* live, only me.

Bell, wordless, hands me a roll of bin liners and I start tipping in the old newspapers, bits of tobacco packets, and am taken aback by a stash of boiled sweet wrappers – I never knew Gabriel Morris would eat a sweet. I sling the whole lot out of the back door. The enamel sink is covered with tea stains and clogged with used leaves, I fix that and apply Bell's bleach. I go from cupboard to cupboard to fridge and back again, the rags getting blacker and blacker with every squeeze. My hands feel as if they'll never thaw, even though I'm using warm water. After two hours, the kitchen is almost passable and that's when I wonder where Bell is.

I find her upstairs. She's in her own room. The floor is swept and mopped, the rug is hanging out of the window. She is kneeling on the bare mattress, rubbing Brasso into the frame. There are holes in her shoes but more joy in her heart and face than I've seen in a long time.

– Bell, why are you bothering with up here?

– It's no bother! And every room has to have a lick! Da said so!

– Da?

– Yes, *Da*!

– You know that Kieran isn't even coming here? He's *not* coming unless he can find time and he won't find it! He has three children and a wife and a job! He's only coming for me? Don't you understand that?

– I don't want to talk about what *Kieran* wants or what *Kieran* doesn't want! I don't care if I never set eyes on him unless he really is the key to us getting out of that bloody bungalow!

I knew she'd hated Carnsore just as much as me. All those years, those squandered years for the pair of us stuck out on the borderline with only a wall of evergreens and my mother's ghost to keep us company. The weight of it, the tedium, the sheer lack of *fun* would crush us if we couldn't keep playacting that we were fine with that. That we had no choice then and no choice now and that it was all my fault. The dust dances between us, spiralling this way and that. Remember, man, that thou art dust and unto dust thou shalt return. We have wasted our lives.

From the bottom of the stairs, Granda Morris bellows out a question. He wants to know how we are doing, just how much longer it will take for *two bloody women* to clean *one bloody house*. I look at Bell, still on her knees, lips pulled into a line, the Sacred Heart only half dusted. I look at my hands, black with a decade's worth of his filth. He will not get his claws into my son, not in a million years. I'll kill him first and plant him next to Granny Tess. They could rot in tandem.

— We're just scratching the surface! Best thing you
  can do is put the kettle on!

Chapter 3

I've never had to wait for someone before. I've often wondered why Bell did it but here I am now, nose pressed against the glass of the front window. I can see practically the whole way to the crossroads, past the deep burn to the thin black line of ancient tarmac cutting through the boulders and briars and whin bushes. Kieran should be here any minute, he should be indicating that he's coming off the main road to Donegal and turning down the bog road, one of the old smuggling roads. Granny Tess herself often took possession of a setting of turkey eggs or a few pounds of tobacco in the days when the pound was much mightier than the punt and people in the Republic were glad to sell their stuff. She robbed them blind because she could.

My back aches from all the shifting and lifting yesterday and Bell is done in. She can barely walk since we scoured every inch of Southfork to reveal it for what it is, a dishevelled farmhouse in the middle of nowhere. But it was worth it – we witnessed the miracle of Gabriel Morris carrying us six mugs of tea.

When he dropped us back on the street at Carnsore we were starving and tired and unappreciated. He'd turned the tractor around the second we had jumped off the linkbox, leaving us to scrabble around in the dark to find the back door. He still didn't know if all 'his' preparations would be admired. He still didn't know if Kieran would find the time to see him. He'd advised that I *do a better job* of selling him the land but I hadn't responded – too busy scrubbing the soap scum from the bathroom sink. Kieran would find out soon enough what a tricky customer his great-grandfather was.

At last, I see a vehicle! It's a jeep of some sort and it can only be coming to this address. I wish I could shout out to Bell but she's sticking to her refusal to be bothered by the arrival of my son. I'm heartened by the butterflies in my stomach – convinced that this time I will be able to reach out to him. The jeep slows down at the stony bridge and I see him looking at Carnsore, this nasty little rectangle of bricks wedged into a corner of bog. He probably can't believe that anyone would live in such a bleak spot, but then he doesn't know we had no choice in the location of our forever home. He rolls forward and drives between the welcoming whin bushes to stop on the street. The long legs appear first then he adds the big chest and the heavy head and he's all present and correct by the time I open the door.

– Well! This is some place!
– It is, isn't it?
– You've no bother with the neighbours!
– Ha! We really don't!
– Those trees are the maddest things I've ever seen!
– We're not short of mad things around these parts, for sure!

I let him through the door ahead of me so I see it when he dips his hand in the Holy Water fount and blesses himself. This boy of mine has not given up on his God. He bashes his head on the low-hanging flowery lampshade in the hall and reaches up to steady it as Bell arrives in the kitchen doorway. She studies him as if he's a specimen in a glass jar but eventually she manages a strange little curtsy and a half-hearted 'You're welcome here' before she turns to put the kettle on. He follows on her heels because I've not warned him that we Morrises are a strange breed. He thinks he's getting a sweet old dear who's kept up with the times but he's actually sharing air with a woman who will tolerate him only because her own father has given him a thumbs-up.

He looks even bigger and wider in the confines of the kitchen as he paces up and down. Bell tuts. She does not like people who don't sit straight down, she doesn't like people who occupy space with ease and confidence, she does not like people who show up at her door empty-handed, especially people who might have known that a gift of some sort would improve their chances of being liked. She's making me nervous and I wish he would stop pacing too, but he distracts us both by being over-familiar and that Northern Irish sin of sins, being *forward*.

   – So, Bell, are you delighted you have a great-nephew?

   – *What?*

   – Me! Are you delighted I showed up? I know Lindy is, aren't you, Lindy?

Although I have had no part in rearing this boy, his shortcomings are still mine. I'm horrified with the jovial tone of voice and huge grin on his face. Has he never had any manners beaten into him? For God's sake! In Carnsore, we do *not* come right out with direct questions. In Carnsore we do not think that we are worthy of being alive. I wish he wasn't so big, I wish he wasn't so loud, I wish he wasn't so damned sure of himself, but I can't say anything other than yes, yes, yes, I'm so glad he showed up.

Bell pales at his lack of modesty and I know what she's thinking. She's thinking this boy has Babs's blood mixed with a gypsy's blood running through his veins and that's just for starters. She doesn't even know what type of horror I slept with in London. If only she had let me *talk* about him, if she'd been able to acknowledge his existence before he pulled up a chair and put his massive feet under her kitchen table, she'd look less like a walking heart attack.

Kieran is blissfully unaware that he's the cat among the pigeons. He's full of chat and doesn't really need either of us as anything more than two sets of ears. We bob heads and pour tea and offer scones as he rambles on about Derry, about his sons, about farming, about his drive down, about how set he was on meeting his real family. He picks up his mug just like Granda, by the lip because he can't get his finger into the handle. He puts it down to punctuate a change in topic or to pick up another slice of scone. This boy of mine can talk and talk and talk. An imaginary dog collar slips around his neck but I shake my head to get rid of it, the violence of the action makes them both look at me so I paste on the freaky-deaky to make them turn away again. Practice makes perfect.

Bell is flummoxed by the spitting image of Granda Morris being friendly, being noisy, handing out information that doesn't involve either of us ending up with some unpleasant job. He clears the plate and drains his cup and he stands up all of a sudden and we scuttle back. Bell still holds the teapot, I have a dishcloth twisted through my fingers, useless defences both. He doesn't seem to find this unusual and waits for us to walk back to him. He wants to have a look outside and Bell pushes me forward as his guide.

There's a freezing air today and we both shiver inside our big coats and wellies. I'm going to walk him across the front of the house and point out the view of Carn Hill before I walk him across the back street to view the magnificence of the coal shed. If I can think of anything to say I might walk him into the forest. He might like the density of the trees as they deaden the outside world and there's no birdsong. We could walk in the carpets of ancient pine needles standing a foot deep and breathe in together. We could watch the crows and rooks and the few pigeons and robins stick to the oak and syca-more trees or hunker down in the blackthorn hedgerows. Maybe then I would feel as if I have been given a second chance? Maybe I can learn how to be a mother? Maybe I'll be a nice granny to his sons?

- God! It's bitter up here! Unbearable! Shall we go in, Lindy?
- Aye! I need to talk to you about something anyway.

Bell has disappeared. She must be in her room waiting for this excruciating morning to be over. She thinks

346

she's done her time. She sat through a whole teapot of tea and didn't embarrass herself by giving in to even one biscuit. Eating would have meant she approved of him while drinking just meant she was being civil. I'm glad we have the kitchen to ourselves. I didn't want to be stuck in the front room with its glaring lack of pictures. We don't have a single snap between us, Bell and me. I keep all the random photos of Miriam's grandchildren in school uniforms, sitting on various Santa Clauses or holding up buckets and spades, in a drawer in my room. Bell keeps her freshly married parents centre stage on her dressing table and everyone else is buried in the divan. I should have been keen enough to shove my grandsons into a frame and have them already displayed on the mantelpiece but it didn't occur to me until now. I'm such an eejit.

– This is a funny little house, isn't it, Lindy?
– Yes! Yes, it is!
– Only … I know Gabriel Morris has a lot of land and the pair of you are stuck on less than half an acre?
– How did you know about the land?
– I asked around. Everyone at the mart knows him. I wouldn't be surprised if we had been standing side by side on more than one occasion.
– I suspect you might have noticed each other.
– Aye! Maybe you're right.

I don't like the fact that my son has asked around about the bloody land. I've yet to find out how the farm in Derry was divvied up when it came to him and the four siblings. There's a look in his eye that reminds me of Uncle Malachi and his boys – all hungry for a pitch of their own. There's no better way to test the water than to plunge straight in.

 – Gabriel Morris has a mind to give you his land. That might sound very strange but you're his only male heir and he's got a bit overexcited and wants you to go and have a look at the place. Of course, I told him it was a lot to ask! I told him you'd be unlikely to uproot your family and shift them all the way down there. He's an old man, very set in his ways. I'll tell him that you need time, that you need to discuss it with your wife …

 – My wife will be on the same page as me.

 – Will she? You'll have to change your name and hers and your boys – that's one of his conditions. You have to become Morrises – the whole job lot of you!

 – I already use a name that's not my own, another won't make much difference.

 – What? Are you seriously thinking about giving in to him, just like that?

 – Giving in to him? He's making me an offer! The least I can do is talk to him!

The clouds over my heart darken. I picture his wife as a quivering little mouse trying to keep herself out of harm's way. Kieran didn't say no right away. I thought we would inch closer to Granda Morris's demands over a period of weeks. Weeks when I would be able to let Kieran know that Gabriel Morris is not to be trusted, but we are already teetering on the threshold of Southfork and all that comes with it.

Granda Morris had been right all along. This boy could taste the land, the acres and acres of it if he would drop a name that wasn't his anyway. If he could just wipe out the parents who had reared him and left him a few fields in Derry. He was not the boy I wanted him to be. But he was no fool. He could see very plainly that he was the answer to a lot of prayers. He was practical, a farmer already with ambitions he didn't bother concealing – Southfork would be like winning the Lottery – he would be paid in cows and sheep and other fodder. What was the point in trying to keep them apart? They were cut from the same bolt of cloth. Cuckoo, chime, ting.

– We might as well go there now?
– Yes, we might as well, Lindy. There's no time like the present.

Kieran dips his fingers into the Holy Water fount again on his way out. He's a man set on a safe journey.

*

349

The jeep is very comfortable. It's at least as comfortable as the ambulances that have taken me up and down this uneven road for my little holidays in the Clinic. I tell Kieran as we drive past field upon field, every one of them getting greener, sheep giving way to cows which give way to grass, that this is all Morris land, and he nods and smiles, a kid in a sweetshop. He hangs his hands on the steering wheel and leans forward, all the better to devour the view. When the turn comes to the farmhouse, he giggles at the pillars set right on the tarmac. He understands instantly that not an inch of land was given up to build them and he approves. The clouds over my heart let loose their rain.

I am drifting. I am rising up out of the jeep and watching the two dark heads, my own and my son's, moving forward down the long lane and spotting the old white house. Although I didn't call, I know Granda Morris will be waiting and sure enough, as Kieran kills the engine he walks out of the kitchen door with a smile so wide it's blinding.

– Kieran!
– Granda!
– Well now! Well now! Let me have a gander at this *boy*!

They shake hands like old friends, pumping palms and holding each other's elbows but thankfully they do not hug. My mind is slipping so fast now that the sight of them cheek to cheek, a monster with two heads, might make me burst. That Kieran called him 'Granda' while I remain 'Lindy' adds salt to the wound. They both ignore me and walk straight past the house to view the land from the top of the lush valley all the way to the horizon. They'll be discussing how to squeeze even more cows on to the pasture, more lives that they can slaughter for profit.

I leave them alone and go into the kitchen to put the kettle on. I know my place. A wall of heat hits me like a furnace when I pull open the door. The range is fairly glowing – it's so stuffed with turf and logs. It's gone from damp to stifling overnight and I have to throw off my overcoat. The smell of yesterday's blitz still lingers, air freshener mixed with bleach and slave labour. The smallest drop of annoying sweat starts its journey down my back. It won't be the last.

It's so hot, the air too dry to take in without gagging. *My wife will be on the same page as me.* I hope this wife-with-no-name is a quick learner. I hope this wife-with-no-name likes violent old men and brand-new rules. I hope she's a braver mouse than I've given her credit for. I'll try to help her, try to be her friend, but mice don't last long in Southfork. There's no tolerance for thieving vermin in the house of Gabriel Morris.

*

351

The sound of laughter wafts in at the door. I cross to one of the windows I cleaned yesterday to watch them. Granda has his big hand flat against Kieran's back as he guides him this way and that, the puppet master. The backdrop is a sea of emerald green. They're delighted with each other. *At ease.* The acid burn of jealousy and anger drips down my throat and sits sourly at the top of my stomach. I wish I'd thought to bring a packet of biscuits but then I spot the bread bin. It's a rounded, wooden thing that's been in this lousy room for as long as I can remember. The lid is not sitting flat. Inside are packets and packets of buns and biscuits and bars of chocolate. More sugar than has graced that box in over fifty years of use. Granda has been shopping! He's no intention of showing how mean he is, for now.

The box never had more than half a scone of bread in it when I was small. The other half lived in a much fancier box, one that was draped with a strange home-crocheted doily with blue glass beads. That was the box that fed Granda Morris and Tess, they called it the *clean bread,* as it was never to be touched by me. *Bell! Get me a slice of clean bread!* I remember him barking at my aunt and being wide-eyed as my mother smiled and roared after her. *Aye, Bell – don't mix up the boxes or we'll all be bokin' before the rosary!* She never missed a chance to make a joke but not one of us ever laughed. The fear of him rising out of the chair and walking towards her made me shake because the first thing she always did was pull me in behind her. I hated that he would have to get through her to get to me.

I was often hungry, before and after she left. I remember the excitement of the bread man on a Wednesday afternoon when Mammy might have been able to stretch to a Wagon Wheel each and we'd lean our backs against the outside of the barn wall, stuffing the cheap chocolate and thin jam into our mouths until every crumb was gone. Then we'd lie back, well pleased with ourselves that we hadn't had to share it with anybody. My mammy wasn't a mammy who would ever tell her child off for eating what Granny Tess called 'rubbish'. Maybe that's how I would be? Maybe I would spoil my little grandsons with too many sweets? I'd have to check with the wife-with-no-name before taking such liberties, wouldn't want to blot my copybook straight out of the gates. We had to be allies. Through her, I could get to know my son.

They're still outside, still pointing at fences and at hills. When they're done pointing, they turn to face each other to talk. The profiles match, although Kieran is straighter in the back and therefore a couple of inches taller on the sod. Have they forgotten that I'm here? The kettle sings. They both turn at the sound and then have a little dance over who should walk in front of who. They both gesture with one big arm – after you,

no, after you! Granda wins, no surprise, and Kieran
sets out for the glory of Southfork with the rotten auld
bastard slavering after him.

- Sorry about that, Lindy! Granda was keen to show
  me the land!
- Great-granda ...
- What?
- He's your *great*-granda, he's *my* grandfather!
- Oh well, that's too much of a mouthful! Granda
  will do!

The man in question is scraping his wellies on the
rough bag outside the door before he starts over on
the relatively clean doormat inside. Another first for
Gabriel Morris. He usually doesn't mind carrying
great clods of *his* land inside anybody's house, especially Carnsore, where he marches across the cream
carpet as if it's a strip of bog. I step back, out of his
way and out of his reach, as he comes into the kitchen
and plonks himself down. He's all smiles and I'm waiting for the act to end so that Kieran can see for himself
that it's time we were off.

I want to get back in the jeep-ambulance and rake up
the muck on the street as he guns the engine and spins
the wheels to get us to safety. But today is not going to
go my way. Today is not going to bring what I want.
Today is all about seeing new things and hearing new
things and trying not to go completely mad.

- Lindy! It's great to see you back in this kitchen! A house is hardly a house without a woman in it, don't you think so, Kieran?
- Oh aye, it's hard to do without one, right enough!
- Ha! Begob, you're not wrong – it is hard! Are you making tea for us, Lindy? I've the bread bin full to the gunnels with all your favourites! This mother of yours has a terrible sweet tooth, Kieran! Not that you would think it to look at her, she keeps herself so neat and tidy!

They both have a hearty laugh at me and my endearing rascally ways and I'm gladder than I've ever been before that it's easy to burn yourself on a roasting hot range.

Chapter 4

Miriam O'Dwyer wants to know why I'm upset. I'm hunkered down behind the front-room door with the phone so that I don't disturb Bell any further and I'm chewing the inside of my face to stop myself from howling. Gabriel Morris has stolen my son. I've only just got him back and I've failed to keep him safe. *Again.* I need the right words. Gabriel Morris has put a hook in my son's cheek and he's reeling him in, reeling him in. I can see the flesh tearing, the blood pouring down his face, but his eyes are empty, his arms hanging limply by his sides as he glides along. Kieran isn't putting up a fight. He wants to be landed.

Miriam implores me to use different words when I've said 'I don't know' about twenty times. I try out a few phrases in my head. *The whole world's tipped upside down.* Too melodramatic. *I think I've lost my mind for good this time.* Tempting fate. *I've made a fool of my short time on this earth!* Too close to the truth. *This boy is not the boy of my dreams.* The absolute truth, which can never be told to anyone, ever. *Everything's just happened too fast.* A tolerable version of the truth that lets out no deep secrets. Cuckoo. Chime. Ting.

— Everything's just happened too fast, Miriam!

— I understand! I do, I really do! But you've got to count your blessings, Lindy! Gabriel Morris could have put you out on the street and then where would you be? It's a modern-day miracle that he's had a change of heart, surely?

— I just don't want Kieran to take anything he says for granted. I can't explain how mad yesterday was. It was like someone had stolen Granda's head and replaced it with someone who gave a shit! He called me *Lindy*! He actually said the word 'Lindy'!

— He said WHAT? What's he playing at?

— God, I suppose!

We have a little laugh because it *is* hilarious. I have been allowed my given name for the first time in fifty-two years. I am no longer 'girl'. I am no longer the wrong child. I have become indispensable and it's the one thing I'd never prepared myself for. One of my main problems is that neither has Bell. We had a shocking evening of teacakes and tantrums when Kieran dropped

357

me back home yesterday. I was already unnerved because 'the men' had left me in Southfork all alone for two hours while they took the jeep-ambulance out for a spin to view this field and that lump of granite and the many miles of good strong barbed wire that framed them.

I had wandered about, thrown by my grandfather's cheery demand to 'make yourself at home'. Not an offer I get every day. I might rob something. I might rifle through the cupboards and drawers and make a mess, I might leave the door of the range open and look away when a burning turf fell on to the rug and set the whole rancid place on fire. Instead, I nodded because it's what I do. I saw Kieran smiling at him and could practically hear him thinking what a nice old chap he was. Sweet, even. Jesus! They patted each other's backs as they walked away. I made sure the jeep-ambulance's doors were slammed shut before I punched the wall.

Miriam tells me that I'm doing alright and that she'll be down to visit tomorrow. She wants to hear all about Bell and why she's making such a fuss. *We'll close ourselves in the turf shed for a fat chat, Lindy, just like the old days!* What she *really* wants to know is what Kieran's like and if I've made any plans at all to go and visit Linus Quinn. She's probably thinking that this is *the thing* which will turn me around. This sudden glut of blood relatives will restore my faith in the world and give me a reason to live. I can stop being 'deep'. She can stop worrying about me at last. I can imagine her and her lovely mammy sighing with relief. Lindy Morris is going to make it. I force a smile on to my face so that my darling friend can hear it in my voice. I'd never bother her with the sorts of images and thoughts that flit through my head but I'll always be able to gossip with her about Bell and the auld bastard and maybe soon about Kieran.

She doesn't need to know that I found myself sitting by the hearth where Granny Tess died as they turned right between the pillars heading for Ballyglen. What would she have made of all this, the auld bitch? *She would be on the same page as her husband!* It didn't take me long to make my way up the stairs and into Mammy's and my bedroom. Bell had insisted on cleaning the bedrooms and they all looked neat and tidy. The thought of Kieran's little boys running about made me smile until I remembered that running was not allowed.

The door to Granny Tess's room fell open without a creak. Her single bed against the back wall looked strange cocooned in its pink bobbly bedspread and there wasn't a single other thing in the room. Even her Sacred Heart was gone. The pale patch above the bed had a hole instead of a nail. I stayed in the doorway. For years after she was buried, I dreamed she was behind doors – ready to slam and lock them shut as soon as I was stupid enough to step into her trap. Her mean little eyes lit up at last with something close to pleasure. I closed it again with no creak.

Granda must have guessed that I would go in to his room. His door didn't creak either. Bell had clearly gone mental with the WD-40 when she saw her chance. I have no idea what it was like when we were all still living here. It never opened unless he was in the house and when he was in the house I was hiding. Now the sight of it is more than I can take. All three walls are lined with holy pictures. So many pictures that the faded wallpaper peeling behind them is hard to spot. He has two Sacred Hearts, his and Granny Tess's, mystery solved. They are hung side by side and a stranger might think it was because he loved her but that stranger would be wrong. I can only guess that he's doubling up on the protection it is supposed to offer.

He has gaudy gold-framed scenes from the Bible: the Last Supper, the Ascension of Jesus into Heaven, St Christopher flanked by St Michael and St Francis of Assisi – hung on the wall by the man who doesn't travel, who detests sick people and sickness and who shoots cats and dogs for setting one paw on his land? He's also a man who's not fond of other trespassers. The fact that Linus Quinn 'was moved on', according to Bell, snags in my mind like a thorn.

There are four crucifixes that I can see, the biggest is directly above the bed and shows Jesus in an agony of suffering, the wounds on His hands and His side are bleeding a startlingly unrealistic red. The bed is sagging in the middle. It is covered with a brown and purple blanket that looks like it was crocheted on the Ark. It reeks of him – tobacco and wet wool, clean sweat and not-so-clean sweat. Every picture has eyes that follow you around the room. For a minute I'm transported back to my lovely little cell in the nurses' home in Putney. I wanted to be guarded by Boy George, Simon le Bon and Paul Young, all Gods in their way. I wanted smiles and kindness even if they were fake. Granda has gone straight to the top of the charts – he only has the cream of the Catholic crop to watch over him.

His shotgun is cracked open and sitting on the chest of drawers. Two brass-tipped orange cartridges sit beside it. He's ready to defend Southfork with one leap from his bed. The thick layer of dust has been disturbed above the top right-hand drawer where he's been leaning on it. I don't need to lean, I just pull out the drawer and see immediately a brown envelope.

It's a draft of his last will and testament. I knew it would be. I open it without pausing. I, Gabriel Bartholomew Morris, being of sound mind and body, blah, blah, blah. He must have nearly beaten in the door of Skelton Solicitor's on Monday morning. Father Boluwaji is his executor. Uncle Malachi can no longer be relied on and Bell and me, the bloody fucking women, have never been trusted. The residue of his estate is passed to Kieran Morris (formerly McCreedy), address to follow. It lists Southfork under its real name, 11 Mourne Road, and Carnsore is put down as 25 Green Road. He's left Kieran *everything*. Every fixture and fitting of both houses and all the land between them. Poor Bell doesn't get anything, not a single penny. I am not mentioned. He couldn't even leave us with a roof over our heads? A roof we could finally call our own?

Hatred is such a queer thing, an ember that can explode into an inferno. The heat of it travels through me from feet to head so fast that every pulse of blood burns and my eyes feel as if they're on fire. I want to tear this paper apart, tear this whole damnable house apart, but I don't. I put the envelope back in its nest and close the drawer. He need never know that I've touched his wildest dream, to finally have a *boy* to hand over to. Maybe the relief will kill him outright? Maybe it was a kindness that Patrick Joseph didn't live to bear this cross?

It was the anger still raging inside me that set off the big fight with Bell when I got home. She was in the kitchen still pretending that I hadn't had a baby or that she wanted to slap me, really slap me hard. She didn't want to talk about Kieran. She didn't want to discuss

362

what had gone on in Southfork. She didn't want to know that Gabriel Morris was masquerading as a decent person. She was only interested in when she could go *home*.

I told her it wasn't going to happen but she shook her head and got on with ironing some more clothes that she'd rooted out for the Africans. They would not be fashionable but they would be neat as pins. I tried to explain that I found it just as difficult to deal with Kieran, this boy who had walked out of my past and into our present. I needed to make her understand that he could also be a big problem in our future. But she would not listen to a woman, *any woman*, complaining about the gift of a child, even an illegitimate one. It was not a gift she had had the chance to give to herself because of me. I got a half-hour on the 'nothing and no one to call my own' tantrum with full-blown water-works and hiccups and assurances that she, *she alone*, had the right to be beside herself, not me. It was a familiar grab. She wanted to keep all the pain to herself. She slammed out of the kitchen and slammed into her own room.

I'd needed to explain what it was like sitting beside Kieran McCreedy in the jeep-ambulance when he finally came back to collect me. He was a changed man. He knew he was the key and he knew the door was Southfork. He was a man with his eye on the prize. He thought he was keeping a secret. He wasn't keeping it from me. I'd seen that look before on the Hazlewell Road when I'd had a Catholic Church at my back. He would be in charge, the captain of his own ship. My nerves were on edge and I didn't want him to hear that in my voice, so I asked him only one question.

– What do you think of the old man?

– I'd say we have an understanding.

He was gone. He was in Gabriel Morris's back pocket. He had not come for me, he had come for the land, and I knew he would do *everything* required to get it. He looked out to the right and to the left, appraising the fields at his leisure, gazing over the hedgerows like a man who had already taken possession. He didn't ask me anything. I was just a passenger.

Chapter 5

I am washing the stones on Mammy's grave. I have manned up and cleared the weeds from Patrick Joseph's head to his toes. He has become the guardian angel I've always wanted and I let him fly free so he can watch my back. Miriam is washing the stones on her grandparents' grave, which is three plots over, a bit closer to the chapel. We're on a promise for heavily buttered barmbrack and a mouthful of sherry with Father Boluwaji when we're done. It's not exactly a wild day out. When she landed on the street this morning I was still tapping at Bell's door and begging her to come out. She must have felt like me a thousand times, trapped in the corridor with a mug of tea and an overwhelming desire for company. I had to get her to come to terms with the idea that Southfork was inching further away from her, not closer.

Miriam traipsed down the corridor to give Bell another rattle but even she came back empty-handed. There was no point in gossiping or making noise if Bell wasn't around to shout at us, so we stepped out. Miriam had promised her daddy that the late Granny and Granda O'Dwyer would be spick and span before the Blessing of the Graves on the following Sunday. So off we went. I heard her call out for me and turned to see her holding a massive nettle by the roots. I answer with a thumbs-up and she goes back to her weeding. She's always happy, even if she's kneeling in the muck with a fine, cold drizzle seeping through every seam in her raincoat.

I'm also on my knees. All the white stones thrown down on top of Babs Morris to keep her in are soaking in bleach in two big buckets. I keep my eyes away from a particularly fat, purple worm as I pull up the dandelions and bits of thistles that are sprouting along the edges of the concrete surround. The dark clay sticks to my fingers and I start to shake. I need to think about her taking walks in the moonlight, not rotting in the ground. I feel her kiss me goodbye. *Don't tell anyone, Lindy!* I always promised I wouldn't and held up the sash window so that it wouldn't slam and give her away. She'd drop on to the flat roof of the pantry, light as a bird, and be away up the lane and out of the pillars, her green coat a perfect disguise. She never waved. I asked her a hundred times, why can't you stay with me and watch the silvery sky? It wasn't the same, she said, she had to go climb a mountain to get really close to it and one day, very soon, I'd be big enough to go with her. Cross her heart and hope to die.

How had she coped with losing Patrick Joseph? Did she think she had ended up with the wrong child? I look to the tiny cleared plot and squeeze my eyes shut to picture her face when she talked about him. An angel who had fallen from Heaven. She had been fine, accepting. He had been gone five years or more by then. As Bell said, such small things as lost babies weren't talked about in their day. God took back whoever He wanted.

I talk to her about my son. If she doesn't understand why I can't seem to love him no one will. I tell the patch near where her head should be that he's like Granda Morris and I can almost see her wrinkle her nose. He's ambitious, he's a grafter, he knows he's on to a good thing. He doesn't know that the bearer of the gift will try to bend him to his will. He doesn't know that he, too, will break.

His wife-with-no-name won't last more than a week in the damp, dark isolation of Southfork. She'll not know that piling the range high with turf only happens twice a year, that the bread bin is always empty, that children should be seen and not heard. I'm not sure Mammy is listening; I hear her sigh, bored by such earthly problems. She wants to be free, to be clear of the clutches of Gabriel Morris and anyone who looks remotely like him.

I change tack. I've found Linus Quinn, I tell her. Now she's interested! If only she'd found Linus Quinn that day, if only he had been on time, if only he had been in the right place. If only, if only. I have a good mind to tell him off for letting her down. When she took off it was his job to catch her. Instead, her lovely green wings had been dragged under the icy waters of the Lace Lakes. If only he had come for me? If he had been brave enough, even Granda Morris wouldn't have stopped him. I could have been with his family; I could have lived my life on the open road without a whole townland gawping at me. I could have had a child that I could keep. I could have been a version of me that I didn't want to hurt.

The drizzle keeps coming. The ground is freezing. Mammy has nothing to say. She has danced off into the trees that sway around the huge graveyard at St Bede's Chapel. To every side, hundreds of crosses stretch to the stone walls. There are some black marble Celtic crosses, higher than all the others because they mark the graves of IRA men who fought and died for Ireland. There are extravagant arches that link family graves together and tall angels where a child is buried. *Granda wouldn't stretch to a headstone. There was no point in drawing attention to another disappointment courtesy of the bloody fucking women in his life.* Of the two of us, he is the true bastard.

The simple tablet that was carved to commemorate my mother says Barbara Anne Morris, born and died on the same day, twenty-seven years apart. She would be seventy-two now and like Bell, starting to rub at painful joints and suspicious of medication. It's a small blessing to die young enough to dodge all that frailty, I think, as the corner of her green coat flaps up in the wind and she skips towards the hill.

– Lindy! Miriam! Barmbrack!

– Coming, Father!

– Coming, Father!

I tip the stones out of their buckets and quickly plaster them back into place. There now. She looks good. She's ready to be blessed in all her pure white get-up.

The front room is cosy in the Parochial House. I can't believe that it's less than a week since I've been here and that I had ripped a handful of bitchy Mrs Barr's hair out for slapping poor auld Bell. That was a beautiful moment. I like it when my rage lets me fly at someone else for a change. It was a different life – one where I felt that things might work out for me and Kieran – but now things will only work out for Kieran and Gabriel Morris. Father Boluwaji has bid us to take the weight off our feet and he didn't have to ask us twice. We sit down, delighted to be spoilt. The smell of burning sultanas reaches us with a few words of exasperation in Father Boluwaji's own language. We smile at each other when the sound of a knife scraping at a toasted slice follows.

He comes in at last with a tray piled high with warm brack and a bottle of golden sherry. We clink and glug a big spicy mouthful. I wish I could stay in this room, in this hour, for the rest of my days with these two angels at my side, but I'm not gone totally daft. I have this hour and no more. We chat of this and that, the state of St Bede's Chapel, the problems with the fleet of elderly Catholic women who demand to run it without interference. He mentions that he's been in talks with the local Protestant vicar, who's as keen as he is about getting the young people of both religions to share a youth club. I know he's keeping the talk light before he asks Miriam if she would mind leaving us and I stiffen for the blast of cold air that this change of direction will bring.

- Miriam? Could you give me and my Lady Lindy a few minutes?
- Of course, Father! I've still to hose down Granny and Pops O'Dywer anyway!

With that, she's off to tend to the dead with a selfless heart. I know why he's cleared the room. He's prepared to break a confidence for my sake. He smiles and makes a great performance of relaxed pootling before he settles down. Gabriel Morris is quite a character, he says, and that makes us both giggle. I'm tempted to tell him that I know about the last will and testament but I don't. He will find a way to let me know that I have been sold on as a job lot with Auntie Bell. The thought of her, trapped in her silent, dusty bedroom, lonely and alone, makes me beg this friend of mine for another favour.

- I need you to visit Bell. She's not coping too well with ... all this. She can't talk about it, especially not to me ...
- I'd be deeelighted to come to her this very day. I find that Confession and Communion let people speak more freely of what's troubling them?
- Thank you, Father.
- On that note, how much ... conversation have you had with Kieran?
- Not much. I'd say Gabriel Morris has taken up as much of his time as I have.
- Yes, yes. I do believe that they want the same thing. It's a blessing, I suppose, that he's taken to the boy? Although, things are moving at a pace that may not benefit everyone. Is there any way you could speak to him and ... how can I put this now ... gauge his wishes?
- I can try. He's coming down again on Sunday, this time with his family. Maybe I can try to talk to his

wife? I get the feeling that she's a gentle sort of girl, someone who could use a friend?

– Yes, yes, talk to his wife. See if you can work out how the land lies.

We both chortle again. We both know there's a good chance that the wife-with-no-name will do as she's told. We both know that if Gabriel Morris doesn't get what he wants, it'll be the first time in ninety years. We both know that Bell and me will have less value than any of the other beasts in the field when we come under the hammer. We both know how the land always lies in West Tyrone.

Father Boluwaji worked a near miracle with Bell. Miriam stayed with me in the kitchen – the two of us more nervous than if we were waiting for a litter of pigs to be born – while he knocked gently on her bedroom door. I was mortified when she didn't immediately come out and sit down with him in the front room. I imagined him hovering uneasily on the rug between her bed and the chest of drawers. He was the first man to set foot in there since Uncle Malachi and Granda had finished plastering the walls. There was nowhere for him to sit but somehow they managed.

She emerged red-eyed but calm and said she understood that I might have had a bit of a rough time of it over the years. *A bit of a rough time?* I nodded my thanks and we got straight back to pretending we were buddies. It's hard to beat an Act of Contrition, a bit of penance and a small floury disc of the Body of Christ to turn the tide. Now we are sitting at the kitchen table with Martha Kennedy and we are *discussing* Kieran's visit.

Mrs Barr and Mrs McCrossan are still in talks, mostly with each other, on whether or not they will ever hover over us like hawks again. A little sliver of hope that I'll be able to forge some sort of connection with this son of mine springs into life as I sit between my aunt and Mammy's dear friend. He's allowed to join us as a *possibility*. In my mind, the little mousy wife hops in behind him followed by the perfect bouncing baby boys, and I almost feel happy he's come home.

We're all wondering if a full meal should be prepared or if we would be alright with something that Martha has heard is all the rage – a cold collation. She can't stop saying it and Bell is feeling feisty enough to fight back against such an easy choice. She insists that a large beef stew with potatoes and an apple tart and custard for afters is the absolute bare minimum for such an occasion, although she doesn't go on to try to describe the occasion. After all, she says, sounding very snotty indeed, there are *children* to consider. I keep my face dead straight and agree with her. Children must be supplied with hot food in December. It's so typical of Bell to go from point-blank refusing to acknowledge someone's existence to setting the table for them in under a week.

The phone rings often now in Carnsore. Kieran calls every day; it's always short and to the point, but at least it's contact. I feel that he wants to love me as much as I want to love him, but neither of us has found the trick of it, yet. He has let me know his wife-with-no-name will be coming. The little boys will eat anything they're given, they're not spoilt, far from it, he's seen to it they have manners. I want to ask how the manners are administered but he's already moved on.

He's busy, there's so much to tie up. I don't like the sound of the 'tie up'. Something is ending but I don't question him. Bell and me have decided on the menu: roast chicken dinner with apple tart and cream, cream is classier than custard. We'll get ice cream for the children, though we don't want to spoil them. Martha is going to drive us to the Co-op and back and we're going to have plenty of time to scrub Carnsore from top to bottom. None of us have mentioned making Gabriel Morris welcome and that's how we leave him. Not welcome.

Chapter 6

I'm back at the window, peering down the long black strip that is the Green Road. The roast chicken dinner is going well. Bell and me had a bit of a row over the best way to roast potatoes. You'd think we would have sorted that out in the last thirty-three years, but it's probably nerves. We've never had anyone here for anything more complicated than a sandwich. The apple tarts, for there are indeed two, are sitting pretty in their foil cases waiting to be warmed up. All butter, says the pastry.

The table is set. We have napkins and glasses at every place. At the very last minute, Bell broke and allowed the use of Granny Tess's good white linen tablecloth that was strictly for special occasions. She stayed my arm when I went to put the first set of cutlery down and returned with the cloth without a word. We took a corner each and floated it on the table as if it was an altar. This could be a sign that Bell is getting over the fact that I'm a dirty cheat like my mother.

Cuckoo, chime, ting. Kieran is late but only by ten minutes, only ten. I hope he's touched by the efforts we've made. Carnsore is immaculate. We left no cushion unturned when we made at the place yesterday. Every surface is polished. Every window cleaned. Every corner emptied of cobwebs and biscuit crumbs. The one common ground we've not lost is that we don't want to shame ourselves in front of strangers. Even with all the effort it still looks what it is, a cheap bungalow filled with second-hand tat. But it's an extremely clean cheap bungalow filled with second-hand tat. Kieran is fifteen minutes late. My nose is getting cold where I have it pressed on the window. It's a vicious December day with grey clouds scudding across greyer skies. I'm not going to leave my post until I see the jeep-ambulance coming.

Bell is faffing about in the kitchen. She's had on three different dresses today already. She started out in flowers, large yellow flowers on a navy background, until she caught sight of herself in the hall mirror. The second outing was also flowers, more muted tones of beige and pink on a brown background. That only lasted ten minutes. Now she is dressed in her failsafe dress. It's a black crêpe thing that comes down over her hands and falls well below the knee. It has a long ribbon of shiny round black buttons that remind me of the dead eyes on today's teddy bears. I'm also dressed head to toe in black, so we're a bit funereal to be greeting a young wife and three small children but we'll have to do. Kieran is twenty minutes late when the phone rings.

– Hello? Is that Lindy Morris?

– Yes! Who's this?

– This is *Mrs* Collette McCreedy. We've called in to Mourne Road and auld Gabriel says he didn't know about any dinner today?

– Well, no ... no ... he's usually so busy—

– He's not going to be busy today now, is he? Not when he has *his family* on the doorstep? Maybe you could bring the dinner to us? I've just put Brian down for a nap and I don't want to be disturbing him anytime soon ...

– You want me to bring a roast dinner and two apple tarts to Southfork?

– We're not going to be calling the farm that any more. It's Mourne Road Farm now.

She signs off by telling me that Kieran will come and collect 'your aunt and yourself and the spuds' in the next ten minutes. Click. My head is banging, my heart too. I knock my forehead against the door jamb to make it stop. I don't like the 'we' in we're not going to be

377

calling Southfork that any more. Who are 'we'? The mouse has been swallowed by a terrier, a terrier bitch.

I have to tell Bell that everything we have done for my son is not good enough. We have to pack it all up – *how?* – and allow it and ourselves to be transported to Southfork again. Bell has come up behind me, I can hear her trying not to cry. So, she knows. There will be no sit-down dinner in Carnsore today. She pats me on the back and says she can't manage on her own. I'm going to have to pull myself together and give her a hand to wrap everything in tinfoil and tea towels. I nod and say of course, I just need a minute. It'll only take a minute to tear a hole big enough to get me through the next few hours.

Kieran's jeep-ambulance is very hot. Bell is pulling at the scarf round her neck as if it's attacking her. We're side by side on the back seat because the roast chicken dinner in its various pots and pans had to be secured with the seatbelt in the front. Three child seats had to be wrestled out and thrown in the boot. Kieran is not very chatty. He keeps his black eyes on the road ahead. He was more bad-tempered delivery boy than attentive newly found son when he was standing in the hall waiting for us. He didn't even find time to dab himself with Holy Water from the fount before he ushered us out. *Mrs* Collette McCreedy was waiting, it seemed, and judging by the harsh voice I heard, she wasn't a woman who would tolerate being kept waiting long.

The fields flash past and the first sign that we're close is the white smoke from the chimneys – both fires are blazing. Kieran turns between the pillars and two small boys dressed in red anoraks look up from where they're playing by the back door. My twin grandsons, Laurie and Donal. I hope the ice cream hasn't melted. I hope the apple tarts aren't squashed. I hope they like me. I hope they like Bell, even though she looks like a bloodless nun. I hope Granda Morris doesn't take a fit of roaring at them and scaring them out of their soft little skins.

I have a sudden desire to turn back time. Not too far, I've long since given up going back thirty-three years and nine months. I only need to go back two weeks and say no, absolutely no, no, no, not ever, to Father Boluwaji when he tells me it's going to be alright. I want to be facing down a lifetime of boredom at the Credit Union with mithery Siobhain and greasy Declan McIvor and the thrill of a Toffee Crisp on a Thursday. I want to go back to battling Bell and to stop hating her for having nothing and no one to call her own. I can't do this. I can't be someone's mother. I can't be someone's grand-mother. *I'm not able*. I'm not so far gone that I don't realise that things can always get worse.

Mrs Collette McCreedy is standing in the doorway. It takes the whole doorway. She has crossed her arms across her chest – two hams on the bone. Face like a family pie, Miriam would say, and she would not be wrong. I look at Kieran's face but it's still straight. Thank God, I thought the family pie comment had come out of my mouth. *Mrs* Collette McCreedy is the sturdiest mouse I've ever seen. I can still make friends with her, though. I know the type. Industrious, no-nonsense, practical, the kind of woman who would scoff at the thought of wearing a dab of lipstick. I chew the swipe of pink off my own lips, which also guarantees I won't say anything stupid for now. Bell has no such restrictions in place.

    – Is that the wife?

    – Yes, that's her!

    – Jeepers! You got your money's worth there if you were buying by the pound, boy!

He reddens but says nothing. Bell is chuckling and rubbing her eyes, and I know she's nervous too. Nervous and put out by this one-woman mountain who has made us heel.

Mrs Collette McCreedy picks up both the children as Kieran swings around to park and before he's switched off the engine Gabriel Morris is standing with his hand on *Mrs* Collette McCreedy's shoulder and with the other one he's waving at Bell and me as if he's missed us. It's going to be a long afternoon. The pots and pans have to be ferried in so we set up a human chain to get them from car seat to range without bothering with introductions. We all know who we are.

The house is warm and Kieran closes the door and stuffs the bottom of it with the meal bag to keep out the draught. They've made tea while they waited for us and the homely smell of it fills the air. Bell is burbling. She's rewriting history, talking of good times that were never that good, forgetting that it was only fear that drew us together. No one's really interested, but she tells them that it feels just like the old days, the days when her mother was still alive and always cooking up this dish or that. *God rest her soul*, says Gabriel Morris, and no one but me sees the cold eye that slides my way. The wolf at my door.

I meet my grandsons in turn, they are solemn little creatures who have been trained to hold out their hands to shake rather than to hug. They are tall for their age, strong too, perfect farmers in the making. Kieran tells them to call me Granny and they nod, although happily they don't repeat it. *Mrs* Collette McCreedy bustles about, pulling cutlery out of drawers and plates from cupboards – all of which she deposits on the bare wooden table. She has no word of greeting for us, no word of apology for us, no word of thanks. The first words I hear her speak in the substantial flesh are 'You're here and you're there'.

- You're here and you're there. Creedy, you're here between Lindy and me. Everybody set? Good. I'll dole it out.

She'd moved Granda out of his chair at the top of the table, he was shunted down the side beside Collette. Bell was at the bottom where Tess had always sat, which wouldn't be cheering her up at all. Kieran, or *Creedy* as she called him, was plonked right down in his place, the new man of the house. I sat on his right side. Collette sat on his left. I was enjoying the disbelief on Granda's face while he waited for food cooked by me to be spooned on to a plate by another bloody fucking woman and a bossy bloody fucking woman at that. Bell was getting paler and paler, the atmosphere in here was settling itself in to be exactly like the good old, bad old days, stormy with a chance of lightning.

There was not a single doubt left in my mind that Mr and Mrs McCreedy had made their decision. He'd leapt at the chance of having his own place, his own rules, and she had been guided by him. Even the tiny boys were acting as if they already owned the place as they rolled around flicking dinner at each other *unchecked*. I could see that as a couple they were more than capable of taking the auld bastard on.

They looked entirely at ease in the uncomfortable silence as they pushed fistfuls of mashed spuds past their baby teeth. Collette ate with her mouth open, eyes blank, a cow at the cud. I was glad of the two apple tarts. Her left arm knocked against Gabriel Morris when she raised her elbows high to work her knife and fork. Southfork rules dictated that meat was cut using only movements of the wrist so that no contact with another family member was made. His face puckered every time a potato fell off his fork and he had to chase it and get it to his mouth before her elbows shot up again.

At last, at last, Gabriel Morris didn't have complete and utter control over his kingdom. My shoulders dropped and a smile that I'd been waiting to feel for weeks rose through my chest on angel's wings and settled on my face. It was my mother's smile, the one she let fly when she had nothing left to lose. He sees it too, my darlin' old granpappy, and the mask slips another inch when I open my gypsy mouth to shame him again.

– So, Collette, have you thought of a new pet name for Kieran when you change yours to Morris?

Baby Brian is awake and he's sitting on my lap. The heavy, hot feel of him leaches into me. I like that he can't talk but instead coos and squeaks. I'd be enjoying this if it wasn't for the 'chat' that I had with Collette. I won't be holding him again for a while. The smile nailed on my face won't last much longer. I am longing for the ride home in the jeep-ambulance. Bell can't stop herself from staring at Gabriel Morris as he giggles and tickles the two other little boys. Her face is bleached out. I need to get her back to Carnsore before she starts crying and spoiling the party. This afternoon has shown her that there's no room for her in Southfork. Southfork is gone, replaced by Mourne Road Farm. Her bed will be made up for one of the new Morrises.

We'd all slogged through the chicken dinner and the best part of two apple tarts and were feeling a bit sick and tired when Collette ordered 'the men and Bell' out of the kitchen and into the front room while me and her 'cleared away'. *Lindy will clear away, won't you, Lindy?* She'd told me off for scraping the chicken bones into the bin. She, *herself*, never wasted food. She, *herself*, would have used them for soup. I apologised for disposing of my own meal in the wrong way. Granda Morris had smirked, glad that I was being slapped down now that he couldn't do it in person.

Collette tells Kieran to bring the twins and he picks them up and carries them away without a glance. I've heard less from him today than I've ever heard. He seems changed because of her, the anti-mouse, but not unhappy. There's not a lot of warmth between them but they seem satisfied to survive on common sense. I imagine him shooting rabbits and her skinning and gutting them with all the concentration of a cavewoman. They both get to eat and that's all that matters. She, *herself*, would fashion a warm hat and gloves out of the pelt, although it might take quite a few rabbits. I was wrong to make fun of her even in my mind. She was not someone to take lightly.

As she stood beside me at the sink, one great arm rubbing against mine as she washed and I dried, she had that lesson to teach me. Don't ever let your guard down. Don't ever forget that appearances are deceptive. Don't dream that things will work out for the best. She was quite the speech-maker, this cavewoman. Cool as you please, she let me know that I wouldn't ever have to be a granny.

– The thing is, Lindy, me and Creedy have found ourselves disagreeing over a few ... aspects of moving to Ballyglen. He thinks it would be great to involve you in the boys' lives. He's convinced you'd be a help while we pull this place into some kind of order. But me, *myself*, I wouldn't feel comfortable letting them near someone who gave up her own child. I wouldn't be able to trust a woman, any *woman*, who could do that. You understand? You were all wrong as a mammy.

The sound of Bell, Kieran and Gabriel Morris all laughing at the noise of the small boys comes from next door. There will be no storms today. I nod and nod, it's what I do. I understand. It's not as if I can be trusted.

Chapter 7

Kieran has asked us if we want to come for Christmas dinner. Thank God it was on the phone so he couldn't see the look of horror on my face. I managed to say no, no, Bell and me are fine up here by ourselves. You settle in, I say. This last piece of advice is hardly necessary. They moved in four days after the chicken dinner and apple tarts. It was Miriam who told me; she'd heard it from her father who'd heard the news doing the rounds in The Forge Inn that Collette and him have already made quite an impression on the few people they've met in Ballyglen. He's already known as a chip off the old block, she's just known as a block.

He didn't grace me with a warning. He'd gone home to Omagh and finished packing. He'd packed his jeep-ambulance full of boxes four times over and done the tedious journey to Mourne Road Farm four times over to unload. The old place filled up with cots, plastic toys, tacky china and ornaments, bags of clothes and an enormous television set. There were several vases full of large silk flowers that Collette was very proud of. She, *herself*, loved them. So much nicer than real flowers, as they were no bother at all even though they harboured dust. He had called me on the second day. He was en route to collect me, just me, Bell was not required. He had a surprise for me, he said.

It was as well that Bell was not required. She had fallen into a walking coma. Her eyes were dead as she wandered from room to room, from cup of breakfast tea to bedtime cocoa with hardly a word. I begged her to watch rubbish TV, I'd even sit through quiz shows with her if she wanted. I read out what the papers had to say about the poor finalists from talent shows, every bit of dirt that had been found and dragged out. She just shook her head because she wanted to do another rosary. She left every room I followed her into.

The surprise that Kieran had for me was *not* that he had moved in, lock, stock and barrel. I was expected to absorb this reality by osmosis. It wasn't that his wife had zero taste. It wasn't even that Gabriel Morris had finally flipped and started kicking furniture as a warm-up to throwing it. No, it was that he had strung a set of coloured lights through the branches of the big sycamore closest to the house instead of having a Christmas tree inside. It reminded me of walking by the Thames the very night I had fallen pregnant. I thought it was a bit stingy, even Bell and me stretched to a Christmas tree, every year except this year. We'd had one too many distractions to focus on glass baubles. We all stood at the kitchen window, me, the children, the anti-mouse, the auld bastard and my son, as the snake of red, orange and yellow bulbs rippled in the breeze.

I'd be surprised if they survived to see in the New Year. The winds that threw themselves down the valley to this farmhouse could knock you off your feet. He'd learn that now that he lived here. Very festive, I said and he smiled.

I was allowed to stay while the kettle was boiled and the water poured over fresh leaves. Wee Brian was napping. Laurie and Donal ran off into the living room where a brand-new fireguard kept them away from the blazing turf. Collette's big back was all I had left to keep me company as Granda and Kieran had to go and see to the beasts that were now in the barn at the back for the winter. They had to be fed and watered and the yellow light poured out across the yard when one or other of them pulled the door open. Evidently, they worked well together.

Collette broke eggs into a pan, which spat oil. I watched her add another thick slice of Cookeen to make sure they didn't stick. The little boys were getting fried eggs on toast for their tea. She didn't ask me to join them.

– Do you think you'll be happy here, Collette?

– Happy? I don't see why not.

– It's a big place. It'll take a lot of hard work …

– It's not hard work when it's *your own place*.

God, I hated her, the giant smug cuckoo. I didn't want to know which room she was sleeping in. I didn't want to imagine her turning and turning to get herself comfortable in me and Mammy's bed or in Bell's bed. I didn't want to imagine her lying under my son. I didn't want to think of her thumping down the corridor, raising the dust. I imagined her getting her arse stuck in the narrow bath and being stuck in there for years.

My time tolerating her came in thirty-minute slots. They might well have had a conversation about that *aspect* of living here? Mr and *Mrs* McCreedy, *herself*, might have decided that twenty minutes in the jeep-ambulance plus thirty minutes in the kitchen plus another twenty minutes back to Carnsore added up to plenty of time for me to spend with my new relatives. I must get to Linus Quinn before too much longer. I hope he finds me more interesting.

I finished my tea. Collette had barged around the room for most of my time without wasting a word. She folded clothes and made them into piles. She felt whether or not they were dry to the touch by pressing them against her

389

cheek. She assembled a pile of not-dry-enough items and spread them out on the rack above the range. Such a weird sight to see in Southfork. Rows of blue and white babygrows hanging there like bunting. If someone had asked me what the last thing on this earth I would see was I couldn't have come up with it. We would never find an inch of common ground, this cuckoo and me. For one thing, she'd be able to block most furniture flying through the air with just one of those forearms at a time.

Cuckoo. Chime. Ting. I must rip the cuckoo clock off the wall and bury it when the first thaw comes. I'm over cuckoos. It's Christmas Day. Bell and me got taken to midnight Mass last night by Martha. The outing did Bell the world of good. She loves seeing the big statues of Mary and Joseph and the Three Wise Men all standing around the hay-filled crib of the pure blond, blue-eyed baby Jesus. Poor Mary has lost a goodly chunk of her plaster nose since last year – the road to Bethlehem must be getting rougher. The stable was decked with holly and ropes of golden tinsel. Father Boluwaji came down off the altar and shook hands with every single good Catholic, sober or not, as they stumbled out after the blessing. He had a big bowl of sweets for the children, tubes of Parma Violets and Love Hearts.

He asked us to come in to the Parochial House for a mince pie and sherry and we did, despite the hour. Bell was reviving. She was pleased enough with her special treatment to remark that she'd tell Bitchy Mrs Barr and the muck-spreader Mrs McCrossan about it the first chance she got. We had hooked arms to get across the icy path as Martha tooted the horn and left us alone again at the end of the line. The evergreens loomed above the roofline of Carnsore. Above their reeling heads, a vast black sky studded with stars guaranteed a bitingly cold night and an even colder Christmas Day. It was *hours* before it would be over for another year.

Bell is in the kitchen stuffing an unfortunate chicken with pork mincemeat from an unfortunate pig so that we can celebrate Jesus's birthday. We make much more fuss of Him than we ever do for each other. My birthday is not judged to be worthy of remembering and Bell's birthday has been rather coloured by the fact that it's the anniversary of her twin sister's death. No point in baking a cake for *that*. I will be called in from the peace of the living room any minute to help peel the spuds and the carrots and tip the marrowfat peas out of their steeping water and into the saucepan. Bell and me might have a little chat. We might pull crackers and throw away the stupid paper hats. We might reflect on how altered our lives are since the last time we had a party for Jesus. Or we might not.

The loss of Southfork has hit her hard and the worm of worry that Carnsore could be occupied by Collette the Cuckoo has worked itself inside my head. I wish it hadn't. I have quite enough inside my head to contend with without picturing Bell being carted off to one of the housing estates at the bottom of Ballyglen. She'd hate being cooped up with other people in a pebble-dash box. One of the things she's always hated about Carnsore is the vertical cliff of evergreens at its back. There's no view, she used to cry, no view. There is a view to the front, a long thin strip of dark tarmac disappearing through the brown and grey rocks, she just didn't want to have to step out to have a 360-degree panorama. In the first few years here I felt as if I'd stolen the whole sky from her and every inch of the light.

Her current sadness is that we're not in the same boat any more. We are not *HMS Spinster Central*. She didn't mind when neither of us got what we wanted, but now she has to die with the knowledge that when I die not all of me has been wiped out. I've conjured the chance to have a life beyond myself out of pure badness. Whether I like it or not, I now have a son and three grandsons. I do not like it.

This son of mine has only been around for three weeks and in that tiny space of time he's somehow scattered the last few pieces of a jigsaw that I'd been using to make a picture of my life. Miriam is furious. Indecent haste, she shouts when I tell her that Mourne Road Farm is under new management. She also knows that

Collette doesn't need or want my friendship. She, *herself*, is totally fine without a mother-in-law hovering about the kitchen. She's always busy, too busy to entertain me. She does not need any help with anything so I can stop asking. Kieran tells me that I don't need to try so hard. The thing is his wife is a very independent sort of woman. It's one of the reasons he picked her from the herd, she's low-maintenance. I mustn't go getting notions that I'm not welcome, though. They'll have the old place in shape soon then I can come over. I can even bring Bell if she fancies a change of scenery.

I haven't been back near the Credit Union. I'm not able. I can't face anyone. Siobhain had sent my bath cubes, same ones as last year, in the post. Greasy Declan McIvor sent a card, which was very nice of him. Merry Christmas and a Happy New Year. He says I'm missed. Not that *he* misses me or that *Siobhain* misses me or any of the other ones shuffling papers for no reason. I'm missed, like a chair whipped away too soon when someone needed to sit down. I'll get a box of Roses in the January sales and drop it in. The awful job will be kept open for me and I'll try to go back when my hands don't shake so much.

I got Kieran to come and collect a pile of presents that I wrapped up for them. I bought clothes and selection boxes in the shape of Christmas stockings for the little boys. For my son, I wrapped up a warm wool scarf. It was *exactly* the same Bananarama primrose yellow of the dungarees I wore when I carried him under my heart. For my grandfather, I sent a pot of home-made rhubarb jam. He hates cloves, so I put in an extra handful. For her, the low-maintenance wife, I sent a pair of huge grizzly bear bedroom slippers and my only dream going into 2019 was to catch her wearing them. I didn't check what size she was, I just needed them to have 'large' stamped on the sole. Kieran had declared me 'too kind' as he chucked them on the back seat and drove off leaving me empty-handed. I'd watched the tail lights all the way to the end of the road, even though the wind was cutting through me.

Maybe I should have said yes to Christmas dinner. His first Christmas in his new home with the children that finally let him feel like life had started for him. It's hard to tell if he's annoyed or not, but on balance it's worth it to have him annoyed. He's promised he'll be in touch on Boxing Day. I could not have sat through a dried-out turkey-and-ham combo while Gabriel Morris ho-ho-ho-ed his lousy head off. Kieran told me that 'Granda' was dressing up in a Santa suit all the better to play with Laurie and Donal and wee Brian with a straight face that I couldn't match.

I remember being in the Clinic with my 'nerves' one time and one of the other customers had bowled through the ward in a very agitated state. There's a flying saucer on the roof! he'd roared. A massive flying saucer! Can't you feel it? We're all going to be ate! We'd all looked up at the ceiling to make sure there were no cracks and to not make him feel worse. That's how I've felt since Kieran came home, like there's a flying saucer hovering just above my head and if I look up to check, all the little green men will swarm out to gobble up what's left of my brain.

– Lindy? I've washed the spuds but that's as far as I'm going!
– Coming, Bell!

The homely smell of fried onions, sage and thyme is grounding. I made a Christmas pudding in November, a month before life took a strange turn, it's steaming in the big pan we usually reserve for jam making. I will peel the spuds, Bell will cut up the carrots. Whoever finishes first gets to see to the Brussels sprouts. We will watch the TV while everything is boiled to ruination. I'll spoon the vegetables out on to the plates while Bell cuts up the meat. We'll clink glasses and tell each other it's the best dinner we've ever made. We're keeping it pleasant, neutral, only the old stories which won't offend or wound are wheeled out for another spin.

When we're stuffed to busting we'll declare an hour's break before we have a big bowl of pudding with cream and custard. I'll be nursing a swollen belly of excess while my grandsons play on the same floor that both Bell and I played on, Babs too. But we're not there today because I couldn't stand to spend a whole day with my son and the unpleasant lump he calls his wife or the rotten auld bastard who he calls Granda. It would be entirely alien even without the flying saucer on the roof.

By the time we're settled back in the living room to watch the dreadful Christmas Day garbage on TV, the sky is a dark purple blanket burned to black when the clouds scud in front of the moon. Bell is peeling the foil from the Green Triangles from the box of Quality Street and smoothing them against her thigh ready to fold. She wants this day to end without incident just as much as I do. We miss our dull lives. The theme music for one of the Indiana Jones films reaches us, familiar as a psalm; there'll be no more need of talk until bedtime. Happy birthday, Jesus.

Boxing Day dawns bright and cold. A fierce silvery sky shimmers from the evergreens to the horizon. Tonight will be bitter. The wind that marked yesterday has died down and we all stand still, me, the chickens and the forest. It's too calm. I check the kitchen window to make sure Bell isn't watching before I pick up the poor auld hollowed-out stone from under the tap to kiss it better. A little disc of ice has formed overnight and I scoop it out. It's about the size of a 50-pence piece and it melts away in a second. Such an ordinary day apart from the fact that a thought has been clattering through my head from the minute it touched the pillow: Kieran is not mine, Kieran is not mine, Kieran is not mine, Kieran is not mine. I want him to be mine but he's not. He's not the child of my dreams. He's not all perfect white teeth and dimples. He doesn't make me feel safe or happy. He's not proof that I did the right thing, that I suffered for good reason.

He's caught between the jaws of Gabriel Morris and Collette. I can't use the word 'deserve' but I can't think of another word. I deserved to be told that he would take everything on offer without considering what I wanted. I might not want to share a small town like Ballyglen with my illegitimate son, for example. I might not want to feel sick every time the phone goes in case it's my allotted thirty minutes. I might not want to have to tell Bell that Collette, *herself*, needs this shitty bungalow for one of her own wans, though they might have a job getting up and down the narrow corridor.

Miriam calls down for an hour in the afternoon. She has three small children with her – her beloved grandchildren – the first time she has ever entered this house with a child of any description. I no longer have to be shielded from the delight of having children in my life. They are decked out in reds and greens and it does cheer Bell and me to watch them whirl around the yard. They play tag to give themselves a reason to run and run. The phone doesn't ring.

When we've waved them off we decide we're going to binge the last of the Christmas pudding and we'll have a glass of brandy too. We're getting back to being Bell and me. I carry in three baskets of turf and set the fire. In minutes the whole living room is glowing and we kick back to enjoy the heat. We're going to survive all this, Bell and me. She feels it too. She sniffs and wipes her eyes and we egg each other on to have another glug of brandy.

I've just heaved myself off the couch to go and fetch the box of Quality Street when I hear a noise. It sounds like a car door. Miriam must have forgotten something. It's only 4 p.m. but it's dark already so I flick on the outside light. It's Kieran! He didn't phone but he didn't forget. The big shape of him wavers behind the glass door and I cross the cream carpet to let him in. If it was the Devil himself complete with horns and a tail I couldn't be more taken aback. It's Gabriel Morris and he's not alone. Beside him sits a single suitcase. He's carrying his wellingtons in one hand and the other one is resting inside his greatcoat just about where his heart should be. What on God's earth does he want at this hour?

– Who is it? Lindy? Who is it?

– It's Granda ...

– Da? What does he want?

She joins me in the hall to peer out at him where he stands on the doorstep. All the heat's escaping and the freezing air wraps itself around our ankles. He steps in and closes the door behind him. Six big mucky prints on the ill-advised cream carpet see him into the kitchen and I know Bell's as scared as I am that we've left the bottle of brandy in there. He doesn't approve of bloody fucking women drinking, we might forget ourselves, forget our place. She motions for me to go ahead of her and tucks herself behind me as if we were going on a boar hunt.

He's standing with his back to the range and with the sheer efficiency of the fluorescent light we can see he's had better days. The big square face is white all bar the grey shadows under his eyes. He's got on his Sunday best but he's not been to a pub, not today. He's sober, which is one sort of blessing. Bell nudges me forward until we are all three standing in the kitchen. There's a smell coming off him, something sour. He won't stoop to explaining himself so I'll have to go first and suffer the consequences.

- What are you doing here?
- This is my house. I don't need to give *you* a reason to stand in it, do I?
- No ... no ... That's not what I meant. I mean why now? Why are you here *now*?
- I'm to live here.

I feel Bell slump against me. Her legs have given out and I hate her for beating me to it. Now I have to keep us both upright. A thousand thoughts clatter through my brain and not one of them makes any sense. How did Gabriel Morris, the Big Man of Ballyglen and all-round auld fucker, let himself be put out on the street? And to end up here with Bell and me? In this shitty bungalow? But I can see what has happened. He's shrunk. He's smaller because my son has cut him down and I can't even enjoy it because I have to live with yet another of his snap decisions. We're all running out of enough spit to swallow this. Cuckoo, chime, ting. I pour out three large brandies and hand them round. There's only one toast I can think of.

– Times have changed, I say. Times have changed.

I can hear Bell. She's crying. I'd like to cry too but I lost the knack of it forever ago. Gabriel Morris has a bedroom that shares a wall with mine. It's the closest he's ever been and I don't want to remind him that I'm still alive. When we'd downed our brandy he had barked at us to get out of his sight and we'd both run to our respective dens. That was four hours ago and it's still only eight o'clock. He'd taken possession of one of the front bedrooms about an hour after that. The dull thud must have been the suitcase hitting the wall. He's pacing around the box he built.

What has gone on at Mourne Road Farm? How has he come to leave there? He didn't even come in his tractor, so how will he go back tomorrow? Kieran dropped him off, an unwanted pet. Is he going back? I need to get to the phone. The television is still on in the living room, the noise of it should cover my footsteps down the corridor but not the sound of my voice as I ask my son – *what have you done?* There's a danger that Collette will pick up and she may not feel inclined to give me any information. She could cite the fact that I've risked waking all three of her perfect sons. It's what she would expect of a woman like me. A woman who can't be trusted. But there will be no sleep for any of the happy campers in this house tonight unless I find out. Is this just an overnight stay or do Bell and me have to suffer the rotten auld bastard for life?

The thought that he could hurt me at any moment makes me brave. If there's pain to be had it's always better to have it up front. I turn the door handle and step out. If I was in the wilds of Africa and staring down a hungry lion, I couldn't feel any more scared. One step, two steps past the door that's holding him in, and I'm back in the living room. The fire has died. There's two empty glasses and two empty bowls – the only evidence that Bell and me had a few moments of enjoyment today.

I register that I'm very thirsty and that I'm not alone in the same second. He's in the doorway. All the pacing has not worn him down to a dull rage, it's still burning brightly. I wonder if he'd agree to more brandy before I remember that I'm not allowed to speak first. What words will come have to come from him and so we both wait. The evergreens creak and sway towards us before they creak and sway back sharpish, too afraid to hear what's coming next. It's a rough night.

— What're you doing up? Answer me, bitch!

— I needed some water.

— Don't even think of touching that phone, d'ye hear me?

— I won't touch the phone.

— When I tell you and that other bitch to get to your beds, I mean get to them and stay there. I don't want either of you wandering about like you own the place! This is my house and from now on, it's my rules.

— Your house, your rules. Times have changed.

We both smile, a first. It won't be long before we get to the fact that it was me who brought a thief to his door. He won't care that he begged him to come in. The dodgy DNA of Linus Quinn will leap into the spotlight. No one will, it seems, ever ask if Kieran McCreedy had a father of his own. I'd be delighted to wheel out my Catholic priest to see if he'd outweigh a traveller. No matter. I'll still have to pay in a variety of ways. Cuckoo. Chime. Ting.

Chapter 8

Kieran walks in on our family scene the next morning. Adopting a Carnsore tradition for Morris men, he doesn't even knock this time. This has become *his* place. We are all three hollow-eyed at the kitchen table, trying to drink tea without slurping and to chew toast quietly enough to not make Granda Morris hit the table with the palm of his hand so hard that the salt cellar jumps. My son doesn't bother with the Holy Water fount now, he's blessed enough. But today he looks wretched and he wants a word. With me. I can think of several, all inappropriate, but instead I nod and pull on my coat so that we can talk outside. My grandfather doesn't even look up from his breakfast and Bell takes her chance to lock herself in the bathroom. This time we make it past the cliff face of the forest and into the dense scent of the pine.

Kieran starts out by musing on the fact that having Gabriel Morris as a lodger won't be easy for us. But the thing was, Collette had caught him kicking wee Brian's cot. The baby had been crying, probably hungry or put out by his new bedroom, and when his wife went to check that's when she discovered that Gabriel Morris couldn't really be trusted. The thing was – why was there always a *thing*? – she was very protective of the boys, so either he had to leave or Collette was going to pack up that instant and move her precious cargo back to Omagh. He didn't need to tell me that she'd go without him if she had to. The big shoulders would have shrugged, the huge feet in bear slippers would be rammed under the table as she reached for the bread bin. I might as well have been in the room. Collette liked to rule.

I wanted to shake him. If he had ever so much as asked me once I could have told him all about Gabriel Morris and his fabulous parenting record but Kieran hadn't asked. Kieran didn't seek advice, he didn't check facts, he just packed his bags and clutched at the first straw he was offered. His father's ambition to be top of the pile ran in his veins. He would be the captain of his own ship no matter the cost. His inability to resist the power it would afford him made me feel queasy. I had to say something to make him give Gabriel Morris another chance. Bell and me could not survive living

with him. He was an ornery bull that would be crashing around making our lives a misery.

– Why didn't you speak to me about any of this,
   Kieran?

– There was no need to speak about any of it. It's a
   good deal for Collette and me – we just can't have
   him behaving like that around the children.

– *You* can't have him? What about *us*? Bell and me?
   The bungalow is the only semblance of peace we've
   ever know! You have to take him back.

– I can't! I promised Collette that I wouldn't buckle
   when you and your aunt played up.

– *Played up?* We're not talking about being pissed
   off here, we're talking about being in danger! It's
   not just babies he lashes out at, y'know? We're not
   safe now!

My son is in a pickle. He runs his hands through his
thick dark hair just like his father did when he found
out that he could lose a whole church for the sake of
one stupid mistake. He is battling with all the scenarios
running through his head, but I know him better than
he knows himself. He'll only ever choose the land. He's
torn but not torn enough to bleed for anyone but himself. Then I see his face twist and he turns away from
me double-quick time. I am not pleasing him. The
memory of how heavy he was as I lugged him, screaming, from room to room at the Loreto, settles on my

chest. I had wanted so desperately to comfort him but I never could. This time I have to try harder.

– Kieran, is this what you want? Truly?

– I owe Collette ... I owe her ... Oh God!

– Why do you owe her? Why? What's wrong?

– A few months ago there was a girl. She was in the Omagh Players and she loved it, just like me ... and anyway, things got out of hand and it got back to Collette, who was stuck at home expecting wee Brian at the time ... and ...

I wanted to ask about the other girl but now was not the time. Even if he had loved her, he had given her up. All I could think of was the timing – 'a few months ago' was when he started to think about me, but it wasn't me who could feather a new nest for him, it was Gabriel Morris. He'd had my name for two years but hadn't acted on it until he ran out of options. The last flicker of hope that he's sought me out because he'd wanted to meet his mother died. He was mine, flaws and all. I didn't deserve any better.

I watch this son of mine struggle to find the words to tell me he's stuck, literally, over a barrel. That barrel is Mrs Collette McCreedy, herself. I could imagine that face hearing the news that he'd nearly skipped away with a slip of a girl who shared his passions. I could imagine she held up the twins in front of her still-rounded belly and threatened him with the thing he feared most: losing his boys. Until they were born, he'd had no kin of his own, he says. He wouldn't cope with seeing them just at weekends, even if Mrs Collette McCreedy had been so kind as to allow him that much. She'd suggested Mourne Road Farm as the only solution. They both needed to be free of Omagh, free of his silly love for acting and free of any knowing looks that she might have to suffer when she was wheeling *his* three waynes around.

— Please try to understand, Lindy – I didn't want any of this to happen the way it did. I wanted to meet you before all this but Collette wasn't keen. And then I got myself into trouble and … and … God, I'm so sorry!

— It's okay—

— It's not okay! Collette's delighted to be shot of him! He was the only real fly in the ointment, as far she's concerned, when you and Bell already had a house of your own!

I link arms with him and he lets me. We head deeper into the forest, both of us quiet for now. The endless trunks groan. The wind is getting up. The soft shush of the water dripping down from the moss that runs in small hills over the roots of the trees is soothing in its way. My mother had run through this same forest on the way to her death, setting in train a life for me that she would have hated. A life with Bell and Tess and

Gabriel that has left me standing out in the cold for as far back as I can remember. I step up on to a broken branch and pull my boy into my arms and he lets me. He isn't the first Morris to get himself in trouble.

– We can sort this out, Kieran. Between us we can sort everything out.

– Do you really think so, Lindy?

– I know so. I know so.

When he left me in the forest we were about halfway through. He weaved between the lichen-furred branches back to Mourne Road Farm, head low. The weather was turning nasty and he battled through it. As I watched, he pulled out the primrose yellow scarf I'd given him and tucked it around his neck. I had quieted him some more, telling him that every life had bad patches, and he'd looked like a much younger man as he nodded and nodded, happy that, at last, he had someone on his side. I was standing in Donegal. I could go back but I couldn't even think the word 'home'. Bell would be out of her mind with worry and fear now that she was trapped alone with her precious 'Da'. I felt the pull of her but instead I turned my feet away. My father, my flesh and blood too, was a good stiff walk away. I'd make it there in a couple of hours. I'd been to Dunalla before. It was a crossroads with a few buildings hugging tight to the four corners. A couple of pubs, a

Parochial Hall, a chapel, a huge feeds factory where everybody worked. Linus Quinn would not be hard to find. I needed to find him this very day.

The forest got boggier and boggier but I pulled every foot up and out of the muck until I got to the other side, where a road ran through it. When I'd walked the length of it, I came to a gate to the main road. Every step in the Republic made me lighter. I was breezing along, lungs pumping; Bell started to fade, him too, the auld bastard. I'd told Kieran to tell them I'd walk to Miriam's to clear my head. Not that either of them would ask. My welfare wasn't exactly on the top of any pile of concerns. He had nodded. He had to get himself back to Mrs Collette McCreedy. He didn't say, but I'd a notion she kept a close eye on the clock when he was out of sight. *There was a girl ...* how many thousands of stories had started with that line?

The rain came, soft at first, but a heavy shower soaked me to the bones before I made it to the crossroads. Dunalla was darkening as I got there. I was determined to get to him before one more hour was lost to me but there was a storm brewing. It was likely roiling over the Blue Stack Mountains even now, gathering speed. There was hardly a light in any window and the feeds factory was shut for the holidays. The bell of a corner shop tinkled and I turned towards it. The owners had a display of buckets and spades outside in too many shades of bright pink and green. The rain plinked and plonked into them, the only purpose they'd ever likely serve. A raft of plastic pinwheels spun themselves into a blur.

I walked past the newspapers framed in tinsel, where a smell of turkey and stuffing still hung in the air. The man must have seen me sniffing, we live above, he said, by way of explanation. He knew Linus Quinn and was even bold enough to make a joke about the fact that he was being 'kept' in a caravan. I laughed too. All I had to do was follow the road up past the chapel; I couldn't miss the house, the caravan was parked right outside it, the doors nearly matched up so he had a short distance to travel when the widow woman was in the mood for love. The caravan is red, said the man. The brightest, most showy red I could ever imagine, the paint so thick it looks wet, it sticks out like a sore thumb, it's *beyond* gaudy.

He wasn't wrong. The little long house with its now slate roof was dwarfed by the outrageous thing. It was cutting out every ray of natural light on its high white wheels with his and her desire to maintain respectability. I knocked the door and every heavily decorated window, nothing. No one was home so I tried the door on the cottage and the widow woman wrenched it open as if she'd been waiting to be annoyed.

– What d'ye want?

- I'm looking for Linus Quinn?
- He's not in. What d'ye want wi' him?
- I just need to speak to him about something ...
- Oh, is that so? You need to speak to him about something. Well, let me tell you, Missy, you're not the first blue-eyed bastard to show up on my doorstep and you're unlikely to be the last! But if you still want to speak to him about *something*, try The Lantern – that's where he makes his best speeches!

The half-door slammed fast in my face before I could thank her for her hospitality and understanding. She was not what I'd expected in a widow woman, her hair was a startling pink instead of grey, for a start. She smelled like forty fags a day. She was well and truly over having *another* blue-eyed bastard on her doorstep? How would I ever find the rest of them? Granny Tess would be so happy for me. She'd been right all along. I'd only another few nervous steps to close the distance between me and him.

The Lantern is small and seems to be lit by a score of different lamps, each fitted with a weak yellow bulb. The carpets are sticky with beer and a few bits of tinsel billowed in the heat from a turf fire. I'd not set foot inside a pub since leaving London. The Railway Tavern in Putney and The Polar Bear in Leicester Square had both been full of life, but The Lantern has a dejected air that probably hung around long before and long after the festive season.

Two men sit together at the far end of the bar and one man sits with his back to me, his long black hair now streaked with silver. *This man's your daddy.* I sit down beside him. His wrists are bare, the thread bangles long put aside for wrinkles and alarming ropes of vein. He's as thin as a penny whistle. He doesn't much care that he's got company. I wait for him to take another three good swallows of his beer before I interrupt his life.

– You might not remember me, I'm Babs Morris's girl?

– Ha! I wondered if I'd ever see you again! What brings you here now?

– I'm not sure! Maybe because it's Christmas?

– Aye, well, it is Christmas right enough …

I remember the absolute punch I felt in my guts when Father Boluwaji told me I'd been tracked down by Kieran, but this man sighs heavily and carries on sitting beside a child he hasn't seen in over forty years as if it's just one of those things. This man is sustained by alcohol. His blue eyes, my eyes, are swimming in a watery red reservoir that's been years in the making. With that he beckons over the barman who's appeared and orders himself another pint of protection and then he asks me what I want. I get a whiskey and we go on sitting beside each other in silence.

Reunions are not what they're cracked up to be. I had decades-long visions of running back to London and finding Kieran's hand in mine again. It was going to be perfect, we would be back together on good terms. I would find the words to describe the numbing loneliness that led me to give him up. He would understand, he would forgive and we'd live happily ever after on opposite sides of the Irish Sea. He would be English and polite and I would be allowed the freedom of keeping my secret. And today, today, this father of mine would leap out of his chair – or off his barstool – and maybe wrap his arms around me with gratitude that I'd sought him out. We'd talk about Mammy and how much he loved her, and maybe he would even remember that he should have loved me too. He'd never even known about Patrick Joseph but he wasn't short of blue-eyed bastards so the loss wasn't worth mentioning.

One of the men at the end of the bar blows his nose noisily into a handkerchief and I immediately feel sorry for the woman who has to wash it. It was one of my hated jobs, boiling Granda Morris's snot rags and ironing them dry. I always kept my face away from the steam in case a tiny drop of him remained. I want to get out of this pub and go back to Carnsore and crawl into my bed, but I can't crawl past Gabriel Morris, not even one more time on this side of Hell.

- Do you remember my mother? Do you remember Babs?
- I do! She was a wild one! It was terrible what happened to her but no real surprise ...
- What do you mean? The only surprise is that you weren't there to meet her! Why did you let her down? How could you let her down? When you knew she was desperate to get away from that auld bastard Gabriel Morris?
- You've got it wrong, girl! It wasn't me she was heading for! She was set to meet up with a man called Vincent Murray – he'd been engaged to her sister but your mother stuck her oar in. The chat was Babs was in the family way again and her and Vincent Murray were going to run off, but he let them both down by buying a one-way ticket to America. People said at the time that she put herself into the water instead of going home ...
- No! No! She wouldn't do that! I was at home! I was waiting for her!
- Oh girl! What you have to understand is that your mother couldn't be handled! She was lying about the ditches half the year. She'd have lain down in nettles if there was nowhere else. I might have been the first but I wasn't the last!
- No, you're wrong. Mammy would never have left me behind. Never.

– Well, it's ancient history now, girl. Take another
whiskey, it'll help you put it to rest.

The sight of Auntie Bell hitting the man in the suit
floated up and blocked every exit I could see. He'd been
dapper and, looking back now, he was distressed too.
Are you scared to come in? I'd asked him. Once upon a
time, in a life far, far away, she, Belinda Margaret
Morris, had had a *beau*. Her sister, her twin sister,
couldn't even let her have that much. Babs had robbed
him out from under her and got herself pregnant again.
Mrs Bitchy Barr and Mrs Muck-spreader McCrossan
had actually done very well to keep their thin lips buttoned. Martha, too; she might have told me but she'd
protected me in her own kind way. There's no point in
speaking ill of the dead.

And Bell? How had Bell been able to stomach even
looking at me, never mind giving up the rest of her life
to rear me? A wave of the purest love for her and all her
slammed doors and teary outbursts broke over me. I
was going to have to leave her with nothing and no one
of her own. I could not meet her eye again, not now.
Mammy had lied when she said she'd be back quick as
a wink. She'd lied when she said she'd die without her
dose of moonlight. She'd trained me to cover her tracks.
Don't tell anyone, Lindy, don't ever tell! She'd spent
her whole life leaving me alone in the dark.

*

Martha was right. I didn't know myself as I walked down the deserted streets of Bundoran. The wind was fierce and there wasn't a soul around. I looked into the sandy windows of the closed gift shops. All the shell ornaments and boxed dollies wore their tinsel with pride. The flashing lights of the amusement arcades were switched off. A seaweed tang blew through the alleyways that led down to the beach. The night was not far off. The van driver who had picked me up where I stood with my thumb out on the Ballyshannon Road had told me it was going to be rough later on and I'd nodded my understanding. It wasn't the right kind of day for a day out at the seaside.

I passed the last of the houses where the bridge was built to let the Bradoge River flow out to the Atlantic, and I turned right to get down to the water's edge. I had not bid farewell to my father, who never got off his barstool. He had talked some more and I didn't like any of the words, wild came up again as did troubled, lively, difficult. I'd had three more whiskeys and none of them helped me put anything to rest. I never offered to buy him a drink. He motioned with his fingers for two more of the same and the barman poured them and left them in front of us. He was sorry to have to think about her again. I never mentioned my brother. I'd already chased one too many ghosts into his path. He sighed, his blue eyes, my eyes, on the middle distance.

— I thought the world of her at the time. You, too;
you were such a funny wee scrap!

He wasn't the one who had let her down. He was the
one who had left me where I was. He had more words
for me, they were meant as a salve. I was 'better off
with my own people' and he'd had 'bother enough of
his own' at the time. Probably chest-deep in other little
blue-eyed bastards. He'd been moved on from a pitch
he'd had at the back of the forest, some brave men with
shotguns thought he shouldn't be using land for free.
He didn't name Gabriel Morris but I could picture the
spent cartridges flying gaily through the air as he
reloaded and closed in on people just trying to shelter
from the cold.

As the years went by, Linus thought it was too late to
even try to visit. He knew he would have to sneak to do
it and he was never great at sneaking. He was kept up
to date on whether or not Gabriel Morris was still looking after me when he met farmers from Ballyglen out on
the road. It had been a comfort to him to know that I
was *safe and warm*. He reckoned I'd not miss what I
never had. At least there was one smile to be had on this
day even though it was the freaky-deaky.

The clouds are angry over the pounding sea. I think
of Kieran in Southfork – sorry, Mourne Road Farm –
stoking the fire and keeping all his little boys away from
the sparks. I see the sadness in him that I had mistaken

for a lack of feeling, my mother's sadness; he was fenced in. I think of big Collette's disgust over not being able to trust a woman like me, a woman who had let her baby slip through her fingers. I was all wrong as a mammy. I imagine her pie-face puckering with joy at the thought she'd got rid of the last blight on her new life. I think of Bell quaking in her bedroom, waiting for me to come in so that we could face Granda Morris together. I think of him and of how he won't waste any time searching for the likes of me.

I can't waste any more time on any of them. I can't ever pay Bell back, what would be the point in trying? I think of Declan McIvor and Siobhain telling people that I was always troubled. They'd use their best hushed voices and Catholic faces and word would get around the town in record time. They'd paint themselves as saints to put up with me all these years. I could not think of Miriam. If I let the kindness in her eyes light on a millimetre of my skin I might turn back to save her the pain. Father Boluwaji would understand. We're just passing through this world, shadows on the land.

The ocean looks like every tear I've never cried. There's not a rock between here and the US of A. It glistens steely and vast except for one faint beam of orange that's bleeding from the sky. There they all are, all the tears I thought I'd lost were just rolling forever in and out. I walk towards them, they call out to me. I would drink them in and they would flow over my head, baptising me as I go.

A change is as good as a break. The freezing water is over my shoes before I know it but I walk on. Might as well, when I've come so far. Did Mammy think of me when she put herself into the water? Did she step in or fall in? No matter, she never came home. The small white stone from her grave is still in my pocket, the little part of her that I've kept with me always. I should leave her on the beach among all the other pebbles, she'd be rounded and smooth in no time, but what good is a stone without a cutting edge? She's been with me from my first attempt to escape, why would I let go of her now when we have a chance to travel so far together in the moonlight? A wave breaks against my chest and soaks my face. My eyes sting and the spray soaks into the ends of my hair. I'm not going to be looking my best when I get to America. Still, it's hard to beat a little holiday.

Chapter 9

The crowds are gathering at Southfork for the funeral. It's going to be a big one. No one wants to miss it. Death is usually so mundane but not this one, this one has drama. The mud from the storm that roared through Ballyglen has been rucked up into ridges from all the cars and tractors that have trundled down the lane and parked, one here and one there, as close as they can to the old farmhouse so as not to be drenched by the rain, which is still pelting down. Father Boluwaji slipped and fell on the way in to bless the remains. He was caked from head to toe on both sides because he had to roll on to his front to stand up and is now drying out like a clay pot in front of the fire. The sight of him is cheering, the story a good one to tell people who still look at him sideways because he is not born and bred Irish. Even men of the cloth can have bad luck.

Kieran and Collette are centre stage, the bereaved ones. There are so many sandwiches and buns that the nastier contingent of mourners are sniggering about the mystery of Collette's immense arse being solved. Kieran is shaking hands, meeting people who will become his neighbours, the people he will turn to when he needs a favour and people he will in turn help. Their twin boys are solemnly watching as plates of biscuits are passed around and everyone is smiling at their pained faces every time a chocolate one is removed.

Kieran was in favour of saving them from the sights and sounds of a wake house but Mrs Herself reckons the sooner they understand the intimate horror of death, the better. They have already been made to kiss the grey corpse. Laurie did well, he kept his nerve, but Donal screamed so suddenly and so loudly that Collette knocked over a vase of lilies when she tried to rush him out of earshot. She needed a wider turning circle.

Bell tutted at the double waste – pricey flowers for the dead and pricey flowers for the dead destroyed as they landed pretty white heads first. Not even one stem could be saved. But she is quiet, quieter than she's been in a long while. She went to Diamond's and made an order for a hundred fresh cream cakes. She knows they will not go to waste as half the townland still has to squeeze itself past the hall door and climb the stairs to the bed-room and its tragic corpse. Declan McIvor from the Credit Union has made a decent start on them. Siobhain gives him a good hard dig in the ribs when the cream splats on to his brand-new black jumper from Leehy's. Mrs McCrossan the muck-spreader and Mrs Bitchy Barr flank Bell, and all three are working overtime on the rosary beads. Their lips ripple in time to their silent, solemn prayers. Lovely Mrs Kennedy couldn't force out even one more Hail Mary and mean it, so she's now set up in the kitchen, drying up the many cups and saucers it takes to toast the dead.

Miriam is moving through the wellingtoned feet as best she can, balancing trays of good hot sweet tea. There's still a bitter wind tearing at the windows and curling itself around people's feet when the front door swings open to let in more folks who can't believe the Mass and the readings they'll have to sit through today. The mumbled talk is of chance, of never knowing when it's your time, of lives lived and mistakes made. Everyone at this particular wake is wiser than Methuselah. Soon the bell will toll at St Bede's. This is the third day.

A hole has been dug as deep as the rain will allow. Bell knows it's filling up with water. She's been told by the undertaker and she has nodded, if that's how it has to be, that's how it has to be. It's not a happy thought, that the coffin will splash down and be covered in sludge rather than being placed down to rot for all eternity with a certain reverence. Father Boluwaji has found a single plot right at the back that no one wanted. No one wants to be alone for all eternity. Bell can pay for it at her leisure. She touches her face lightly where a blackened cheek is fading already to a nasty yellow. She was lucky to escape with such a small wound, the bone did not break.

I have told her that she looks fine. It's a lie and we both know it, but we smile when we lock eyes. We are better matched than ever. I have the fat warmth of wee Brian squashed against me. We've rather fallen in love these past two days, the baby and me. His mother was so busy that she needed a hand, even if that hand with those slippery fingers was mine. The whole of Southfork had to be made ready to be viewed and Collette had barely had time to scrub it out *properly* after the lax lick it had from Bell and me. I almost felt sorry for her as she ran in every direction with her dusters and mop. Almost. She has had a wake-up call and I had the pleasure of delivering it. It was one of the best moments of my life and I can say that with ease because I've just watched my life flash by.

Wee Brian is ready for his nap so I heft the gorgeous weight of him on to my shoulder and make my way to the stairs. Everyone nods and smiles at me; times have changed. It's fine these days to have a baby out of marriage and we can hardly be policed by the Catholic Church when they've had their own bits of bother to cope with. These people are deeeelighted for Auntie Bell and me, we're finally free of the rotten auld bastard that was Gabriel Morris. I have retired the freaky-deaky so I can acknowledge their warmth.

Brian sleeps in me and Mammy's old room. His cot is solid wood and that makes me soften towards Collette just a touch in my heart. She wants the best for her boys, just like I want the best for my boy. He goes off without a whimper, such a good baby, and I get to stand a while and stare at him and to put the last three days correctly into my memory bank. They were so good, the best three consecutive days I've had for thirty-three years, that I can hardly trust the joy they've brought me.

When the water of the Atlantic had reached my neck and my feet were finding it hard to stay on the sand, I fell in love with my life. I had a son. I had held him and promised him things would get better. I would not let him down again. I would not be Babs. I had an aunt who loved me against the odds and who needed me right that minute. She would not survive Granda Morris without me. I had to go back. I had a father, he seemed a useless article but he was mine and he was more than Kieran would ever have. I'd had a mother who showered me with whatever kindness and devotion she could muster with her flawed heart. I had Martha Kennedy who was all kindness. I had Miriam, I would not break her heart for all the tea in China. I was desperate for more chinwags with Father Boluwaji. There was a lot left to be said.

Being tall finally paid off. Another woman might have been submerged this far from the shore, but not me. I turned for land, panic rising as it dissolved under me. I ploughed on, long legs, stupid big feet and arms pumping, and finally got spat out by a wave and all I could do was laugh. Lindy Morris, the ticking time bomb, my whole breed is riddled with crazy. I lay awhile, loving the feel of the sand at my back. The moon came and went as the clouds flew past it. It was white and brown and Mammy was right, the sight of it would make any outing special.

It's not easy to get from the Donegal coast to West Tyrone when you're soaked to the bones and you've no money, but I managed it. One of the big hotels hurried me away in a taxi when I pitched up shivering in their tacky foyer and didn't drop the freaky-deaky for a second, even though they were not smiling back. The driver wouldn't cross the border, even though it no longer existed. I was dropped off at the pink-haired widow's house and had the pleasure of getting her and Linus Quinn out of their illicit love bed. The storm that was building all day was in full swing and I had a job being heard above its screech. I beat on the half-door until my hands ached and between the two of them, her fussing and being furious, they got me some dry clothes and another shot of whiskey. He was wide awake and paying attention this time. Sobering by the second. I liked the way he put his coat around my shoulders like a cloak. He'd more than a notion that it was saltwater that had nearly done for me.

- Don't come back here again, says the lusty widow.
- Don't speak to my girl like that, says decades-absent Daddy. She's welcome here any time when she's my blood!

He drove me home to Carnsore in a truck that felt like it was going to be lifted clean off the bog road. We laughed together when he put on the wipers to get rid of the pine cones falling like hail.

- That was hopeless, I said.
- Or hopeful, depending on where you're standing!

One of the wipers snapped and flew off into the dark and we laughed some more. I liked the smell of beer that kept us company. As we drove past the forest all the big evergreens were swaying in the silvery light as if they were slender shoots of barley. It was quite the sight to see. A piebald moon can bring good luck or bad, says Linus Quinn, his eyes, my eyes, devouring the sky.

The bungalow was in pitch darkness, a telegraph pole had likely snapped so Bell and me would be in the dark with Granda Morris for a few days. We were always the end of the line. Linus turned the truck around, he needed to be heading home to his high maintenance widow in case it got any rougher. She didn't like leaving the cottage but a caravan's the best place to sit out any kind of ruckus. We stared at each other for a minute in the light from the dashboard and then we both smiled. I held out my hand and he took it.

– I'll see you again, Daddy?
– You will, girl, you will!

The path to the back door was covered with pine needles, thousands of them rolled in spiky waves. I walked my hands along the pebble-dash and past the outside tap where it dripped on the poor auld worn-down stone until I came to the back door. I called out for Bell as I pushed it closed against the night but inside was just as dark as out. Bell hadn't even lit a candle or a Tilley lamp and I called out for her again. The whole place was freezing and I pulled my father's coat and its smells of him and The Lantern closer around me.

– Bell? Bell? Where are you? BELL?
– I'm here!
– Why didn't you answer me?
– Oh, Lindy! I thought you'd never come home. Never! I thought you'd left me all alone for ever!
– I'll never leave you again, Bell. *Never, ever, ever.* I promise on my life!

427

She started sobbing just beside me so I felt along the worktop to the cupboard by the fridge where we kept the torch and I turned it on her before she got a chance to hide her face. A sore bruise closed her left eye. My grandfather was right-handed and always had a good aim. She'd got into trouble when I hadn't appeared back with Kieran. She'd got into even more trouble when I hadn't appeared back after nightfall. Gabriel Morris didn't tolerate girls who liked to be out in the moonlight. Any bloody fucking woman who couldn't prevent that happening deserved a punch.

- He only hit me *once*, to be fair, Lindy, it was only once!
- Where is he?
- I don't know – there was a terrible thunderclap and the power went out and there's not been a peep out of him since!
- Can you stand?
- Aye.

I lit some candles for Bell and pressed her rosary beads into her trembling hands. A gale was blowing under the kitchen door, and as soon as I opened it I knew what had happened. This was not thunder. One of the massive evergreens had finally had enough. Its trunk had crashed through the middle of the house, an inch of tiny cones and pine needles covered the corridor. I couldn't see the top of it when I shone the torch

428

into corners that weren't there any more. Deep cracks ran from cream carpet to ceiling. My bedroom was cut off, though Bell's looked like it had survived. The room Granda had picked out at the front was in one piece too. I called out for him and heard a low moan. I pushed at the bark of the tree to test that it was solid because I didn't know what else to do and started to climb. Stray branches sprang back and clipped me a few times, but I dropped on to the other side, scratching my whole back where I slid down. The thought of my skin tearing suddenly made me sick. I called out again and realised that he was in what had been my cell.

The roof on this end of Carnsore was gone. The bungalow had been sliced in half as neat as a sponge cake. He shouldn't have built something so flimsy. The tree that couldn't take any more weather was wide enough to squash the bathroom, its wall that was shared with me and the wall on the other unused front bedroom. The curtains whipped about at the broken windows, their flowers twisting. Gabriel Morris was pinned to my bed. His black eyes were mad with rage or pain or shock or all three. There was a lot of blood where he'd been speared by a splintered bough. The ominous gurgle in his throat told me he wasn't long for this world.

The thing about being put out at the edge of a hundred acres is the isolation. By the time I'd run to Southfork he'd be dead. There was no phone because of the storm, there was no neighbour for miles who could help. There was no real need to save him. I sat by his feet and waited. The grey clouds passed overhead, getting slower and slower as we enjoyed the piebald moonlight together. He's aware it's me who's keeping him company. His hand claws at the distance between us. He'll never be able to touch me again.

    – I went to see my father today, Granda. Linus Quinn? We've plans to get to know each other. I was telling him that my son's come home. It's not every day a boy gets handed such a big parcel of land. Daddy says he can't wait to walk the length and breadth of it. He might even come and stay when the weather brightens up.

Gabriel wasn't too happy at the thought, but times change. He spent all of the minutes he had left trying to reach me. He didn't find any last words of his own. When he was done, I closed his eyes, black coals no more. If only he'd known his place, if only he'd not been nosy-parkering I wouldn't have to tell Bell that her father was gone to join Granny Tess in the Happy Hunting Grounds. She took it well enough.

We have come home, not just for the wake. We are here to stay. Father Boluwaji has taken us all to one side and pointed out a small problem with Gabriel Bartholomew Morris's last will and testament. It was unsigned. The torn up remains of a previous will, now inadmissible. As his only surviving child, it is Belinda Margaret Morris who gets to say what happens to Southfork. As owner she will need a farmer who can work the place, and she has no problem with that farmer being Kieran McCreedy if her and me never have to go back to Carnsore. That its remaining walls are being lashed by wind and rain and hopefully returned to the boggy ground is cheering. But *I'm cheeeered* by so many things now. I have become the key. As long as I stay with her, Kieran's safe. I'll even make sure there will be no more little holidays. Bell doesn't like being left all alone with no one or nothing of her own.

For now, we are living in a huge, beautifully kept psychedelic red caravan. Linus Quinn towed it here himself when news got abroad that I was homeless. He razed a patch of nettles to stubble to make our pitch. I love it. What's not to love about a house that can be shifted overnight? It's parked at the front, right at the end of the rotten lane so no one can miss it. It is an assault on the senses for the whole of Ballyglen. I see them gawping at it, a rainbow taking root.

– Lindy? It's time …

– Thanks, Kieran. I'll be right there.

Father Boluwaji has gathered the immediate family for the final goodbyes. We stand in a row, Bell, me, Kieran, Mrs Collette McCreedy herself, the little twins, Uncle Malachi who has become an old man overnight.

If Gabriel can be stopped in his tracks so can he, and the reality of that has shrivelled him. I don't listen to the prayers, the mumbled replies are drowned out by Collette who shouts the responses as if she's on parade. She's lost plenty of her bluster now that a return to Omagh is not possible and she has a mother-in-law and a great aunt to contend with. I'll be good unless she makes me go bad.

When the remains of Gabriel Morris are doused in Holy Water and Father Boluwaji has done everything he can to commend him into the Hands of God, the undertaker comes in to fasten the lid on the coffin. Collette starts to cry but it is *me* who Kieran wraps his arm around. This is my beloved son in whom I am well pleased. I saw him shake hands with my father and my heart had filled up with love for them both at last. It's just one of the memories I'll keep from the last three days. I'll put the Atlantic and what nearly happened at its edge away until the day I take my grandsons down to the beach for a picnic.

I'll look forward to resuming the Saturday-morning cream cakes with Mammy's old friends just as soon as me and Bell are settled to our own satisfaction. I'll keep the smiles on all the faces who got a good look at me at last and who now know I'm just as dull as they are. I'll try not to laugh every time I see Collette McCreedy holding her hefty head like she's stumbled into a nightmare. I'll keep the conversation we had on the first night of the wake polished like the jewel it has become. Mrs Herself will not be allowed to roll over *my family*.

- Just how long are you planning on staying at Mourne Road, Lindy?
- At *Southfork*? Oh, I'm not going anywhere, Collette. Don't you worry about that! You'll not be left *all alone* to rear my grandsons for the foreseeable future. I'll be right by your side. You can trust me on that score alone.
- But you can't just *live* here?
- Oh, but we can. This is our place now.

As the coffin is lifted and Granda gets to leave feet first, never to darken our door again, the best memory is a simple one. It's Bell and me lying side by side in the double bed, the rain gentle on the curved roof of the cosy caravan. We have wheels beneath us and a brightly painted ceiling of stars that we could touch any time we wanted to.

- Goodnight, Bell.
- Goodnight, Lindy. Sweet dreams.
- You too, Bell. You too.

Epilogue

1966

From their stand at the kitchen window, Tess and Bell could see Babs. Babs was on her knees. Tess and Bell knew that's where she would end up but not where she'd start. Now she had nowhere to go unless she could find a way of taking the bull by the horns. They tried to block out the baby grizzling on the sofa in the good room. The other one was already in his shroud, poor little slip of a thing. Granda Morris has set him on top of the old brown suitcase as if she'd just take him with her when she left. They kept watching and wished the rain was falling harder so that the sight of her and him would be washed away entirely. Bell cowered behind her mother and the two of them shivered in tune. The drips on the pane only smudged Babs and Gabriel

Morris where he stood over her. He was hitting her with something but they couldn't make out what. They didn't really want to know.

– Don't do this! Please don't do this! She belongs here. You have to keep us. She's mine, she's yours!
– She, she, she! You're like a bloody plague! The lot of you! What's a man supposed to do when he's visited by a plague?

He hit her again and she fell off to one side. Her face was in the muck, her long black hair too. She'd catch a chill being outside but when you're dragged out there's no option. Her mother and sister had been told not to interfere and that's what they would do. His hand came up again and they could see that he held a hatchet by the head and was thinking of bringing the wooden handle down on her again when he seemed to sag. He threw it into the wheelbarrow and the metal of it clanked and settled.

Babs straightened herself and tucked two hanks of wet hair behind her ears. She rolled on her hands and knees and got herself to her feet. Patrick Joseph had died in the night but she still had Lindy. Lindy would live, Lindy would thrive. Gabriel Morris would come to understand she was just as good as a boy. The rain was coming down harder now, heavier, and it drove itself into her eyes and nose and mouth but it wouldn't drown her. She'd stand her ground. She knew that her father would come round, one day. Everyone has a breaking point. They'd talked about it so often, her and Bell and Tess, how exhausting it must be to be so angry all the time. They'd done their best over the years but the truth was he didn't like them. He'd liked Patrick Joseph, though, traveller blood and all. He could have lived his life as Patrick Joseph Morris and been of service to his grandfather. He'd have been allowed to do that if the name of Linus Quinn was never uttered in Southfork again. If Da could have found a use for Pajo then he could find a use for Lindy eventually, Tess and Bell could too. She'd be part of the family.

The baby started crying then, she howled and howled, she was most likely hungry or chilly or both. Or just lonesome. She'd never been away from Pajo's warmth before. They'd been so tightly wrapped around each other that morning, it had taken Babs a minute to realise he was cold. Gabriel Morris turned towards the north gable of the farmhouse as the watery sun bounced off the windows. His face twisted in rage at the sound. He was back to square one with bloody fucking women.

Babs edged past him, her whole body aching to be back inside with her little daughter. Her heart broken over her little son when she'd been so careful with them both. She had nowhere else to go. She needed the price of a small funeral and a place to live or she was done for. Linus Quinn had already told her, he had trouble enough of his own. He didn't even know he was a father to twins, no point in ever telling him now. Tess, Bell and Babs had all smelled Gabriel Morris coming back from his night out with Uncle Malachi. The stink of cordite followed him for hours. She needed to say something to save herself and the scrap of Linus she had left before Da changed his mind and went for the hatchet again.

– She'll never trouble you! I'll keep her away from you! You'll hardly know she's in the house, she won't make a peep. Please, Da, please?
– She's the wrong child! I don't want her! I'm not feeding another bloody fucking woman.
– She'll be no trouble! On my life, she'll be no trouble.

He turned, seeing that he wasn't getting his point across. Babs ran after him, the sound of Lindy now screaming fit to burst leaving them both in no doubt that they were against the wall. It was now or never. Bell and Tess knew not to comfort her. She was tainted right up until Gabriel said she wasn't.

– Da? Please, I'm begging you …
– Stay then, damn you! Damn the pair of you and that fucking useless mother and sister of yours! Don't let

438

me hear or see that brat. She's nothing to me. Nothing! I'll die before I claim her as kin. Do you hear me? It'll be over my dead body that a woman inherits so much as a *teaspoon* of Morris land.

Acknowledgements

My thanks are due to my agent Lizzy Kremer at David Higham Associates for her invaluable input and to my editor Charlotte Cray who, together with Rose Waddilove, Klara Zak and all the team at Hutchinson Heinemann and Cornerstone, has been a pleasure to work with.

Thanks also to my wonderful and wise first readers: Rachel Abbott for her unending help, Sarah Simpkins for her help with the ending, Shane Marais for saving me from being shunned by devotees of *Smash Hits* magazine, Liz Winters, Mary Bradley, Kiera McGoran, Ria Bradley, Genevieve McPhilemy, Jo Jordan, Sarah Kelly, Sarah Vooght, Paul Paterson, Sherry Flewitt, Rosemarie Egan, Ann Hodgson, Clare Hanbury, Jane Crust, Lee Flewitt, Alex Birch, Nor James, Clare Evans, Angela Stanley, Fiona Paterson, Charlotte Newton,

Gerry Gaudion, Jackie Davy, Moira Sleeman, Emily McHale and Anderida Hatch.

And for diamond geezer Neil Paterson, always, for everything.